Liath Luachra

Liath Luachra: The Grey One

Prequel to the Fionn mac Cumhaill Series

BRIAN O'SULLIVAN

IrishImbas Books

ISBN: 978-0-9941258-2-8

ACKNOWLEDGEMENTS

Special thanks to Marie Elder and Susan Hutchinson-Daniel.

Thanks and credit also to Chiaki & Nasrin (Chronastock) for the use of their image on the cover.

Many ancient Fenian Cycle texts were essential for the completion of this work. These included *Macgnímartha Finn* (The Boyhood Deeds of Fionn), *Acallam na Senórach* (The Colloquy of the Ancients), *Fotha Cath Cnucha* (The Cause of the Battle of Cnucha) *Aided Finn meic Chumail* (The Death of Finn Mac Cumaill) and many more.

Foreword:

This book and its characters are based on ancient narratives from the Fenian Cycle and in particular from the *Macgnímartha Finn* (The Boyhood Deeds of Fionn). The *Macgnímartha Finn* was a twelfth century narrative that attempted to collate a number of much earlier oral tales about the legendary Irish hero Fionn mac Cumhaill and the Fianna. It was originally edited by Kuno Meyer in 1881 for the French journal Revue Celtique.

Many of the personal and place names used in this novel date from before the 12th century although many have common variants (Gaelic and English) that are in use today. **For those readers who would like to know the correct pronunciation of some of these names, an audio glossary is available at http://irishimbasbooks.com/.**

A number of ancient (and more contemporary) Irish terms are also used in this novel. A glossary for the more common ones is available at the back of this book.

Please note that throughout this book, the terms 'clan' and 'tribe' are used interchangeably.

Chapter One

Liath Luachra, the Grey One of Luachair, watched the raiders slip in before dawn. Blurred figures barely distinguishable against the shaded grey background of the surrounding forest, they slid through the grass at the edge of the clearing like wolves on the hunt.

Wolves.

She considered that for a moment. It seemed … apt. This particular band of raiders styled themselves in the manner of a wolf pack to the point of naming themselves *Na Madraí Allta* - The Wild Dogs. Their leader, a big man with black hair and a distinctive black beard, even went so far as to insist on being called *An Mactíre Dubh* – The Black Wolf.

As she watched, the Grey One chewed quietly on a stale slice of oat bread. The texture of the loaf was tough and leathery and she could feel pieces of the original kernel when she crushed it between her molars. Her belly twinged. She hadn't eaten since noon the previous day and her stomach, flat at the best of times, had recessed even further into her torso. Fortunately, the morsels she was chewing would keep the worst of the craving at bay, hold the hunger weakness off until she had a chance to eat again.

Or didn't need to eat again.

With that depressing reflection, she resumed her scrutiny of the raiders. Sprawled on her belly, she was lying in the treeline on the forested southern crest of a high, U-shaped ridge. The ridge formed a natural enclosure around a wide clearing and from that height she had an unobstructed, if murky, view of the little settlement situated directly below. In all, the settlement consisted of three rectangular thatched buildings and a number of lean-tos lying off to the side. The larger buildings formed a rough semicircle around a well-established fire pit located at the centre. Low flames cast a dull orange glow onto the mud and straw-daubed walls.

A herd of about fifteen cattle milled about the buildings and out around the pasture in the rest of the clearing. A squat figure was silhouetted against the fire. A sentry for the cattle, he'd proven unforgivably lax in his responsibilities. Overly confident in the security offered by the settlement's relative proximity to the *Uí Bairrche* stronghold and the natural concealment of the encircling ridge, he'd simply left the cattle to fend for themselves and retired to the fire to doze.

'One, two, three, four.' A pause. 'Five, six … shit!' Another pause. 'One, two … three.'

The Grey One turned a sideways glance to Canann an Súil – Canann the Eye – who'd paused in his counting to scratch an itch through the thick fistful of whiskers enveloping his chin. Foiled by the bushiness of his facial growth, he settled for a quiet curse instead. The Grey One made no comment. Something of a simpleton, Canann was one of the least effective members of their *fian* – war party. He rarely said anything worth listening to and was beside her uniquely because of his exceptional night vision. Canann, it was claimed, could make out the contours of a pig's arsehole at the end of a deep mine shaft. There was no pig to be found anywhere for any great distance – except, perhaps, in the settlement below – but that claim would be sufficiently tested by his ability to identify how many raiders they faced.

'By The Great Father's testicles, shut your gob, Canann.' An infuriated whisper, laden with venom, this time originating from her left.

The Grey One frowned as she considered the darkness beside her. Bressal Binnbhéalach – Bressal SweetTongue – of the *Uí Loinge*, was usually the most articulate and self-disciplined of individuals. Almost completely obscured by the shadow beneath the forest canopy, she struggled to make him out.

'Calm, Bressal. They approach from the northern gap. They're too far away to hear us.'

'They'll hear us if that cretin doesn't stop counting out loud.'

The Grey One left the discussion at that. As *rígfénnid* – leader of the *fian* – Bressal could demand what he liked of its various members. For the most part a reasonable man, his current belligerence belied an intelligent mind and a superior facility when it came to sheer rat cunning. Despite his intellect however, she'd noticed a recurring pattern of abominable hostility over the course of the current season. Usually just before a fight.

It was the tension of course. Bressal was no fool. It was he, after all, who'd organised this particular action, who'd conceived and developed the plan for taking down the raiders. Now unfortunately, just prior to the battle, his behaviour was becoming a dangerous liability.

Liath Luachra reached across and placed a hand on his. The slim man's forearm was greasy with nervous sweat, the skin about his wrist warm and slimy. She forced herself to hold it there for a moment or two. As a general rule she avoided close physical contact with others and particularly with Bressal for the man had been seeking her caress for almost two years. Over that time, she'd done everything in her power to discourage such interest but right now he needed to be distracted.

As she anticipated, he started at her touch and with the shock of that contact she sensed the tension gush out of him. The leaves crackled softly as he shifted his weight and she pulled her hand back before he could interpret it for something more than it was or, worse, respond in kind. To prevent any further interaction, she turned away to face Canann. The keen-sighted buffoon was still counting but at least he'd reduced his voice to a muted whisper.

'Nine, ten, eleven … eleven, twelve.' He was silent for a moment. 'Twelve,' he declared suddenly but with obvious satisfaction. 'There are twelve men, Liath Luachra. Twelve men.'

'Are there twelve men or is it that you can only count to twelve?'

A momentary silence passed between them.

'There are twelve men,' he insisted, an aggrieved tone to his voice.

'Good, Canann. Good. She tossed him the compliment thoughtlessly, much as she'd toss an unwanted bone to a hungry dog. Despite the fact he was more than twice her age, the warrior lapped the praise up like an excited puppy, moaning softly and nodding to himself as though in confirmation of his count.

Ignoring both men, Liath Luachra turned her focus back to the approaching raiders. She didn't have Canann's keen eyesight but she still managed to catch glimpses of movement in the moonlight as the raiders spread out from the clearing's northern entrance and formed a rough arc along the treeline on either side. When they were ready, they'd swarm out around the settlement in that formation. For the moment however, they seemed happy enough just to sit and observe.

The guard should have been waiting at the entrance. Not warming himself by the fire.

That simple negligence irritated her, which was unusual. Few things roused the Grey One's emotions one way or the other but acts of carelessness in a combat situation occasionally worked their way under her skin to provoke a stir of anger. She frowned, placating this uncharacteristic indignation with the knowledge that the guard would probably be the first to die. For the settlement below however, she felt no particular sense of sympathy, no empathy. By ignoring the most fundamental of responsibilities, they'd brought the consequences on themselves.

Crawling forwards, she edged out of the enclosing shadows until she could look down on the base of the ridge where the other *fénnid* – the other members of the *fian* – were concealed. Like the raiders, the settlement's inhabitants were unaware of their presence, an instruction from Mical Strong Arm who'd also shown them the secret route up from the far side of the steep ridge. Her *fian* were spread out down there, having formed a similar half-circle sometime after nightfall.

My fian.

She felt a momentary twinge of frustration at that. Bressal's *fian*, she corrected herself. *Na Cinéaltaí* of the *Uí Loinge* clan. Even their name – The Kindly Ones – bore Bressal's typically caustic sense of humour.

Raising her head again, she looked across the clearing to the trees where the incoming force was assembled.

Twelve raiders.

She bit at her fingernails. *Na Cinéaltaí* had seven *fénnid* in total, eight including Bressal. Two of these – Senach and Sean Fergus – were concealed off to the right. Three more – Murchú, Conall Cacach and Biotóg – off to the left. Although numerically inferior to their enemy, the odds didn't overly disturb her. *Na Cinéaltaí* would be working with the element of surprise. Absorbed in their slaughter, the raping of women and the pillaging of property, any possibility of opposition would be the last thing on the raiders' minds. She was also comforted by the fact that each of the *fénnid* carried two metal-tipped javelins. With the initial volleys, any numerical advantage would quickly be countered.

She experienced a small sense of satisfaction at that. The javelins had been her suggestion. Bressal, who'd laid out the *fian's* original placement, had made a big deal of humming and hawing as he'd considered it but he'd approved it in the end, as she'd known he would. Over the previous season of engagements, he'd increasingly deferred combat responsibilities to her. Despite his agreement, he'd also made a point of letting the other men know that he was accepting it only because it aligned well with his own plan.

And that his own plan was a good plan.

Liath Luachra wasn't too sure about that. It certainly wasn't so good for the settlement. A sub-branch of the *Uí Bairrche* clan, its people had been cruelly sacrificed as bait to ensure the destruction of *An Mactíre Dubh*. Mical Strong Arm, the *rí* – king – of *Uí Bairrche* had even gone so far as to increase the likelihood of a raid at that particular settlement by spreading false rumours of a treasure cache hidden within one of the buildings.

Liath Luachra had initially been surprised by Mical Strong Arm's callousness towards members of his own clan until Bressal, always well connected, had informed her of reasons behind it. According to one of Bressal's many cousins, the leader of this particular branch was a potential rival to Mical's son for the future leadership of *Uí Bairrche*. By allowing the settlement to be destroyed in the course of the raider's destruction, the *rí* was killing two birds with a single sling shot.

Liath Luachra tried to wipe the fatigue from her eyes. Following reports of *Na Madraí Allta's* incursion on *Uí Bairrche* territories, it had taken two days of frantic travel to get here in time for the raider's assault. There was little prospect of rest any time soon.

With an effort, she turned her focus to the distant trees. Now that the movement of the raiders had ceased, the clearing had taken on a derelict, deserted appearance. Settled comfortably in place, they'd most likely wait for dawn to have sufficient light to launch their attack.

The Grey One pulled her grey wool cloak about her shoulders. The autumn season was upon them and this would be the last *fian* action before the pre-winter dispersal. If they survived this next battle, the *fian* would travel back to Bressal's home place at the *Uí Loinge* stronghold where any loot would be distributed and the *fian* would disband, some members drifting back to their tribal territories for the winter, others *éclann* – clanless – like her, finding alternatives to pass the frozen months.

She shuddered at the thought of winter. For her, the cold season would involve a return to Luachair, a desolate valley by the marshes far to the south-west. She'd spent the previous two winters in a small cave there. With a flap over the entrance passage and a low fire, the cave could, on occasion, feel relatively warm but mostly the cold would drive her to her blankets to sleep like a hibernating animal. In the heat beneath her furs and blankets, she'd nibble on *Beacáin Scammalach* – Cloud Mushroom – to smear her mind and avoid any chance of self-reflection. Most of her time would pass in an incoherent blur and, on occasion, she would not see daylight for days.

In the past, Luachair had contained four separate families, scattered in small farms along the length of the forested valley floor. A band of passing marauders had put paid to most of them. Nowadays, an old couple – the only other survivors and the last occupants of the valley – would come up to the cave every three days or so to leave food at the entrance: vegetables, broth and if she was lucky some kind of meat. The smell of food would eventually rouse her from her blankets although, once or twice, absorbed in her dream oblivion, she'd managed to ignore hunger for periods of up to four days.

Later, sitting beside the fire, she'd gobble the food down until she felt strong enough to venture outside and walk the valley before returning to the warmth of her blankets.

As a child, Liath Luachra too had lived in that valley. Now, with sixteen years on her, it was the only place that retained any semblance of home although 'home' was already a concept she no longer truly believed in. The old couple had been friends of her mother from a time before she could truly remember. Nowadays, she rarely spoke to them

14

and avoided their attempts at conversation. The interaction she wanted with them was simple and very limited. In exchange for the food, firewood and privacy they provided over the course of the winter season, they received her share of booty from *fian* activities: the skins, the goats, metal, anything of value. It was a relationship very much stacked in the old couple's favour and although she was aware if this she didn't really care. The arrangement was a means of surviving the winter and prolonging her existence for another year, although the ongoing futility of the latter was something that was never far from her mind. All the same, it wasn't as though she had any realistic alternative.

Apart from an offer to share Bressal's bed.

She shivered.

Stop thinking. Focus on your enemy.

She looked across the clearing to the northern trees.

Soon.

***

The raiders made their move shortly after dawn, just as Liath Luachra had predicted. The attack was faultless, carried out with methodical coordination and precision. The twelve men rose from the trees in response to some silent, predetermined signal. Advancing at a crouch, they moved forward in a wide semicircle, creeping purposefully towards the unsuspecting settlement.

By that time, Liath Luachra, Bressal and Canann had already worked their way down the ridge, using a slight dip to conceal their descent. Rejoining the others, Bressal had the *fian* form a curved line just inside the southern treeline so they had a clear view of the raiders' advance, unobstructed by the bulk of the buildings.

Crouched behind the bulky buttress of an ancient oak, Liath Luachra could feel the hunger for violence building inside her, the physical and emotional 'stretch' as her nerves pulled on her muscle tendons, twitching for release.

At Bressal's insistence, Murchú – their most recent and inexperienced recruit – was crouched alongside her. The *rígfénnid*'s nephew, he was a handsome youth of fifteen years or so but inexperienced and overly nervous. He repeatedly twisted the javelin haft

15

between the palms of his hands and every now and again he'd raise the weapon as though preparing to cast it then quickly lower it again.

Patience tested by that irritating repetition, Liath Luachra released a feral growl from deep within her throat. Startled, the boy looked toward her and, noting the fearful widening of his eyes, for the briefest of moments she wondered what he saw. A girl in faded leathers, no doubt. Probably bigger than most girls he knew, lithe as a whipcord and strong.

She knew that most young men like Murchú didn't really know what to make of her. Her fine features and lack of facial hair revealed her gender for what it was but the contrast of those austere features with hair cropped close to the skull, the mass of white scars along her lower back and the tangible ferocity in her smoky grey eyes often left them confused as to how they should act with her.

'Breathe,' she instructed him and although it was expressed in a whisper it lacked no authority for that. 'Breathe in, breathe out. Focus on your breath and try to relax your muscles until I tell you what to do next.'

In the colourless light of dawn, Murchú's face looked pale but he dipped his head in acknowledgement. Satisfied that he wasn't going to panic, the Grey One turned away to check her weapons, making sure that the sword pulled freely from its scabbard, that the metal tips of the javelins were firmly affixed and wouldn't break loose under pressure. She also slid the leather sling coiled around her left arm further up towards the elbow to make it sit more securely. A small bag of stone bullets lay inside her tunic but she doubted she'd have opportunity to use them in the coming engagement.

With that, she focussed on her own breathing for she could feel how her body had grown rigid from the mounting tension, the muscles of her neck and shoulders involuntarily cramping to the point where they felt as taut as deerskin on a tanning frame. The sensation was one she was familiar with but no less uncomfortable for that. Her body always reacted in this manner before battle, tightening up like an enraged but restrained hound just prior to being unleashed.

In a strange sort of sympathetic symmetry, her mind also seemed to coil tighter at such moments, as though her intellect was battling to repress the animal bloodlust inside her. Ironically, she always felt that her mind never functioned as well as it did leading up to that point of release. Just before battle, her thoughts were pure, crisp and as sharp as the finest blade. At the surrender to that physical action however, all reason was discarded as she reverted to a slavering force of violence.

A hand tapped her left thigh and she twisted on her heel to find Bressal regarding her with mute intensity. A slender, sallow man with a narrow face that was always freshly shaven, his misleadingly benign appearance gave no hint to the depths of fury that could erupt if he was obstructed or displeased. He jerked his head towards the settlement fire pit. Following the gesture, her eyes locked onto the indistinct form of a large man with a black beard, crouched in the shadows near the sleeping guard, a long knife in his right hand.

The Black Wolf.

She nodded her understanding. Bressal was instructing her to mark the man, to prevent him from escaping in the turmoil to follow. She repressed a quick flicker of irritation at that. If he'd followed another of her suggestions – concealing one of the *fénnid* by the clearing entrance – they could have effectively sealed the battleground. Fearful of the raider numbers however, he'd insisted on having all of his force to hand.

With these last instructions transferred, Bressal hissed, held her eyes then abruptly made a sharp passing gesture with his hand to alert the others that he was turning combat leadership over to her.

She stared at him but Bressal simply repeated the gestures with greater insistence and turned back to study the raiders.

The Grey One breathed deeply as she attempted to absorb what had just happened, but looking down to the settlement, she saw that she had little time to do so. By now, had he been awake, the guard would have been alerted by the uneasy shuffling of the cattle as the dark shapes moved towards them. One or two of the animals began to low quietly but the dozing guard slept on. Liath Luachra watched in silence as the black bearded man crept up behind him. Moving forward with ruthless efficiency, he clasped a hand about the guard's mouth, yanked his head up and sliced his throat open from ear to ear.

Disturbed by the smell of freshly spilled blood, the cattle started moving again, this time crowding towards the southern side of the clearing, obstructing both the *fian's* proposed route of attack and their view of the settlement. Liath Luachra hissed in frustration. Through the milling of the frightened cattle she could see the raiders cluster around the entrances to the dwelling where the settlement's inhabitants still slept soundly. This would have been the perfect time to launch their initial javelin volley but now the opportunity was lost, the field of casting ruined by the position of the shifting cattle. On either side, the men glanced towards her, waiting for her lead. She, in turn, looked to Bressal but he completely ignored her. Scowling, she made a pressing motion with her right hand. They would have to wait.

There was a sudden roar from the settlement as the raiders surged into the various buildings, a roar echoed almost immediately by shrieks of agony or the screams of women and children as the settlement's population awoke to their fate.

The screaming did not last long as *Na Madraí Allta* once again upheld their fearsome reputation for ruthlessness. Soon, the only cries were the victorious yells of the raiders and an occasional scream of pain. Frightened by the noise and the violence, the cattle had shifted position once more, this time stampeding off to the grassy area beyond the buildings, closer towards the entrance of the clearing.

Na Cinéaltaí waited, concealed in the thick undergrowth just inside the treeline. They watched in silence as the raiders dragged bodies from the buildings, piling them in an untidy heap by the fire. The Black Wolf had settled himself on a low grassy hummock, laughing and talking loudly with two of his men while he watched the others rummage through the buildings and ransack the little settlement.

The Grey One forced herself to unclench her javelin, conscious of the fact that if she continued to grip it too tightly the tension would strain her arm muscle, throwing off her cast when it was time.

And it wasn't yet time.

Despite the tempting proximity of the Black Wolf, too many of his men were still scattered in places she couldn't see, inside the longhouses or out of sight on the far side of the buildings. For the javelin volley to achieve the effect she wanted, it was essential that the raiders were clustered more tightly together. They would have to bide their time.

As she continued to watch, a high-pitched scream came from the nearest building and, a moment later, two females were dragged through the doorway and into the open. Both were skinny, fair haired girls, dressed in loose wool shifts. The older girl looked to have no more than seventeen years on her, the younger less than fourteen. Both were almost out of their wits with fear.

Their captors dragged them to where their leader was sitting and cast them onto the ground to cower before him, weeping and clinging desperately to each other. The Black Wolf scratched his beard while he looked them over. Slowly, he rose to his feet.

With surprising alacrity, the big man reached down and ripped the shift from the eldest girl, provoking a cheer of delight from his men. The girl screamed and desperately tried to shield her breasts from the guffawing raiders who'd started to gather around, eyeing her with undisguised hunger.

From the corner of her eye, Liath Luachra noticed Murchú turn his head to look at her but she ignored him. Further along to her right, she heard an evil chuckle and a whisper from one of the *fénnid*. 'There's a pair of beauties worth waiting for.'

Conall Cacach. No surprises there.

Her lips compressed as a snicker of laughter repeated down the line. She made a sharp hissing noise and they settled down.

'Where is it?'

The Black Wolf's voice carried surprisingly well in the stillness of the clearing, his deep, bass tones reverberating loudly in the windless morning air. Petrified, the girl turned her head away and wailed and he had to slap her across the face to get her to stop.

'Where is the treasure?'

Given the absence of any treasure, the girl's stricken confusion was understandable, from Liath Luachra's informed perspective at least. The raiders, lacking her insight into the matter, were less generous in their interpretation.

The Black Wolf sighed. With menacing deliberation, he lifted a heavy wooden club, hauling the head up from where it rested on the earth beside him. A brutal but effective weapon, it looked to be about the same length as his arm and terminated with a large knob carved into the shape of a mallet with a short metal spike indented at its centre. He hefted it threateningly in his right hand then poking it under the girl's jaw, he forced her head up so that her eyes met his. He bent down slightly. 'Where is it?'

'Grey One!' Murchú whispered urgently. She flashed him a furious glare and he flinched, hurriedly lapsing into silence. Turning her gaze back to the settlement, she refocused her attention on the position of the raiders, counting them out in a silent whisper.

'Your final chance. Where is the treasure?'

The panic-stricken girl released a terrified wail, provoking a flash of anger in the big man's eyes. Swinging back the club, he brought it crashing down.

The sound of the smashing skull carried clearly across to the trees and caused even the battle-hardened members of the *fian* to flinch. The warriors watched wordlessly as the girl toppled to one side, hitting the ground with a heavy slap, the left side of her head a broken, bloody mess.

'Well, that's a waste!' A bitterly disgusted whisper from Conall Cacach.

Liath Luachra would have turned on him but she was too preoccupied with her count of the raiders. The black-haired leader, meanwhile, had turned his attention to the second terrified girl who, traumatised by the sight of her murdered sister, sat soundlessly clutching herself, staring at the body with a blank expression. The raiders closed in, curious to see what happened next.

'Javelins', whispered Liath Luachra. Taking a fresh grip on her weapon, she stood and raised it, drawing the haft back until her right hand was well behind her ear. She held it there, noting the action reproduced down the line of waiting men. '*Scaoiligí!*' she hissed. Release!

And cast.

The whistle of the incoming hail must have alerted the raider standing closest to them for he turned around and looked towards the treeline. A puzzled expression had barely formed on his face when the first missile stuck him in the chest, the downward momentum of the metal head punching it through his sternum to emerge two hand-widths from the base of his spine. The other raiders had no time to register what had happened for the other javelins were already falling in amongst them.

The second volley hit them before they had time to react to the first. Six raiders were down, three unmoving, three screaming in agony as though in counterpoint to the screams of challenge from *Na Cinéaltaí* charging out of the trees towards them.

Surrendering completely to the battle frenzy, Liath Luachra led the charge, literally frothing at the mouth as she stormed across the open space to where the shocked survivors were gathered. Her throat was already raw from roaring, her vision reduced to a blinkered red haze. Consumed by her desire to reach the raiders, she was barely conscious that she was running.

By the time she bowled into the remnants of *Na Madraí Allta*, they were over their initial shock but she could almost taste the despair that filled their eyes. They knew they had no hope of survival, that no quarter would be given, no mercy spared. In a retaliatory surge of desperation and fury at the unfairness of it all, they brought their weapons up to bear, intent on going down fighting.

A skinny man with a face coated in black tattoos lunged at Liath Luachra with a metal-tipped spear but consumed in the throes of her battle frenzy, to her he seemed to be moving ponderously slow. Even as the wicked looking metal point came up to take her in the gut, she'd dropped to the ground, hitting the earth with her haunches and sliding forwards on the dewy grass. The warrior attempted to change his grip and jab downwards but she'd already slid past his left leg, gouging a vicious gash along the rear of his knee. Even as the hamstrung warrior toppled, the rest of the *fian* broke over him and his comrades in a violent wave of screaming violence and sharp-edged metal.

21

The Grey One used her remaining momentum to regain her feet, her eyes flickering around to locate the Black Wolf. Unlike his comrades, the bandit leader had not frozen in shock at the first volley of the javelins but responded with impressive instincts of self-preservation. Recognising their predicament, he'd bolted, ducking behind one of the buildings so that he was not only hidden from sight but sheltered from any further javelin cast. By the time Liath Luachra caught sight of him, he'd already cut around the corner of the longhouse and was galloping at full speed for the gap leading out of the clearing.

Good plan, Bressal!

She took off after him, leaping over the body of a raider with a javelin through his skull, careering past a protruding lean-to. Finally on open ground, she yelled and waved to scatter the startled cattle who once again had gathered to obstruct her path.

Because of his size, the Black Wolf would most likely have outrun her if he hadn't been hampered by the wicked gash in his arm, the result of her first javelin. She had hoped to hit him in the chest but because he'd turned at the last moment, the missile had streaked past, ripping a deep streak of skin from his arm. The resulting wound wasn't lethal by any means but it was enough to upset his usual running gait, slowing him down.

She pursued him through the gap, in her excitement releasing a bloodthirsty ululation.

Glancing back over his shoulder, the Black Wolf now realised his sole pursuer was a single female. This seemed to provoke some misplaced sense of outrage for he suddenly slid to a halt and twisted about to confront her.

'You threaten *me*?' He roared as she drew towards him. 'You threaten *me*, little girl!'

With this, he lunged for her, swinging the wooden club with wild force. Once again, her swift reactions vastly exceeded those of her opponent and she slid into a crouch, driving forwards with *Gléas Gan Ainm* as the club whistled overhead in a poorly calculated overextension. Realising the danger he was in, the big man belatedly attempted to pull himself back from the swing but he was too slow. The sword plunged a

22

full finger length into his gut and the twisting movement he made as he attempted to pull back caused the blade to slice along the skin, opening his belly even further.

He pulled back with shock even as the Grey One was reversing her hold on the sword. She smashed the hilt into his face, so savagely that he tottered backwards and tripped over a fallen branch. And then she was on him, stabbing and stabbing, repeatedly, sinking the metal blade deep into his chest.

She was still stabbing when the blood haze finally cleared and she became conscious of Murchú and Bressal standing nearby, observing her with shocked expressions. Straddling the corpse, her hands were coated in a thick sheen of blood and entrails, her clothing and face drenched with blood. Pushing herself off the body, she rose on trembling legs, her chest heaving.

'She's cut him to pieces,' Murchú looked up from the shredded carcass to her blood–stained face but, cowed by the insane venom of her glare, dropped his eyes again almost immediately.

Bressal shrugged. 'She's left the head. That's all we need.' He turned a glance towards the panting woman warrior. 'Good work, Grey One. You've saved the day.'

***

After the earlier shrieks and brutality, the settlement seemed relatively calm when she returned although it was hard to ignore the iron stink of blood, the smell of gore and shit and the corpses strewn about in contorted poses. *Na Cinéaltaí* had come out of the battle exceptionally well, the single casualty a simple gash on Senach's arm. Their victory was substantial.

Unhampered by the wound, Senach – a lean, dark-haired *Uí Loinge* man with more than thirty years on him – was down on his knees, working with Biotóg to rifle the corpses, looting both raider and settler alike. Sitting off to the left on a pile of firewood, Sean Fergus – Old Fergus – watched them with an exhausted, worldweary expression. The eldest member of the *fian*, his grey hair was tied up in braids and he sported a heavy moustache – also grey – drenched and dripping from the bucket of water he'd just immersed his head in.

23

Conall Cacach and Canann were standing by one of the longhouses with the troubled young girl. They had her up against the wall and Conall, a big muscular streak of malice with rotting teeth and greasy black hair, was groping her small breasts through the shift as she stared blankly into open space. With a brutal twist, Conall ripped the hindering garment to shreds. The girl displayed no reaction.

'Uncle!' Murchú nudged his uncle and gestured angrily towards the scene. Bressal slowly shook his head. 'No survivors,' he said quietly.

'But, Uncle! You can't let Conall Cacach have –'

'No survivors,' Bressal insisted. 'Such was my agreement with Mical Strong Arm. If Conall wants to yield a share of the booty for the girl then that's his decision. I'm not going to –'

He broke off suddenly for Liath Luachra had brushed past, striding purposefully towards the warrior and his prize. The two *Uí Loinge* men stared in shock as she pulled a razor-sharp knife from her belt but before they could even call out a warning, she'd barged in between the two *fénnid* and slashed the mute girl's throat. A great spurt of blood gushed out over Conall and Canann, causing both men to jump back in alarm. The girl collapsed without a sound, folding over onto the ground with a gentle thump. Conall Cacach stared down at the shuddering corpse in disbelief, breathing in heavily before raising his eyes to the woman warrior.

'You can't have her,' said Liath Luachra.

Conall Cacach's jaw almost dropped to his chest. 'What?' he bellowed. Furious beyond belief, he lunged forward, swiping at her face with one meaty fist. Anticipating this reaction however, the Grey One had already stepped lithely to one side. As the fist swept past her head, she jabbed the haft of her javelin up into his guts.

With a whoosh of expelled air, the warrior dropped to his ground, crouched on all fours as he whooped and gasped desperately for breath. Liath Luachra stepped forward again, gripped a handful of greasy hair and held her knife up to his throat. 'Do you want to challenge me?'

Wheezing, Conall quickly shook his head.

Releasing him, she stood up straight and turned her eyes to Bressal. The *rígfénnid* was watching her intently, all emotion concealed behind a

24

mask of complete impassivity. She was suddenly aware that the other *fénnid* were also watching her, gaping in fascinated silence. 'I claim this girl as my share of booty,' she said.

The *rígfénnid* stared at her then down to the corpse by her feet which had finally gone still. Shaking his head in bafflement, he gave a noncommittal shrug. 'Very well. Conall gets your share of the remaining booty. As for the rest of you, get your equipment together. Our work here is done but we have a great distance to travel.'

Chapter Two:

On the morning of the *fian's* triumphant return to the *Uí Bairrche* stronghold, Mical Strong Arm gave them a warm reception, praising them lavishly in front of his people at the news of the Wild Dogs' destruction. The *rí* of *Uí Bairrche's* personal satisfaction at the Black Wolf's demise was evident not only in his welcome but from the obvious pleasure he obtained impaling his enemy's head on a stake outside the stronghold entrance. Roaring jubilantly as the crowd cheered him on, Mical's subsequent victory speech was short but effective, the single low point his half-hearted attempt at regret for the annihilation of the *Uí Bairrche* sub-branch. Even to Liath Luachra's ears, those particular sentiments rang hollow.

In contrast to his actions in terms of family competitors, Mical Strong Arm proved honourable in his dealings with *Na Cinéaltaí*. Over the course of the morning, the reward for the *fian's* services - twenty deer skins, five goats, ten swords, five iron daggers and numerous other products - was handed over without dispute. Organised as ever, Bressal had an *Uí Loinge* vassal, three horses and three strong slaves awaiting them at the *Uí Bairrche* stronghold to help transport the booty. Mical had insisted on retaining the cattle and other possessions from the destroyed settlement but, all in all, it wasn't a bad haul combined with the bounty of arms, clothing and other belongings already retrieved from the bandit group.

Following the transfer of the booty however, the warmth of the relationship began to wane as Mical quietly urged Bressal to take his men as far from the stronghold as possible before nightfall. Envisaging a night of festivity at *Uí Bairrche* expense, the *fénnid* weren't pleased when they learned of this development although the Grey One understood the *rí's* motivation well enough. It was common knowledge that *fian* tended to celebrate their victories in an excessive manner and that such celebrations had a tendency to spiral out of control and end in violence. Mical wasn't such a fool that he didn't apprehend the potential threat to his people of having a dangerous group like *Na Cineáltaí* within his walls at such a time.

Shortly after noon therefore, the *fian* departed for the journey back to Briga, an easy march of about four days. The stronghold of Bressal's *Uí Loinge* clan, Briga was the unofficial staging point for the initial raising of the *fian* and its subsequent place of disassembly. Setting these rituals at the *Uí Loinge* stronghold served not only a symbolic tradition but also a practical one as it allowed the *Uí Loinge* leaders to oversee their share of any booty obtained from the *fian* raised under its name.

Given the well-established relations between the *Uí Loinge* and the *Uí Bairrche*, the trade route between both strongholds was a well-worn and frequently travelled trail that allowed the *fian* to cover a respectable distance over a short time. That first evening, they halted by the bank of a slow-flowing river that carved a serene path through the forest. A clearing of trees provided an excellent site to camp with ample supplies of fresh water and firewood. The open view to the west allowed them to catch the last rays of sunshine before Father Sun slid behind the distant hills.

Although it was relatively early when they called a halt, Liath Luachra knew that Bressal was keen to set up camp as quickly as possible. The *fian* were angry at their expulsion from the *Uí Loinge* stronghold and needed to vent some of that resentment before it manifested in bloodshed.

The *Uí Loinge* vassal and slaves set up the camp with the ease of practiced repetition, unloading the horses, setting up the campfire and preparing the basis of a large meal. When they were done, they established a second fire for themselves upriver from the *fian*. While they worked, the *fénnid* lounged by the river bank or bathed in the shallows.

Rearranging the contents of her pack, Liath Luachra noticed Bressal standing by a cluster of grey boulders just ten paces downriver from the fire. The *Uí Loinge* man made a subtle gesture for her to join him, grinning broadly with a full set of white teeth as she approached and settled on one of the rocks alongside. The *rífénnid* was quite a handsome man and generally made the effort to keep a clean-shaven jaw, although the previous days of travelling meant his features were now shadowed with stubble. In the gleam of the late evening sunshine, she noted that his hair was thinning above his forehead and realised he'd be bald in his later years. If he managed to live that long.

Bressal, unaware of such matters, appeared in exceptional good humour, chuckling happily to himself as she made herself comfortable.

And well he should. It has been a good fighting season.

Like Bressal, she knew *Na Cinéaltaí's* reputation would spread as a result of their recent accomplishments. If a fresh *fian* was raised after the winter season, there was a high likelihood of numerous *óglaigh* – young, unblooded warriors – and other individuals lining up to join *Na Cinéaltaí*. The *rígfénnid*, consequently, was becoming a person of influence both within and beyond his own tribe.

'Come closer, Grey One. I would have quiet words with you.'

With some misgivings, Liath Luachra shifted a little closer. Bressal reached into his pack, pulled out a tanned waterskin and tossed it to her.

Grasping it with one hand, she pulled the stopper loose with her teeth. Raising it to her lips, she paused, wincing at the unusually strong smell of alcohol that assailed her nostrils. One deep swig sent a mouthful of the acrid liquid to the back of her throat, burning a trail down her gullet. She wiped her lips and regarded the *rígfénnid* with suspicion. Whatever Bressal had in mind, if he was offering her this taste from his own personal stash, he was clearly hoping to soften her up beforehand.

Or rut her.

'The season has been a great success, Grey One. A great success.'

An image of the young girl from the *Uí Bairrche* settlement popped unbidden into her head. For one brief, grisly moment, she recalled the sensation of her blade cutting through skin and gristle. She hurriedly took a second swig from the skin.

'But it is also a time of opportunity,' the slender man continued. 'Future opportunity for a group such as *Na Cinéaltaí.*'

Knowing what was expected of her, Liath Luachra took a deep breath and dutifully asked the question. 'Is it?'

'Yes, *mo láireog léith* – my grey, young mare. With our achievements this season, tales of *Na Cinéaltaí* will spread through the country like fire in dry brush.' He looked at her with an intensity that unsettled her. 'It is my intention to help spread those flames.'

Liath Luachra shrugged, unclear what point he was trying to make.

Bressal absently tapped his hand against his thigh. 'I have been pondering the future of *Na Cinéaltaí*. I believe it has potential to become the most famous *fian* of all time.'

'Uh-huh.'

Liath Luachra took another swig. Bressal's ambition came as no real surprise. The man was always scheming, planning his machinations for power play and leverage. What she didn't understand was why he was bothering to share such thoughts with her. She was his creature and obeyed his orders without question. That was how it'd worked for the previous two years and that was how she'd imagined it working for the foreseeable future – although she still struggled to imagine a future beyond the immediate day or two.

She looked down at her feet and dug her bare toes into the soft, sandy soil.

Bressal seemed put out by her visible lack of enthusiasm. 'Don't you see?' he demanded. 'With this most recent *fian* we fulfilled a task for a *rí* that his clan could not have achieved, even if they'd raised a *fian* of their own.'

They were fast enough to get rid of us once the deed was done.

The *rígfénnid* suddenly reached forward and grasped the skin from her hand. 'Stop slugging that down, Grey One. I need you coherent, for a little while at least.' He raised the skin and swallowed a mouthful of the caustic liquid himself, grunting and shaking his head at the sting of it. 'Where was I. Ah, yes! It is my belief that there are other *rí* who will reward us well for similar services. Think about it! *Na Cinéaltaí* can offer a band of seasoned warriors to protect tribal lands from raiding parties and other threats. And then of course …' He paused. 'There are those tasks we could fulfil for a *rí* that a tribal *fian* could not.'

Liath Luachra continued to look at the ground for she didn't know what to say. She'd noticed a slight trembling in her hands and fingers as

29

her body reacted to the alcohol, already pre-empting the heady disassociation that lay so tantalisingly within its grasp. She ached for the oblivion the drink offered but she also knew she had little chance of getting it until Bressal was satisfied with her response.

Pushing the craving aside, she forced herself to focus on the *rígfénnid's* argument although much of what he was saying made little sense. A *fian*, generally, tended to be clan-based or, on occasion, multi-clan based. Raised primarily in response to an identified threat such as bandit groups like *Na Madraí Allta*, a perceived grievance or an injustice, a *fian* was also – on occasion – raised simply to raid a competing clan for cattle and goods. In a general sense however, a *fian* lasted only as long as the threat existed or until the grievance was settled and was disbanded almost immediately afterwards.

In that respect, *Na Cinéaltaí* was – admittedly – something of an oddity. Originally raised by *Uí Loinge* in response to attacks from an unusually savage wolf pack, it hadn't disbanded immediately after destroying the animals but, on Bressal's suggestion, offered assistance to a neighbouring sub-tribe suffering from a similar predicament. By the time Liath Luachra had joined them, the *fian* had already been raised on three subsequent occasions and although it had consisted predominantly of *Uí Loinge fénnid*, the proportion of *éclann* had also grown substantially. With the *Uí Bairrche* action, Bressal had also taken the unprecedented step of offering *Na Cinéaltaí* services to other clans.

'What sort of tasks?' the Grey One asked carefully.

Bressal glanced towards the campfire. The flames were still building but the other *fénnid* had gathered close around it, shouting at each other and roaring with laughter. It wasn't possible that they could overhear the conversation but he lowered his voice nevertheless. 'We could fulfil tasks for a *rí* which would not generally be spoken of in the light of day. Secret tasks, acts of depredation that would permit his personal goals to be achieved while at the same time protecting his honour. Enforcers, persuaders. That would be our role.'

'So you would transform *Na Cinéaltaí* from *fian* to *díberg?*'

Bressal's expression darkened. Unlike *'fian'* – a term generally referring to a clan-sanctioned war-party, *díberg* was a term used to describe a band of simple marauders such as *Na Madraí Allta* or those men who'd laid waste to everything in the valley of Luachair. 'Of course not! No. Well … not exactly.' He paused. 'Something in between. We would provide service directly to the *rí*, not to the clan. Just as we did with Mical Strong Arm.'

Liath Luachra shuffled uncomfortably. Bressal knew of her strong hatred for marauders. 'Why do you tell me this? I am a simple sword wielder. As *rígfénnid* that is your decision.'

'Because I want you to take the role of *rígfénnid*, battle leader for *Na Cinéaltaí*.'

She stared at him, genuinely shocked. 'But it is an *Uí Loinge fian*.'

Bressal returned her stare with a somewhat affronted expression. '*Na Cinéaltaí* is *my fian*. It's been my *fian* far longer than it's been an *Uí Loinge fian*.' He hesitated, looked at her guiltily as though he'd given something away. 'But that hardly matters.' His right hand made an expansive gesture. 'What's important is that I wish to take … a less visible role. I'll continue to raise the *fian* of course but otherwise I'll remain hidden in the background, a shadow whispering instructions. You however…' His eyes drilled into hers. 'You will act as battle leader, the person people will see as leading *Na Cinnealtaí*.' His eyes continued to pierce her, as though seeking to compel her agreement on the strength of conviction alone. Unable to bear that scrutiny, Liath Luachra nervously averted her gaze, grunted and nodded vaguely in an effort to buy herself some time to think.

'You have nothing to say?'

'The … the other *fénnid* will not follow a woman.'

He laughed at that. 'Yes, they will. They followed you during the attack on *Na Madraí Allta*. They're scared of you but more importantly, they respect your fighting ability.'

Uncharacteristically flustered, the woman warrior gazed longingly towards the forest and shook her head in confusion. Bressal misinterpreted the gesture. 'You do not care for my proposal?' His voice had grown cold.

31

When she didn't answer, Bressal tugged his chin and mused aloud. 'Let me see. You've been a *fénnid* for … How long has it been? Two years? Three?'

She shivered, kept her head down and made no response. Bressal knew very well how long she'd been with him. He was simply playing his games.

'You are in my debt, *mo láireog léith*' – my grey, young mare. He gave a sour smile. 'You were nothing when I found you. A ragged savage. Now, I offer you a rare opportunity, the chance to carve a name, to lead a *fian* of reputation.'

Liath Luachra said nothing, recognising the truth in what he was saying but liking none of it. She had no desire to lead the *fian* but it was true that Bressal had probably saved her life. For his own ends, admittedly, but still, she was in his debt for that.

She chewed on the inside of her cheek, recalling how the *Uí Loinge* man had discovered her at *An Áenach Tailteann* – The Tailteann Fair –, a three-yearly festival where inter-tribal bickering was temporarily put aside to trade, socialise and engage in competitive bouts. Liath Luachra had washed up there more than a year after the raid on Luachair. A solitary, damaged refugee, she'd been in a bad way, so desperate for supplies that she'd entered a competition of hand-to-hand combat with another woman far bigger than her. The prospect of a vicious fight between two women had been a big draw, hence Bressal's presence in the excited crowd, cheering on the brutal competition that followed.

Through sheer desperation, Liath Luachra had somehow succeeded in winning that vicious bout. Spurred by her feline looks and fighting ability (and no little amount by the flask of *uisce beatha* he'd consumed) Bressal had stood on a high mound and publicly pledged his intention to offer her a place in *Na Cineáltaí*.

The following morning, although the sincerity of his offer had dwindled with a correspondingly escalation of sobriety, Bressal had no choice but to hold to that pledge. Grumbling and resentful, he'd engaged her with few expectations, equipping her with little more than a rusted sword. Over the course of the remaining season however, instead of getting herself killed she'd proven a surprisingly effective fighter.

Taller and stronger than most others of her gender, her natural physicality gave her a distinct advantage in combat, as did her capacity for, and her ease with, violence. When Liath Luachra fought, she fought to maim and destroy. She gave no quarter and displayed a total absence of mercy.

Sensing greater potential within the silent girl, Bressal had organised additional lessons in combat with an old *Uí Loinge* veteran in debt to him from a previous service. Once again, Liath Luachra's natural martial ability took everyone by surprise when a mere two seasons later she succeeded in defeating her instructor.

Although Bressal had tried to hide it, Liath Luachra had sensed the *rígfénnid's* satisfaction with his investment. Within half a year of her joining the *fian*, he'd gained not only a competent fighter with a natural aptitude for warfare but one with an innate strategic 'knowing' of where to be and when to be there. More importantly, from Bressal's perspective, he also had someone who obeyed his every instruction without question and who, because of her gender and prowess, added an appealing mystique to the reputation of his *fian*.

From her perspective, Liath Luachra too benefited from the outcome. Unaccustomed to success in any form, the fact that she had a skill which others appeared to appreciate – albeit a brutal and potentially short-lived one – was a tremendous comfort. More importantly however, she now had a purpose of sorts. True, it was a twisted and poorly formed one but it was more than anything else she'd had for a very long time before that.

Desperate to remain in Bressal's favour, she'd refused no task, no matter how demeaning and trained with relentless fervour. Naturally, being the person he was, Bressal had also attempted to ease that fervour into other areas, more specifically his bedroll. It was here however that he'd finally encountered the limitations to her acquiescence. Unaccustomed to refusal, he'd not taken it well and, a short time later, deep in his cups, he'd attempted to force the issue only to end up with a split lip and a black eye for his efforts.

That incident had marked a particularly low point in their relationship and although she'd disguised it well, Liath Luachra had been terrified at the prospect of expulsion. Bereft of hope or goals and barely capable of interaction with people who weren't as broken as herself, the *fian* was her sole connection to other human beings, her sole connection to life itself in fact. This was a situation she'd always instinctively known to conceal from the *Uí Loinge* man. If Bressal had any inkling of her true dependency on him and the power he potentially wielded over her, he wouldn't hesitate to call her bluff. If he did, she knew she'd have no choice but to submit to his desires or leave.

In the end, to her immense relief, Bressal had refrained from any further untoward action. Although infuriated by the Grey One's rejection, he'd had the wit to reflect both on the value of his investment and the little matter of his wife. Daughter to a senior member of the *Uí Loinge* tribal Council, it was a strategic relationship he'd nurtured for a considerable time and one which he'd have jeopardised if he'd involved himself in an open dalliance with another woman, even a broken *éclann* [clanless one] like Liath Luachra.

Subsequent to their unfortunate fracas, Bressal had maintained a more correct interaction with the warrior woman, restricting himself to the odd leer and occasionally referring to her as *mo láireog léith* or, more disparagingly, *mo láireog deas gleoite* – my pretty young mare. Every now and again however, she'd catch him studying her with hungry eyes and on one occasion, she'd overheard him bragging to some *Uí Loinge* comrades, referring to her as his *lián ghraí* – his stud mare. At that point, she realised that the matter had never truly been resolved.

'I… I'm aware of the debt I owe you,' she answered the *Uí Loinge* man at last. 'But I don't understand. Why you want me to lead your *fian*.'

Bressal shrugged, 'It's very simple. First, if the *rígfénnid* is *éclann*, other clan leaders will see the *fian* as less influenced by *Uí Loinge* goals and will be more open to seeking our service. Secondly, I know I can count on you to obey me - it's in your own best interests to do so. Thirdly, having a female *rígfénnid* of proven prowess distinguishes *Na Cinéaltaí* from other *fian*. Potential *fénnid* will be intrigued and will travel far to join us. That can increase our numbers and our influence.'

Noting the silent disbelief in her eyes, he added, 'I've already overheard people speak in hushed tones of the Grey One and her battle

34

prowess. They say you're a giant woman with great breasts and flaming red hair. They don't know you're a flat-chested whelp with a boy's arse.'

An arse that you want.

She said nothing. She knew from experience that there was no stopping Bressal when he had the flow of words on him.

'So,' he continued, playing his strongest card. 'The choice is simple. Should you wish to lead *Na Cinéaltaí* you will do as I command and take on the role of *rígfénnid*. If you do not, you will no longer be a *fénnid* of this *fian*.' He raised his eyebrows and gave her his gravest consideration. 'What is your answer?'

For a long time she did nothing but stare at the ground. Finally, with evident reluctance, she dipped her head a single time.

'Excellent!' Satisfied with her capitulation, Bressal was all smiles again. 'Believe me, Grey One, you will not regret this decision.'

Liath Luachra continued to stare bleakly at her feet.

'There is one more thing, however. A minor issue that barely merits mention. To lead *Na Cinéaltaí*, you will need to let your hair grow out.'

Liath Luachra raised her eyes to stare at him blankly.

'To look like a true member of your sex, Grey One. I need a *rígfénnid* who will inspire men, who will stir them to surpass their abilities. Do as I ask and warriors will be fighting each other for a place amongst us.'

Liath Luachra shuffled awkwardly, increasingly disturbed by the direction the conversation had taken and resenting Bressal's evident enjoyment of that discomfort. 'Long hair catches,' she protested.

'Then tie it up in braids. It's hardly an onerous task.' The *Uí Loinge* man rose to his feet and took a step backwards as though to better examine her. His gaze transferred from her face to her chest and then down to the sword strapped to her side. 'And you must have a sword, a decent sword. You'll use a weapon with a hero warrior's name. *Gléas Gan Ainm* is a foolish name.'

Liath Luachra felt a stir of irritation at that. *Gléas Gan Ainm* – Tool Without A Name – had been the first sword, the first object of any value she'd ever owned. The prospect of losing it was repugnant to her. 'A name like *Slisneoir na Mhagairlí*,' she suggested in a rare expression of recalcitrance.

'Testicle Slicer? Yes,' the *rígfénnid* agreed with enthusiasm, oblivious to the sarcasm. 'That would be an excellent name.' He raised his hand as though about to slap her heartily on the shoulder. Thinking better of it, he dropped it again.

She glanced glumly towards the fire where the other *fénnid* were chatting and laughing. 'Is there something else you wish to ask of me?'

'Yes. There's a little matter of your reward.' Reaching inside his leather tunic, Bressal pulled out a small leather pouch tied up with string. He laid it casually on the stone beside him. Despite herself, Liath Luachra couldn't help staring hungrily at it and although she tried to pull her eyes away, found herself unable to do so. Her reaction, to her dismay, did not go unnoticed by the *Uí Loinge* man. Given the creaky smile spreading like a stain across his face, it had probably been anticipated. His lips curled. 'You see your reward, Grey One? *Beacáin Scammalach*. Cloud Mushroom. I always keep a special reward for my favourites, don't I?'

He seemed to mull on that for a moment. 'Actually, I do, don't I? I always provide you with your reward, I treat you well, I show you favour.' He frowned and rubbed the stubble on his chin. 'And yet I feel that, of late, you show less respect than I deserve. I mean, what was all that with depriving Conall Cacach of his prize back at the settlement? Honestly! It's as though my efforts mean little. After all I have done for you.'

He sighed.

'I have been considering this ... this lack of fealty. I have come to the conclusion that you should make some fresh display of fidelity, some evidence to demonstrate your loyalty. I think it's the least I deserve, don't you?' He gave a broad smile and reaching across, he cupped her chin in his hand, lifting her head so that she had to face him.

'Now, as you know, I am a simple man. I do not demand great ceremonial rituals like the tribal leaders, so let us keep it simple. Bend your head here and kiss me.'

Liath Luachra stiffened, her loose posture suddenly as tense and contorted as a twisted storm tree.

'Just here,' continued Bressal touching his lips with the tip of his forefinger. 'Nothing more.' He continued to watch her and she could feel her entire body start to tremble. She kept her eyes down to avoid looking at him. In her lap, she could see her hands were shaking, quivering uncontrollably like the rest of her body.

Bressal roared with laughter. 'Gods, Grey One, you are an odd one. You are the most ferocious fighter I know, you throw yourself without thought into the thickest part of battle and yet the prospect of a simple peck on those lips is enough to send you into convulsions of fear. You comport yourself like a ten year old virgin.'

He picked up the pouch and tossed it into the ground before her. 'Here. Take your reward, *mo láireog deas gleoite*. I know I have your fealty and never let it be said that Bressal denies those most loyal to him what they truly desire.'

Liath Luachra scrambled for the pouch, grasped it and took off at a run towards the trees. Heart pounding, eyesight blurring, she pushed deeper and deeper through the undergrowth, further into the forest, ignoring the thorns and branches that scratched her arms and face, desperate to get away from Bressal's laughter.

A natural parting through the trees led her further from the campsite and the sound of the guffawing *Uí Loinge* man.

Pretty Young Mare!

She shivered, made to spit and then changed her mind. Pretty, ugly – the terms were meaningless from a man's perspective once he had the blood horn on. At that point all most men really cared about was plunging their *slat* into some soft, moist orifice and, from her experience, neither the precise location nor the form of it had ever caused much grounds for consideration.

Such reflections stirred up a quiet pool of bitterness and she felt a cold sliding hatred. For a moment, she had to physically stop and lean against a tree trunk while she struggled to refocus her thoughts, pushing that dark combination of memory and reflection back into the slimy crevice from which it had emerged. She cursed bitterly, for such thoughts led to places of shadow, places from which it was not so easy to come back.

Eventually, she started walking again, following a vaguely natural trail through the trees, regularly looking up to study the forest canopy until she located what she'd been looking for. The oak tree she selected was ancient, its bark gnarled and twisted and so ideal for climbing. She clambered easily up to one of the higher boughs, a wide platform she could walk along for several paces before it narrowed to a point where it wouldn't support her weight.

Sitting on the mossy crotch at the intersection of the trunk and the bough, she opened her backpack and removed a coil of woven flax which she then knotted around the stubbed remnant of another long-broken branch. Tugging it to make sure it was firmly attached, she tossed the remainder of the coil over the side of the branch and used it to slide back down to the forest floor.

Hitting the ground, she immediately started back towards the campsite, mentally marking prominent natural features that would help her relocate the tree when she returned that way again.

She was almost back at the river when she heard the sound of voices and instinctively slithered into the shadow of one of the nearer oaks. Crouching low in the undergrowth, she scanned the surrounding forest until two figures emerged from the thick undergrowth off to her left: Sean Fergus and Biotóg both carrying armfuls of wood that were destined for the fire.

Rising to her feet, she stepped out into the open. Sean Fergus was the first to notice her. He raised his head and squinted. 'Grey One,' he said with a nod of greeting.

She returned his nod with one of her own. 'You're not celebrating?'

He shrugged. 'No-one has *uisce beatha*.'

'Bressal has a supply.' She transferred her gaze to Biotóg, a thin faced youth with large, protruding eyes and an unshaven chin that was liberally sprinkled with pimples. Originally from a sub branch of *Clann Morna*, he'd been fostered to *Uí Loinge* but by all accounts his family were in no particular hurry to take him back. The *Uí Loinge* leader responsible for his care had asked Bressal to instruct him in the warrior path by accompanying *Na Cinéaltaí*. Pleased at the prospect of having a clan leader beholden to him, the *Uí Loinge* man had happily obliged.

38

Liath Luachra had no strong feelings, positive or negative, towards the youth. She didn't particularly trust him but then, she didn't trust any of her comrades-in-arms. He was, admittedly, something of an odd one. He listened carefully to everything but spoke very little himself. When the booty from the *Uí Bairrche* settlement was being distributed, he'd surprised everyone by requesting the clothing of the dead womenfolk be included in his share.

'Go ahead to the campfire,' Sean Fergus instructed the youth. 'I wish to have words with the Grey One but I'll catch you up.'

Although curious as to what the old warrior wanted of her, Liath Luachra remained silent, waiting patiently with him as Biotóg walked out of earshot. The pimply youth paused at the edge of the camp and looked back over his shoulder. His eyes rested on the Grey One for several moments before he turned and entered the camp. Sean Fergus shook his head. 'Strange lad, that.'

When no response was forthcoming from the woman warrior, he turned his gaze to her.

'Can I ask you a question?'

'Yes.'

'Do you feel remorse?'

She regarded him in confusion. 'Remorse?'

The old warrior compressed his lips. 'The *Uí Bairrche* settlement. The girl.'

Her grey eyes considered him coldly, giving nothing away.

'I know why you killed the girl.'

'Then you know nothing.'

'Bressal made it clear there could be no survivors. You didn't want her to suffer and Conall would have made her suffer. I respect you for that.'

They continued to regard each other in silence, the older man curious, the woman warrior hostile, unwilling to concede anything. 'Go away,' she said at last. 'There's nothing to talk about. That girl is dead. As you will be if you don't stay out of my path.'

With that she spun around and stalked back into the forest.

***

39

The men had slipped into a surly mood, bellyaching bitterly about their dismissal from the *Uí Bairrche* stronghold when Bressal approached the fire with a set of bags strewn over his shoulders. At that point, their blood was up, roused by Conall Cacach's suggestion of a retaliatory return later that night.

'Shut your ugly gob,' snapped Bressal contemptuously. Pulling two skins of *uisce beatha* from the bags, he tossed them in amongst the gathered *fénnid*. The complaints ceased instantly as the men pounced on them, fighting savagely in a free-for-all for the triumph of the first drink.

Chuckling at the consequence of his contribution, the Uí Loinge man quickly edged away from the spillover of violence, joining his vassal and the slaves at the safety of the second fire. There he sat on a long log and watched the scuffle ensue.

From the shadows of the treeline, Liath Luachra also watched the boisterous brawl, chewing nervously at the inside of her cheek. Following her brief discussion with Sean Fergus, she'd been unable to return to camp and lingered uneasily on the outskirts, salivating silently as her comrades filled their bellies on the roast pork and tubers prepared by the slaves. Ignoring her own hunger, she fought down the rising sense of anxiety that always accompanied the post-combat celebration. For Liath Luachra, this was the period in which she felt most exposed. After the savagery of a *fian* season, the *fénnid's* blood was up and this event almost invariably involved a cathartic expulsion of the bloody residue of fear and the relief of survival through any means available.

On such nights, anything could – and did – happen. Over her two years with *Na Cinéaltaí* she'd seen one man who'd survived countless battles die from alcohol poisoning, another murdered by his best friend during a drunken argument. There'd also been less lethal injuries, the result of accidents from fire, falls and, occasionally, self-inflicted wounds.

Standing upright, she growled, unsheathed her sword then nervously replaced it almost immediately. Once more, she dropped to a crouch, almost pulled the sword free a second time but forced herself to leave it sheathed.

Foolish. Foolish.

Had she been a man, there wouldn't have been an issue. To vent the season's toxic residue, she could have simply strode into camp, sat with the others and let herself slide into the welcome stupor of drunken inebriation. As the single female in a company of violent men however, that course of action just wasn't an option. She had to manage the conditions of her own 'release' more carefully.

As a *fénnid*, she expected death, she expected violence. These were realities she dealt with on a daily basis but she was also realistic enough to know that she was just as likely to die at the hands of her own comrades as she was from the weapons of her enemies. Bressal had delusions of enticing the sons of powerful families into *Na Cinéaltaí* but, in reality, most of the current *fénnid* were fugitives, murderers or thieves. They followed *Na Cinéaltaí* not out of loyalty but out of a love for bloodshed or simply because, like her, they had nowhere else to go.

For herself, she had no illusions. She knew that, despite their shared camaraderie, at the slightest sign of weakness her companions would be all over her like the rabid wolves they were. The only sure way to prevent that from happening was to make them more terrified of the consequences than the action, to intimidate them, to swagger and display a set of balls so much bigger and tougher than theirs, they'd think twice before attempting to challenge her.

With a quick curse, she swallowed her fear and lunged forward into the circle before she could change her mind. Having committed herself fully, her body took on the brasher, more aggressive mannerisms she unconsciously adopted when she was with the others. Stepping into the illuminated circle around the fire, she slid confidently onto a fallen log alongside Senach. As the others were watching Conall Cacach smash Canann in the face, no-one but the po-faced warrior with the missing ear even noticed her sudden reappearance and he didn't say anything. Looking around the little company, she realised that most of them were already half-cut. Even Bressal, returned to the fire to join them, was red-faced from drink and tears of laughter streamed from his eyes. The only one who didn't look completely sozzled was Sean Fergus and he simply looked sad. Sitting off to one side, he drank with silent determination, as though complete inebriation was a goal that could only be achieved through sustained effort.

Liath Luachra settled in straight for the *uisce beatha*. It was rare enough to get a fresh supply although Bressal, through his contacts, always seemed to manage. She shared the skin with Senach, Sean Fergus and the young *fénnid*, Murchú. With all four passing it around and taking it in turns to drink, none of them noticed the fact that she was swallowing far less than they were, taking one draught for every two of their great sucking swallows and merely moistening her lips and pretending to swallow the rest of the time. It was some indication of the strength of the alcohol that, even with this restraint, she soon felt its heightening wash in her blood, the warm flush in her cheeks and the tightening of the skin between her lips and her nose. Fortunately, for her, this minor intoxication was a smoothening balm, dampening down the fury in her head and allowing her to think, if not lucidly, at least less feverishly.

The night was dark and the blazing red of the fire looked blurred, yet oddly intensified, through the sheen of the alcohol. Her stomach felt hot when she rose to her feet and pulled the sword from its scabbard, dragging its blade along the base of a nearby boulder to create a scraping metallic sound that drew the others' attention. Most of the men, seeing her stand, started to leer and catcall. Swaying and grinning, she commenced a wide circle of the fire and the men gathered about it.

Bressal and one or two of older *fénnid*, having seen all this before, sat back to watch the spectacle.

The Grey One stopped and felt the heat of the fire burn against the skin of her knees and the inside of her thighs. She stared about at the surrounding circle of hideous faces, features looking deformed and even more hellish in the flickering red light of the fire. 'I seek blood!' she bellowed 'What scumfucker takes my challenge?'

Someone groaned. 'The Grey One's completely addled.'

'Who said that?' she snarled, swinging around to where the voice had seemed to come from. 'Was that you, Canann? You wanting to challenge?'

The burly simpleton held up two placating palms. 'Not me,' he protested. She sneered at him, noting the silence of the surrounding men grow increasingly turgid. 'Not me,' he repeated but she continued to glare at him until he dropped his eyes to the ground.

Scowling belligerently, she started a fresh circuit of the fire, her habitual reserve overridden by the *uisce beatha*.

She circled the fire twice in total, strutting with an exaggerated swagger, brandishing the sword in her right hand, swinging the blade carelessly but with a control that only the most drink-muddled could miss. Each man she passed looked down or pretended to be otherwise preoccupied. In some cases they actually were. Biotóg was stretched out cold at the edge of the ring of light thrown out by the fire. As to whether this was from the drink or an earlier disagreement with his brothers-in-arms, she couldn't tell.

The single exception to them all was Conall Cacach who stared brazenly back at her when she stood in front of him. Cruel mouth twisted, he regarded her through narrowed eyes and a surliness fuelled by a full day of fermenting resentment fortified by *uisce beatha*. Liath Luachra realised she must be drunker than she'd thought for she experienced a sudden, irrational hatred for that pig-ugly, sneering face. Her nostrils flared and her eyes took on a dangerous, unhinged gleam but when she saw a bead of sweat break out on his forehead, somewhere behind the fog of alcohol a sudden realisation surfaced.

He's scared. He's scared of me but even more scared of backing down before the others.

'Try your luck, Conall?' She poked his knee with the tip of the sword but he made no response to the provocation. Possibly the sharp prick had hurt him and he'd simply hidden it, possibly the *uisce beatha* had dulled his senses to the point that he couldn't feel anything anyway. Either way, he continued to glower at her, eyes full of hatred.

With a sneer, she spat on the ground in front of him, waited, and when he didn't make his move, continued her circuit.

By the time she'd completed her third round of the fire, she hadn't received a single challenge. She'd expected that but there was no harm in reminding them what they could expect. Two previous summers, at

43

the start of her first season with the *fian*, an *éclann* by the name of Callach An Thóin Mhóir – Callach Fat Arse – had responded to similar provocation with a drunken hatchet swipe. Her own instinct-driven response to that clumsy assault had been sudden and to the point: a steel-tipped finger length of *Gléas Gan Ainm* straight through his throat.

That particular incident had shaken *Na Cineáltaí* and even Bressal had paled at her viciousness. From her perspective however, the subsequent verbal abuse she received had been worth it. Earlier that evening, she'd overheard Callach An Thóin Mhóir boasting of his intention to take her by force when she was drunk, much to the delight of the other *fénnid*. Her action had forced them all to drastically reappraise her potential availability for cocksplay.

'Cowards!' She spat. 'Half-men!' She brandished her sword, swung it loosely as through she wasn't in complete control of the action but even that didn't incite anyone to challenge her. She spat again, unsure whether she was relieved or disappointed. Either way, she knew that for the moment at least, she was safe.

She retrieved her seat beside Senach. 'Move!' she snarled. The *Uí Loinge* man stared at her then hurriedly shoved up the log.

After that it was back into the alcohol and this time, like the men, she lapped it up. Within moments her challenge was forgotten, the raucous mood re-established and the boisterous laughter scaring the wildlife as though nothing had changed.

But she knew better.

As the alcohol flowed, the talk grew bawdier and a rowdy song was sung, followed by another and then another again. Soon everyone, including Bressal, was in a state of complete inebriation and even the surly Conall Cacach cracked a smile and laughed hoarsely. If any enemies had happened to pass, the Grey One realised during one brief moment of lucidity, they'd have been doomed, completely incapable of defending themselves.

But she didn't care. They didn't care. For the moment, they were alive and mindlessly carefree. And that was all that mattered.

Later, when she was barely able to distinguish physical darkness from the hazy fog behind her eyes, she left the others, peeling herself out of the firelight to plunge into the shadows at the edge of the forest. She staggered forwards into the darkness until she managed to get her bearings then turned to peer blearily back at the camp site. Monitored by Bressal's *Uí Loinge* servant and the slaves, the fire was still blazing and the *fian*, an odd set of distorted black silhouettes, roaring with laughter around it.

Within the shadows of the trees, she felt her earlier anxiety subside, her sense of control slowly return. Many considered her strange for spending so much time within the Great Wild. Most, understandably, saw the wilderness as a dangerous and hostile place where death lurked for the unwary in every dappled shadow. Liath Luachra agreed with that interpretation but at the same time she knew that, for all its lethal nature, the Great Wild was not cruel. The true predators inhabited those spaces where people gathered. Out in the Great Wild there was no subterfuge. You always knew what dangers you faced and you fought, you ran, or you hid in order to survive them. She regretted the absence of such candidness in her other interactions.

With a grunt, the woman warrior finally managed to relocate the path she'd marked out earlier, tripping over a root and then crawling on her hands and knees until she found the oak tree. Somehow, she managed to clamber onto the bough, pull up the fibrous rope and attach herself to the makeshift platform. Lying back against its mossy bulk, she stared up at the heavens through a hole in the forest canopy. A distinct patch of sky was visible, the stars winking madly at her as though sharing some great joke she didn't quite understand. Fumbling about in her tunic, she located Bressal's pouch, poked her fingers inside and pulled out a morsel of fibrous organic material.

Beacáin scammalach. Cloud mushroom.

Breaking off a segment, she popped it into her mouth, chewing half-heartedly on the tasteless material before she swallowed it.

As always when she partook of cloud mushroom, she felt a certain forlorn regret. Back in Luachair, her father's use of the substance had intensified dramatically on her mother's passing. A harsh and brooding man at the best of times, the cloud mushroom had exacerbated those qualities and within a short period of time, she and her brothers had

45

been obliged to tiptoe around him to avoid his increasingly erratic rages. At times, towards the end, he'd suffer from fits, falling and thrashing about on the ground, spitting and foaming at the mouth and catching the whiff of mushroom on his breath she had a fair idea what had been responsible. Other times, at night, he'd leave their hut, slip out into the forest and join the distant wolves up on the hills howling at the moon.

Such memories didn't prevent her own use of cloud mushroom, of course. Ironically, if anything, they seemed to provoke an even greater use of the substance. Such behaviour, she knew, could only be damaging and, yet, she remained powerless to change it. She was her father's daughter and she could feel that same self-destructive madness within herself at times. That was her destiny.

There was no impact at first but she knew this was just a normal part of the process. While she waited for its effect she remained lying on her back, staring up at the flickering stars that were faint and blurred from the *uisce beatha* she'd consumed. After a time, she realised the mushroom was starting to act, for the clarity and the detail of the stars had increased dramatically. A short time later, she heard the thunderous sound of crickets and the swish of owl wings as they spiralled through the trees around her. A little later again, she thought she heard voices, children's voices that called her name from some place very far away. The sound caused her heart to pound and she struggled to calm herself as the flush of her pulse pumped loudly in her ears.

It's the beacáin scammalach, the beacáin scammalach.

The voices persisted however, growing increasingly louder. Suddenly, she found that she'd slipped free of her constraints although she had no recollection of doing so. Sliding down the flax-fibre rope, she landed effortlessly on the forest floor and started walking in the direction from which the voices seemed to come. The voices were happy, carefree, punctuated by wicked giggles and the erratic, delighted whoops of children at play.

Soon, she came to a tall stretch of holly bushes and, dropping to a crouch, eased her way through the bulk of them. The leaves prickled and stung but she ignored them as she pushed deeper into the vegetation. Reaching the edge, she used her hands to part the branches

46

before her and discovered a small clearing with a wide pond off to one side. For some reason, it was daytime within the clearing, sunshine pouring down on some children at play in the mud flat beside the pond.

There were three children in all: two fair-haired boys with about five and six years on them and a dark-haired girl about six or seven years older. The girl was instructing the two boys on the proper method of making mud cakes, rolling the mud out on a large flat stone that, judging from the tracks in the earth, had been dragged from the forest.

'It's like this,' she was saying, demonstrating with a large handful of mucky wetness. 'You roll them flat and then … No, Feirgil. Like this. See?'

Liath Luachra trembled for she recognised this scene: the boys, the mud pool, the girl. The latter, in particular, she recognised for it was herself as a child, from what now seemed an impossibly long time ago. She continued to stare, her hands unconsciously moving to mimic the actions of her younger self, accurately recreating the movements from recollection alone.

'Num num,' one of the boys was burbling softly. He pointed at the mud cake his sister had just completed. 'Num num.'

The girl lifted the flattened circle of sludge and lifted it to her teeth. 'Should I eat it?' she asked her brothers. 'Should I eat this wonderful, tasty cake?' The two boys giggled and nodded enthusiastically. 'Num Num.'

'Num num,' she repeated, placing the mud into her mouth and biting down on it. The action provoked a marvellous response from the two boys who absolutely squealed with laughter. Spitting out the gritty sediment, the younger Liath Luachra began to laugh as well.

In the bushes, Liath Luachra turned and headed back towards the tree, the children's laughter haunting her like ghosts in the night.

Chapter Three

When her head cleared that morning, Liath Luachra found herself strewn sideways rather than lengthways across the bough of the oak tree. Both of her legs were dangling from one side of the great branch, counterbalanced on the other by her head and arms. Only the tightly fastened flax rope and knots had prevented her from falling.

Breathless from the constrictive pressure against her chest, it took several attempts before she managed to lever herself back onto the bough. Even then, when she was upright, she found her legs entangled in the contorted coils of her rope and, trembling from the aftereffects of the cloud mushroom, had to use a knife to extricate herself.

Free at last, she clumsily worked her way down to the forest floor, relieved at the firm touch of solid ground beneath her feet. Leaning forward to support herself against the trunk, she carefully squinted around. Despite the aching hangover, the forest seemed unusually peaceful, the chirping of birds, the drone of bees, the play of wind through the leaves all combining to create a remarkable sense of tranquillity. Further through the trees, she saw shafts of sunlight cut through gaps in the canopy, showering the green fern and forest floor detritus with a warm, yellow glow. Fighting off a creeping nausea, she was unable to appreciate the beauty of it and took a deep breath instead as she replayed the visions from her dream.

I saw the clearing again.

Why do I always see the clearing?

Curious, she studied the ground around the base of the tree. There was a single recent set of footprints: clumsy, stumbling tracks left from her drunken return the previous evening. There was no trail leaving the tree so she hadn't physically departed from her refuge during the night as she'd imagined.

Rifling through the undergrowth, she found Bressal's pouch but also – to her dismay – her sword, which had somehow worked its way loose from the scabbard and fallen while she slept. Staring at the weapon, she slumped against the oak's rough bark, furious that she hadn't even noticed its absence.

Pushing herself off the tree, she started back towards the campsite with a heavy heart. Stalking though the greenery, she slowed abruptly, transfixed by an unanticipated flash of insight that halted her in mid-step. Standing in one of the warm shafts of sunlight that pierced the forest canopy, she felt her shoulders slump.

Of course.

Exhaling heavily, she shook her head and released a sour laugh. She finally understood why the memory of the clearing always followed her ingestion of the *beacáin scammalach* but that knowledge was a bitter, poisoned gift. She saw the clearing because it was the last time she could ever remember being truly happy.

***

The *fian* campsite resembled a deserted battleground with comatose bodies, scraps of food, possessions and clothing scattered throughout. The single area untouched by the detritus of the previous night's celebration was in the immediate vicinity of the second fire where the slaves had been sleeping. Displaying a rigour and energy unshared by the *fénnid*, all three were already up and about, preparing breakfast and packing for the *fian*'s imminent departure under the oversight of Bressal's *Uí Loinge* vassal.

There were other signs of life too. Sean Fergus was still sitting by the oak tree where she'd seen him the previous evening, grunting softly to himself and wiping his face with his hands as though in pain. With cloudy detachment she noted the vomit stains down the front of his tunic. His long grey-streaked hair had torn loose from its binding and now lay coarse and tangled about his shoulders.

Conall Cacach was completely unconscious, spread face-down in the mud by the riverbank. Further upriver, Biotóg was lying across Murchú, his hands loose around his throat as though he'd been attempting to strangle him but had passed out before he'd finished. Canann and Senach were lying alongside one another, snoring softly like exhausted lovers.

Bressal was up too, of course. Although his eyes were bloodshot he'd reclaimed his seat on the log and was staring down at the black scorch marks that marked the site of the previous evening's fire. Every now and again, he lifted his head and thoughtfully rubbed his chin.

Probably working on another scheme. Always scheming that man.

Hearing the tread of her feet, he raised his head and watched as she approached and took a seat on another log lying on the opposite side of the scorch marks. Liath Luachra reached down to a nearby bucket of water and, dipping her hands inside, splashed some of its contents onto her face. Unfortunately, the liquid was too tepid and lacked the bracing impact she'd been hoping for. Annoyed, she kicked out and knocked it over then watched as the liquid soaked into the dry earth beneath.

One of the *Uí Loinge* slaves approached and offered them both a bowl of steaming porridge. Thanking him, Liath Luachra poked her hand into the bowl, scooped out two fingers worth and slipped it into her mouth. She chewed the lumpy gruel for a moment then abruptly spat it out. The bland flavour of watered oats had been polluted by the residue of the previous night's drinking and now had a distinct aftertaste of *uisce beatha*.

Laying the bowl aside, she fought the urge to vomit. Sensing the weight of the *Uí Loinge* man's eyes on her, she blearily raised her head to find him watching her.

Always scheming, always watching.

She stared stonily back at him. Her head hurt, her stomach was churning and he just sat there with a knowing smirk on his face. At that particular moment she truly felt that she hated him.

As far as she was able to feel anything, of course. Without motivation or purpose it was hard to feel much beyond the most basic of sensations: fear, anger, hatred. The only time she could recall experiencing anything akin to happiness was when she was inebriated, clouded on cloud mushroom or on the survival side of fighting. Even then, that wasn't really happiness so much as the absence of anguish, the absence of emotion in fact.

And what are you going to do about it?

Nothing, of course.

With a glum exhalation, she gazed about at the sprawled bodies of her comrades. The *fian* season was almost over. In a few days' time, following its dissolution back in Briga, the men would drift away singly or in pairs, returning to tribal lands or family to pass the worst of the winter. Some of them would return when Bressal made the call for a fresh *fian* in the summer season. Some would not. Constrained by family, duties or perhaps because they hadn't made it through winter, they would simply not turn up.

And what about you, Grey One. Will you survive another winter?

Conscious of Bressal's presence, she repressed a shudder. The prospect of spending another winter alone in that cave, dosing herself with cloud mushroom, was enough to fill her with despair. The first winter she'd endured there had been hard, the second even harder. She wasn't sure she'd survive another.

'Where will you go, Grey One?'

Bressal's voice was thick and phlegmy but the question caught her completely by surprise. She threw him a quick, panic-stricken glance, terrified that he'd somehow divined what she was thinking. Fortunately, he'd turned his head to spit a gob of phlegm into the grass, so he missed the rare expression of fear on her face. By the time he was facing her again, she'd recovered her composure and her features, impassive at the best of times, combined with the numbing effects of cloud mushroom to make her thoughts even more impenetrable. 'I return to Luachair,' she said at last.

'You have other family there?' He observed her carefully, as though gauging her response.

Liath Luachra felt her body tense. Bressal knew little to nothing of her background. This being an aspect of her life over which he had no direct control, he was always intensely curious, always seeking a chink in her silent reserve. As *éclann*, of course, he knew she had no clan to return to or on whom she could call for support. Given the circumstances under which he'd found her, he'd also worked out that she had no immediate family to speak of. Over their two year relationship, she'd deflected many such questions and despite the continual probing, he never really knew for certain how or where she spent the winters.

'Friends.'

'You have friends?' He regarded her with undisguised scepticism.

'Old friends,' she insisted. At least the first half of that sentence was true. Bressal continued to scrutinise her, as though he'd discovered something new and unexpected. 'Good friends.' She reached for the porridge again and although her stomach recoiled at the prospect of eating it, she stuffed a large mouthful between her lips to have an excuse not to talk.

The *rígfénnid* grunted. He sounded unhappy. 'Back in Briga, I know of a free hut where you would be wel-'

A sharp shake of the head cut him off.

Bressal compressed his lips and said nothing more but she could tell that her response had angered him.

For a time they continued to sit, silent except for Liath Luachra's exaggerated chomping. 'My cousin was waiting for me at the *Uí Bairrche* stronghold,' the *Uí Loinge* man said suddenly.

Liath Luachra raised her eyes over the bowl but displayed no other reaction.

'He came bearing whispers of another task. Apparently ...' He lowered his voice. 'The *rí* of the *Éblána* seeks a service.' He threw her a sideways glance. 'You know of the *Éblána?*'

Dropping her eyes, Liath Luachra shook her head.

'They are a coastal tribe led by Rólgallach Mór, a man also known as the Great Boar of the *Éblána*. They hold territory up along the coastlands to the north. My cousin married into them.'

Liath Luachra grunted noncommittally. The territory and its people meant nothing to her.

Her lack of curiosity seemed to irk the *Uí Loinge* man. 'You might ask why a man like Rólgallach Mór would seek the aid of *Na Cinéaltaí* outside of *fían* season,' he said as though thinking aloud.

Realising that he was intent on discussion, the Grey One conceded a nod. 'The warm weather is fading. The men will soon disperse.'

'Yes,' agreed Bressal, warming to his subject. 'But he does not seek the aid of the *fian* so much as the service of a small number of *fénnid* with ... skills for his task.'

Liath Luachra finally experienced a sliver of curiosity. 'What is his task?'

'He wants a man who is breathing to stop doing so.'

'And the *rí* of the *Éblána* cannot kill a man himself? Does he have no house guard?'

'It is not so simple. The man in question leads a *díberg* in *Éblána* territory but he is also Rólgallach Mór's nephew and a popular figure within the tribe. It would not look well for the *rí* of the *Éblána* to shed the blood of his own kin. Such a task would be better served by strangers so that Rólgallach Mór's name remains untainted.'

'What does he offer for such a task?'

'Land.'

This time she raised her eyes and looked at him directly. As tribal property, land was rarely offered in exchange for a service. Particularly in dealings with someone from outside the tribe.

'Rólgallach Mór is willing to trade some deserted land in their southern territories. The distance from the *Éblána* stronghold means they have little use for it, particularly as its isolation makes access difficult. Still, I have seen that land. It's good land, enough to maintain a fine herd of cattle if the right person was to work it.'

The Grey One put the empty porridge bowl aside, impressed despite herself. That was a substantial reward. Any land, particularly a holding with the makings of a sustainable farm, could set its owner up for life. 'You intend to accept Rólgallach Mór's task?'

Bressal shook his head. 'The killing of a popular figure from another tribe could have substantial consequences. I do not wish my name or that of my *fian* tarnished. I have my future position to consider. I would like you to do it.'

Because I have no name. No future.

She said nothing for she had nothing to say. As always, Bressal intended to use her, just as he used every other person with whom he ever came into contact. A natural manipulator, he had no par when it came to cajoling, intimidating or bending people to his needs.

Sensing her reluctance, Bressal hurriedly added honey to his words. 'Clearly,' he said, his voice sweet and oily, 'this task earns me the goodwill and gratitude of a powerful man in a powerful tribe. Having a friend such as Rólgallach Mór is an important part of my future plans.'

He coughed several times but the Grey One knew they weren't genuine. He was simply giving himself time to work out an approach that would ensure her compliance.

'I am not an ungenerous man,' Bressal said at last. 'This is a delicate endeavour and thus, the importance that my name and that of Rólgallach Mór are not linked. If you fulfil Rólgallach Mór's task, I propose that you receive the land he offers in reward.' He studied her face to assess her reaction but she could tell he was frustrated, stymied by its impassivity.

'Imagine that, *mo láireog léith!*' His voice sounded hearty, enthusiastic, full of excitement for her prospects. But she could tell it wasn't genuine. 'Although you are *éclann,* you would have your own holding, your own territory to do with as you wished. In future, instead of travelling back to Luachair to winter with your friends, your very good friends, you could winter in comfort on your own land.'

Liath Luachra closed her eyes and suddenly wished that she was gone, did not exist. Bressal wanted to use her and in order to do so, he was probing dangerously close to an area in which she felt exposed. Clearly, he had doubts about the existence of her 'friends' and driven by his natural instincts he wanted to test it further, honing in on some weakness he could exploit against her.

She knew she should feel angry or, at the very least, aggrieved at the *Uí Loinge* man's undisguised attempt at coercion but she felt nothing, nothing beyond a profound fear.

When she opened her eyes again, Bressal was still watching her carefully, struggling to read features that were so void of emotion. 'Will you take the task?' he asked at last.

Liath Luachra pretended to think it over but she already knew she had no choice. The prize from the *Éblána* task offered the prospect of an alternative to Luachair, not only for this winter but for all future winters, a potential refuge where she could retreat and hide from the Bressals of the world.

And that was the other consideration. If she didn't accept the task, Bressal would continue to hound her out of spite. Focussed on such a goal, it would only be a matter of time before he eventually wore her down and discovered her secrets. Once he learned the true nature of her pathetic existence and her dependence on the *fian*, his control over her would be total. Accepting the task, at least, would put off the inevitable.

She nodded.

'Excellent!' Bressal almost whipped the air in satisfaction which made the habitual flavour of capitulation taste that much fouler. The *Uí Loinge* man quickly recovered his earlier aplomb, suddenly all business again. 'You will need support. Three men. Who will you take?'

She took a deep breath then slowly turned her head to survey the battered campground and the sprawled assembly of bodies. 'Canann,' she suggested. 'And...' Drawn by the noise of coughing, her eyes drifted towards Sean Fergus. 'And Sean Fergus. And...' She frowned. 'Murchú.'

Bressal shook his head. 'Murchú is *Uí Loinge*. He will not be accompanying you. Besides, his father's sent word that he's to bond with a woman from another branch of our tribe.' He leered. 'He'll be too busy pounding her loins to swing a sword.'

'So, my choice is limited to *fénnid* who are not *Uí Loinge*?'

He smiled sourly but refused to answer her query. 'Canann is a good choice. He'll do as he's told and, like you, he is *éclann*. His people lie deep in the earth and he has no other commitments.' He tossed a quick glance over towards the prostrate warriors. 'Sean Fergus is also a good choice. I have a sense this will be his last *fian* with *Na Cinéaltaí* for I have smelt death on his breath.' He folded his hands into his lap. 'There is a condition I should have made mention of before I spoke of this task. Rólgallach Mór insists on the absence of flapping lips. He demands that those who have taken part in the endeavour be silenced.'

When she realised what Bressal was saying, Liath Luachra stared. 'The loss of almost half the *fian* causes you no concern?'

He shrugged. 'Given our recent successes I'm confident we can replace all three with new, better *fénnid*. Provided you remain close-lipped, of course.'

She regarded him silently.

And must I be silenced? Will you replace me as callously as the others?

Bressal seemed to guess what she was thinking for he raised his eyebrows and gave her an aggrieved look. 'You are too important to me, Grey One. Do you honestly think I would replace my new *rígfénnid* after all the time I've spent preparing you? I think not.'

Liath Luachra held his gaze then turned to look over to where the *fénnid* were sprawled. Conall Cacach was sitting up, rubbing at his eyes but Sean Fergus was the only one actually on his feet. Standing slightly back from the others, he held one hand against a tree to prop himself up, his face grey and haggard, the same colour as much of his hair. Given his age, he was surprisingly sprite in battle but, like Bressal, she too had noticed his increasing slowness over the course of the previous season. Still, what he lacked in speed, the warrior made up for in reliability and she could depend on him to follow her orders. 'If Murchú is not the third man, then who?'

She scanned the scattered bodies, her eyes falling on Senach.

Uí Loinge man.

Biotóg.

In Uí Loinge fosterage. As good as one of the tribe.

Moving on, her eyes came to rest on the final *fénnid*, Conall Cacach.

Her reaction was immediate. 'Not him!'

Bressal gave a tight smile, clearly anticipating this reaction. 'We both know Conall Cacach is a shitpiece but he's a good man to have at your side in a fight. More importantly, no-one will miss him when he doesn't return. Remember the *Éblána* condition.'

'As it was with the *Uí Bairrche*. "No survivors".'

He paused to scrutinise her, unsure whether she was being facetious or simply stating a fact. Unable to read her, he defaulted to the latter interpretation. 'Exactly like the *Uí Bairrche*,' he said.

'I don't trust Conall.'

'Then you are wise for I don't trust him either. My counsel would be to keep your guard. Promise him what you need to convince him to follow you. When the task is done, get him drunk and cut his throat.'

He leaned forward and held her eyes. 'Remember, Grey One. If you're successful you gain land. More importantly, you get what I suspect you truly crave; independence from those around you.'

Liath Luachra looked at him impassively, unwilling and unable to express the true sense of powerlessness she felt. 'Very well,' she said quietly.

***

As always after an extended conversation with Bressal, Liath Luachra experienced a great yearning for solitude. Hurrying away from the camp, she cut through the trees and worked her way downriver, eventually coming to a long, grassy clearing with a section of bank that sloped gently into the river. Approaching a rotting tree stump by the water's edge, she took a seat, stared at the smooth current drifting by and tried to let it scoop up her anxieties and carry them away. Try though she might however, she couldn't dislodge the conversation with Bressal that repeatedly played itself out in her head.

Rising brusquely to her feet, she stripped off her weapon belt, the sleeveless leather tunic and leggings, dropped them onto the stump and walked down into the river. Wading in up to her waist, the coldness of the water struck her like a punch to the chest. She hadn't expected it to be warm but it was far icier than the tranquillity of the current and sunshine suggested, certainly cold enough to get her heart pumping and cause goose pimples to break out on her skin.

Kicking out from shore, she swam to midstream then ducked underwater, diving deep until she touched the silt of the river bottom with her hands. Initially, she just followed the flow, kicking out occasionally to keep to the centre of the waterway. The current wasn't particularly strong but she could still feel herself being pulled downstream. Grasping a rock, she used it as an anchor and allowed herself to hang horizontally in the drift, feet floating out languidly behind her.

She remained like that for a time, enjoying the absence of sound, the translucent quality of the light and the sensation of being immersed and cut off from her life onshore.

Is this how death tastes. As peaceful as this?

She toyed with the idea of staying there forever, of slowly falling asleep and drifting off to the Black Lands but her body was having none of it. Desperate for air, it pushed her to release her grip on the rock and swim up to the light. As her head broke surface, she whooped in a great lungful of air then let herself drift aimlessly while she panted and struggled to fill her lungs.

When she looked up again, she found that she'd been pulled more than five-hundred paces downstream from where she'd originally entered the river. Striking back to shore, she hauled herself onto the bank by grasping the branch of a fallen beech tree lying at an angle into the water. Pulling herself onto the trunk, she clambered up its steep length before setting her feet back on solid ground.

Gasping for breath, she stood at the end of the trunk, Father Sun's touch a warm caress against her skin. Water ran down her back and stomach, dripping onto the rough grass beneath her feet. She twisted her head in a slow circle, pleased to find that the exercise and the chill of the river water had eliminated the headache and shaken the web of fuzziness from her mind.

Leaning against the angled trunk, she regarded the silver swirls on the river's languid surface. The day was truly rare for the cusp of autumn. Father Sun radiated heat as though determined to mark the passing of summer with his most impressive display of sunlight and the forest throbbed with life. She was able to make out the distinct descending 'pew, pew, pew' of *an ceolaire coille* [the wood warbler] but also the beautiful trill of *an fuiseog* [skylark]. The forest leaves rustled in a gentle breeze and the air was heavy with an earthy after-rain perfume tinged with the sweet scent of wildflowers.

She sighed. These were the rare moments of pleasure, the moments of peace and clarity when she could lose herself in the sheer physical beauty of the Great Wild. And yet, despite such joy, she could feel a shade settle over her mood at the thought of her imminent return to the campsite.

Her earlier euphoria withered and for a moment she simply stood, confused by the intensity of her own reaction. Over her previous seasons with *Na Cineáltaí*, she'd felt herself growing inside, albeit tortuously slow, like a damaged seed. Despite the danger, the bloody violence and the mind-numbing substances she took to erase them, her time with the *fían* had its positives. It had provided her with a sliver of hope, the possibility of a future other than an overwhelming sense of dread. It had offered her a sense of belonging, of self-worth; something entirely absent for a substantial proportion of her more recent life. The other members of the *fían* – with the exception of Conall Cacach, of course – appreciated her fighting skill, respected her, even if they didn't actually like her. Certainly, she knew her 'comrades-in-arms' would take advantage if she let them, but she hadn't let them and at least some of them grudgingly respected her all the more for that.

But now, for some reason, it too felt like the turning of a season. That sense of inclusion she'd always clung to, had deteriorated. The situation with Bressal was becoming increasingly complex and she could sense his grip on her growing ever tighter. The offer of *rígfénnid* might have been flattering had it not been such a blatant element of his own plans, plans in which she was little more than a pawn to be manipulated. She shivered, an uneasy nausea souring her stomach at the prospect of the increased responsibility and the associated interaction that role would necessarily entail.

I could run.

She considered that for a moment. The idea held some appeal. She could run, slip into the shadows of the forest and simply walk away from the *fían*.

Except that she had nowhere to go, nowhere to return to but Luachair. Her stomach give an involuntary lurch.

So what else are you to do?

She chewed thoughtfully on the inside of her cheek.

The Éblána Land.

In a sense it was the perfect solution. It offered everything she needed; autonomy and independence. If she had land to support herself and the tacit consent of the most powerful tribe in the vicinity, she could retreat there, living safely and shunning all human contact. The isolation wouldn't be a problem. After so much time alone, she didn't feel loneliness in the way the others did and if anyone entered her territories she could always hide and ...

She paused then, suddenly conscious that what she was envisaging bore an uncomfortable resemblance to her existence in the cave at Luachair.

She started walking.

It didn't take long to make her way back upriver. Although beech trees proliferated along the bank, there was plenty of space between them and the ground was free of impassable undergrowth. A short time later, she caught her first glimpse of the stump through the trees and was about to increase her pace towards the clearing when a sudden, unmistakeable chill tingled the back of her neck.

She dropped to the ground.

Slithering into the undergrowth, she crouched and waited, eyes scanning the surrounding forest.

A long time passed but nothing moved amongst the trees and she heard nothing out of the ordinary. Despite the forest's apparent calm, she sensed a certain discordance, an underlying menace to the happy chatter of birds, a particular stillness to the air that she'd only ever previously noticed just before the start of battle.

Moving at a crawl, she worked her way closer to the clear strip of river bank, coming to a halt behind a thin cluster of ferns spread beneath the expansive branches of an unusually gnarled beech. She gazed across the open ground to her clothing and equipment. *Gléas gan Ainm* was in its scabbard, propped up at an angle against the rotting stump, tantalisingly close yet too far away to be of any use. Chewing nervously on her lower lip, she considered the precariousness of her situation. Naked and without a weapon, she was at a distinct disadvantage.

Her eyes examined the ground to her right where a broken branch lay amongst the leaf clutter, a solid length of wood that looked solid enough to wield as a club. She considered it for a moment, assessing its potential before, finally, deciding against it. Stealth and agility were her most effective responses right now. The club – despite its reassuring solidity – would only be effective if she had the advantage of surprise. It wouldn't help against an armed man of any competence.

A sudden shuffling in the bushes at the far side of the clearing drew her eyes and her throat tightened when she saw Conall Cacach step out into the open. A shiver rushed through her as though the winds had changed and a cool breeze had gusted in off the river.

Maintaining a wary eye on the surrounding forest, the greasy-haired warrior ambled slowly towards the riverbank, one hand resting on the hilt of his sword. Approaching the stump, he swiftly bent down to grasp *Gléas gan Ainm* and, with a single yank, pulled the sword free from its sheath. He held the weapon at arms' length, gazing down the length of the blade as he moved in it in a wide horizontal arc that took in the surrounding trees.

'I know you're out there, Grey One. Slinking though those bushes.'

He glanced down at the weapon, nodding appreciatively as he wielded it in his hand. Taking up a battle stance, he proceeded to whip the sword thorough a series of complex combat manoeuvres, moving with impressive dexterity before he finished up, chest heaving. Raising the sleeve of his filthy tunic, he wiped the sweat from his forehead.

'Very good, Grey One.'

Resheathing *Gléas gan Ainm*, he dropped it onto the ground and his hand returned to the hilt of his own weapon. 'Your sword has good balance. I commend you.' He waited for a moment, staring around the trees as though waiting for a response. When none was forthcoming, he shrugged and turned back to the little pile of clothing.

'I'm sure it causes you no disquiet that I explore your kit, Grey One. As comrades of the trail, I'd like to think we can share what little we have.'

Concealed behind the screen of ferns, Liath Luachra continued to watch, fury scalding the pit of her stomach. With fierce eyes she

61

observed Conall Cacach remove his own sword and use it to poke her clothing, shifting the various items about with the tip until he'd located what he was looking for. Angling the weapon in, he prised her loincloth free, raised it up on the sword and tossed it in the air to catch it with his left hand. Lifting it to his nose, he inhaled deeply and his face broke into a creaky, gap-toothed smile. 'Ah yes! Mmmm, that's ripe. Ripe enough for the plucking I'd say.' He laughed, a harsh unpleasant laugh. 'A good thought to take a swim, Grey One.'

'You should rethink what you're planning.'

Conall Cacach spun about, eyes latching onto the Grey One's slim form at the far side of the clearing where she'd emerged from the ferns. The *fénnid's* eyes dropped from hers, slipping down to her chest and plunging straight for the apex of her thighs. After a prolonged gawk he deigned to raise his gaze and consider her directly.

'Oh?' He widened his eyes in a poor caricature of surprise. 'And what do you think I'm planning?'

'Something ill-considered.'

'Just a quiet talk in the woods, Grey One. Nothing more.'

The Grey One stepped forward a little further out of the ferns. 'We can share words back at camp.' She kept her voice soft, carefully neutral. 'Besides, Bressal intends to call a gathering. He has a proposal to lay to the *fian.*'

'No, he doesn't. Bressal's off planning with that spineless vassal of his and you know as well as I do how that man likes to talk. So, no. There's no hurry. We have all the time, all the privacy in the world.' He beamed at her but this time there was an edgy hunger to that gap-toothed, yellow-stained smile.

'Then say what you want to say. I have no mood for your company.'

The leer broadened at that but the Grey One simply stood unresponsive, returning his stare without expression, no give to her at all.

'You owe me.'

'I owe you nothing. What you earn as booty is under Bressal's command.'

'No,' he insisted. '*You* owe me.'

She sneered. 'What do I owe you?'

'Back at the *Uí Bairrche* settlement, you killed that girl. I had plans for her.'

'You were compensated.'

'Not to my satisfaction. You have to make it right by me. You'll pay your dues …' There was a malicious slowness to his movement as he lifted the loincloth to his nose and sniffed again. 'One way or t'other.'

Liath Luachra felt a cold knot in her stomach with the realization that her attempt to brazen it out had failed. Secure in the knowledge that she couldn't reach her weapon, he'd called her bluff and now she had but two options left to her: flight or fight. Neither held much appeal. If she fled back to the *fian*, naked and routed, she'd lose all respect and any credible authority she'd built up over the preceding seasons. The *fénnid* would more than likely revert to their baser natures, turning on her while they had the advantage. Bressal might step in to save her, of course. But he'd want something in return and without her ability to control the men, she'd have lost her usefulness to him.

Fighting – without a weapon – offered even less as an alternative. Although big for her age and gender, Conall Cacach was much bigger, even if she did manage to get past his sword. Despite his obnoxious and toxic character he was also the most dangerous man in the *fian*, except perhaps for Sean Fergus, although the latter's heyday had been and gone.

A sudden call rang out from the trees off to their right, followed by a scuffle of movement as someone worked their way through the forest towards them. Conall Cacach's black eyes flared in furious resentment and he tossed her a look full of venom. 'It seems this is a popular spot.'

She made no response.

A moment later, the bushes at the northern edge of the clearing parted and Sean Fergus pushed his way through. The old warrior was facing Conall Cacach when he first emerged from the trees, but his eyes quickly flickered to the Grey One, drawn by the sheen of her skin. His jaw dropped as he saw her full nakedness.

'What do you want, *a seanstrompa?*' growled Conall Cacach, his usual belligerence intensified by his rage at the grizzled warrior's untimely intrusion. Distracted, Sean Fergus glanced at him briefly before his eyes returned to Liath Luachra. Despite her lack of clothing, the young woman stood coolly observing them as though both were beneath her interest.

'Bressal calls a gathering. He wants you both back with the others.'

'A gathering?' Conall Cacach shot the Grey One a look of dark suspicion.

Sean Fergus shrugged. That's all I know, big man. You can come or you can stay. Makes no difference to me but if you're wanting your share of the booty it'd be wise to follow sharply.'

'Of course, of course,' said Conall Cacach, his words tinged with bitter sarcasm. 'When *rígfénnid* Bressal calls, his *fian* come a-running, loyal men and true that we are.' Surprised by the venomous response, Sean Fergus turned to consider him more closely but the broad-shouldered warrior ignored him and stalked off into the trees. 'Next time, Grey One,' he spat over his shoulder although he made no attempt to look back at her.

Sean Fergus watched him go then, with a shrug, started to move off after him. He paused abruptly, twisting about to look at Liath Luachra. 'You coming, Grey One?'

'Go ahead.' She waved vaguely in the direction of the camp. 'I'll follow shortly.'

The greying warrior looked at her uncertainly but then he nodded and continued on his way.

Liath Luachra remained where she was, watching the forest until she was sure the two men had left. Turning on her heel, she walked slowly towards the stump, grasped her clothing and equipment, then holding the bundle in her arms, started for the opposite side of the clearing.

She managed to make it half-way across that open space before she faltered and broke into a run, plunging panic-stricken through the treeline and deep into the forest. Unable to stop herself, she kept on running, brushing through the branches and scrub that obstructed her path, raked her skin and scratched the side of her face. In the end, it was a tree root in the darkest shadow of the forest that stopped her, catching her foot and tripping her up so that she hit the ground hard, the breath knocked out of her. Wheezing, she shuffled into the tight, leaf-lined space between two buttresses of a giant oak, curling up with her knees drawn close to her chest. She lay trembling, eyes screwed tight shut, shivering violently, jaws clenched in terror. The scars on her back, insensible for so many years, suddenly burned as hard as they had on the day she'd received them.

She must have passed out briefly for when she came to her senses, she was lying on her side, cold and damp, coated in a sticky layer of dead leaves. Sitting up, she wiped a crust of dried snot, spit and tears from her face. Numb and exhausted, she got to her feet, pulled on her clothes and strapped her sword belt around her waist. Her hands were no longer shaking but her head was empty. After the traumatic outburst she had nothing left to spill.

She drew a shaky breath, conscious of how fortunate she'd been. If Sean Fergus hadn't turned up when he had, events could have worked out very differently. It was possible she'd have got away had she made a break for it but, then again, it was just as possible she might not. Conall Cacach moved with the lethal agility of a river eel when he needed to. Naked and without a weapon, she wouldn't have stood much of a chance. She'd have fought him to her last breath but in the end, when he'd had his revenge, he'd have slit her throat and left her body in the woods to rot. No-one would ever have known.

No-one would have cared.

***

With his plans made, Bressal had wasted no time putting them into action. By the time Liath Luachra returned to the camp, Conall Cacach and Sean Fergus were seated with the others by a newly-set fire, chewing on a fresh batch of the gritty porridge. The former looked at her coldly as she joined the circle of *fénnid*. Drawing on a confidence she did not truly feel, she forced herself to return that look with a baleful glare until he finally averted his eyes, although any sense of triumph she might have felt was undermined by his open sneer.

I have to kill him.

That much was evident. She'd managed to keep him in check in the past but, following her actions at the *Uí Bairrche* settlement, his hatred of

65

her had finally spilled over to overwhelm his instinctive wariness. Foiled at the river through circumstance rather than through any kind of effective defiance, he'd seen her at her most vulnerable. Now, he wouldn't be able to prevent himself coming after her again.

The Grey One bent forwards from the log on which she was sitting and massaged her temples. Conall Cacach wouldn't risk approaching her head on. He had wit enough to know that good fighter though he was, with a weapon in her hand, she was more than a match for him.

She sniffed.

No. He'd go with what had worked for him in the past, watching her constantly until she dropped her guard. Then he'd make his move.

Knowing there was nothing she could do about it at present, she pushed such thoughts aside and considered the other *fénnid*. The wet patches on their clothing suggested that they'd been roused with buckets of river water. Now however, they sat quietly, nursing bowls of porridge and hangovers with equal intensity.

Noting the return of the final member of his *fian*, Bressal stood up and called for silence. When he had their attention, he wasted no time introducing the intended change of plan, outlining the *Éblána* request for a service and his intention to place Liath Luachra as *rígfénnid* of a smaller *fian* to fulfil that service. After that, he proceeded to describe in great detail the potential awards that awaited those who volunteered.

At first, the *fénnid* sat listening morosely, making no comment, asking no questions. As the plan was outlined in greater detail however, their leader's great understanding of the kind of men he was dealing with and the impulses that drove them, became evident. Although he appeared to give every *fénnid* a choice on whether they should continue on to Briga or follow her on the *Éblána* service, Liath Luachra couldn't help but notice that he worded it all in a manner that emphasised the rewards of women, wealth, land and − most of all − respect, rather than the risks associated with the venture.

As someone who struggled to express herself on any topic outside of martial action, she appreciated the *Uí Loinge* man's talking skills. Bressal's fluency with words took on an almost otherworldly quality to her ears. Bressal Binnbhéalach, sweet-tongued indeed.

66

At the same time, despite her respect for his speaking skills, she experienced a growing uneasiness as the true depth of his duplicity became more apparent. Because of the words he was using, Bressal came across as a concerned leader, direct but trustworthy, someone who had his men's best interests at heart. Nevertheless, he was effectively sending three of those men gathered to their deaths

The *fénnid*, for their part, responded with almost tragic thoughtlessness. Stirred by Bressal's rousing speech and promises of wealth and glory, Canann volunteered immediately. Conall Cacach sneered and made his usual sarcastic comments but, in the end, his greed too got the better of his innate rat cunning and he consented to join them. Sean Fergus simply shrugged and nodded as though the matter was of no great concern to him either way.

As for the *Uí Loinge* men, she couldn't help noticing that although they listened intently, none of them actually volunteered for the *Éblána* service. Bressal, clearly, had prepared his fellow tribal members in advance and instructed them to say nothing.

Scheming. Always scheming.

Despite her disquiet at the *rígfénnid's* ruthlessness, the Grey One couldn't help but be impressed by his sense of organisation. He'd evidently been planning this action for some time for the siting of their current campsite – the nearest point to *Éblána* territory on the *Uí Bairrche - Uí Loinge* trade route – could hardly have been simple coincidence. Bressal must have intended to halt there all along so that he could organise a *fian* to dispatch to the *Éblána*.

Which means he must have known I would concede to his bidding.

The thought that she was so easy to manipulate weighed heavily on her shoulders and she slumped backwards on the log, watching quietly as her suspicions were confirmed with the arrival of the *Uí Loinge* slaves, bearing four parcels of food; five or six days' worth of supplies for each volunteer. The journey would take longer than that of course but the weight of those packages was as much as each *fénnid* could reasonably carry and still make speed, supporting it with what they hunted and foraged on the trail. What interested her most however, was the fact that the food had been prepared – smoked salted and packed – well in advance.

In hindsight, of course, it was now obvious why he'd chosen the *éclann* for this particular task. Despite their viciousness and fighting ability, none of them were particularly smart. More importantly, none of them had anywhere else to go and nobody would miss them if they did not return. The *éclann fénnid* were essentially expendable and as long as Liath Luachra held them to their task and ensured their silence on its completion, Bressal had nothing to fear.

The Grey One felt a mounting apprehension at her own part in this plan. It was true she despised most of the *fénnid* and, had the situation been reversed, she doubted any of them would have blinked an eye before silencing her. Nevertheless, the prospect was one that filled her with misgiving.

Having said what he wanted to say, Bressal invited them all to spend the remainder of the day and that night to recover for their separate treks the following morning. As the group broke up and drifted apart to reflect on his words, the *Uí Loinge* man insisted on taking Liath Luachra aside, reminding her of his expectations and then, surreptitiously slipping her another pouch of *beacáin scammalach*. Standing before her, he momentarily raised his right hand but then abruptly let it drop to his side. With a start, she realised that he'd probably intended to caress her face but had decided against it at the last moment.

He gestured at the little leather pouch. 'Don't overdo it. I want you back here in one piece.' He leaned forward, brought his lips to her ear. 'Come back, Grey One. But come back alone. You and I have further matters to discuss on your return.' He considered her intently. 'And I would have you closer.'

Chapter Four

It took twelve days of hard travel for Liath Luachra and her companions to reach the low hills that marked the western border of *Éblána* territory. The trek across the Great Wild had been arduous, one of the most gruelling she'd ever undertaken and a poor omen for the harsh days to come. Despite the residual warmth of early autumn's mantle, the terrain had been more severe than anticipated, surprisingly empty of game and not without its own lethal diversions. On one occasion, inadvertently stumbling upon the den of a large wolf pack, the group was obliged to fight off the animals in a vicious battle that left the warriors exhausted and coated with gore but, fortunately, without serious wounds. A few days later, unfamiliar with the territory and confused by a heavy mist, they'd wandered off course and ended up on an isolated promontory surrounded on all sides by impassable swamp. With no other option but to retrace their steps to firmer ground and work out an alternative route, they were delayed a further two to three days.

The mild weather had also caved in and the rains started in earnest while they were still some distance from their destination. For the remaining three days of the journey, they'd trudged through puddle-infested ground, mud-coated slopes and incessantly dripping forest. Despite the hooded wool cloaks they wore, nothing could prevent the rain from trickling in, saturating their clothing and causing chafe rash from the constant movement.

By the time they reached the foothills, the group was sodden, starving and at each other's throats, particularly Conall Cacach who glared repeatedly at Liath Luachra with hatred but took his frustration out instead on the feeble-minded Canann. The Grey One was obliged to extend herself beyond her habitual silence, forcing herself to harry the surly *fénnid*, utilising all manner of threats to keep them in line. Unable to conceive of anything beyond their immediate discomfort, it was a struggle to keep the men focussed on their task. Bressal's promised rewards were too intangible a carrot to use as a meaningful bribe and it was up to her to support the *Uí Loinge* man's assurances with threats and promises of her own.

For this reason, although she concealed it well, the Grey One was just as relieved as the others at the sight of the nearby hills. The burden of leadership and responsibility had proven an even greater yoke about her neck than she'd anticipated. Despite the fatigue and discomfort that she shared with the others however, she did have the advantage of being able to take a more distanced and pragmatic view of their situation. She was alive, she wasn't back in Luachair with the cave and the cloud mushroom and for that, at least, she was grateful.

Working their way up into the hills, they found a narrow, passage-like cave below the treeline that offered shelter from the unrelenting rain. Here, given the lateness of the afternoon, the continuing downpour and the bedraggled state of the *fénnid*, Liath Luachra called a halt. Tired, soaked to the bone and caked in filth, they collapsed inside the rocky shelter, relieved to find the makings of a good fire – dead leaves, twigs and dry moss – strewn across the floor. Building up a small fire, they soon had it blazing hot enough to add larger – if damper – pieces of wood.

Hanging her sodden cloak from a ledge above the flames, Liath Luachra scraped layers of caked mud from her legs and feet as she stared out at the torrential rain. With the group's food supplies exhausted, she knew she had little option but to send the men out to forage. Despite the angry moaning, she had everyone pull straws and ended up directing Sean Fergus and Canann to set snares while she attempted to scavenge some food in the lower trees. Aware that they were going to be saturated no matter what they did, all three left their cloaks behind to dry, looking forward to the heat of them on their return.

As the one who'd drawn the short straw, Conall Cacach had the relatively luxurious task of remaining in the warmth of the cave to protect their equipment and tend to the fire. When they left, he sent them off with an evil chuckle.

Given the weather, the Grey One wasn't expecting much success from the snares when she returned some time later, saturated and lugging a small pile of edible, if somewhat tasteless, roots. Fortunately, it turned out that the local wildlife was also obliged to venture outside in the rain for both Sean Fergus and Canann came back with a hare in each hand. Divesting themselves of their sodden clothing, all three wrapped themselves in their cloaks and sat by the fire to warm up. That night they dined on roast hare, dry and comfortable for the first time in many days.

Although she wanted nothing more than to retire to her own company at the far end of the cave, Liath Luachra forced herself to make an effort to speak to the *fénnid*. To her surprise, she'd noticed that they'd started to defer to her judgement – even Conall Cacach – in terms of the longer term decisions and the overall direction of the service. While they chewed on the smoky meat therefore, she outlined the proposal for the following day: essentially to continue east until they could see the sea. Once the Great Blue was in sight, her instructions had been to search for sign of smoke from the *Éblána* stronghold and to work their way towards it until they caught sight of a large *bod*-shaped [penis-shaped] outcrop on the upper hills. There, at the designated meeting point, they would signal *Na Éblána* of their arrival and wait until they were contacted.

Heartily sick of each other's company by then, there was little conversation after the meal and with the exception of Canann, who held the first watch, they retired early.

Wrapped in the cocooning warmth of her flame-dried cloak, Liath Luachra cursed Bressal repeatedly as she mentally worked through the necessary steps for the following day. According to the *Uí Loinge* man, the *Éblána* stronghold was located directly east of the hills, essentially another half-day's march. If they left early, it was possible that they could be at the meeting place sometime before mid-day.

Drowsy, she closed her eyes and pushed such logistical details away. With a sigh, she relaxed and slept well for the first time since leaving the *fian*.

***

The following morning, it seemed as though their luck had finally turned for when Liath Luachra awoke, she found the rain had ceased.

Tossing her cloak to one side, she got to her feet and made for the cave entrance where Sean Fergus was taking his watch. The old warrior was sitting on a flat rock, cloak clutched tight about him as he stared out at a heavy mist. Noting her approach, he glanced up and scratched his beard. 'It'll clear,' he assured her. 'The forest and the hills still hold moisture from the rain but I've been watching the breeze pick up. That'll shift the mist soon enough.'

Liath Luachra grunted. Since her previous conversation in the woods with the grizzled warrior, she'd intentionally avoided any further discussion with him. Undiscouraged, Sean Fergus looked back into the cave to ensure the others were sleeping. 'What do you think then, Grey One?'

She considered him with a non-committal expression, loathe to encourage further conversation.

'Of this *Éblána* service,' he persisted.

'Just a service.' She shrugged. 'Just like any other.'

'But it's not, is it?'

She eyed him curiously.

'No-one forced you to join us, Sean Fergus. If you didn't like it you should have continued to Briga with the others. Besides, you swore fealty to Bressal.'

'True enough,' he conceded. He plucked a sliver of dried clay from his beard and tossed it aside. Liath Luachra started to edge away but before she could escape he hit her with another question. 'And you, Grey One. Did you swear fealty to Bressal?'

'Of course. He is *rígfénnid*. I follow his direction.'

'Would you follow his direction if you believed it was the wrong one?'

'That is the bond of *fénnid* and *rígfénnid*.' She looked at him, her discomfort growing. These were trying questions to pester her with, particularly as they mirrored some of her own reservations.

'Even if it was to your own detriment?'

She rubbed her eyes with the heels of her palms. 'Shut up, Sean Fergus. You make my head hurt with your *ráiméis* – your nonsense talk.'

72

Leaving him, she wandered back to where the others were sleeping and roused them both with a kick to the side. 'Get up off your arses. We leave shortly.'

Canann grunted and Conall Cacach snarled, but sensing her mood both had the wit to restrain their discontent to whispered insults and did not challenge her.

As Sean Fergus predicted, the mist dispersed rapidly with a strengthening breeze. After a time, wide shafts of golden sunlight pierced the remaining cloud cover and soon even this had faded away to blue skies, a warm sun and almost perfect visibility. Settling down to an unappetising breakfast of watercress and tubers, they ate quickly, packed their remaining gear and set out from the cave.

The warm, dry conditions helped to improve the group's morale immensely and there was a minimum of the usual bickering and crabbishness. As they trekked uphill, the *fénnid* talked openly about their plans for the reward from their service. Liath Luachra listened in, her stomach tightening, but said nothing.

'What will you do with your rewards, Sean Fergus?' Canann wanted to know.

The old man scratched at the pale skin of his belly through a hole in the woolly material of his tunic then turned to empty a nose-full of snot into the grass. He shrugged. 'I don't know. Nothing.'

Canann shook his head in incomprehension as he scratched the stubble of his skull. 'I'm going to get my mother a cow. Maybe two cows. What about you Conall?'

'I'm going to get your mother. And then, rut her senseless.'

Canann looked at him, visibly offended but too cowed to retaliate.

'Or maybe,' continued Conall, casting a smile like an obscenity in the Grey One's direction. 'I'll get myself a nice, flat-chested wife to go down on her knees and suck the wits from me.'

'That'll be quickly done then,' Liath Luachra countered.

The big warrior snarled but said nothing more.

Achieving the summit of the plateau, they traversed the high country in an easterly direction. The terrain was coated in heavy beech forest and undulated dramatically at times but without the rain and marshes, the trek was markedly less onerous than it had been over the previous days. The sun was at its highest point when they broke out of the trees and onto a rocky promontory at the top of some high cliffs. Looking down, they saw a narrow strip of flatland stretching out from the base of the cliff to the distant coastline.

As the others gathered about the lip of the cliff, Liath Luachra stared down at large sections of unforested flatland drenched in a soft, crisp yellow light. Glancing to her right, she noticed Canann shielding his eyes against the glare as he stared towards the sea. The dim-witted warrior was stretching his neck forward, eyes bulging in concentration, as though by trying harder he'd be able to see even further. She was about to ask him what he was doing but Conall Cacach's poisonous growl got in before her.

'What are you doing, *a dúramán* [half-wit]?'

Canann didn't turn to look away. 'The sea,' he said. 'I've never seen the sea before. I want to see it better.'

Conall Cacach rolled his eyes.

'My mother told me it was blue,' Canann continued. 'Like a giant lake. But that's green. A dirty green.'

Conall scoffed. 'Like the inside of yer snotty head!'

'My mother said it was full of fish.'

'Then I bet it smells just like her an all.' With a snort of disgust, Conall Cacach turned away and moved further along the cliff top.

Distinct traces of smoke to the south indicated the location of the *Éblána* stronghold so Liath Luachra led them in that direction, keeping to the hills but moving parallel to the sea while they searched for an outcrop that looked like a male sexual organ. The search provided a major source of amusement for the *fénnid*. 'Wouldn't be the first time you were out searching cock, Grey One,' Conall Cacach laughed harshly.

'I shit on your head, Conall. Now shut your gob or I'll cut your scrawny balls off.'

As they drew closer to the source of the smoke, it became evident that it originated from not one but from four separate fires, suggesting a stronghold of significant size. Liath Luachra fretted, concerned about approaching too close for fear of being spotted by someone other than Rólgallach Mór. From their raised position on the hills, there was already plenty of evidence that the coastal land was occupied: large sections of forest had been cleared and empty fields showed the remains of recent harvests.

In general, the presence of strangers on tribal territory was treated with suspicion and often outright hostility. No tribe appreciated their territory being traversed or hunted without their consent. There were exceptions of course; individual travellers or traders were generally accepted but no-one was likely to mistake the *fénnid* for anything other than the warriors they were.

It was fortunate therefore, that just when she was on the point of calling a halt, the rock they were seeking loomed into sight beyond another forested outcrop several hundred paces to the south. To the Grey One's surprise, the rock did indeed have a distinct phallic shape. An enormous stone column that had split away from the main cliff face some time in the past, subsequent erosion had smoothened it into the form of an erect *bod* poking out at an angle from the cliff. That impression was heightened by the presence of two giant boulders at its base which bore a surprising resemblance to a pair of *magairlí* [testicles].

Moving closer, they found that the structure was located at the centre of a deep, U-shaped cleft in the hill, the high, curving cliffs on either side the key reason for the time it'd taken them to discern it. As the little group moved further inside the enclosing grotto, Liath Luachra noticed a small stone altar at the base of the boulders covered with votive offerings; bone or stone bracelets, brass necklaces and wrist bands. The Grey One frowned and bit her lip. This location was clearly something of a sacred site for the *Éblána* and there was little doubt in her mind that if they were caught trespassing, they'd immediately be taken for thieves or looters. Growing increasingly uncomfortable, she fingered the hilt of her sword and looked around at the semi-circular enclosure. The site offered good concealment but if they were discovered and trapped within the grotto, they were going to be in trouble.

She exhaled heavily, forcing such misgivings from her mind. It was obvious this was the location described by Bressal so they really had no alternative but to follow his instructions and hope for the best.

She quickly directed Conall Cacach and Sean Fergus to gather wood and kindling to build a fire while Canann was sent further downhill to take up position where he could alert them should anyone approach. The warriors had the fire lit quickly enough and once it'd taken hold, she tossed grass and green leaves onto the flames and watched the resulting smoke rise into the air. Thick and dark from the green material, it formed a strikingly dense column that would be more than enough to alert the *Éblána* to their presence.

In fact, it took a surprisingly short time for the *Éblána* to make their appearance, the haste of their arrival suggesting that they'd been anticipating the *fian* for some time. Not long after the smoke had risen above the lip of the surrounding cliffs, Canann came rushing back to inform him that strangers – three warriors and a man on horseback – were approaching at speed.

Taking no chances, Liath Luachra had the *fénnid* form up in battle position on the inner side of the fire, the altar and the two large boulders at their backs. They didn't have to wait long. A few moments later, a man riding a tall roan – clearly Rólgallach Mór – entered the grotto at a canter, followed closely by three hard-faced warriors – his personal house guards – running breathless behind him. The Grey One watched with curiosity, relieved by the presence of such a small welcoming party. It confirmed Rólgallach Mór not only knew who they were but that the encounter was one he didn't want news of to spread.

Behind her, the *fénnid* watched uneasily as the newcomers drew closer, hands on their weapons. As the horseman approached, Liath Luachra gestured for them to keep them sheathed. About twenty paces from the fire, the *rí* of the *Éblána* hauled back on the reins of his mount, bringing the animal to a sharp and brutal halt. Agitated, the horse briefly skirted sideways before it stopped moving. Ignoring the skittish animal, Rólgallach Mór regarded the four strangers to his territory with cautious eyes. Liath Luachra noted that they seemed to linger on her far longer than on the others.

76

The *rí* of the *Éblána* was a giant of a man, strikingly tall and stocky with long, curly brown hair tied up in a ponytail. His eyes were unusually narrow-set and with his thin lips, gave his face a somewhat petulant appearance. Despite this, he carried himself with that assured air of authority so common amongst the tribal leaders and it was easy to see why he'd earned the title 'The Great Boar'.

As the horse came to a stop, he leaned forwards, his right hand resting on his left knee and called out to them: 'I see you strangers. I am Rólgallach Mór of the *Éblána*.' His voice was deep and boomed loudly in the rocky confines.

'I see you, Rólgallach Mór,' Liath Luachra responded in the traditional manner. 'I am named Liath Luachra. These are my comrades Sean Fergus, Conall and Canann. We've travelled from the central lands to be here.' As instructed by Bressal, she made no mention of his name or that of *Na Cinéaltaí*.

Rólgallach Mór nodded but she thought she saw a slight scorn in his eyes at the lack of any reference to a clan affiliation.

Ah, of course. As éclann, we are lesser people.

Whatever his views on their origins, the *Éblána* leader made no mention of them. Reaching around behind, he pulled some leather sacks from where they lay draped across the horse's rump and tossed them to one of the panting warriors: a dark, black-bearded man with a circular tattoo in the centre of his forehead. Dismounting from his horse, Rólgallach Mór retrieved the sacks, approached the fire and handed them to Liath Luachra. Over a head taller than her, she found herself having to look up at him as she received them.

'A gift from the *Éblána* to welcome you to our lands. You've travelled far and are, no doubt, burdened by hunger. Please sit with us and partake in the hospitality of the *Éblána*. Afterwards we can talk.'

The *fénnid* stared hungrily as the Grey One opened the sack and handed out pieces of cooked venison wrapped in leaves, still warm from recent cooking. The sacks also contained a basket of smoked fish pieces, several cooked tubers and a skin of water. Fulfilling the tradition of hospitality, the *Éblána* men sat by the fire with their guests and although

77

they ate sparingly, they chatted easily enough on the local hunting practices and other non-contentious topics.

Before the food had been consumed, Rólgallach Mór reached over to tap the woman warrior on the arm. 'Let us talk to one side.'

Rising to their feet, they ambled slowly towards the southern cliff and out of hearing of the others. The Grey One studied the *rí* of *Na Éblána* from the corner of her eye, noting the swagger in his stride, the way he held his chin up, chest puffed out as though he was majesty of all he surveyed.

Which, she supposed, he was.

Up close, she could also see that despite his stocky build most of that bulk was muscle. The loose folds of flesh around his eyes however, suggested that he hadn't lacked for sustenance any time recently.

As they approached the grey rock face, Liath Luachra slowed to a halt. To her surprise, Rólgallach Mór advanced further, obliging her to back up to maintain a space between them. She sensed the confining closeness of the rock face against her back and was suddenly conscious of how close the looming the *Éblána rí* had come. Clearly accustomed to towering over women, she knew he was intentionally trying to intimidate her.

'So you're Bressal's little mare.' He made a soft whistling sound between his lips but it sounded high and off-key. 'Let's have a look at you.' He abruptly reached out with one hand, catching her under the chin. He forced her head up, swivelling it from one side to the other. The Grey One stiffened and felt her heart pound inside her chest but somehow managed to control her temper.

'Take off your tunic,' he ordered.

Casually, so casually it might have been taken for a simple accident, she let her hand drop to the hilt of *Gléas Gan Ainm*. Over by the fire however, everyone was watching and nobody mistook the threat for anything other than what it was. All six men quickly rose to their feet, the earlier fireside camaraderie discarded as both groups pulled apart. Canann and Conall put their hands on their swords, ready to draw from their scabbards. Sean Fergus suddenly had a knife in his hands and although he was pretending to use it to clean his fingernails, he wasn't fooling anyone. The three *Éblána* men meanwhile had tightened their grips on their spears. The two groups weren't actually facing each other off across the smoky flames but they weren't far off it.

Distracted by the scuffling sounds behind, Rólgallach Mór twisted his head to see what was happening and stiffened as he grasped the situation. Before things could deteriorate any further, he called out to his men. 'Flannán! And you others. Put your weapons down. Sit at your ease. These people are our friends.'

The *Éblána* warriors looked at him uncertainly then, with evident reluctance, lowered their weapons and retrieved their seats by the fire. After a few moments, the *fénnid* cautiously joined them but they remained on their guard as they watched the *Éblána* closely.

Rólgallach Mór chuckled once more as he returned his attention to the woman warrior. 'Bressal said you were a prickly one.' He shrugged. 'I am simply a curious man. I wished to know you were not just a pretty boy.'

Despite his playful tone, the *rí's* eyes glittered with the harsh sheen of polished metal. Liath Luachra stood terse and silent, muscles trembling, poised to leap into action. At the best of times, she struggled with small talk and, right there and then, it went against all her instincts to exchange pleasantries rather than blows with this man. Nevertheless, Bressal would not forgive her for resorting to violence, no matter the provocation. Sucking a lungful of air in through her nose, she suppressed the urge to attack, resorting instead to the single topic of conversation she had in common with him.

'Who is the man you want dead?'

The *rí* of the *Éblána's* eyes narrowed, unaccustomed to such direct interrogation. Although his gaze didn't waver she could tell he was weighing up whether to give into his sense of outrage or bide his time for more practical benefit. A seasoned politician, the latter won out.

'He is named Barra. He is my second cousin and a traitor to our clan.' He paused as though expecting her to say something but she simply stood watching him impassively.

'My spies report that he is attempting to raise a *díberg* to raid against his own people and-'

79

Liath Luachra shook her head abruptly, cutting him off. 'Your motivations are of no interest to me. Those are the affairs of *Na Éblána*. I need only know his name, his looks and where I might find him.'

Once again, Rólgallach Mór's stance grew rigid with stifled anger then, surprisingly, the tension eased from his shoulders. He considered her with fresh appreciation.

'Barra holds coastal land at Gort Na Meala – Field of Honey – to the north of here. A trade trail running up the coast from our stronghold will lead you where you need to go. Four day's travel will find you at a great yellow rock where a second trail branches off to the west. This marks the start of a wide valley running directly inland from the sea. The hills are not high so the valley can also be accessed from several points either side.'

'How will I know this Barra?'

'He is tall, young. He has brown hair that falls to his shoulders and boasts a wide moustache. He is ...' He paused. 'He is considered by some to be handsome.'

That cost you some effort, big man.

'He tends to a red-coloured cloak of wool.'

'What forces does he have to call on?'

Rólgallach Mór shrugged. 'Four warriors. Some servants and slaves but probably no more than three or four at most, none of them fighters.'

Hardly a serious threat against Na Éblána then.

She kept that thought to herself as she regarded the stocky man. *Na Éblána* politics were unimportant. 'We require a guide.'

Rólgallach Mór's eyes narrowed. 'Why do you require a guide? I have given you his likeness and placement.'

'That's true but a mistake may still arise. Your cousin might discard his cloak or he might have shaved his face on the day we seek him out. No, we require someone to point him out, someone who knows his face.' She paused then, startled by her own coherence. Generally, she avoided conversation, particularly with people she didn't know. In social situations she could not escape, she generally remained tongue-tied or restricted her contribution to monosyllabic responses. Here however, discussing murder with a man she loathed, she found she was able to articulate clearly. That insight was something of a revelation.

Meanwhile, the *rí* was frowning. Unable to find purchase on the blankness of her features, his careful scrutiny had fallen away. 'You are a cold stone,' he said with a shrug. 'But very well.'

He called out to the bearded man with the tattoo on his forehead. 'Flannán, you will accompany these ...' He almost said 'men' but caught himself at the last moment as he considered Liath Luachra. 'Visitors.' He scratched his nose and sniffed. 'Remain with them to point out my cousin and return to me when all is done. Do not,' he added, 'let yourself be seen.'

Flannán nodded obediently but when he glanced at Liath Luachra she could see the resentment in his eyes. The *Éblána* man was not overjoyed at the prospect of being dispatched with the *éclann*.

Rólgallach Mór started back to where his horse was cropping noisily on a patch of grass beside the altar. 'Flannán will lead you to a cache of supplies that have been prepared. Before you go however, there is one other matter to discuss.'

The Grey One raised her eyebrows.

'Barra holds a prisoner at Gort Na Meala, a fair-haired kinswoman by the name of Muirenn. When my cousin's blood mingles with the dirt, let the woman return here to the safety of her own people. Everyone else you can kill. And take what booty you wish. It should look like another *díberg* raid.'

So, díberg we are, after all.

The *Éblána* leader paused and eyed her closely. 'Has Bressal instructed you on the matter of loose lips?'

Liath Luachra returned his stare without expression. 'Yes,' she said simply.

Rólgallach Mór's eyes flickered back to the campfire where the *fénnid* were sitting, chewing the remnants of the meal with wary eyes fixed on the *Éblána* warriors. 'And there will be no ... talk from your men after the deed.'

'Once the task is done I will take it upon myself to ensure that.'

'How, then, do I trust in your silence?'

The Grey One looked at him blankly.

'You don't say much, girl, do you?'

She ignored that.

'My words are in jest. I know you're Bressal's filly.' He shrugged. 'Just tell your master that Rólgallach Mór honours his agreements but, should the need arise, he can muster thirty fighting men, most of them battle experienced. If the vassal tribes are called in, that number can be doubled. He would do well not to forget that. That holds also for you.'

She opened her mouth to clarify that Bressal was not her master but those words melted on the tip of her tongue as the truth of it struck her. 'I will pass on your words,' she said at last.

'Good.' He seemed satisfied with her apparent capitulation.

Returning to his mount, he clambered onto its broad back. Responding to a sharp jerk of his head, the two men accompanying him ran to place themselves at his rear.

He stared at her chest again before raising his eyes. 'Farewell, Grey One. I will not see you again.'

***

The departure of Rólgallach Mór and his men left a brief silence in the rocky cleft, one that Conall Cacach, as ever, was ready to fill with intellectual contribution.

'*Cén breall*!' What a cunt! 'From the head on him you could plough a field with that one's *slat*.'

'*Slat*!' repeated Canann unnecessarily, beating his knee in mirth. '*Slat*! *Slat*!'

Conall Cacach threw him a contemptuous sneer. Liath Luachra ignored them both, her attention focused on Flannán. Standing tersely to one side of the dying fire, the *Éblána* man was regarding the *fénnid* with a mixture of disdain and revulsion as he fingered the hilt of a long knife in an elaborately stitched scabbard tucked at an angle inside his belt. Noting the woman warrior's observation, he immediately adjusted his pose to take on a more haughty air.

'We must leave. Now. The *rí* has no desire for your *fian* to be seen here.'

The *fénnid* looked at him then turned to observe Liath Luachra's reaction to the condescending command. She merely shrugged. It made no difference to her when they departed. Nevertheless, she subjected him to careful scrutiny. 'You have a route in mind?'

'We should drop lower from the hills. Into the forest where we cannot be so easily seen. But first we should travel north, put some distance between us and the settlement.'

'You don't have scouts patrolling that territory?'

'When your signal was spotted, Rólgallach Mór directed them to the south and the west. The path north will be clear for some days.

She nodded in satisfaction. 'Very well. Then there's nothing to keep us here. *Ar aghaidh linn.*' Let's go. She lifted a hand and gestured for him to proceed ahead. 'This is your land, *Éblána* man. You know the route so you take the lead.'

The bearded warrior seemed to take this as a given for he made no argument as he led them off into the western hills, following a long, circuitous route that skirted them well clear of the *Éblána* settlement, so far in fact that they lost sight of the smoke. The Grey One looked back at the untainted blue sky. Flannán was haughty but he was no fool and she respected the fastidiousness he displayed in his efforts to avoid being seen. On several occasions, he asked – demanded – that they stop and disappeared into the forest to scout ahead, returning after a time with a nod to start them moving again. Although she suspected the actual risk of being seen was minimal, it was clear Flannán didn't intend to take any chances on being spotted by some solitary hunter. Given that he knew the country far better than her, she decided it was best to trust his judgement on the matter.

Later that afternoon, they finally intersected the trade trail, a rough but well-beaten path headed in a northerly direction. Their speed increased dramatically at this point and they made good progress until Flannán slowed then abruptly led them off the western side of the trail to a narrow gully a hundred paces into the forest. There, hidden beneath a small mound of stones, they retrieved the supplies that had been prepared by the *Éblána*: several days' worth of smoked meat and dried tubers stored in flax baskets. Given the darkening sky and the prospect of a hot meal, there was a general consensus to remain there for the night.

The gully turned out to be a good place to camp for it contained a small spring at the base of its southern wall, plenty of fern to make a comfortable bed and numerous rocky overhangs spread along the cliffs on either side they could retreat to if it started raining again. From the large number of ancient campfires that dotted the gully floor, the site had been used extensively in the far past. Fortunately, none of them looked as though they'd been used any time over the last twenty years or so.

Although nobody asked him, Flannán assumed the cooking duties that night. While he was in the process of preparing a stew made up from some of the smoked fish and mushrooms, Liath Luachra directed Sean Fergus and Conall Cacach to retrace their steps to the trail and remove any evidence of their presence.

'What the hell for?' moaned Conall Cacach. He was lying stretched out on his bedroll and showed no inclination of moving. 'It's not as though anyone is going to find us out here in the wilderness.'

'Because I told you, 'the Grey One answered.

The warrior snorted dismissively and rolled over on one side. Flannán and the two other *fénnid* watched as Liath Luachra regarded him in hostile silence. Spinning on her heel, she returned to the trade trail and started doing the clean-up herself, wiping away any imprints and removing any broken twigs or debris they might have stood on. By the time she got back to the campsite the meal was completed and a delectable smell was wafting through the trees. She stood in the shadows for a moment, watching the *Éblána* man dole out the helpings, slopping the stew into a wooden bowl for each man.

Joining them at the fire, she sat with them and slurped over her stew as the *fian* men reverted to their favourite past-time: baiting Canann.

'Canann, it's not that you're fucking the cursed animal,' Conall Cacach was musing aloud, 'so much as the fact that you have romantic notions towards it afterwards.'

'But I'm not fucking a sheep.' The slow-witted *fénnid's* forehead wrinkled, his hairy brows furrowing down close over his eyes. Despite a

84

whole season of taunting, he never seemed to understand that his comrades were teasing him.

'The only good thing from this situation,' continued Conall Cacach, 'is that after the tender clinching of hips, you have a soft pillow on which to lay your weary head. That's good, that's thinking ahead.'

'But I'm n-'

'Or something to eat,' suggested Sean Fergus. 'Don't forget that. That's very clever too.'

'Thanks,' said Canann, nodding dubiously, his voice betraying his confusion.

Sitting off to one side of the gully, Liath Luachra regarded the interplay without interest, turning her attention instead to the *Éblána* man. Loathe to share the company of the other men, Flannán had situated his bedroll on the opposite side of the narrow gully where, wrapped in his cloak, he glumly watched the proceedings. He had his knife out again and was sharpening the edge with a whetstone, drawing it down the side of the blade with a facility that spoke of extensive practice. Turning his head, he noted the Grey One's scrutiny and took her apparent interest as an invitation. Rising to his feet, he crossed to sit down beside her and offered her what she assumed was his most charming smile. 'Why do they call you Grey One?' he asked. 'I would have thought it too drab a name for one with your fine cheekbones.'

She regarded him without warmth. 'Because I wear a grey cloak.'

'But, but you all wear grey cloaks.'

Liath Luachra turned away.

Realising that he'd misread the situation, the *Éblána* man got to his feet again and, without another word, returned to his place. Stretching himself down on his bedroll, he pulled his cloak around him and turned away towards the gully wall.

Still weary from the extended days of travel, Liath Luachra too felt the call of her bedroll but had a task of her own to attend to before she could relax. Moving backwards into the shadows away from the fire, she eased herself up and into the trees, working her way around by the route back to the main trail. Here she waited, trying not to yawn as she listened to the *fénnid's* conversation. Finally, their discussion started to dwindle and the men decided to call it a night and retire to their beds. She watched as Conall Cacach carried out his usual night time ritual, tramping past where she was shrouded in shadow, moving off into the forest to relieve himself so that he could sleep with an empty bladder. He didn't go very far from camp, no more than four of five trees deep at most. Coming to a halt, he pulled down the front of his filthy trousers and, with a great sigh, began to urinate against a pine sapling.

When he'd finished, grumbling and muttering under his breath, he was tucking his *bod* back inside his trousers when the Grey One eased out of the trees behind him, a heavy branch in her hands.

'Conall.'

Startled he turned, just in time to receive the full impact of the branch. There was a solid thwack as it connected with his head and he toppled to the ground, lying on his side as he held his head and moaned in pain. As the worst of the pain faded, he sat up shakily, spat out a mixture of spit and blood from where he'd bitten his cheek and looked at her with undisguised hatred.

'We have a service to fulfil, Conall. You seem to forget the oath of fealty you swore to complete the task.'

'I piss on you, Gr-'

He'd started to rise but she quickly moved in to kick the leg out from under him causing him to topple face first into the mossy forest floor. This time, he sat up slowly, wiping dead leaves and dirt from his face and mouth. 'Stay down,' she warned him, lifting the club threateningly.

He fixed her with a low-lidded stare. 'You weren't so brave back at the river in your skin.'

'You were treacherous, caught me off guard without a weapon. That won't happen again.'

He growled.

'It's time to make your choice, Conall. Bressal has named me *rígfénnid* and I do his bidding. Defy me and you defy him. Break your oath to me and you break your oath to him.'

Conall spat, leaving a wet glug of mucous and spit glistening like a slug trail on the ground. 'A titless girl leading a *fian* of warriors!' he scoffed 'Truly our ancestors mock us. How has it come to this?'

'Make your choice, Conall. Stay or leave but refuse a directive from me once more and I'll kill you where you stand. You'll get no other warning.'

'I'll stay, damn you. I want my booty.'

'And follow my bidding?'

'Yes.'

'Say it.'

'I follow your bidding.' He snarled. 'Until this service is done and I have my prize. Then I'll spit in your eye and laugh.'

'Then you'd better enjoy it to the full for it'll be the last physical pleasure you ever feel. In the meantime, mull on this should you feel your conviction falter.' She slammed the club into his stomach causing him to collapse to the ground again. As he lay there writhing, she crouched down on one knee. 'You know I can best you, Conall. Any time. You just say the word.'

Rising to her feet, she tossed the club into the trees and started walking back to camp, the pained cries of the injured warrior tainting the air behind her.

'Grey One!'

She stopped and twisted about to regard him coldly.

'The stew you ate tonight. I pissed in your bowl. While you were outside of camp.'

She shrugged. 'I know. I saw you do it. That's why I exchanged bowls with Canann.'

She continued walking. From behind came an anguished howl of fury.

Liath Luachra's lips twisted into a genuine grin.

Chapter Five

They left in the dim, grey light of dawn, Flannán hurrying them, fearful of being discovered by other travellers from the *Éblána* settlement. In this regard, although his caution was commendable it was also unwarranted for they moved far too fast to be overtaken.

Over the course of the morning they travelled without encounter or incident, covering good ground. At noon, with the increased risk of meeting people coming from the other direction, Flannán insisted on scouting ahead, returning to the group to urge them off the trail whenever he spotted anyone approaching.

The first time this happened, the little group hid in the shadowed bush off the trail, watching as a trio of bearded men – hunters – passed by. Two of the men carried wild pig carcasses on their backs, the forelegs slung over their shoulders and bound in place around their chests, the hind legs secured about their lower back and waist to support the weight. The third man carried the other's javelins and equipment.

They passed quickly, heads bent, visibly weary from their hunt but pushing themselves hard to reach their destination. When they'd disappeared from sight, Flannán confirmed that they were *Éblána*, people from his own settlement.

Later that afternoon, they hid from a second group of travellers, this time three men and a woman. Two of the men led packhorses loaded with furs and a number of bulky objects concealed beneath woollen blankets. The remaining man and woman carried javelins and swords and eyed the forest, wary of ambush.

Traders. And two warrior guards.

Liath Luachra examined the female warrior with professional curiosity, noting the padded leather battledress she wore and approving of the methodical manner in which she scanned the trees on either side of the trail. The woman looked much older than her, twenty to twenty-five years old at least. She also had distinctive tattoos running down both cheeks and long, auburn hair tied up in a tight plait. The Grey One unconsciously raised a hand to run her fingers through her own tightly cropped fuzz, recalling Bressal's instruction to grow it out with a fresh swell of resentment.

That night they camped off the trail, laying out their bedrolls in a section of forest far to the west where there was little chance of being spotted. The site they chose differed from the rest of the surrounding forest only in that it had a gap in the canopy that allowed sunlight to reach the forest floor. Here a thick layer grass provided a soft bed and a view of the stars when they lay down to stare up at the night sky.

Flannán offered to prepare the meal again that night but on this occasion the Grey One declined, instructing Sean Fergus to undertake the task instead. The *Éblána* man seemed put out at her refusal and, having tasted his previous dish, even the others looked disappointed but she wasn't moved. They might be dependent on *Éblána* supplies but she had no intention of leaving responsibility for their food with someone she didn't entirely trust.

After a quiet night and another early start, they repeated their precautionary approach with Flannán scouting ahead. Over the course of the day they encountered but a single traveller: a dark-haired man with sun-weathered skin who pounded south, a look of grim determination spread across his features.

'What wolf's been chewing on that man's bollox?' muttered Conall Cacach, studying the traveller from the shelter of the treeline. Liath Luachra said nothing although she too watched with a certain degree of curiosity. There was something strangely compelling about observing strangers who were unaware of your presence and ascribing stories to fit their faces. To her mind, this man looked like someone intent on revenge for an insult or some wrongdoing. She thought about that for a moment then shook her head, amused at the extent of her own imagination.

When the man disappeared from sight, she led the *fénnid* back onto the trail and they continued their journey. It felt strange to be travelling on such an undemanding and well-travelled track. She'd always heard the territories along the eastern coast were more populated and more connected than other lands but she'd never actually believed it until now. Further inland, where she'd spent the greater part of her existence, there were no trails or paths apart from those nature provided. There, the wilderness – the Great Wild – consisted of forest, swamp and rough terrain where generally few but hunters, fugitives, or those desperate to eke a living, ventured.

On their third night in *Éblána* territory, the little band camped by a shallow cave and it was Liath Luachra who prepared the evening meal, a stew of mushrooms and smoked meat from the *Éblána* supplies. The meal was adequate, inferior to Flannán's previous culinary contribution, but the others ate it dutifully without complaint.

As always after eating, the Grey One sat apart from the others, curling into a comfortable nook created by the twisted nest of roots around the base of a giant oak. Using one of the wooden bowls supplied by the *Éblána,* she sipped on a hot herbal infusion, the strong flavour stirring her tongue and warming her belly.

It had grown colder over the course of the evening and now the air was cool against her skin. Her cloak lay off to one side by her bedroll but she was feeling too comfortable, too lazy to make the effort of rising from her seat to retrieve it. She sniffed at the air, noting the heavy scent of moisture. It would rain again soon, she decided.

Yawning, she stretched her legs, enjoying the light strain of her muscles, from her thighs all the way down to her ankles.

She looked across the campfire to where Flannán was sitting, staring into space with a slack frown on his face. A stiff and unsocial man, like her he'd intentionally placed himself apart from the others, distancing himself from their unsavoury company. As she watched, a peal of raucous laughter from the *fénnid* caused him to raise his head and stare at the warriors. For an instant, the *Éblána* man's expression slipped from bland introspection to one of absolute loathing. He recovered almost immediately however, dampening his features to soft reflection once more.

The Grey One turned her head away but she continued to observe him from the corner of her eye. Over the course of their travels, Flannán had maintained a polite demeanour but it was evident to everyone that he despised his travelling companions. That didn't particularly bother her. Flannán was something of a horse's arse but she felt pretty much the same way about them.

With a groan, she got to her feet and circled the fire to halt beside the rock where he was sitting. The *Ébléna* man glanced up at her in surprise but said nothing. To avoid another misunderstanding, she remained on her feet. 'Are we far from Gort Na Meala?' she asked.

He chewed the question over with a mouthful of oat bread.

'If we leave at dawn tomorrow, we'll most likely strike *Carraig An Fhírinne Buí* – Rock of the Yellow Truth – by mid-morning.'

'What's this Yellow Rock you talk of?' demanded Conall Cacach from his seat near the fire. Like the other *fénnid*, he'd stopped talking and was unashamedly listening in on their discussion. 'Is it some sort of tribal pissing post?'

The *Ébléna* man threw him a filthy look. 'It is a sacred spot, a site of the Ancient Ones.'

Conall Cacach chuckled contemptuously then spat a lungful of phlegm off to the side. 'Sites of the Ancient Ones litter this land like deer shit litters the woods. What's so important about this one?'

Flannán considered the warrior coldly then pointedly ignored him by returning his attention to Liath Luachra. 'We call it *Carraig An Fhírinne Buí* but in fact there are three stones. Two have fallen and now lie on their sides, coated so heavily with moss they're barely visible to the eye.'

'Is it a site sacred to the *Ébléna*?' the Grey One asked.

'Not as sacred as *Cloch a' Bhod.'* The Cock Stone.

'*Cloch a' Bhod*. That was the place we met with Rólgallach Mór.'

Flannán nodded. 'Yes. It's a fertility site. When our young people couple for the first time or if they seek the blessings of the ancestors for a healthy child, they spend the night at *Cloch a' Bhod.'*

Liath Luachra took a moment to think that over. 'If the site is so important to your people why would Rólgallach Mór risk profaning it by meeting there with strangers?'

Flannán gave an off-handed shrug. 'My master desired a meeting place that was free from intrusion He instructed our *draoi* to place a *geis* on *Cloch a' Bhod*, a prohibition preventing our people from venturing there until it was lifted.'

91

Liath Luachra grunted. 'And *Carraig An Fhírinne Buí?* Does this hold significance for the *Éblána?*'

Flannán shook his head. 'No particular significance. Although there are some who say the stone is a marker.'

'What does it mark?'

He shrugged. 'Boundaries. Spaces that are different. I don't know. You would have to ask the *draoi.*'

There was a snigger from the others at this and even Liath Luachra had to wonder at the *Éblána* man's obtuseness. A *draoi* was the last person anyone would approach for information. Jealously possessive of their restricted knowledge, they resented any efforts to make them share their secrets. Powerful in terms of magic and tribal authority, everyone knew they were best avoided.

Flannán bristled, misunderstanding the reason for their laughter. His lips formed a thin line and his forehead furrowed so deeply that the circular tattoo halved in size. 'You can laugh but I tell you sites like *Carraig An Fhírinne Buí* are best avoided. That stone marks the entrance to a pretty little valley and yet none of the *Éblána* dare to venture there.'

'How do you know?' asked Sean Fergus, scratching his beard with thick fingers.

'What?'

'How do you know there's a pretty valley? You said your tribe do not venture there.'

Flannán looked at him askew. 'A kinsman of mine entered the forest beyond the stone by accident, when he was hunting and veered astray. He saw the valley through the trees but he was too fearful to go there for he swore it was haunted.'

'Haunted?'

The *Éblána* man paused, as though struggling to recall something he'd been told a long time before. 'He said the air was wrong. My kinsman is not a man prone to false embroidery of a tale. Neither is he one to panic easily so his words bear the weight of truth for me.'

'What did he see?' asked Canann, his eyes bright with nervous curiosity. 'Your kinsman. What did he see?'

'Nothing.'

'Hah!' roared Conall Cacach.

Flannán tossed the large warrior a heated look, infuriated by his blatant disrespect. 'My kinsman did not see anything but he felt something.'

'He felt something? What did he feel?' Canann was leaning forward eagerly now, like a child hearing a ghost story for the very first time.'

'He felt a coldness, an unnatural texture to the air. It frightened him deeply.'

Conall Cacach snorted. 'Your kinsman must shit himself every time the wind shifts to the east.'

Flannán reddened. 'If you are a man of such courage perhaps you would spend the night at *Carraig An Fhírinne Buí* by yourself.'

Conall Cacach sneered. 'I have better things to do than sit around a piss-coloured rock, *Éblána* man.'

'Of course, of course. You are so very, very busy.'

The bickering continued until Liath Luachra growled at them both to shut up. Furious, Flannán retreated into himself and said nothing more. Conall Cacach, for his part, led a fresh discussion on a subject that was the *fénnid's* unfailing favourite: their plans for their newfound wealth and reputation following the completion of their service.

Liath Luachra listened to the men's conversation with growing discomfort then noticed the *Éblána* man looking at her with a kind of repressed glee. At that moment, she understood that he too was aware of the *fénnid's* fate and the duty Bressal had set upon her. The muscles in her neck and shoulders tensed. Unable to remain where she was, she left them, returning to her seat in the oak roots where she fretted, struck by a sudden craving for cloud mushroom.

No.

With an effort, she repelled the temptation. It was too dangerous to take it in camp for she couldn't anticipate how she might react to the substance, what she might reveal or say to the others. More importantly, she couldn't take the risk of leaving herself open to attack. Conall Cacach wouldn't have forgotten what happened by the river and he certainly wouldn't have forgiven the beating she'd given him the previous evening.

With that, her eyes flickered over to where the big warrior was sitting, slapping Sean Fergus heartily on the back and roaring with laughter at some joke the older warrior evidently didn't share for he looked savagely unhappy.

I should have killed him. Last night, I should have killed him.

Deep down, she recognised the truth of it. Unfortunately, the focus of their service – Barra of the *Éblána* – had at least four warriors and, potentially, another three or four slaves he could call on to fight. And that wasn't counting any family or supporters that might be visiting Gort Na Meala. Conall, despite his volatile and toxic personality, was her best fighter. Canann was adequate but nowhere in the big warrior's league. As for Sean Fergus … She sighed. It was true, Sean Fergus had always been a competent fighter but over the course of their travels to *Éblána* territory, it'd been hard to ignore the fact that he was slowing down even further.

He's dying.

Of that there seemed little doubt. She'd seen him coughing up blood twice over the last few days, despite his attempts to conceal it. He'd also become increasingly clumsy, tripping up, dropping things, tiring more rapidly than he used to. The other two *fénnid* appeared to have picked up on his fading abilities as well, for the wary respect with which they once had treated him had dwindled to the point of veiled derision.

She exhaled heavily. For the moment at least, she needed Conall. Afterwards, when the service was complete, if the big warrior survived, she'd follow her instincts and Bressal's direction at the same time. Without hesitation.

Ironically, having made the difficult decision to avoid cloud mushroom, the Grey One now had to watch Sean Fergus pull his own supply from inside his tunic. Opening a thin, leather pouch, he poured several slivers into his palm and generously offered them around to anyone who wished a taste. Conall Cacach and Canann accepted the offer readily, Flannán shook his head, unwilling to partake in any further activity that might include the *fénnid*.

Don't.

Liath Luachra felt her own hands tremble as she stared at the smooth, white fungus but drawing on a reserve of self-control she hadn't hitherto known she'd possessed, she pushed the craving away. Somehow she managed to shake her head and when she saw the the the old warrior's supply consisted of several smoked slivers – a process that somehow tended to fortify its effects – she was suddenly very relieved that she'd declined. The previous summer, following a particularly vicious skirmish with a *díberg* in *Uí Loinge* territories, she'd tried that variety in an attempt to erase all memory of the slaughter. Instead of wiping the memories away however, the smoked substance had seemed to intensify them, manufacturing visions and hallucinations so terrifying she'd refrained from ever using it again. In some respects, she realised that she'd probably just been unlucky for it was well known the impact of cloud mushroom varied erratically. Over her time with *Na Cinéaltaí*, she'd seen several *fénnid* swallow the stuff to no detrimental effect while others who'd merely nibbled on a sliver had ended up in a delirium, crying and screaming for long dead mothers or wives. On one occasion, shortly after joining the *fian*, she'd seen Callach Fat Arse swallow a huge segment on his own. He'd ended up sexually aroused by the sight of a nearby ash tree and woken them all with his screams the following morning as he attempted to remove the splinters from his most sensitive parts.

As the fire died down, so too did the *fénnid's* conversation. The three men sat close together about the fire, sitting on fallen logs, chewing quietly on the dreams the mushroom produced. Suddenly, Conall Cacach cried out, his voice heavy and cracking with uncharacteristic emotion. 'Sing us a song, Sean Fergus. Sing us one of your songs.'

Curious, Liath Luachra raised her head. She'd had no idea Sean Fergus could sing and she doubted he was well enough to raise a tune, particularly given the cloud mushroom he'd consumed. To her surprise, the old warrior levered himself up off the log, hawked to clear his throat then placed one hand on his chest as though to ground himself. He started off with a monotone hum that slowly, very slowly, increased in volume. As the pitch began to fluctuate, Liath Luachra fancied she could hear individual words although his voice seemed to produce little more than a mumble. Suddenly the old warrior's voice swelled and he startled them all as he began to sing a tune of heart-breaking melancholy.

Liath Luachra sat up with a start for she recognised the tune, a lullaby her mother had sung to her when she was still very young. The song was old, so old it was said to originate from the time of the Ancient Ones. No-one knew the exact meaning of the age-old words although there was no mistaking the depth of the emotion behind them, the deep-rooted yearning for someone or something that was no more.

An inexplicable puffiness filled her chest and for a moment it seemed as though there was some magic to the old man's song for it had stirred up old desires and memories she'd thought long-forgotten. Rising to her feet, she knew she'd have to leave the campsite before she broke down in front of the others.

Pushing her way into the trees at the edge of the camp, she forced her way deeper through the solid darkness until the campfire was little more than a dim glow to her rear. There she halted, confused and, taking a deep breath, turned to look back at the campsite. In the distant yellow-green glow, barely audible now, Sean Fergus's heartrending tune was finally drawing to a close.

A strange hush settled over the forest when the old warrior finished, as though it'd somehow been struck dumb by the sheer poignancy of his song. The silence continued for a time before it began to fade, replaced by the more natural rustle of small animals, the hoarse bark of a fox, the distant hoot of an owl.

When the Grey One finally returned to camp, everyone but Sean Fergus lay fast asleep on their bedrolls, their rumbling snores and incoherent mumblings a sharp contrast to the earlier melody. The old warrior was sitting by the fire, his gaze locked on the dancing flames. He made no move when she took a seat on the log beside him and she made no effort to speak with him. Shivering, she poked the embers of the fire with a stick and allowed her mind to roam, surprising herself by the topic it latched onto.

The Éblána land.

Closing her eyes, she sighed aloud as a mental image formed in her head, a stretch of flat, green pasture drenched in sunlight, bordered by solid oak forest and framed beneath a clear blue sky. A soft breeze rustled the long grass where a small herd of cows was grazing. Birds chittered and twittered, the background drone of bees hung lazy in the air. The scene struck some essential part of her, appealing so strongly on an emotional level that she immediately felt her heart lighten. All of this was almost within her grasp. All she had to do was complete this one service, maintain her focus and do as Bressal had directed.

Then, she could truly be free.

Engrossed in her reveries, she didn't notice the movement behind her until a pair of hands suddenly draped a cloak around her shoulders. Panicked, she recoiled in fright, leaping to her feet and drawing *Gléas Gan Ainm* free, even as she grasped the fact it was Sean Fergus standing before her. She stared at him in bewilderment, belatedly registering the surprising gentleness with which the cloak had been applied. 'What are you doing?'

The old man seemed surprised by the question. He stared at her with bleary, bloodshot eyes, overhung with bushy grey brows. Some of his hair had worked loose from the braids again, poking out like the threads of a frayed rope. 'It's cold. You were shivering.'

'I can feel the chill on my skin, old man.' Her hand gripped the hilt of the sword so tightly her knuckles shone white through the skin. 'I will decide if I'm cold or not.'

'I sought only to help.'

'Why?'

'Eh?' He looked at her in confusion.

'Why do you seek to help me?'

The old man stared at her again and looked lost for words. Finally, his eyes dropped to the ground and he poked at the grass underfoot with his right leg. 'It was the cloud mushroom. I thought ... For a moment I thought you were Lann.' He stopped and rubbed his nose with the back of his sleeve. 'I thought you were my daughter.'

The Grey One continued to regard him but with no easing of her bristling stance.

'I had a daughter,' Sean Fergus continued. 'About your age. She survived the plague that took my wife and my other children. A few years back, she caught the cold and then the flux but ...' He paused suddenly, swallowing emotion. 'She started coughing, a small cough at first but it got worse. By the third day she was coughing up phlegm, by the fifth she was coughing up blood. After seven days she was dead. She'd coughed her life out.' He exhaled then, long and hard. 'I didn't want you to catch the cold.'

The Grey One pierced him with a dark look. 'I am not your daughter.'

The old warrior said nothing, his face bleak and pale.

Still trembling from the shock of being caught unawares, Liath Luachra resheathed her sword but her eyes continued to burn into his. 'And you are not my father.'

He sighed. 'Yes,' he said after a time. 'Yes, I know. But all girls should have a father to care for them and I know you have none.'

Liath Luachra glared at Sean Fergus then with such frightening intensity that he unconsciously shuffled backwards, disconcerted. She abruptly shucked the cloak from her back, letting it drop to the ground behind her. Despite the cold, she lifted the hem of her tunic up and twisted around so that he could see the mass of white scar tissue spread across her lower back. 'You see that?' she snarled. 'That is how my father cared for me. I cursed his stinking breath until the day the raiders came and slit his throat.'

She twisted her head and saw the old warrior staring in horror at the shredded flesh.

'Don't touch me again,' she said. Turning on her heel, she stalked back to her bedroll.

***

As Flannán had promised, they reached *Carraig An Fhírinne Buí* sometime before mid-morning. They'd moved quickly despite the intermittent showers that softened the ground and lined the trail with puddles. Flannán had scouted ahead while Liath Luachra – still raw from the previous night – transferred her anger into a rapid pace that ate up the trail. The three *fénnid* had followed her lead with uncharacteristic docility, still mellow from the residue of cloud mushroom.

The trail was narrow, little more than a gap through the scrub and bushes that brushed constantly against their shoulders. Suddenly, it widened out again, delivering them onto a broad semi-circular clearing with a flat section of grass. Because she'd been actively seeking it, Liath Luachra spotted the tight path on the left, cutting through the scrub in a westerly direction.

The route to Gort Na Meala.

Excited, she turned to her companions but found that none of them had even noticed. Their attention was completely taken up by the tall stone standing to the rear of the grassy semicircle: *Carraig An Fhírinne Buí.*

A *gallán* – a standing stone – it was certainly an impressive structure. At least twice her own height, it was much taller than any others she'd ever seen. Dominating that section of the clearing, it loomed ominously over the little group gathered before it.

The Grey One bit her lip, considering *Carraig An Fhírinne Buí* as she masked a frisson of animosity. Back in Luachair, her family had worked a piece of land near a site with a similar, smaller *gallán* and she had nothing but bad memories of that particular stone.

But there had been no triskele.

She stared at the triskele symbol engraved at head height in the flat surface. Curious, she waded through the ankle high grass, approaching the stone to rub her fingertips across the symbol with its three distinctive interconnecting spirals.

It's deep.

That was unusual. The engravings on every other standing stone generally tended to be worn smooth or erased to a faded imprint by countless years of erosion.

'Come back, Grey One,' Canann called out nervously. 'It's haunted.'

She rolled her eyes but did not turn around.

'It's not yellow!' Conall Cacach sounded affronted, as though he'd caught someone attempting to cheat him. 'Why would they name it *Carraig An Fhírinne Buí* if it's not yellow?'

99

Flannán stared at the stone, perplexed. Apparently, he had never given the matter any serious thought. Finally, he came to terms with the quandary and he shrugged listlessly. 'I don't know. It is an ancient name. Perhaps it was yellow when my ancestors knew it. Or perhaps it was the truth that was yellow rather than the rock – whatever that means.'

'Perhaps your ancestors were inbred.'

'Shut your beak, Conall!' the Grey One snapped, in no mood to deal with the warriors' bickering. Conall Cacach's lips turned down at the rebuke but, sensing her mood, he kept his lips sealed.

Casting the stone one final bleak stare, Liath Luachra dismissed it with a shrug. There were more important things to do than sit around gawking at the works of the Ancient Ones. Turning back to address the chatting *fénnid*, she opened her mouth to order them onto the Gort Na Meala path when a sudden peal of laughter from further up the trail silenced them all.

'Someone comes,' hissed Flannán. Muttering under their breath, the little party once again let him drive them off the trail, into the forest directly opposite *Carraig An Fhírinne Buí*. They'd barely managed to get into hiding when the source of the laughter appeared. More travellers. An older man with about forty or fifty years on him, accompanied by a pair of pretty, dark-haired girls who couldn't have had more than fourteen years on them. The similarity of their facial features identified them as close relatives, as did the easy, close-knit nature of their interaction. They ambled forwards at a relaxed pace, laughing and chatting, visibly comfortable in each other's company. Bent forward against the shadowed trunk of a fallen elm tree, Liath Luachra watched the family with an ache of longing, moved and, in a strange way, envious of their closeness. It took an effort to prevent herself from stepping out of the trees to speak with them.

Where is the mother? Why does she not accompany her family?

The most obvious answer saddened her. Her own mother had died when she was still quite young, worn down by a protracted illness and her brutal husband's fondness for *uisce beatha*. A gentle woman, she'd loved her children deeply and did her best to shield them from the

100

worst of a harsh existence eking a living on land reclaimed from the edges of the Great Wild.

Her mother had seen three sons die: a stillborn, a boy of less than two years who'd passed away from the flux, and a seven year old who'd fallen from a tree during a freak accident in the forest. She'd never really recovered from the oldest boy's death and it was only a short time after that incident that her health began to fade, her own grief eroding her from the inside. The eldest child, Liath Luachra had ended up taking on much of the burden, mothering her two younger brothers when she wasn't helping her father in the fields or carrying out the tasks her mother was no longer able to manage.

The Grey One mused on those memories quietly. Her mother had been a beautiful woman yet by the end of her illness she'd been reduced to little more than a withered husk. The woman warrior could recall the day her mother had passed away with perfect clarity. She remembered the tears that she, her father and her brothers had shed but, oddly enough, she was unable to remember any of the emotions, any of the sadness or grief she must have felt. Like everything else, it all felt distant now, very far away.

Another life.

She watched the little family approach *Carraig An Fhírinne Buí*, noting their increasing nervousness as they drew closer to the towering *gallán*. The laughter and the chatter died and, bowing their heads to avoid looking at it directly, they increased their pace and hurried by, out of her line of sight.

The Grey One sighed and was about to straighten up when she heard a strange fluttering, flapping sound from behind. Twisting her head, she looked to her rear where Canann was standing, leaning against a tree with his eyes fixed firmly on her rump. The warrior was panting raggedly and when she dropped her eyes to where his hand poked inside his trousers, the jerking movements left little doubt as to what he was up to.

Without thinking, she grabbed a stone on the ground beside her and hurled it at him. The missile struck him in the crotch of his trousers, just below the pumping hand and the resulting screech of agony confirmed the hit. Canann folded, his long shriek trailing into a soundless moan as he gripped his crotch with less energetic but more focussed attention.

Nostrils flaring, she advanced and kicked him in the ribs. Taking a ragged breath, she fought down the urge to kick him again, knowing that if she did she'd keep on kicking until he was a broken, bloody mess. Instead, she turned and crashed forwards through the bushes, emerging onto the trail once more. Glancing up to her right, just beyond the point where the clearing ended, she spotted the old man and his daughters staring, wide-eyed, back in her direction. Seeing the woman warrior, the old man grabbed his daughters by the shoulders and quickly pushed them forwards. All three took off at a run, quickly disappearing around the curve and out of sight.

Liath Luachra stared after them with an inexplicable sense of loss. Before she could make sense of the reaction however, Flannán came barging out of the bushes towards her, his face livid with rage. She rounded on him immediately, the ferocity of her expression enough to make him skid to a halt. 'Open that gob,' she snarled, 'and I'll gut you where you stand.'

Although he'd almost certainly intended to berate her, the *Éblána* man stood on the trail, staring at her uncertainly. Shaking her head in contempt, Liath Luachra turned her back on him and stalked away in the opposite direction, past the towering *gallán*, funnelled by the natural curve of the surrounding trees to the apex of the semi-circular clearing. Crashing into the woods, she stomped through the dappled shadows, eager to get as far from the *fénnid* as possible.

Canann. Twisted cur.

Because of his simple-minded character most people tended to underestimate the true nature of Canann the Eye, however no-one remained within *Na Cineáltaí* for long if they couldn't fight or worried about the shedding of blood.

And she knew Canann didn't worry about the shedding of blood.

There was something genuinely disturbing about the simpleton warrior, something truly perverse but, hidden beneath so many layers of idiocy, most people never discerned it. When she'd first joined the *fian*, the Grey One too had been guilty of such blindness, blithely believing the wiry warrior relatively inoffensive until an encounter in the forest had revealed another side to his character.

Coming upon him by chance while hunting for venison, the woman warrior had instinctively slipped into the shadows when she'd spotted him. Unaware that he was being observed, the *fénnid* had been sitting on a log with a young hound from the *Uí Loinge* settlement cradled in his hands. Reluctant to engage in conversation, Liath Luachra would have continued on her way if it hadn't been for an odd gleam in his eyes which roused her curiosity.

Watching from the shadows, she saw Canann place the pup on the ground and proceed to tie its legs to four separate saplings. An uneasy sensation of nausea had blossomed in her stomach as she saw the trusting animal lick the warrior's fingers. A moment later, the happy yapping abruptly changed to an agonized whine for Canann had tightened the ties, stretching the puppy's limbs beyond breaking point. As the *fénnid* started to giggle hysterically, the woman warrior hurriedly backed into the forest and turned to leave. With her last glance, she saw Canann pull a gleaming knife from his belt. Moving as fast and as noiselessly as she could, she had hoped to escape the terrified screeches of the puppy. Unfortunately, it'd been a windless day. The noise had carried well and it had taken a very long time to get out of earshot.

Even now, she still regretted not confronting the nauseating warrior although she knew it had been the right thing to do at the time. Still fresh to *Na Cinéaltaí*, she'd been frightened and attacking a fellow *fénnid*, a warrior of unknown fighting ability, had never been a realistic option.

Slowing her vigorous tramp though the forest, she gradually eased to a halt. Preoccupied with her thoughts, she'd progressed much deeper into the forest than she'd originally intended.

It's quiet.

It was quiet. There was no birdsong, no scuttling of mice, no brush of leaves from the wind; nothing. Now that she was aware of it, she wondered why she hadn't noticed it sooner. The absence of sound was conspicuous.

Unsettled, she slid towards the closest tree, pressing her body close against the prickly trunk. This hush was unlike any pre-battle silence,

103

certainly nothing like the silence she'd experienced at the river with Conall Cacach. No, this was something completely different. The air felt dense, still and slightly cooler and even the sound of her own movements and breathing seemed oddly muffled. She carefully scrutinised the surrounding trees. The forest shadows didn't present any immediate sense of danger but there was an almost imperceptible impression of ... wrongness.

Anxious now, she kept one hand on the hilt of *Gléas Gan Ainm*, her breath tight as she continued cautiously forward, maintaining her original course. All of a sudden, she froze, convinced that she'd heard voices through the trees off to the right. When she concentrated to listen more carefully, there was nothing to hear.

Flannán had the right of it. This place is haunted.

She shivered then, feeling a sudden prickle at the back of her neck. Swinging around, she wrenched the sword free, bringing it to bear on whoever was creeping up behind her, then slowly lowered the weapon in bewilderment. There was nothing there.

Nervous but undaunted, she moved forwards again and after several paces, she thought to hear voices once more, speaking gravely, the cadence rising and falling as though one or more people were arguing heatedly. This time, instead of halting, she kept moving, switching direction to head directly for the area from where the voices seem to originate. For some reason, the closer she got, the more the voices seemed to wane until they had finally faded away altogether.

Frustrated, she chewed silently on the inside of her cheek, studying the shadows beneath the trees around her. Finally, unsure what to do next, she decided to continue forward again.

She'd only taken ten or twelve steps when she spotted patches of green and blue and, with relief, realised she'd reached the edge of the trees. Eager to break free of the uncharacteristically frightening forest – a place she normally felt most secure – she lunged forwards. The growth abruptly opened to scrub and isolated wildlings and then she was through the treeline, into the open air.

Stepping out into the sunshine was like stepping into summer. The air was suddenly much warmer and full of birdsong. A gentle breeze blew in from the south, heavy with the distinct scent of beech. Her relief at escaping the eerie confines of the forest was mingled with immediate appreciation for the splendour of the view before her. She was in a narrow valley, a beautiful valley. Bordered by a range of high hills, it was dotted with strikingly large patches of yellow flowers she'd never seen before. It was also thriving with wildlife and judging from the strength of the birdsong, the lushness of the vegetation and the visible deer spoor, hadn't been visited by man for a very long time.

The valley ran east towards the coast, although a long curve at the furthest point prevented her from seeing the sea. Most of the land on the southern side was occupied by dense beech forest. On the northern side, a narrow lake followed the bend of the forested hills until it, too disappeared around the distant curve. Several tiny islands dotted the lake and the northern bank at the base of the hill was choked with reeds. The water was dark and placid although the occasional squall sent ripples shivering along its surface to lap gently against the stony shore.

Liath Luachra closed her eyes and breathed deeply, absorbing the scent of beech and the briny smell from the water and enjoying the brittle, pink haze playing against her eyelids. The intense vivacity of the valley after the morbid forest was striking.

Curious, she returned to the treeline and edged her way in through the undergrowth to see if she could recapture the eerie sensation she'd experienced earlier. She took two or three careful steps into the deeper shadow and, almost immediately, felt it again: a kind of sinister, empty stillness to the air. Returning to the treeline, she took several steps north and repeated the process. Sure enough, as soon as she moved a few paces into the trees the air seemed to drop in temperature and the noise became more muffled.

Retracing her steps she emerged by the edge of the lake and stood looking back at the forest, clucking her tongue in puzzlement. This place was unlike anything she'd previously encountered and she was at a loss to explain the phenomenon. A *draoi*, no doubt, would have come up with an opinion on the matter, some kind of explanation involving gods and ancestors and special powers but she suspected such an account wouldn't satisfy her.

Squatting by the edge of the lake, she idly gathered stones while she mulled over the situation, picking out twelve or thirteen similarly-sized flat ones that fitted snugly in the palm of her hand. Rising to her feet, she took up position at the water's edge, braced herself and snapped her hand forward to send one of the stones skimming across the surface. It hit the water at least seven or eight times before sinking and the woman warrior nodded in satisfaction. As Canann had learned to his detriment, she had a very good throwing arm.

She continued the *sciotar uisce* – skimming stones – until her supply was exhausted then, exhaling heavily, headed back towards the trees. Having passed through the forest once, she had no qualms about repeating the process but the thought of the waiting *fénnid* was enough to darken her mood. No doubt, they'd have questions about what lay beyond *Carraig An Fhírinne Buí* although, knowing her temper as they did, they'd refrain from asking straight away. Later, when she had calmed, they would question her again.

She knew she would never tell them.

***

The men were still concealed in the trees opposite *Carraig An Fhírinne Buí* when she returned. They looked at her with a guarded wariness as she drew closer, except for Canann who was tenderly rubbing his ribs with a wounded expression that made her want to hit him again. Repressing the temptation, she halted, considered them all with a stony expression then jerked her head sharply towards the rough path heading off to the west. 'Flannán, you lead. Take us to Gort Na Meala.'

The new route – little more than a deer track – continued west for a considerable time and Liath Luachra noted how the low ridge poking above the trees to the south grew progressively broader and took on greater height until it was looming high above them. A similar ridge came into view above the trees on the far side of the broad valley.

Eventually, Flannán led them off the track and onto the ridge, clambering up the steep, forested slopes until they cut above the treeline and reached the top. The summit was surprisingly flat. An uneven plateau comprised mostly of bare rock interspersed with isolated clusters of mountain ash and scrub, it also provided an unrestricted view in every direction.

A plume of smoke to the south-west pinpointed the location of Barra ua Éblána's holding. Keeping to the centre of the plateau so their silhouettes couldn't be spotted against the brightness of the skyline from below, they followed the ridge, finally coming to a halt when the smoke plume was almost directly off to their right. Liath Luachra set the *fénnid* to waiting in a small clump of ash trees then she and Flannán dropped on all fours and crawled to the lip of the nearest cliff. From there, they peered down into the valley.

Barra's property occupied the better part of a wide clearing located about two or three hundred paces north from the base of the cliff. The central area was relatively small with two rectangular thatch longhouses, a few lean-tos and a single, fenced enclosure that currently lay empty. The clearing was immediately surrounded by dense oak forest although several paths fed directly into it.

Plucking a stem from a nearby patch of grass, Liath Luachra crunched it between her molars, enjoying the grainy texture of it as she studied the holding below. From her vantage point it was difficult to judge the size of the buildings but both looked big enough to hold ten people or more.

West of the longhouses, the valley had been extensively cleared and held several wide, cultivated fields separated by a number of shallow ditches. With the harvest completed, the fields were bare and empty apart from a number of cows chomping on the remaining stalk and chaff. It was an impressive herd. Liath Luachra counted thirty-two animals although she couldn't see any bulls.

The cattle were guarded by a pair of young boys sitting on a low haystack to one side of the ditch that separated two of the larger fields. Although both were chatting, they held wooden staves that seemed ridiculously long relative to the size of their little bodies. The Grey One squinted, trying to make them out more clearly for they had an unmistakable ragamuffin air to them that reminded her of her brothers. Her siblings, she reflected sadly, would be of a similar age to these boys had they survived.

A flicker of movement to the left of the haystack drew her eyes and she frowned when she saw a small hound sniffing patches of grass at the side of the ditch. The hound looked young and scampered about in excited, energetic movements. Whip-thin and full of energy, such animals were invariably alert and watchful, always eager to warn their masters of any potential threat.

Such as a fian lurking in the environs.

The Grey One and the *Éblána* man remained at the edge of the cliff observing the activity below while the *fénnid* lounged in the shadow of the ash trees, conversing softly amongst themselves. Canann, in an attempt to ingratiate himself, approached and started to count the people he could see until a hostile hiss from Liath Luachra sent him scuttling away. Sulking, the warrior retreated, muttering and wringing his hands in an agitated manner.

The Grey One ignored him. So far, she'd observed a total of five people: the two boys, an older woman who'd briefly poked her head out from one of the buildings and a pair of thin men who'd arrived at the homestead via a small trail from the north. Both had been hauling a rickety cart loaded with firewood which they'd then set to stacking inside a lean-to to the left of the longhouses. From the foreign cast to their features and their subdued mannerisms, she'd assumed they were slaves. They certainly didn't look like fighters for they were quite elderly and didn't move with that rolling swagger so typical of fighting men.

A fresh flurry of movement pulled her eyes to the corner of the furthest building where another pair of men and a woman had appeared. The men, dressed in mud-spattered working clothes, looked to have twenty or thirty years on them. The woman, also wearing mud-spattered clothing, had her hair bundled up in some kind of headscarf but looked to be much younger.

The captive? Muirenn?

It was hard to tell. She certainly didn't behave like a captive for she was laughing and her body language suggested she was very much at ease in her surroundings.

Liath Luachra glanced across at the *Éblána* man who, bored, had laid his head his arm and was dozing quietly. Picking up a pebble, she tossed it at him and hit him on the nose, jolting him alert.

Jerking upright, Flannán caught her urgent gesture and turned, following the direction of her pointing fingers. By the time he was looking down into the valley, the woman had disappeared inside one of the buildings but the two men remained outside engaged in earnest conversation. The *Éblána* man stared for a moment before turning back to the warrior woman. He slowly shook his head. Liath Luachra frowned.

'Perhaps,' suggested Flannán in a low voice, 'Barra walks his land or prepares for another raid. We should make our camp, settle in for a longer wait.'

Liath Luachra grunted unhappily. The prospect of an extended delay did not fill her with joy. After so much time travelling, she was eager to complete Bressal's direction in short course and leave. All she wanted now was to be gone from *Éblána* territory and to claim her reward, her land.

Oh, so it's my land now, is it? Not that of the Éblána.

Her lips twisted into a cynical grin at that irony. Misconstruing her expression, Flannán grinned back. He pointed further along the ridge. 'We passed a small hollow down in the trees of the northern slope. It would be a tight camp but well hidden from this valley.'

Liath Luachra considered the suggestion. 'Very well. Take Canann and Conall and the supplies. Set camp but set no fire. Do you hear?' She waited, obliging him to nod to confirm his acknowledgement, something that, from the stiffness of his stance, he resented. Despite his apparent amiability, he did not appreciate taking orders from her.

'Go,' she told him. 'Sean Fergus will remain with me. He'll follow to fetch you if I see one who matches Barra's likeness.'

Flannán didn't look particularly enthusiastic at the prospect of spending time alone with Canann and Conall but he nodded obediently. 'Very well.' Shuffling back from the edge of the cliff, he rose to his feet and moved off to join the others. The woman warrior watched him go with silent unease, knowing that beneath the *Éblána* warrior's thin veneer of comradeship lay a lethal and potentially treacherous man.

At Liath Luachra's beckoning, Sean Fergus hurried forward to take Flannán's place but as he stretched out on the hard rock, he gave an involuntary grunt of pain and clutched at his chest. The Grey One turned him a curious stare but he stoically repressed any further reaction.

It struck her then that, despite her antagonism towards him the previous evening, the old warrior had been surprisingly civil – certainly more civil than she would have been in his place – over the course of the morning's march. She regretted that harshness towards him now for of all the *fénnid* in *Na Cinéaltaí*, Sean Fergus was the only one who'd never sought anything of her, who'd never subjected her to a threat or menace of any kind. If anything, he'd been a rare source of reason, a calming influence within the group and, hence, one that Bressal had used for the more complex tasks such as mentoring Biotóg or monitoring the distribution of *fian* booty.

And then discarded without a second thought.

With some discomfort, Liath Luachra wondered how she would deal with the old man if he survived the forthcoming violence. Fearful of appearing weak, she'd always treated Sean Fergus as she'd treated the others, refusing any offer of assistance, rejecting any attempt at interaction and generally responding to his politeness with a distant stiffness. But could she really kill him? Would she really be able to dispatch him, spill his blood dispassionately?

For once, she wasn't completely sure.

I need that land. If I have to, I will spill his blood.

She sniffed and put such thoughts aside. Given the old man's failing health there was little realistic chance of the situation arising in any case.

'This does not sit well,' the old warrior muttered suddenly.

Roused from her thoughts, the Grey One examined him from the corner of her eye. Sean Fergus was staring down at the holding with a furrowed brow. Ever reluctant to encourage further dialogue, she refrained from comment.

'The thread of Bressal's story does not unspool true,' he continued nevertheless. 'This is a farm. I see no warriors here, no defences, nothing but boys and slaves, old women and farmhands. Hardly a threatening force.'

She frowned for now she had no choice but to step in.

'Rógallach Mór says that this is Barra's base and the assembly point for his *díberg* raids. It's possible he's out raiding even as we sit here watching his cooking fires.'

'This does not have the air of a *díberg*.'

She looked up again, surprised to find that he was looking at her intently, as though to assess her reaction. 'We have a man to kill, a captive to rescue. Does the prospect of heroic action not quicken your pulse?'

'Heroic action?' He stared at her, looked down at the holding, then back at her again. A burst of laughter escaped his lips but was stifled almost immediately as he closed his eyes, wincing in pain. '*Na Cinéaltaí* is not a *fian* to encourage heroes.'

'It was your choice to join the *fian*, Sean Fergus.'

'Was it?' His eyes glazed momentarily as he pondered the statement but then he shrugged. 'Sometimes the river of life scoops you up when you least expect.' He considered her closely, cocking one eyebrow as though to emphasis the imparting of some great gem of wisdom. 'You can fight its watery tow but, one day, when it finally deposits you on some desolate outcrop, you look around and realise you're in a place you never intended to go.'

The Grey One scowled. 'We follow Bressal's direction.'

'Even when it's wrong.'

She ignored that. 'If we see Barra, we move in at dawn.'

'To kill them?'

'Except for the blond *Éblána* woman. That is the direction.'

'Even the old woman? Even the boys?'

That caught her. She wanted to say yes, she wanted to shut him up, to blunt his argument with some pithy, definitive response but the words just caught in her throat. She glared at him, swallowing. 'Dawn,' she managed to spit.

111

Shuffling back from the edge of the cliff, she got to her feet and considered the old warrior coldly. 'Stay here,' she ordered. 'And keep a sharp watch for Barra. You've heard the account of his likeness. I'll send someone to make sure you're relieved later.'

Sean Fergus looked at her with soft eyes. 'Too late for that Grey One,' he said. 'Nothing and no-one can ever relieve me now.'

Chapter Six

That night sleep came fitfully to Liath Luachra. When, at last, she fell into slumber, her dreams were agitated, plagued by nightmares old and new. It was early morning when she woke, roused by an insistent tapping against the sole of her foot. Choking down an involuntary cry, she stared blearily up to where Canann was standing. It had been his soft kicking that had disturbed her.

'What?' she growled.

He looked at her in an odd, almost apologetic manner and a shudder-like a premonition ran through her. 'It's Sean Fergus.'

She stared at him blankly.

'He's dying. He wants to see you.'

***

The trek back along the plateau seemed interminable but it was a clear night and the silver glow of a three-quarter moon allowed her to work her way along the pitted surface. With the absence of cloud, the night sky was stained with stars, vast splashes of silver pin pricks that merged with the moonlight bathing the land in liquid silver. She cursed then for she'd liked to have paused to study such a rare view.

But she had other commitments, of course. Sean Fergus deserved that much.

The grey streak of dawn was slipping in over the horizon, blurring out the beauty as she arrived back at the cliff where she'd left the old warrior the previous evening. Locating him wasn't particularly difficult. The distant wheeze of laboured breath from the cluster of ash trees was audible even before she could make him out through the shadows.

She closed in on the noise, picking her way towards the trees with care until she found him sprawled in a rough nest of leaves and foliage at the base of a particularly gnarled pine. Stepping closer, she paused to stare down at the dozing warrior, unnerved by his sickly appearance. Sean Fergus had looked unwell for some time but here, lying back against the trunk in the grey gleam of dawn, he looked more corpse-like and wasted than ever before. Regarding him now, it seemed odd that

113

she hadn't previously noted how worn he'd become over the past few days.

'Sean Fergus.'

The warrior started awake and opened his eyes. Seeing her, he raised one hand in greeting but with obvious effort. 'Grey One.' He attempted a tight smile but on that haggard face, the resulting expression looked more like a grimace. 'It seems we come to a fork in the path, Grey One.' His voice was raspy and had a disturbing chesty gurgle. 'I will soon go my way, you will go yours.'

She sniffed, awkwardly shifting her weight from one foot to the other. 'I'm sorry you're dying, Sean Fergus,' she said simply. While traversing the plateau, she'd considered whether it might be easier not to acknowledge his impending death, to feign ignorance and circumvent any attempt to speak of it directly. Looking at him now, she could see how deeply insulting that would have been.

'Come now, Grey One.' He flinched briefly, his hand pressing on his chest as he attempted to shift himself upright. His low, strictly modulated voice hid the true extent of the pain she knew he must be feeling. 'This way at least you do not need to cut my throat yourself.'

She stared, opening her mouth to deny it, but nothing came out.

'Rest easy. I take no offence. If anything, the thought of an end beneath your blade settles softer than the prospect of an offing from the likes of Conall or Canann. Or Bressal himself.' He paused to inhale slowly, clearly struggling to manage the pain. 'Not that Bressal would dirty his hands on the likes of me.'

'It's true. He would have someone else do it for him.'

'Someone like you.'

'Yes,' she admitted.

'It is my belief, deep down, that you would not have killed me.'

'No. It would have weighed heavily but I'd have done it.'

He made as though to respond to that but as his lips parted he broke into a fit of harsh, liquid coughs. She winced in sympathy at the sound. 'Pain?' she asked.

'No,' he wheezed. 'I have my fill.'

She looked at him blankly.

114

'A joke, Grey One. One of poor taste that falls back on me but …'
His shoulders twitched, the phantom of a shrug. 'As a young man, I
enjoyed jokes. Nothing pleased me more than a deep-rooted belly laugh.
Until my family passed, of course. My humour died with them.' His eyes
momentarily grew distant. 'Odd, now that I'm Breathing Dead, I should
regain an appetite for humour.'

'I'm sorry you're dying, Sean Fergus,' she repeated. 'If I could, I
would make it not so.'

'I wouldn't. My song is sung. I am tired and yearn to rest with my
ancestors. I had hoped to pass to the Black Lands with a sword in my
hand but the blood cough allows no easy route to a warrior's death.'

Liath Luachra shuffled uncomfortably. 'Canann said you wished to
speak with me.'

'Ah, the odious Canann. I had to offer him my knife to convince him
to go and fetch you.' Sean Fergus paused to wipe a globule of saliva that
had dribbled from the corner of his mouth. Liath Luachra couldn't help
noticing that it was flecked and foamy with blood. 'Yes. I have two
items of counsel I would offer should you hear me out. Then, perhaps,
a boon to ask in exchange.'

She waited but he said nothing for several moments and she could
sense his hesitancy. 'Share your first counsel then,' she urged him.

'You must leave *Na Cinéaltaí*.'

Liath Luachra's lips gave a sardonic twist. 'This is your wise counsel?'

'If you remain with the *fian* you will die.'

'If I leave the *fian* I will die,' she countered. 'Probably by my own
hand.' She caught herself then and glowered, irritated by the
uncharacteristic slip, the release of such an intimate admission.
Addressing a Breathing Dead, it seemed, had a way of encouraging
uncommon candour.

Fortunately, she saw that her words had also served to pause the old
man's ramblings for he was looking at her with troubled incredulity. 'I
have no wish to leave the *fian*,' she continued, taking advantage of his
silence. 'And I have no reason to do so. Bressal has promised me the
opportunity to carve a name.'

115

'And you trust the cuckoo tune Bressal Sweetongue whistles in your ear.'

She bristled at that. 'Bressal has named me *rígfénnid*. *And* granted me leadership of this *fian* service.'

'This is a tainted service. None of us are meant to survive this encounter.'

'None of the *fénnid*.' Her eyes hardened. 'But I am *rígfénnid*.'

'You are also *éclann*,' he reminded her. 'Bressal's first loyalty – and my use of that term stretches its meaning – is to his tribe.'

'*Éclann* have their value. Bressal recognises that.'

'As blade fodder. And such value founders for witnesses to secrets that are best kept secret.'

'He has no fear of loose lips from me. He has promised me *Éblána* land to ensure my silence.'

'Bressal dangles that carrot you crave most before your eyes. It's his way to blind people to the fact that his milk is watered.'

'No!' She shook her head, angry now. 'Bressal knows he has my loyalty. And more, he has need of me. He requires a *rígfénnid* he can depend on, a female *rígfénnid* to attract and gather other potential *fénnid*.'

'And when the *fénnid* are gathered? What then? What would prevent him from removing the threat of knowledge you pose?'

The prospect of rutting me.

She kept this particular insight to herself but, confronted by the reality of her predicament, she had to acknowledge it was a poor prospect on which to gamble her survival. A scowl crept up one side of her face. 'If this is the sum of your counsel, old man, I have no need of it.'

'You must leave *Na Cinéaltaí*,' he insisted.

'I've lasted this long.'

'You have lasted this long only because of me.'

She stared at him and although from long habit her features displayed no hint of what she was thinking, she was genuinely astonished by the old man's assertion.

'Do you truly believe a green sapling like you could have survived unaid- ' He paused as he saw the look in her eyes. 'Ah! I see. You did.'

He shook his head, an action that seemed to provoke a fresh bout of coughing. When he finally looked up at her again, his eyes were watering and the grey of his beard was stained red below his lips. He tried to speak but choked, struggling for breath. Taking a deep breath through his nostrils, he tried again.

'The elders advise us not to underestimate the brashness of youth. Now I see the truth in their wisdom.' He sighed and absently rubbed at his knee as though it too ached to the bone. 'But another truth, Grey One, is that I have held your flank within the *fian* these last two years. You are a sharp blade, well able to bite back at the hand that threatens you but alone, in a band of vicious, damaged men ...' He shook his head. 'I recognise that you have hardened, that your ferocity has grown. But when you first set foot within our circle you were an unguarded settlement, ripe for sacking. This is why, from the very first day, I made it clear to the other *fénnid* that they would answer to me if they troubled you.'

'That's a grand claim,' Liath Luachra mocked. 'And yet I know such threats cause little disquiet to the likes of Conall Cacach.'

'Not now perhaps, but not too long ago, it did. Back when I had my full strength I could have stopped any one of them.'

'You didn't stop Callach Fat Arse.'

'No, you handled him well enough but that was after two full seasons with us. During the first half-year of your tenure with *Na Cinéaltaí*, I prevented three separate attempts to accost you of which you knew nothing.' He closed his eyes and sighed heavily. 'My strength has faded but I've continued to do what I can till now.'

Liath Luachra snorted, causing the old man to open his eyes and regard her with an expression of surprisingly fiery resentment. 'Do you truly believe it was simple circumstance that I should appear by the river, just at the moment Conall Cacach was preparing to attack you?'

Liath Luachra stared at him, unsure what to say. She wanted to refute it, reject everything the *Seanstrompa* – the Old Fart – was saying but, instinctively, she knew he was telling the truth. Deep down, she suspected she'd always known it, even if it was an unconscious knowing.

She had certainly always slept easier when Sean Fergus was present in camp.

Despite his illness and her mask of stoic implacability, the warrior remained perceptive enough to see the emotions he'd stirred. 'Forgive me. It is not my intent to sour your thoughts. I have only ever sought to help you.'

'That is the second time you make such a declaration. Why do you seek to help me? Do not say it is because I remind you of your daughter for I don't believe it.'

'Of Lann?' Sean Fergus paused to rub his heart with a trembling hand. 'There is a close resemblance between you but no, you have the truth of it. The real reason is linked, I suppose, to my second counsel.'

The woman warrior regarded him suspiciously.

'My second counsel is this: you do not carry your father's madness.'

Liath Luachra stiffened and she eyed him with cold hostility. 'How could you know? What do you know of my father?'

'I know of a man who lost his wife and then his mind, a man who drowned his thoughts in cloud mushroom and *uisce beatha*. I know of a man who chained his only daughter to a rock, who whipped her till he flayed the skin from her back.'

Liath Luachra stared at him in shock, her posture rigid as iron, her hands balled into fists. 'How...?'

'I, too, hail from Luachair.'

The Grey One's jaw dropped. She stood looking at him, her mouth hanging slack.

'I have returned but a single time since the day I left the valley.' Sean Fergus' face took on a distant expression. 'Many years ago now. I knew your mother when we were children and, later, your father. That man and woman who look after you in winter – the friends of your mother – that man is my brother.' He paused to examine her face for some reaction but when he saw no give in her, he continued talking. 'I would ask you not to hate him. He and his woman sought to aid you but you've seen him. He's old and even in his youth, he was no warrior. He feared your father's rages.' He paused to cough again and when he'd finished, he slowly wiped the blood from his lips. The Grey One's face

118

had reverted to its habitual stoniness and now she watched him with a falcon's gaze, tense and blank but still saying nothing.

'You may not recall but, over the three nights you lay chained to the *gallán*, they would creep into the clearing while your father slept or lost himself in *uisce beatha* and tend to your wounds and feed you scraps of food.'

The Grey One had begun to tremble, pain-clouded scraps of memory revived by the old warrior's words. She'd always wondered why she hadn't died in that clearing. Starved and bleeding profusely, she should have bled out or at least caught poisoned blood from the wounds on her back alone.

But she hadn't. And the old man's tale offered a credible, if unwelcome, explanation.

She took a deep breath. The vague memories of sensations she'd always thought were dreams; the touch of a poultice on her bloody back, the taste of bread and water, they'd all been real.

Her shoulders dropped and she sagged against the tree, letting her weight drag her down the rough trunk until she sat crumpled on the ground. She could feel Sean Fergus's eyes on her and tried to brush his presence away but the old warrior hadn't finished.

'My brother had planned to release you, to hide you and your brothers in that cave where you now spend your winters smoking cloud mushroom and awaiting death's cold touch. Had the *díberg* not come to Luachair that very morning, blocking his path, your brothers might still be alive today. As it was, he barely got himself and his woman to safety.'

Liath Luachra closed her eyes, unable to prevent the unleashed memories from rushing up to envelop her. Despite the mind-numbing suffering from three days of brutal whippings and beatings, she too had observed the arrival of the *díberg*. A band of seven warriors, they'd eased in out of the dawn mist, halting at the edge of the clearing to regard her in silence like curious ghosts. Barely conscious and half-mad from pain, she'd blearily regarded the line of assembled men, numbly marking the dew glinting on their metal swords, the cold windburned features that returned her regard without compassion. After a moment, the leader had jerked his head in the direction of Luachair and the *díberg* had

119

moved off, following the track down into the valley where her family's holding was located.

It was only then that her mind had begun to function properly, the true ramifications of the *díberg* presence working its way through the dishevelled fog in her head. She'd struggled to get to her feet but her legs had refused to support her. Instead, she'd tried to scream a warning but after three days of screaming her throat was raw and swollen and the few feeble cries she'd managed to produce had been cast back at her by a westerly wind. Later, that same treacherous wind had carried the smell of burning to her nostrils, the distant screeches of pain and terror.

By mid-afternoon, the *díberg*'s work was done. Four of the warriors had returned to the clearing and, secure in the knowledge that she couldn't escape, they'd taken their time with her, raping her in turn until they were spent and all that remained of her was one great flaring wound. By then, the agony had completely overwhelmed her, reducing her to a deadened insensibility that prevented her from feeling anything anymore. At some point, the *díberg* men had left and night came in to shroud the land as though shamefully cloaking the bloodshed that had preceded it.

Don't think of it!

Her fingers dug into the dirt, piercing the mossy surface at the base of the tree and somehow the sheer mass of the Great Mother helped to steady her, anchored her sufficiently to recover her equilibrium. Raising her head, she opened her eyes to find Sean Fergus watching her in silence. 'Have you completed your counsel, old nettle-tongue,' she snarled, acid in her voice. 'I would have you go follow your path now and die.'

'And there lies the boon I seek of you.'

She sneered and shook her head, unable to speak for several moments. 'Nothing,' she said at last. 'You get nothing from me.'

He looked at her with an air of exhausted desperation. His face was tight, the skin around his eyes shiny with sweat. 'Will you hear me out? You owe me that at least. My words may sting but you know I speak the truth.'

120

The woman warrior looked as though she was about to strike him but she somehow regained control of herself. 'Speak, then!' she spat.

'The blood cough fills my lungs and eats me up from inside. I've managed the pain with cloud mushroom but my supply is exhausted and it grows unbearable. I ask you … to end it.'

She gave a curt shake of her head.

Sean Fergus released a sudden, involuntary giggle then he started to cough again, a liquid cack that wrenched his entire body.'

Liath Luachra looked on, her lips rolled back in a silent snarl, teeth bared.

The old warrior leaned forward, hands on his chest and hissed at the pain bubbling up inside him. When he stopped and turned his eyes to her again there was something brittle in his gaze. Something had gone out of him after that last attack.

'You grit your teeth and admit reluctant acquiescence to my murder yet when I seek a boon on this same matter, you falter. Truly, you are as consistent as the Spring rains, Liath Luachra.'

He wiped the sweat from his forehead.

'I am not your enemy, Grey One. I need your help. And there is even no need to bloody your blade. I ask only that you pass me your own supply of cloud mushroom. Then I will trouble you no further.'

Her nostrils flared several times as she considered his words but she displayed no other emotion. Finally, she reached one hand inside her tunic, rummaged around the left side above the belt, and withdrew the leather pouch that Bressal had given her, what now felt like many lifetimes ago. Without a word, she undid the ties and poured the little pile of white fungus into his waiting palms. Raising his eyes, he nodded at her in thanks.

They sat in silence as he slowly filled his mouth, chewing and swallowing until the entire contents of the pouch were gone. Neither spoke for a time. Both understood that Sean Fergus was now truly Breathing Dead. He would not survive the lethal quantity of cloud mushroom he'd ingested.

Liath Luachra turned her head to the east. The sun was peeking over the horizon, imbuing the world with fresh colour and bringing life back to the land. A true irony under the circumstances.

'You said you knew my mother?'

Sean Fergus looked up, surprised by the sudden question. 'Yes,' he said, before turning his eyes once more to the ground. 'A good woman. In truth she had my heart. I'd have taken her hand in a moment, raised a child with her and- ' His gaze flickered momentarily towards her but she ignored him. Instead, I left the valley and had my family elsewhere. I often wonder how things would be if she'd not made another choice.'

'My father.' There was no disguising the quiet hatred in her voice.

Sean Fergus took a moment before responding. 'You should know that the man who chained you to a rock and flogged you was not the man I knew. I can't claim to understand what drove him to do what he did but when I knew him he was generous and courageous. He never made visit without gifts and he never once retreated from a clash of spears. I suspect your martial sense is inherited from him.'

He caught the shudder of revulsion that ran through her.

'My counsel was sincere, Grey One. Whatever madness overtook him, it is not one that you carry within you. You have too much of your mother's touch in every other matter.'

'My father was a contorted briar, a bent blade.'

'Try to show sympathy, girl. Your father was a broken warrior who tried to live a life of peace and ...' He hesitated. 'And failed. Every old warrior you meet still fights the hard battle. Most will hide it but the wounds are always there, deep beneath the layers of scar tissue.'

'Warriors like Conall Cacach?' she asked, her voice scathing.

Sean Fergus chose to ignore that particular barb, slyly turning her words another way. 'Beware Conall Cacach. He watches you at all times, waiting for you to put your weapons aside.'

She made a dismissive gesture and turned her eyes away as though the topic warranted little attention. 'I can take Conall Cacach. He is driven by his blood horn and it makes him careless.'

'He is driven by more than that. He wants to hurt, to humiliate.' Sean Fergus paused again, gasped a little but managed to stifle the cough in his lungs before it could take hold. 'There is something burning that man up from the inside. He is black, fire-twisted metal, beyond help or pity. Nothing but death will ever give him peace. I think …'

Noting the pause, Liath Luachra looked up and saw the warrior's eyes had softened, the intensity of his gaze dwindling as the *beacáin scammalach* took effect. Sean Fergus too appeared conscious of its influence for his lips broke into a weary smile. 'The tide ebbs,' he told her. 'And the pain fades.' He looked down at his hands and seemed to sag a little. 'Not long now.'

'Whist, you grow melancholic.' She reached forward as though to take his shoulder and steady him but, at the last moment, drew back and bit her lip instead.

'Ah, whist yourself. If there's a time for a man to grow melancholic, I'd think this would be it.' When she made no response, he shook his head as though in regret. 'You don't talk, Grey One. It has always been so with you. You talk the shallow-talk, shun those who dare to come too close. You take the untravelled path, side-step all contact. You do your dance of avoidance and think yourself so very clever when all the time it is you alone that you avoid.'

He grew quiet again and she saw his frame was trembling but couldn't tell whether it was the effect of the cloud mushroom or the illness.

'Grey One,' the old warrior said suddenly. *'Cén maitheas uisce nuair atá uisce beatha le fáil?'* Why have the water when you can have the whiskey?

'What? What do you mean?' She looked at him in confusion but he made no answer for several moments and when he did it was on another topic entirely. 'I'm scared, Grey One. I'm glad you're here. It's a hard death to pass alone.'

Then my own death will not be soft. That's a future set in stone.

Sean Fergus' thin frame trembled briefly again. At a loss how to respond, Liath Luachra remained silent beside him, finally opening her mouth to make an attempt at some threads of consolation. Before she could speak however, Sean Fergus's hand reached out to grasp hers and hold it weakly in his own. 'Lann.' His eyes were glazed now, his voice a whisper. 'Come home. I miss you.'

123

She looked down at his hand, a clumsy, warm weight in her palms. 'Lann,' he whimpered. 'I miss you. Are you there?'

Liath Luachra sighed. 'Yes, father.'

***

Sean Fergus passed away some time before the sun peeled free of the eastern horizon. Shortly after taking her hand, she'd felt his body go limp but the death rattle in his chest continued for a little while after. When this too had ceased and she could detect no heartbeat, Liath Luachra busied herself, cutting a shallow grave in the dirt beneath the trees and wrapping the old warrior in his cloak. She rolled him gently into the depression, laying him on his back so he could face the heavens, his weapons in his hands. Fortunately, there was no shortage of stones and she was able to gather enough to cover the body with a hard protective shell.

When her work was completed, she sat and stared at the resulting mound, battling with conflicting feelings of pity for Sean Fergus and anger that he'd chosen to die at a time when she needed him most. In truth, she wasn't sure how she felt about the old warrior. She thought she might miss him but, then again, she couldn't be certain. What was clear to her now was that he'd helped her much more than she'd ever imagined. At the same time, she couldn't help resenting his defence of her father and his secret familiarity with her own tortured past. The unanticipated dredging up of her history had truly shaken her and, even now, the memories caused her heart to pulse, the muscles in her neck and shoulders to clench tight, and a bitter taste of metal to flood her mouth. The old warrior's call for clemency had cast salt on the wound for she knew she'd never forgive her father. Sean Fergus might speak of forgiveness and compassion but he hadn't endured the hellish years that she'd been obliged to live through on her mother's passing, he hadn't seen the beastlike insanity in her father's eyes as he struck her again and again and again.

She paused then and drew a deep breath. Even now it cut raw and deep to think of the days after her mother's death. Within half a year of her passing, her father had started imbibing self-made *uisce beatha* and cloud mushroom in equal quantity on an almost daily basis. A season before the *díberg* raid, his descent into the madness had already reached a terrifying stage. By then, he'd already started complaining about a strange taste to the food Liath Luachra prepared although nobody else could find fault with it. Over time, those complaints had grown in frequency, gradually becoming more vocal and violent to the point that family meals were a terrifying affair where the children huddled in fear while their father bellowed with the fury of mounting paranoia.

Convinced of his daughter's intent to poison him, he'd dragged her from her bed one night. Although dressed in little more than a thin shift, he'd hauled her through the late autumn chill to the clearing with the lichen-coated *gallán* at its centre. There, he'd chained her to a hole in the stone using an old set of rusted manacles retrieved from a skeleton in the forest years earlier. Over the next three days, he'd repeatedly whipped her senseless with an old horse whip, screaming at her to confess.

Initially Liath Luachra had pleaded with him, tried to reason with him. Later, cowering in pain, she'd begged. Finally, when her back was little more than a ragged, flaming sore, she'd just gone silent, her heart growing colder with every bite of the lash, every meaty strike against her back.

Forgiveness.

Her lips rolled back in a feral snarl. Sean Fergus' suggestion felt like having the scab of an old injury ripped from her heart.

So, no. She wouldn't be forgiving any time soon.

She was struck then by a sudden longing for a *sliog* – a slug – of *uisce beatha*, a physical need for its scalding splash against the back of her throat. Or even a sliver of cloud mushroom.

But Sean Fergus, of course, had finished her entire supply.

With a sigh, she left the trees and crawled to the edge of the cliff, recovering her previous vantage point over the valley. There was some activity down in Gort Na Meala. A southerly wind had picked up and she could hear the low of cattle, the distant tinkle of metal on metal, the sharp thud and crack of an axe splitting wood as the two slaves from the previous day carried out their tasks. Beyond that there was little else. Her mouth and jaw set grimly.

125

Sean Fergus had the right of it. This does not have the feel of a díberg camp.

As she watched, she saw the two young cattle herders emerge from the nearer longhouse, long staves in hand as they made their way towards the fields where the cattle were located. Several paces from the building however, a high cry stopped them and both turned to wait as a third child – a little girl – came running out of the building after them. As she watched each of the boys take one of her hands, Liath Luachra felt her heart break. The *díberg* had killed her brothers. According to the old couple, they'd hacked the little bodies into even littler pieces. Taken captive by the *díberg* for use as a slave, she'd never seen the bodies, never got back to bury them and their absence was a hole in her heart, even today.

Stop this! The past is dead. As will you be if you do not fulfil your service.

With a black heart, the Grey One pulled back from the edge of the cliff and rose to her feet. Taking a deep breath she released it slowly and focussed on what she needed to do. She did not have the luxury of grieving the past or even Sean Fergus. She had to concentrate on the task at hand. Find Barra ua *Éblána*.

And kill him.

She chewed thoughtfully on the inside of her cheek. By rights, she should return to camp, inform the others of Sean Fergus' passing and do her best to convince Flannán to join them and take his place. She needed another fighter if Rólgallach Mór's information was correct. In the meantime, she'd also have to set someone else on the lookout point to monitor the holding.

But first, scratch the itch that tickles you.

She could not ignore her curiosity any longer. She had to learn more about the holding, identify whether it truly was a *díberg* site or not. It didn't look like one but a smart man might disguise his base, conceal his weapons and fighting men until they were needed. Picking up a twig she clamped it between her teeth and thought about it further.

Before returning to the *fénnid*, she could descend to the valley, carefully work her way closer to the longhouses. The dog was away with the boys and the thick growth around the clearing would allow her to get up close. She was confident she could edge in without being seen

126

and find a hidey-hole. From there, she could study the holding, assess the fighting ability of the people and identify whether this truly was a farm or not.

Casting one last glance towards the silent cluster of trees – now a silent burial ground – she said her farewells to Sean Fergus then slowly started back along the ridge to find a spot where she could work her way down to the valley floor. Unfortunately, the steep cliffs stretched much further than she'd anticipated, forcing her to retrace her steps all the way back to the original path where the little *fian* had first commenced its ascent to the plateau.

It wasn't long before she found herself back at that section of the plateau just above the spot where the *fian* camp had been established. Although loath to engage with the men, she moved closer, thinking that since she was there, she might as well order one of them back to the lookout point. When she peered over the lip of the plateau however, she was surprised to see that not only were the three men awake but sitting together talking earnestly around a small fire.

She frowned then, curious at the sight for she knew the men detested one another. For a moment, she attempted to hear what they were saying but could make out nothing more than a distant mumble and an occasional cackle of laughter. She scratched at a piece of dry skin on her knee cap.

Now what are those three talking about?

She glanced up at the sun. Whatever it was, it would have to wait.

Moving back from the edge, she turned and traversed the plateau to the northern edge. She followed that for a time, finally finding a route through a steep gully that provided access to the valley floor.

The descent was rapid if invigorating, for she had to slide down at an angle at the steeper parts. She hit the base of the ridge without much warning. One moment she was skidding downwards, the next the terrain had flattened out and she'd slowed to a point where she could straighten up and walk upright again. Ignoring the scratch and tug of tangled branches, the prickle of briars, she pushed forward through the dense undergrowth for several paces before suddenly emerging out onto the narrow trail back towards *Carraig An Fhírinne Buí.*

Finally.

She cast a quick glance east along the trail to check that it was clear then turned and started west, following the curve of a tight bend. Normally, she'd have taken the time to move more carefully but, conscious of the late hour and the urgent need to find a hidey-hole before the holding became more active, she increased her pace, speeding up to a brisk trot.

She took the bend at a sprint, pushing herself faster and as she came out of the curve onto the straighter section of the trial she skidded to a desperate halt. Standing directly before her, at a distance of less than ten paces, was the fair-haired young woman from the *Éblána* holding.

Spotting her at exactly the same instant, the other woman too stumbled to a startled halt. She took an uncertain step backwards, defensively raising the wicker basket in her hands before her like a shield. Her eyes narrowed as she examined the woman warrior with a mixture of suspicion and curiosity. For her part, Liath Luachra too had responded instinctively, her hand automatically reaching down for her sword. The weapon was already half-drawn from the scabbard by the time she'd realised the senselessness of the action. The fair-haired girl clearly posed no threat. In fact, if anything she seemed slightly bemused by the woman warrior's reaction.

'What is this, boy? You intend to menace me with that sword?'

Surprised by the fair-haired woman's boldness, the Grey One took time to examine her before answering. More of a girl than a woman, she couldn't have had more than seventeen or eighteen years on her, little more than a year or two older than Liath Luachra herself. She was tall and quite beautiful, her slender figure hugged by the tight, green dress she was wearing. Her eyes, bright blue, displayed intelligence but also a certain playfulness and a possible wilful streak. She struck the warrior woman as surprisingly assured for, despite the potential precariousness of her situation, she regarded the Grey One more out of curiosity than fear. 'I'm not a boy,' Liath Luachra retorted, unable to keep a note of irritation from her voice.

The other woman inspected her with more careful scrutiny then slowly nodded her head. 'No, you're not. What are you doing here, little sister?' When she spoke, her voice was surprisingly husky, like a cough soothed with honey.

'Travelling. Going home.' The lie came easy, easier than it should have. But it was the right lie. Unlike larger groups, a single individual travelling through tribal lands – although unwelcome – was not usually considered as much of a threat and hence a little more latitude was generally offered.

The fair-haired woman regarded her carefully then took one or two steps forward. She was clearly intrigued at the presence of this stranger on her tribal land. 'You're a woman warrior,' she said at last with quiet conviction.'

Liath Luachra nodded. There seemed little point in denying the obvious.

Her response seemed to please the *Éblána* woman. 'My mother was a warrior,' she declared with unexpected enthusiasm. Liath Luachra looked at her warily, unsure how to respond to this piece of information.

'Fíne Surehands was the name on her. A talented warrior, renowned among the *Éblána*. Did you know of her?'

Liath Luachra shook her head. The name meant nothing to her. 'I'm not *Éblána*,' she said by way of explanation. A non-tribal member would hardly be expected to be familiar with the warriors from a particular tribe unless they'd clashed in battle or a warrior's reputation was truly exceptional.

'You must meet with her,' the girl declared effusively. 'My mother's speech would flower in the company of a fellow woman warrior.'

Taken by surprise by this brash invitation, Liath Luachra struggled to come up with an excuse to decline. Fortunately the girl did it for her. 'But not just now. I make my way to the beach to bathe.' She briefly hoisted the wicker basket in her hand. 'Would you care to accompany me or are you too pressed in your travels. I have food enough for two.'

Liath Luachra shuffled uncertainly.

The older girl studied her, cocking her head to one side. 'You don't know what a beach is, do you?' she said, misinterpreting the Grey One's shuffling.

129

'I know what a beach is. It's the side of the sea.' Liath Luachra straightened up and puffed out her chest, a barely perceptible difference given the resources nature had given her to work with. 'I come from inland, far from the coast. And I have seen a beach. I've just never walked on a beach.'

'You have never walked on a beach. Truly you are an intriguing person.'

Liath Luachra regarded the svelte young woman with her pretty green dress and silver-blond hair. Accustomed to dealing with men, she felt oddly awkward and apprehensive in her presence. 'I never had need to,' she said with a little more force than was necessary.

'Then here is an opportunity to experience something new, little sister. Now you must certainly come with me.' She beamed and seemed about to sweep forward to take the Grey One's arm but then seemed to hesitate and hold back. 'But first, tell me how are you named?'

'Liath Luachra.'

The girl waited for the tribal affiliation. When it became clear none was forthcoming, she shrugged. 'I see. Well, Liath Luachra, I am Muirenn ua Éblána.'

Muirenn?

The Grey One managed to conceal her surprise but she considered the girl with fresh curiosity, wondering if this could possibly be the same woman Rólgallach Mór had instructed her to watch out for, the girl they were supposed to break free from captivity. She immediately discounted the possibility. Muirenn was a common enough name and this girl, out walking the trails on her own, hardly looked in need of rescue.

'Shall you accompany me, Liath Luachra?' asked the *Éblána* girl.

Liath Luachra continued to regard her without expression, unaware that she was chewing the inside of her check as she considered her options. She could continue the role of solitary traveller, make an excuse to press on and slip away without raising suspicion. Alternatively, she could play this out, potentially learning more of activities at Gort Na Meala from this oddly over-trusting girl. In some respects, the encounter was something of an opportunity. Through Muirenn she could learn more of Barra ua Éblána, his current location and the true nature of the opposition that awaited them. Great rewards often awaited those brave enough to grasp the nettle offered them. Finally, she nodded stiffly. 'I am not pressed for time,' she said.

Chapter Seven

The *Éblána* woman led the way, returning east along the path in the direction of *Carraig An Fhírinne Buí*. Emerging onto the grassy clearing, they turned left, taking the direction from which Liath Luachra had watched the old man and his two daughters arrive the previous morning. She couldn't help casting a quick glance towards the south to see if they were still there but there was, of course, no sign of them.

The trail north wasn't much better than the one from Gort Na Meala, rough and overrun with foliage from the summer growth. Despite this, the woman warrior observed the occasional footprint suggesting it was a route used by someone on a relatively regular basis.

After a time, the trail seemed to veer east, weaving its way closer towards to the coast although the sea remained out of sight. While they walked, Muirenn swung her basket loosely in one hand and maintained a constant excited chatter. 'I walk this trail often,' she informed the warrior woman. 'Most often when I need to escape the dreariness of farm life.' She sniffed somewhat unhappily. 'Something that seems all too frequent.'

Liath Luachra mumbled vaguely, not trusting herself to open her mouth and not even entirely sure what Muirenn was talking about. The woman chattered like an excited sparrow and, for one accustomed to the company of brutal, monosyllabic men, she was at a loss how to behave.

Nevertheless, the *Éblána* woman was pleasant enough, strikingly attractive and her happy chatter proved an effective antidote to the Grey One's own sombre reflections. More importantly, as they continued north, the Grey One managed to glean some useful information with respect to the Gort Na Meala holding. Keen to obtain further detail, she decided it was time to press the fair-haired woman further.

'Do you feel no fear out here?'

Muirenn looked at her in confusion. 'What do you mean?'

'You walk alone. On empty paths.'

'I walk paths on our land.'

132

'Your land?'

Éblána land. Our tribe patrols the territories strictly. That is why we have no wolves in the region, except in winter. And even fewer strangers. You're the first fresh face I've seen in over a year.'

'You do not fear … *díberg?*'

In response, Muirenn laughed then transferred the weight of her basket from one hand to the other. 'There are no *díberg* in *Éblána* territory. Even if there were …' Using the thumb and forefinger of her free hand, she raised one corner of the cloth draped across the circular rim. Inside, amongst the cheese, the bread and the cold tubers, Liath Luachra caught the gleam of sharp steel. 'My man has taught me the use of the knife.'

'You have a man?' asked Liath Luachra. For some reason she found herself oddly disappointed. She had difficulty imagining Muirenn with a man of her own. Despite the two or so years she had on the warrior woman, she still had an air of childish frivolity about her.

'Yes. Barra ua Éblána. He is a man of some importance among the *Éblána.*'

They were climbing a steep incline at that point so both had their heads down, breathing hard. As a result, Liath Luachra was able to mask her shock at the *Éblána* woman's response.

Barra ua Éblána!

This Muirenn was the woman of the man she'd been dispatched to kill.

She swallowed, cleared her throat to hide her internal disarray. 'You do not prefer to pass time with your man?'

Muirenn turned and gave her a playful smile. 'Why would I want that when I have your pretty company?' She laughed then, amused by the Grey One's startled reaction. 'Besides, Barra is away. He travels north trading bulls with his cousins.'

Or carrying out a raid.

The woman warrior dropped her eyes as they continued up a particularly steep incline, struggling to make sense of Muirenn's revelation. It was difficult to be certain but she didn't think the girl was lying. That meant she was either telling the truth or her man was misleading her.

She hid a frown at that. The latter seemed unlikely. She might appear somewhat spoilt and frivolous but Muirenn didn't strike her as a fool. She certainly doubted the woman could be duped over an issue of such significance.

So Rólgallach Mór was lying. There is no díberg at Gort Na Meala.

She bit her lip nervously, disturbed by the conclusion. If Rólgallach Mór had lied to her about Gort Na Meala's role as a centre for *díberg* activity, what else was untrue? Even more disturbing, if Rólgallach Mór had lied to her, had he also lied to Bressal or was Bressal, too, aware of this particular machination?

The woman warrior nervously grasped the pommel of her sword. Although reluctant to acknowledge the possibility, she wasn't foolish enough to discount it entirely. Bressal was aware of her undeclared loathing for *díberg* even if he didn't know the reasons behind it. He was also well versed in concealing the truth to achieve his own ends. It was entirely possible he'd sent her to sack Gort Na Meala in the knowledge that her hatred of *díberg* would dissuade her from asking too many questions.

And had it not been for Sean Fergus, he'd have been correct. The possibility that she might have been so easily manipulated once again, cut deep.

He needs me. He wouldn't do that to me.

She chewed anxiously on the inside of her cheek.

Yes, he would.

Before she could consider the matter further, the women emerged out of the trees and onto a flat section of cliff overlooking the sea.

Oh!

Liath Luachra halted and stared, all thought of Bressal and Rólgallach Mór whipped from her mind by the blustery offshore breeze. Preoccupied with the *rí* of the *Éblána's* deception, she'd lost track of how far they'd travelled, how high they'd climbed. The cliff on which they were standing was located at the tip of a towering promontory that stretched out to sea. She found herself physically struck by the sheer impact of blue, the great slab of aquamarine against the vastness of empty sky. Spread in a wide semicircle for as far as the eye could see, the horizon was a flat line between the two contrasting expanses, a sight that, for some reason, caused her heartbeat to quicken. Any other time she'd ever been near the sea, the body of water had always seemed much further off, its immensity minimised and tamed by framing headlands or other sections of coast. Here, it seemed to stretch into infinity, further than the eye could cope with.

Beside her the *Éblána* woman smiled, genuinely pleased by her reaction. 'A beautiful sight, is it not?'

'It's …' Liath Luachra swallowed, unable to complete the sentence. She closed her mouth, opened it and then closed it again as spicy, salt-tinged air flooded her throat and nostrils.

Muirenn gave a knowing smile then reached out to press her gently on the shoulder, a surprisingly intimate gesture given they were practically strangers. 'It's pleasing to share this sight with another. Sometimes I think I'm the only one to see this beauty. That makes me feel selfish for what value has beauty if it cannot be shared?' She exhaled softly and a barely perceptible trace of sadness flickered across her face. 'Let's go down to the beach.'

She moved forwards to a nearby crag. Behind the grey, pitted rock, a narrow goat track of a path twisted its way back along the side of the promontory, descending to a section of golden sand far below. Still numb from the beauty of the view and her earlier consternation, Liath Luachra followed quietly, feeling like a small child trailing in the footsteps of its mother. To her surprise, despite its apparent steepness, the rocky path was relatively easy to negotiate and it took less time than she'd imagined to reach the bottom. There, it levelled out, merging with a triangular section of sand that led into a passage created by two enormous black rocks arched in towards each other, their tips almost touching. The passage was short and at the far end, the blue-green water was illuminated in brilliant sunshine.

Stepping onto the sand, Liath Luachra enjoyed the grainy, almost powder-like sensation between her toes for it seemed much softer, much finer than the sand on some of the Great Wild's internal waterways. It squeaked softly underfoot as she followed Muirenn through the dark passage and out onto the beach.

The first thing that struck her was the sound. From a distance, beaches had always looked tranquil places but here, close up, she appreciated the coast's true dynamic vitality for the very first time. Waves hurled onshore, slapping the land with a voluminous, foamy roar before subsiding into a great whispering *hissss*. The din was offset by the plaintive cry of seabirds, the flutter of wind and the muffled bark of sleek seals sunning themselves on a rock at the base of the cliffs.

She turned her head and looked around. The beach stretched north from where they were standing to two separate, lichen-coated outcrops that jutted into the water. Although these effectively broke it into three individual strands, all were easily accessed by the broad strip of sand running down from the base of the cliffs. Further to the north, a distance of more than a thousand paces, another sheer headland poked into the sea. Combined with the encircling bluffs and the promontory from which they'd just descended, it effectively sealed the beach off from any possible incursion.

Liath Luachra stared at the distant cliff with curiosity for although it was devoid of vegetation it seemed to undulate with shifting layers of black and white. It took her a moment to realise that she was looking at the movement of a large number of birds, clinging, shuffling or shifting along the ledges of the cliff face.

'Rinn na gCánóg,' said Muirenn. Headland of the Puffins. 'It's quiet now but in spring when the puffins nest they make a noise like a thousand people shouting at once.'

Liath Luachra continued to watch. She recognised some of the birds – guillemots, razorbills, shags and fulmars but there were a number of strange looking ones she'd not seen before.

Beside her the *Éblána* woman licked her lips. 'The puffins taste delicious in soup. My brothers hunt them in spring. Barra and his men lower them down from the cliff tops in *cliabhán* – cradles – so they can reach into the burrows.'

'You have brothers?'

'Two. Two rascals. They came to live with my mother and I when we moved to Gort Na Meala.' Muirenn glanced at the woman warrior and a fond smile flashed across her face. 'That's the name of the valley where we live,' she added by way of explanation. Liath Luachra turned away and said nothing.

The *Éblána* woman seemed to know where she was going so Liath Luachra let her lead the way and followed slowly, keeping a wary eye on the turbulent waves in the same way she'd maintain a watch on a distant wild animal.

'We'll make for the next strand,' Muirenn said over her shoulder. 'The surface has less sand but the outcrops to the sides protect it from the worst of the swell and it's safer to swim.'

As they drew closer, the woman warrior could see Muirenn had the right of it. The long, rolling waves did, indeed, seem to break on some underwater obstacle beyond the rocks. Crushed and subdued, they washed ashore as limp wavelets, lapping up the beach in creamy tongues.

The seagulls keened eerily overhead, circling in lazy spirals as the two women walked along the sand. Having mostly observed them in the aftermath of battle, skirmishing with ravens over the bodies of the dead, the Grey One had never been particularly fond of the birds. Here, in this environment however, their presence seemed more natural, more … fitting.

A number of shags skimmed along the beach, just above the crashing waves. Further out to sea, a solitary gannet plunged vertically out of the sky to hit the green water in an explosion of white spray.

Liath Luachra watched, absorbing the sounds and physical sensations of this unfamiliar environment in quiet fascination, unable to voice what she was feeling. She could sense the emotions flitting about inside her, like butterflies trapped in a cupped pair of palms, but it felt as though she didn't have the words to release them properly. 'Beautiful …' she murmured although even that seemed ineffectual, laughably inadequate to express the sensation.

Muirenn seemed pleased by her reaction for she smiled and nodded her approval. 'It's pleasant to have the company of another woman. I feel lonely here sometimes.'

Her words brought Liath Luachra back to the precarious reality of her situation and, fearing the *Éblána* woman might detect her mounting nervousness, she turned her face away and gazed straight out to sea. Rólgallach Mór had lied about the *díberg* and it struck her now that it was just as likely he'd lied about Muirenn. This woman, mate of Barra ua Éblána, was probably the woman they'd been instructed to 'rescue' and send back to the *Éblána* stronghold.

Stones clattered underfoot as they strolled onto the second strand, two hundred paces or so of sea-smoothened shingle and cobble. Curving around the first lichen-coated outcrop, Muirenn took several steps towards the water before dropping her basket onto the sole patch of sand. Brushing the thick mane of silver-blond hair back from her brow, she reached up and loosened the tie that held it in place. Released, the gleaming strands billowed out in the wind behind her.

Liath Luachra, regarding her profile against the blue background, was struck by a sudden_suspicion. 'You have no other female company where you live?' she asked, doing her best to keep her voice neutral.

'At Gort Na Meala?' The *Éblána* woman responded with a loose shrug. 'There's my mother, I suppose. And my sister, Lerben, but she has less than seven years on her. No-one near my own age.'

And with that, Liath Luachra suddenly knew she'd got to the heart of the matter. The *fian* had not been dispatched to rid the *Éblána* of a troublesome *díberg*. They'd been sent to kill Barra, destroy his settlement and ensure Muirenn was returned to her tribal stronghold.

Where Rólgallach Mór awaited.

She shook her head, wondering how she'd missed it for, in hindsight, it now seemed so obvious. All of this came down to nothing more than a powerful man's lust for his cousin's woman.

Oblivious to her companion's reflections, Muirenn was brushing down her skirt, still dwelling on the woman warrior's earlier question. 'I have my man of course, and his kin to exchange pleasantries with. But they talk only of practicalities.' She pursed her lips in thought, crinkling

138

the soft pink of them. 'Sometimes there needs to be beauty, don't you think? If life is truly one long struggle for survival then surely there must be some beauty to counter that burden?'

Liath Luachra felt a sudden surge of fury. The *Éblána* woman's entire existence was on the cusp of destruction and yet, here she was, warbling on about a life dictated by beauty, a notion so alien to her own experience that she wasn't entirely sure she'd heard her correctly. A wrinkle bridged the woman warrior's brow.

Enough! I must know for certain.

'Do you remain at Gort Na Meala by choice?'

The *Éblána* woman's left eyebrow angle upwards at that. 'Of course. Why else would I be here?'

'You're not a prisoner?'

She laughed out loud at that. 'Of my heart, perhaps. Why? Would you come to rescue me?'

'I'd rescue you.'

She'd answered automatically, without thinking and she blushed when she saw the expression of surprise on Muirenn's face. 'I mean' she added quickly, 'If you were a prisoner.'

'*A laoch, go deo,*' the fair-haired woman laughed, but not unkindly. My hero, forever.

Despite Muirenn's frustrating naivety, Liath Luachra felt her earlier anger fade. For a moment, she could almost understand why Rólgallach Mór had gone to such extreme lengths to possess this woman. There was something truly compellingly about Muirenn, a dynamic combination of sheer physical allure and personal charisma. The fact that she appeared completely unaware of the effect she had on others only seemed to make her all the more beguiling.

Reaching down, the Grey One picked up a fist-sized stone and cast it out to sea. The distance and the noise of the waves beyond the outcrop however, drowned out any noise of it hitting the water.

Beside her, Muirenn leaned forward to consider the woman warrior with fresh interest. 'You have fine cheek bones, Liath Luachra. You should let your hair grow out.'

Liath Luachra wrinkled her nose.

139

'You disapprove?'

'Others have offered such advice of late.'

'Well, then they had the right of it. That stern grooming leaves your face too harsh. Having body about the sides will soften the hardness from your features.'

'I do not think that would overly trouble this individual.'

Muirenn chuckled. 'You have a secret admirer?' she teased.

Once again, Liath Luachra found herself at a loss for words. Uncertain how to respond to such playful mockery, she simply scowled and the *Éblána* woman had the grace to change the subject. 'Shall we bathe?' she asked. Without waiting for a response, she started to undo the belt around her waist, dropping it onto the sand alongside her basket. She pulled the loose, green dress up to her hips and then over her head. Like the belt, it too joined the basket on the ground.

Liath Luachra regarded the fair-haired woman's firm bosom as she unwrapped her loincloth from around her hips and experienced an uncustomary embarrassment at the flatness of her own chest. For the woman warrior, her sexuality had always been something to be concealed, to be stifled. Yet now, in that particular place and time, she had the oddest feeling, as though some fundamental part of herself was somehow lacking.

Sensing the warrior woman's discomfort, Muirenn considered her with a worried expression. 'Do you not swim where you come from?'

Liath Luachra gave, what for her, was a disgruntled look. 'I am no unbathed calf. I may live far from the sea but there are many rivers in the Great Wild, many great rivers.' With this, she awkwardly unbuckled her own belt. Loosening the leather strap, she removed it and the two scabbards holding her sword and her knife, laying both carefully on the stones beside Muirenn's dress. Conscious of the fact that the other woman was watching her, she quickly climbed out of her leggings, pulled the tunic off over her head and, naked, started down the stony shoal towards the sea, driven by years of conditioning to hide her body in the water. Suddenly, she halted mid-step, some instinct alerting her that Muirenn's gaze had somehow changed or intensified. Turning

140

about, she found the woman staring, horrified, at the scars on her lower back.

'By the Gods! Who did this to you little sister? Who treated you in such a brutal fashion?' She moved forward, raising her hands to touch the ragged skin but Liath Luachra stepped out of reach, shrugging off her hands. 'I don't like … to be touched.'

'Tell me! By my word, I swear I will have Barra cut the culprit's head from his shoulders.'

'Barra will find that a formidable task. The head of the man who did this was separated from his shoulders more than three years ago. It lies rotting in bogland far to the west.'

Muirenn looked at her in surprise but then she gave a sharp nod of satisfaction. 'Did your clan catch him? Give him just reward for his brutality?'

The assumption took Liath Luachra by surprise. 'We were *éclann*. There was only ever my family and I.'

'Your father then? He took vengeance on the one who did that.'

'It was my father who did this.'

Muirenn continued to stare at her but the confusion in her eyes revealed her struggle to absorb what Liath Luachra was telling her. 'Your father did this?' she gestured vaguely towards Liath Luachra's back. Her voice sounded strained, high-pitched.

Liath Luachra nodded.

'But … why?'

In response, the Grey One could only look at her. There weren't enough words in the world to describe the enormity of what she'd endured and, even if there were, this beautiful but naïve and sheltered young *Éblána* woman would understand none of them.

The Grey One turned her eyes down and stubbed her toe into the grainy sand, noting the fine, regular imprint it left in the surface. 'I don't speak of such things,' she said at last.

There was a prolonged and uncomfortable silence as Muirenn attempted to digest her response but it was obvious she was struggling to comprehend what she'd just been told. At a loss, she resorted to a clumsy smile. 'Let's play *Dúiche Sheilge'* – Hunting Ground.

141

'Wha-?'

Before the Grey One could react, the *Éblána* woman had slapped her on the shoulder and taken off down the beach. Liath Luachra stared open-mouthed after the receding figure and although she felt no desire to partake in the game, some inner predatorial instinct seemed to kick in for she suddenly found herself tearing down the beach in pursuit.

Lithe and nimble from years of hunting rough terrain, she pounded powerfully across the cobbles that rattled and clacked underfoot. She caught the fair-haired woman a little way down the third strand, tackling her lower legs to send them both tumbling into the spray. Taken aback by the odd taste of salt on her lips she relaxed her grip, allowing the *Éblána* woman to wrench free and wade further out into the water, laughing hysterically as she did so. Licking her salty lips in numb fascination, Liath Luachra followed, pushing her way out through the rippling fronds of seaweed to where the water was clearer and reached to her waist. Unlike the second strand however, this section was exposed to the full force of the sea and it wasn't long before a substantial wave rolled in and struck her head on, knocking her backwards into the water.

Gasping, she resurfaced, coughing seawater from her lungs and wiping the sting of salt from her eyes. Muirenn took the opportunity to swim past, taunting and splashing her. Disentangling herself from the seaweed, the Grey One lunged but the fair-haired woman was fast and got past, stumbling up out of the water and running up the strand with Liath Luachra once more in pursuit.

The woman warrior rapidly found herself becoming caught up in the other woman's enthusiasm and soon everything else was forgotten as the two threw themselves into the game, chasing each other through the shallows, splashing water, shrieking, wrestling in the rock pools. It was only later, when both slumped exhausted onto the sand, that she realised how much she'd given in to the moment, how completely she'd let herself go.

As she sat panting for breath she struggled to recall a similar period of such unrestrained laughter and realised it was the first time since the death of her mother that she'd truly felt free of the black burden, the *tuirse croí* that weighed her down. For one moment she'd allowed herself the luxury of forgetting who she was, what she was. Ironically, the recollection was now all the more painful for that.

Liath Luachra glanced over at the naked *Éblána* woman, noting her flat belly and long, tanned shanks, the drops of seawater set like dew in the curls of her pubic hair.

You are a fool. You allow this woman to befriend you. And yet you intend to slaughter her man.

Her stomach curdled.

But you want that land. The Éblána land Rólgallach Mór promised for your service.

She felt her back and shoulder muscles clench.

But Rólgallach Mór is a liar.

She thought about that for a moment. It had actually been Bressal who'd promised her the land and she hadn't sensed any deception to his words. It was quite possible the promise of land was valid and, in fact, her instincts supported this. Although Rólgallach Mór might have lied to her, it would have been a far greater risk for him to pass untruths to a *fian* leader like Bressal Binnbhéalach.

'You could stay at Gort Na Meala, tonight,' said Muirenn suddenly, disturbing that particular train of thought. Taken aback by the unexpected offer, the Grey One stared at her.

'I mean,' Muirenn added hurriedly. 'If there is no hurry on you to depart.'

Struggling to adapt to this turn of events, Liath Luachra twisted around and allowed her gaze to drift up the sand towards the mouth of the passage through which they'd originally come. A sudden frisson ran through her. Three dark figures were standing there, three men staring towards them with unnerving intensity.

The fénnid!

A quick flare of anger overwhelmed her initial alarm.

What are they doing? They're supposed to remain at camp.

She sniffed as she wiped salt water from her upper lip. Over the course of the journey north, Flannán had been obsessive about remaining hidden and yet there he was, out in the open and clearly

143

visible. From the manner in which the *Éblána* man was standing, the two *fénnid* behind him, it was also clear that they were now following his lead. Circumstances had clearly changed dramatically and from the belligerent hostility of their stance, she could tell it wasn't in her favour.

Treacherous cur. I knew you were not to be trusted.

Her eyes slid across to the second strand where the cloth on Muirenn's basket fluttered in the breeze like a twisted battle banner, just beyond the little pile of her weapons and her clothing.

Beside her, Muirenn's laughter faded abruptly as she too caught sight of the encroachers. She peered and that joyful face went taut and still as a mask. Something flickered in her emerald eyes, those perfect lips gave the slightest twitch of fear. 'Who are they?' she asked, her voice tight.

The woman warrior's eyes didn't move from the distant figures. 'Evil men.'

'You know them?'

'Yes.'

Muirenn shuddered, even at that distance sensing the malevolence of those stares. 'Do they threaten us?'

'Yes.' She turned to look directly at the *Éblána* woman. 'If you want to live you must follow my lead.'

'Maybe we can talk to them. Maybe when th-'

'No,' said Liath Luachra with inarguable finality. 'They're not here to talk.'

Muirenn glanced fearfully towards the three men and noting the swell of panic in her eyes, the woman warrior slapped her across the face. With a gasp, the *Éblána* woman drew back, her hand moving up to her flaming cheek. She stared at Liath Luachra with a wounded, offended expression. The Grey One ignored it. 'If you want to live you must follow my lead. Do you understand?'

Muirenn regarded her with evident disquiet but she slowly nodded her head.

Liath Luachra turned her gaze back to the men and assessed their situation. It did not look good. The *fénnid* could see that the two women were naked and unarmed. Their sole advantage, in fact, was that their clothes and her weapons were out of the warriors' line of sight,

144

obscured by the first outcrop. Given that they couldn't be certain she didn't have her weapons close to hand, they'd probably hold off from an immediate attack.

She considered the terrified *Éblána* woman from the corner of her eye. Muirenn couldn't be counted on for help. With a sigh, she cast her eye back towards the flapping picnic basket. At three to one, the odds were still very much in the *fénnid's* favour but if she managed to get to her sword and sling she'd be in an appreciably stronger position, possibly strong enough to talk her way out of the situation.

With a forced bravado she did not feel, she slowly got to her feet and started forward, gesturing for Muirenn to follow. At that exact moment, the three men also started to advance.

Cursing, the woman warrior quickly increased her pace but in the pit of her stomach she already suspected her cause was lost. The *fénnid* were much closer to the distant outcrop and almost certain to reach it before her.

Bereft of any workable alternative, she continued forward but they'd barely made it onto the stony strand by the time the three warriors reached the outcrop. Almost immediately the men came to a halt and stared down the strand, drawn by the flapping cloth on the food basket.

With a sinking heart, the Grey One continued across the noisy cobbles, Muirenn to her side. After seven or eight paces however, her foot shot out, catching the *Éblána* woman's ankle and sending her crashing forward onto the stones. The warrior woman crouched quickly, catching Muirenn by the elbow and helping her to her feet but as soon as she was upright, the fair-haired girl tugged her arm free. She glared at the woman warrior in anger. 'You did … Why?' The question froze on her lips as her eyes caught a movement from the three men who were still watching them. She started to tremble, her anger forgotten.

'Courage, Muirenn. Be prepared to act on my word.'

The fair-haired woman looked at her dubiously. Ignoring that display of doubt, the Grey One squared her shoulders and led on again, subtly angling her trajectory towards her weapons in the vain hope her intention wasn't immediately obvious.

Unfortunately, despicable loudmouth though he might be, Conall was no fool. Even as she drew closer, she could see how he led the others to match her movements, adjusting the angle of his own path so that he could cut off her access to the weapons. She was still more than twenty paces away from the little pile of clothing when the three warriors reached it and she had to watch as Conall kicked it aside and rested one predatory foot on the scabbard of her sword.

The Grey One slowed her approach, prompting the gruesome warrior to respond with a sick smirk and she knew he was recalling the incident at the riverbank. As they drew closer to the *fénnid*, Muirenn growing ever more terrified, began to lag behind, the crunching sound of her footsteps sounding increasingly hesitant.

I hope you have speed on the run, Muirenn.

The two women came to a halt, a distance of ten paces or so still separating them from the men. Transferring her gaze from Conall to Flannán and Canann, the Grey One observed how completely at ease the *Éblána* man appeared. A regal-looking wolf cloak adorned his shoulders and he was poised comfortably with his weight pressing forward on his right foot. His right hand rested on his knife, fingers beating an excited tattoo on the ornate pommel as his eyes flashed in self-satisfied glee at the way things had worked out.

Canann meanwhile, was standing uncertainly, three or four paces behind the other two, eyes flicking repeatedly from Conall to her and back again. Never one to waste words, the Grey One got straight to the point. 'It's a dangerous game you play, breaking your bond to Bressal,' she said, addressing the two *fénnid*

Conall Cacach's evil cackle polluted the air. 'Hah! Bressal can go fuck a pig. We have a better offer, a much more generous offer.' He made a mocking gesture towards Flannán.

'With Rólgallach Mór? That will be a short friendship.'

'What would you know, *a rígfénnid.*' The last word was spat out with unmistakeable venom. 'You're a poor leader, a poor warrior.' To emphasise his point he tapped her scabbard twice with his foot. 'Careless with your weapons.' He snorted. 'Here is a riddle for you, Grey One. What good the sword you cannot grasp when truly needed? Eh?

146

What good.' Using his foot, he flipped her belt up off the ground and, grabbing the scabbard in his left hand, unsheathed *Gléas Gan Ainm*. 'No good's the answer. These weapons are mine now. You do not deserve a named weapon and by the time I'm done, you'll have no further use for them.'

The Grey One's eyes narrowed and she stared at him with chilling stillness. 'Do not test your luck with me, big man.'

Conall seemed surprised by her boldness. He gave her threat brief consideration but the subsequent look in his eyes told her he'd discounted it as bluster. Dismissing her words with a sneer, he flicked his gaze over her shoulders to where Muirenn was standing, doing her best to use the warrior woman as a shield. The fair-haired woman had placed herself almost directly behind her so the Grey One sensed rather than saw her raise her hands to cover her breasts, an action that prompted the ugly *fénnid* to guffaw loudly. He tossed a smug smile at Canann. 'You see, Canann. Flannán promised us an interesting stroll in the Grey One's wake and it seems he's a man of his word. Look at what he delivers? Two prime dairy cows.'

'Don't be a fool, Conall. You cannot trust Flannán. He's Rólgallach Mór's man. That knife of his will silence your *bladhmaireacht* – loud talk – once your work is done.'

Flannán's confident laughter resounded off the cliffs. 'Hear the desperation in the Grey One's tone,' he gloated. 'Rólgallach Mór is an honourable man. What need would he have to kill men who sack his enemy's house, who deliver the woman he's hungered for these many silent years?'

'He's lying. You are *éclann*. He will betray you.'

'No! He will reward you generously.' Flannán beamed mockingly at the woman warrior, as though daring her to reveal her own secret agreement with his master. She shot him a look of helpless fury but he took no notice. 'And should this circumstance trouble you,' he continued, 'console yourselves in the knowledge that you take the Grey One's share of any spoils as well.'

That particular point seemed to appeal to Conall Cacach for he rolled his head back and roared in gleeful laughter.

'Conall, you kn-'

The *fénnid* turned and spat with impressive accuracy given the distance between them. His spittle hit the woman warrior on the breastbone, splattering across her bare skin. Repressing the urge to wipe the repulsive mess away, she focussed her most commanding glare on the other *fénnid* instead. 'Canann,' she snapped. 'Stick your sword in the *Éblána* pigshit's back.'

The order didn't have the impact she'd hoped for. Canann blinked in momentary confusion but then his eyes hardened and he looked at her as though to say 'You had your chance.' Conall, however, startled by the command and untrusting at the best of times, was forced to change his stance, angling himself around so that he could keep an eye on the other *fénnid* should he, for some reason, take it into his head to obey her. The *Éblána* man, ever confident, didn't even trouble himself to turn around but shook his head sadly like a disappointed parent scolding a foolish child. 'You are over-enamoured with your own importance, Grey One. Bressal must truly be foolish or smitten to make you *rígfénnid* when he-'

'Yer nuttin!' Conall's sudden roar took them both by surprise. 'Nuttin but a flat-chested vessel for Bressal's seed. That's the only reason you hold the title.' He spat again. This time onto the cobbles. 'The title that should have been mine.'

Satisfied with this contrary outburst, the big warrior seemed to calm himself temporarily and his gaze drifted back to Muirenn once more. His eyes lingered he leered at the *Éblána* woman, a prominent stiffening visible in his leggings. 'You, though. You've got udders a man could cuddle up to. Come to me, honey flanks. I'll suckle on those golden nipples.'

This time, Flannán was quick to step in. 'Leave her, Conall. She's Rógallach Mór's woman now. He wants her untainted.'

'Hardly untainted if she's been spreading her legs for your master's red-cloaked cousin.' He guffawed. 'Just a little taste. He need never know.'

'He would know. And if you have a care for your reward you'd best put such thoughts aside.'

148

Even in this, his moment of victory, Conall couldn't help but revert to his normal cantankerous self. 'Bad cess to your reward, then. *Tá drúis chráite agam.* I could plough a field with the horn on me.'

'Then plough that one.' Flannán gestured loosely at Liath Luachra. 'You've bored us often enough with all your talk of that intent.'

While the men were arguing, the Grey One had slowly been shuffling sideways, working her way towards the basket. Her sword was beyond reach but Muirenn's knife lay in that basket and she would use its cold steel to spill the blood of at least one of her opponents. If all was truly lost, she'd thwart them by leaving nothing but a lifeless corpse on which to slake their passion. She glanced quickly at the trembling *Éblána* woman.

And take Muirenn with her.

Once again, Conall Cacach seemed to discern her desperate objective. 'What's this, Grey One? You grow impatient for my touch?' He turned his head slightly, calling to the other *fénnid* from the side of his mouth. 'Canann, secure the blond heifer while I deal to the Grey One. Quickly now.'

Liath Luachra turned to Muirenn. 'Run,' she mouthed.

Muirenn looked at her in confusion and glanced over her shoulder, back up the beach. Her bewilderment was easy to understand. There was nowhere to run to. The beach was enclosed on either side, the single egress obstructed by their opponents.

'Run!'

Spurred by Liath Luachra's roar, the fair-haired girl turned and started to sprint away from the startled warriors. Taken by surprise, Canann stared in shock. Conall roared at him. '*A cabóg!* She went past you like a cow past a heifer. Get after her!'

Abashed, the wiry warrior took off in pursuit. Flannán, frowning, initially stared after the fleeing girl and her pursuer then, fearful of losing his master's prize, he too joined the chase.

Taking advantage of the momentary distraction, Liath Luachra shifted sideways again, another two paces closer to the basket. Conall however, had spotted the Grey One's headway and the sword in his hand angled directly towards her once more. Although he said nothing, the greasy-haired warrior sneered contemptuously for through her movements, the Grey One had trapped herself between the beach, the *fénnid* and the rocky outcrop. He was still laughing when she flung the first of the stones she'd palmed after tripping Muirenn on the cobbled strand.

The egg-sized missile flew true with the Grey One's habitual accuracy. It slammed into the warrior just above the bridge of the nose, producing a meaty 'thunk' and driving him several steps backwards. Although not a fatal wound, she knew it had to have been painful, certainly painful enough to addle the warrior while she made to tackle him.

Unfortunately, Conall Cacach had a hard head and despite his painful disorientation, he flailed wildly with the sword blade so that she couldn't get close enough to attack. Increasingly desperate, she was about to try a lunge for his legs when a terrified scream from behind stopped her in her tracks.

Muirenn!

The Grey One threw her second stone and this one also hit the staggering *fénnid* in the head, provoking a fresh bellow of outraged pain. Without a second glance, she turned and fled up the beach after Muirenn.

Terror seemed to have empowered the *Éblána* woman with increased athletic prowess for she was moving far faster than when the Grey One had been chasing her, despite the cobbles slipping and shifting beneath her feet. Canann, a natural runner, was gaining on her slowly. Flannán, weighed down by his weapons and heavy clothing, was already falling far behind.

The warrior woman broke into a powerful run that ate up the distance. By the time, she'd traversed the cobbles and made it onto the more solid footing of the third strand, Flannán was less than twenty paces ahead while Muirenn was rapidly approaching the distant headland. Confronted by sheer cliffs that were too steep to scale and a section of coast battered by a dangerous, white-waved swell, she found herself trapped, unable to do anything but watch in desperation as her pursuers drew inexorably closer.

150

Oblivious to what had taken place behind him, Flannán kept running, labouring painfully on the hard-packed sand. As Liath Luachra closed in however, some instinct must have alerted him, for he slowed and glanced over his shoulder, his eyes widening when he saw her.

The Grey One released a shriek of pure visceral excitement as he skidded to a halt and attempted the pull his sword from its scabbard. The folds of his cloak, unfortunately, hung in the way, restricting his hand, and that delay gave her the precious moments she needed. As the weapon slid free, she threw herself at him. Too fast and too close for the *Éblána* man to effectively swing his weapon, he attempted a clumsy stabbing motion instead but was unable to line it up before she slammed into his left shoulder.

Flannán staggered backwards, desperately trying to regain his balance and get the space he needed to strike her. Weaponless, she stuck close, ducking in under his arm and using the remainder of that momentum to force him backwards, attempting to keep him off-balance. She felt a desperate slash of the sword whistle past her ear and grabbed his waist as he tried to spin away from her. By chance, her hand fell on the hilt of his knife and without even thinking, she wrenched it free. Flannán yanked himself from her grip and raised his arm to strike. Before he could do so, she lunged up out of her crouch, punching the blade of the knife directly into his heart.

Stunned from the impact of the blow, Flannán stumbled back and stared with disbelief at the hilt protruding from his chest. Slowly, he raised his eyes to look at her. His mouth opened and he tried to speak but she had no time to listen. Snarling, she wrenched the weapon free from his chest, barged past him and was already ten paces up the beach by the time the *Éblána* man hit the ground.

Flannán's knife was still clenched in her fist, blood streaming down the blade and onto her wrist and fingers. She ignored it as she focussed her full attention on what was taking place directly ahead. Canann had reached the headland, cornering Muirenn in a rocky alcove at the base of the cliffs. The *Éblána* woman was doing her best to fend him off but unaccustomed to violence, her resistance looked distressingly ineffectual.

The *fénnid* made several attempts to try and coax her out to no avail. Growing impatient, Canann reached into her refuge, brushed her scrambling hands away and attempted to drag her out. When she reacted by scraping her fingernails across his face he responded with predictable brutality, smashing his fist into her belly and whipping her out so violently that she went tumbling over the sand, hitting her head on a protruding stone to lie face down and unmoving on the strand.

Hurrying after her, Canann, straddled the unconscious young woman, taking the opportunity to fill his hands with the curve of her buttocks as he did so. The shuffling sound of the Grey One's feet on the hard-packed sand alerted him to her approach but the *fénnid* took his time turning to look. When he did, the expression of complete shock confirmed that it'd been his assumption Flannán was following him.

There was no time for mercy, no place for anything other than violence. Even as Canann rose to his feet, she launched herself onto his back, clamping him tight around the neck with her left arm and wrapping her legs around his waist. He staggered under her weight but before he could even attempt to shake her off, she was stabbing him in the side, punching the knife repeatedly into his rib-cage in short, violent thrusts.

Canann screamed, a startlingly high-pitched scream. Unable to bear her weight, he collapsed onto his knees and she rode him down, landing with a foot on either side. Consumed by his agony, he made no effort to defend himself and she offered no quarter. Wrenching his head back, she jammed the full length of the knife through his neck, the point of the blade emerging on the other side.

A gush of blood spurted out sideways over the Grey One's face, temporarily blinding her. Released, the *fénnid's* dead weight fell forward onto the sand. When the Grey One crawled off his body and smeared the blood from her face and eyes, she saw his left leg continue to spasm violently for a moment before it finally went still.

Gasping for breath, the Grey One struggled to her feet. Her right hand was coated in gore to the elbow, the rest of her body spattered in blood. Her heart was pounding but she could feel the surge of adrenaline leaking away to leave her shivering and exhausted.

Conall Cacach!

Panicking, she spun round, expecting to find the big warrior bearing down on her but, to her immense relief, he was still sixty or seventy paces down the strand, striding towards them at a measured pace. Leaning forward over the dead *fénnid*, Liath Luachra undid his sword belt and, getting to her feet, she strapped it on. She pulled the sword from its sheath and, using her wrist, weaved the blade in a series of complex circles to get the feel of its weight. The weapon was heavier than *Gléas Gan Ainm* but Canann had been a smaller man than most and the difference wasn't substantial.

Shuffling over to the *Éblána* woman, Liath Luachra plunged the sword into the sand and used both hands to turn Muirenn. As she rolled her onto her back, the fair-haired woman's head flopped to one side, a purple bruise visible on her forehead. Liath Luachra cursed. Muirenn was breathing regularly but she was unconscious, in no position to flee the approaching warrior.

Rising to her feet, the Grey One cast a fresh glance up the beach to where Conall was walking determinedly towards them, now less than forty paces away. She picked up a handful of sand, using the gritty material to wipe the blood and sweat from her palms, reducing the chance of the leather-thonged pommel greasing up and slipping from her grasp.

She started towards the warrior, keen to put as much distance as possible between him and the unconscious *Éblána* woman, knowing that he'd use the threat of potential harm to Muirenn against her if he could.

Passing Canann, she glanced down at the contorted body. A small pool of blood had formed beneath his head but the gush from his throat had slowed to a trickle and the sand was already absorbing the fluid faster than his body was discharging it. The *fénnid's* face lay sideways, his eyes open and staring vacantly into the distance. To the Grey One's surprise, the sight prompted a brief flush of regret, although one that she quickly dismissed. Canann had been her comrade-in-arms for over two years and they'd fought side-by-side under some horrific circumstances. Nevertheless, she'd also seen that black streak of

153

meanness to him, the joy he got from inflicting pain on others. For that reason alone, she felt no need to waste sympathy on him.

Besides, my other one-time comrade beckons.

If Conall Cacach felt any surprise or trepidation at her decision to confront him directly, he didn't show it. He was glaring at her intently, eyes locked on hers, which surprised her to some extent. She had expected his attention to be focussed on her pelvis once again. It struck her then that his feelings towards her were no longer of a sexual nature. His sole physical interest at this time was to harm her, to kill her.

The sword was suddenly very heavy in her hand and for the first time in what felt like years, she felt a genuine lack of confidence in her own abilities. Although she knew she had no choice, taking Conall head on went against all her instincts. He was much bigger than her and although she was probably more nimble and more skilled with a sword it wouldn't count for much. That was the problem with single combat. It always came down to basics: strength, staying power, sheer brute force. That was also why she'd always preferred ambush or... or trickery, anything that worked to her own strengths, anything that gave her the edge over those more physically powerful than her.

He feared me once.

But not now. She took a deep breath to steady her nerves and tightened her grip on the hilt of the sword. On the open beach the weak glare of the autumn sun showered down on them and the sound of the rolling surf seemed even louder than before.

It is a good place to die.

Except she didn't want to die. If she died, Conall would get Muirenn and she had to prevent that. For the first time in her life she had a genuine reason to survive the combat and, in a strange way, that knowledge somehow seemed to undermine her usual fighting fury.

When she and the big *fénnid* were about five paces apart, they both came to a halt. Conall stood staring at her with murder in his eyes. Although he seemed to have recovered from the stones she'd thrown at him, a deep red blotch was visible above his nose and a crust of dried blood lay on the lower lobe of his ear. When he finally spoke, she could hear the effort it cost him not to scream.

154

'Yours will be the painful death, Grey One. When I've cut you down I will rut that blond heifer on your bleeding limbs. Afterwards, I'll slit your throats and plug your vulva with dirt. None of your line will taint this land ag-'

She attacked.

Although taken by surprise, Conall responded with impressive alacrity, stepping back and raising his own sword to block her downward strike. The clash of metal on metal echoed off the nearby cliffs.

With the failure of her initial attack, the Grey One retreated to assess her options. Conall didn't allow her any opportunity however, for he immediately attempted to circle around her.

Instead of retreating, she advanced but this time it was he who attacked first. He lunged forward, his longer arms giving him an advantage in reach but, anticipating the movement, she sidestepped it easily and managed to counter the follow–up attack as he whipped the blade back up to cut her. The edge of her own weapon intercepted it, arching it away and sparks flew where the two blades scraped a fingers length along each other. Conall didn't stop there. He followed that furious attack with another and then another, hacking and thrusting at her with such force that it was all she could do just to deflect them and move back to keep out of reach.

The *fénnid's* intention quickly became clear. As she'd feared, he was driving her backwards, closer and closer to Muirenn. Eventually, unless she stood her ground, he'd push her to a point where she couldn't defend the prone *Éblána* woman. Even as she deflected another attack, the Grey One desperately sought a suitable countermeasure and wondered at the continued ferocity of his assaults. Conall's rage was propelling him, fuelling his attacks but he couldn't sustain them indefinitely. The effort it took to instigate them was far greater than that needed to repel them.

But all he needs is to drive me another ten paces back. Then Muirenn is in his reach.

Conall initiated a fresh assault but this time rather than pulling back one or two steps, the Grey One retreated a full five paces. She saw the

155

suspicion blossom in his eye as he automatically slowed his attack, his caution giving her just enough time to whip Flannán's knife free from the back of her belt and fling it at the advancing warrior.

Conall Cacach reacted with stunning speed, stepping back and whipping his sword up to knock the knife out of the air. With a gleam of triumph, he turned on her again.

Just in time to receive a face full of sand.

Coughing and spluttering, the big warrior retreated but not fast enough to prevent her reaching him. Lunging forward at an angle to his right, she whipped past, slicing her blade deep into his shoulder. Conall yelped with pain and surprise and although blinded by the sand, he thrust out instinctively. Through good fortune rather than skill, he struck her.

The Grey One gasped as she felt the sword's steel tip enter her, tearing deep into her side above her left hip. It was all she could do not to shriek in despair but, by some perverse instinct, instead of retreating she pushed forward at an angle, ignoring the agony in her side as she slashed her own sword upwards to connect with Conall's chest. She vaguely registered a gobbet of flesh and other material fly into the air before wrenching herself backwards to feel the burning metal slide from her body.

Bleeding, both warriors backed off, eyeing each other cautiously while, at the same time, assessing their own wounds. The Grey One could feel blood pumping from her side but she didn't dare take her eyes from the *fénnid* to investigate the injury further. He was also bleeding profusely. Blood trickled from the wound in his shoulder and she could tell from the strain on his face and the way he was favouring his right hand that she'd badly damaged some muscle. There was a large gash in his tunic which was bleeding seriously, just at the point where his nipple should have been. That was gone, of course. Lying somewhere on the golden sand now, no doubt.

The Grey One shifted her weight from one foot to the other and back again, testing her ability to move. The results were not reassuring. She could step forward on her right foot easily enough but when she tried to move her left the pain in her side caused shadows to form in her eyes. She took a deep breath, preparing herself for the inevitable pain to come. The next assault would decide things one way or the other. Both of them were now too badly injured to sustain the fight much longer.

Five paces away, Conall spat, watched her with an analytical eye and attacked again.

The initial strike was a downward slash from Conall's right hand side. Fortunately, given his wound, she'd anticipated that, for the momentum of the descending movement allowed him to apply greater strength to the strike. She stepped back, avoiding the slice and, knowing he'd struggle to raise his weapon again, moved in for her own strike.

Some instinct, some gleam of satisfaction in the *fénnid's* eye alerted her that she'd misjudged. Even as she swung her sword in, she attempted to pull her body back again but her injuries had slowed her usual cat-like reactions. Too late, she realised Conall wasn't trying to pull his sword up as she'd expected. Instead he'd continued forward, slamming into her with his left shoulder, knocking her backwards and then – then – slashing up with his sword.

Spun around by the force of his shoulder-ram, the blade sliced into her lower back and side, carving a bloody route through the mass of scar tissue. Using the momentum of the initial blow, she continued the spin and then jabbed her sword forwards with all its force. It sank into the *fénnid's* mid-riff.

Too fast, the weapon was wrenched from her hands and she fell to the ground. Something smashed into the side of her head and she momentarily blacked out. She couldn't have been unconscious for more than a moment or two but when she came to she was surprised to discover she was still breathing. Her head pounded and her left eye seemed to be sealed shut. All sight though her right was tainted translucent pink. She grasped around the sand with both hands, desperately trying to find the sword.

'Bad cess to you, Grey One.'

She froze, anticipating the killing blow.

A moment passed, then another. But no blow came. Tentatively, she turned her head, trying to identify where the voice had come from. Through the pink haze she eventually spotted Conall sitting with his

157

back against a smooth grey rock that protruded up out of the sand behind him. The lower section of the warrior's belly was bathed in red.

'You killed Canann. *And* you killed Flannán. I had business with that *Éblána* man.'

She attempted a shrug but failed. 'I warned you it'd be a short friendship.' Looking down, she saw blood dripping onto the sand from the wound in her side.

'And sand! That was no *gaiscíoch* action.' Conall seemed personally affronted. 'A child's trick.'

'It served.' The Grey One held her palm over the wound to stem the flow but blood continued to seep through her fingers.

'Perhaps. But no-one will sing songs of your endeavours, you cold bitch.'

'Our likes don't have songs, Conall Cacach.'

Conall growled at her use of the epithet. He'd always hated it even though it had been his nickname long before she'd joined the *fian*. She realised then that he was incapable of movement. Otherwise he'd have already come over and killed her.

'I curse the day you entered my life, Grey One. From the moment you joined *Na Cinéaltaí* I knew you were trouble, nothing but a burden for this back.'

She snorted. 'You hated me because I wouldn't open my legs to you. You're an ugly man. No-one would unless forced on them. Lonely, lonely Conall Cacach. Solitary milker of bulls in the wood.'

'Shit on you nettle-crotch.'

'Pig fucker!'

'Seed swallower!'

They kept it up for a few moments longer but, eventually, exhausting their supply of insults and succumbing to the pain of their wounds, they lapsed into silence. Through the haze of pain, Liath Luachra heard the roar of the surf, surging up onto the beach nearby.

I am glad I saw this place before I died.

She raised her head. 'Are you dead yet, Conall?'

'I'm not going to die, Grey One. You are the only one travelling to meet the ancestors today.'

'Brave words. But I see your life-blood spilling onto the ground when you speak.'

'You see nothing. Your left eye is mangled. Blood coats your right. Had you lived, you'd have been blind.'

That much was true. A pink foamy haze had formed about her sight and she could no longer see anything.

I'm blind. And dying. But what use a blind warrior?

She started to shiver.

'You grow cold now.' Conall chuckled. 'Do not fear. I'll come and piss on your corpse to warm you up.'

She snorted again but the action caused a wave of pain to flush through her and it took several moments before she could respond. 'You'll not piss again. I pierced that poxy bladder of yours when I gutted you. Whatever putrid, yellow piss you had has already dribbled down your leg.'

He emitted a croak of laughter at that. 'More insights from the blind eye.'

Silence fell between them once more.

Liath Luachra could feel her concentration wavering, her mind leaking away as black fog moved in to replace the pink in her eyes. The agony flaring up her left side was becoming unbearable and blood dripped freely onto her outstretched hand from the wound in her back. She suddenly wanted to cry, wanted her mother to take away the pain and the only thing that stopped her was the thought of Conall's mockery if he saw her shedding tears.

'Conall?'

'What?'

'Just fucking die!'

'I'll die when I'm good and ready.'

'Well, hurry on. I can't wait all day for you to vomit up your ratty soul.'

'Actually, I'm feeling better.' Conall's response was surprisingly upbeat. 'A *bean feasea* showed me a trick once, how to control my breathing and slow my heart beat so my wounds would clot.' He coughed and cleared his throat. 'Didn't seem to help much when I

159

gutted her, mind. Anyway, any moment now, I'll be strong enough to get up and come over there and deal your last breath.'

'You have breath enough for both of us, you tumultuous fart.'

'If you weren't already dead I'd kill you again.' This time, when he responded, his voice seemed weaker, more indistinct. Or maybe it was her. It was hard to tell. The pink in her vision was almost gone and she could feel the weight of darkness pressing in. An involuntary whimper of fear almost escaped her but she swallowed it in time. Damned if she'd give Conall Cacach the satisfaction of hearing her pain.

'Conall?'

'What?'

'You're an arselicker of pigs.'

'Piss on you, you poisoned heifer.'

Silence.

'Conall?'

'Shit on your head, you wrinkled sack for cocks.'

'No. this is serious. I hear your death rattle.'

'By the Gods, I preferred it when you never spoke. Now that you're dying I cannot hear myself think. Return to the Great Mother, you soiled milk calf. Your bits and blood will feed her soil.'

'So speaks the man with intestines around his ankles.'

'The worms will grow fat on you, Grey One. They'll feed well tonight.'

They receded into silence again. Liath Luachra could feel the air, the anger and hostility easing out of her. Unable to turn her head, she called out.

'Conall!'

'What now?' He sounded tired.

'You really are an arselicker.'

Conall started saying something but then, suddenly, it didn't matter anymore. Her mother was calling her and she had to go. Back to Luachair, back to her brothers who were playing mud pies in the clearing.

She lifted one of the flattened circles of sludge to her teeth. 'Should I eat it?' she asked her brothers. 'Should I eat this wonderful, tasty cake?' The two boys giggled and nodded enthusiastically. 'Num Num.'

'Num-num,' she agreed.

Chapter Eight

The first trickle of awareness was accompanied by a persistent, deep-rooted ache. For what seemed like an interminable period of time, she drifted in and out of the sensation. Too indistinct to truly hurt, it simply clung about her, an unpleasant background haze.

As she became more lucid, the pain surged in with force, burning an angry streak through her left side. Like an insanely tenacious rodent, this new pain gnawed incessantly at her edges, bit and chewed until it nudged her back to consciousness.

Opening her eyes, she saw nothing but darkness. Striving to make up for the lack of sight, her other senses rushed in but their intrusion proved unwelcome. Physically, she was in a bad way. This much she could tell even through the fog of confusion. Her ribs were aching, her lips were dry and cracked. Her back was sore, her cheeks bruised. Her left eye was swollen and puffy, much more than the right although she couldn't see out of either. Her mouth and throat were parched, her skin tender from after-fever. In her stomach, when the pain didn't obscure it, hunger competed with nausea.

That shrill pain in her side obliterated the throb in her skull. It felt as though someone had pressed hot metal against her, pressed so hard it'd passed through the skin and lodged deep inside her rib-cage. As the pain swelled to excruciating levels, she felt her initial coherence begin to falter and wither.

'You're awake then.'

The shock of hearing that voice pulled her thoughts back together again. Pain momentarily forgotten, she listened carefully but no other words came. She frowned, wondering if she'd imagined it. It had sounded female, unfamiliar but calm.

Her throat caught as she tried to speak. Her lips, sticky, wouldn't part at first and it took several attempts before she managed to get the words out. '*An bhfuilim marbh?*' Am I dead?

Her voice sounded pathetically weak, like the reedy gasps of a feeble old woman. She waited for a moment but no response came.

'*An bhfuilim marbh?*' she tried again. 'Are these ... the Dark Lands?'

'Do you feel dead?'

She took a moment before responding and when she did she did so with care for she had to concentrate on articulating each individual word. 'No. I. Feel. Pain.'

'Talk to me of pain when you've eased a child from between those hips.'

It was hard to make sense of that particular response but, in truth, it didn't matter. The conversation had already used up what little energy she had and Liath Luachra could feel her reason slipping away.

'I... Do I...?'

'Whist.'

Darkness.

***

The second time she drifted back to consciousness, her thoughts were battered things, tender as the bruises on her body. Still exhausted, she didn't try to move for she instinctively knew that to do so would revive the pain in her side, now mercifully dormant. Her head still hurt and she couldn't see anything so she remained prone, ignoring the discomfort while she listened.

The patter of rain was audible somewhere overhead but she was unable to tell what the falling drops were striking. It sounded like some kind of man-made shelter. It wasn't cold and there was no flow of air, suggesting it was sealed or closed up. The strongest smell in her nostrils was that of her own fever-stained sweat although the earthiness of burning turf was also discernible. A comforting weight of heavy fur pressed down on her chest and from the touch of it against her skin she was relatively sure she was still naked. Relaxing back into the dull fog of fatigue, she was close to drifting off again when the faint sound of breathing stirred her back to alertness.

'Who's there?'

'Who do you think is there?'

It was the same voice she'd heard before. Female. Calm and soft but tarnished now with an underlying hostility.

163

'Muirenn?' She asked hopefully although she was almost certain it wasn't the young *Éblána* woman.'

'Not Muirenn.'

Whoever she was, she seemed in no mood to converse. As Liath Luachra lay wondering what to do next, the furs were abruptly lifted off her chest. Fingers slid across her belly and down to the painful area on her left side. Someone had wrapped strips of wool around her waist and the fingers tested them, shifted a bulky poultice to one side and then eased it back into place. The movements were gentle but they still hurt. She did her best not to flinch.

'*Bhí an t-ádh ag rith leat.*' Good fortune ran with you.

The voice again.

'The sword did not pierce your organs. The battle-wound sickness was on you for a time but you fought it off.'

'How long have I … How long?'

'Five days.'

Five days!

For some reason that seemed important but it was difficult to think straight or work out why. 'Muirenn,' she said. 'Where's Muirenn?'

'Not here.' There was a pause and, even blind, Liath Luachra could sense the sudden tension to the other woman. 'We found her on the beach. And three dead men.' The voice seemed to catch momentarily. 'And then there was you.'

Struggling to keep her thoughts together, some inner instinct urged the warrior woman to remain tight-lipped.

'Nothing to say, now?' asked the voice.

Liath Luachra felt her own body stiffen, her muscles tensing involuntarily in anticipation of a blow. Surprisingly, none came. Instead, she felt the shift of air as the other woman moved away, then heard the sound of a flap being brushed aside. The heavy swish as it fell back into place confirmed she was alone once more.

She strained to detect any noise outside but apart from the soft patter of rain and the crackle of fire it was surprisingly quiet. That disturbed her. If she was at Gort Na Meala, it seemed odd that she couldn't hear the sound of other voices, the unavoidable bustle of farm activity or even the noises of animals.

Unless I am not at Gort Na Meala.

With a sigh, she let that thought slide to one side. Instead, she focussed on working her right hand free from beneath the furs and, although she succeeded, it cost her in pain and sweat. Bringing her fingers up to her face, she discovered another strip of wool wrapped around her head and covering her eyes. After several attempts she finally succeeded in tugging it loose and light, blurry and bleary, leaked into her eyes.

I can see!

The relief was such that she actually started crying. Unable to roll over, the tears slid down her cheeks to her ears. She wept for what seemed an endless time and had anyone asked, she knew she wouldn't haven't been able to answer if she wept from pain, from self-pity or from simple relief.

***

By the next day, the last symptoms of fever had left her body and although she was weak she found that she could think more clearly. The pain had also lessened although any movement of her torso shot streaks of agony through her left side and back. In a strange way, knowing that she wasn't blind helped to alleviate the physical discomfort. She'd replaced the woollen strip over her eyes but she hugged the knowledge close in the dark like a delicious secret.

The air had the smell of morning about it. Overnight, the fire had died for she couldn't hear it crackle and the air was cold against her face. Beneath the furs however, her body was warm and snug.

Lucid but helpless, she spent her time trying to remember, for her memories flitted past in snatches: meeting Muirenn; the beautiful beach; the *fénnid*'s sudden appearance; her combat with Conall Cacach and the other warriors. Somehow, despite her apparently hopeless situation, she'd managed to survive but her memory remained hazy. She couldn't recall what had happened to Muirenn and she had no recollection of arriving wherever she now lay.

Despite the fact that she couldn't see, Liath Luachra could sense walls tightening around her like a snare on a hare's neck. Ever since her abduction from Luachair and the subsequent year in chains as slave to the *díberg*, even the thought of being constrained was enough to make her break out in a cold sweat.

As time passed, she grew increasingly restless. She tried to sit up but when she attempted to use her stomach muscles the pain in her left side drove her back down again. The effort left her lying on her back, shivering in a puddle of her own sweat.

Later, when she'd recovered her strength, she tried again, this time rolling onto her stronger side before attempting to sit up. On this occasion, she succeeded in getting upright and, ignoring the pounding of her skull, forced herself to breathe hard until the pain subsided. Although her head was still spinning, she decided to remove the woollen strip around her eyes. She wanted to find out where she was and, in hindsight, it seemed unlikely that whoever was holding her would care if she could see or not. If they hadn't beaten or killed her by now, she reasoned, they were unlikely to do so.

Pulling the woollen strip from her face, the woman warrior opened her eyes and waited. When her blurred vision finally cleared, she found herself in a conical hut, the curve of the roof formed by a number of arched saplings secured together at the apex to a central support pole.

The hut was small, the end of her bedding – a mound of heather covered by a flax over-blanket – less than two paces from the entranceway: a narrow gap in the mud-daubed wicker walls overlain with a thick leather flap. A small fire pit was situated to her right and although it contained little but cold ash now, there was a reed basket with a few sods of turf sitting alongside it on a roughly woven flax mat.

And that was it. Apart from the bedding, the mats and the fire, the little hut was empty. Liath Luachra chewed thoughtfully on the inside of her cheek as she sniffed the air. The hut had the feel of a relatively recent construction, a suspicion supported by the lingering tang of sap from the freshly-cut wicker and mud.

Her attention was drawn then by another, less familiar scent and she looked down to her side where a moss compress applied at the point of

166

the wound was held in place by the woollen strips around her waist. A similar compress had been placed over the wound in her back. Both smelled oddly stringent, but, fortunately, lacked the tainted smell associated with blood rot.

The entrance flap parted abruptly and Liath Luachra looked up in alarm for she'd heard no sound of footsteps, no indication of anyone approaching in fact. A tall woman with dark, braided hair stood in the open entranceway. She was dressed in leather tunic and leggings and a wolf-skin cloak draped over her shoulders gave her an imposing, striking appearance.

As the woman's blue eyes scrutinised her, Liath Luachra noticed grey flecks to her hair. She appeared physically strong and trim but she was probably older than she looked, with forty to forty-five years on her at least.

Moving into the hut with a single, easy movement, the woman quietly kicked the turf basket aside and took a seat on the mat. Sitting cross-legged, she regarded Liath Luachra in silence. Her face was strong and would have been attractive but was marred by a vicious scar down the length of her left cheek. There was also a familiarity to her features that left the Grey One in no doubt as to whom she was facing. 'You are Fíne Surehands,' she said. 'Muirenn's mother.'

At first, the dark-haired woman displayed no reaction at the mention of her name but then she nodded in acknowledgement. 'Yes. And you are the Grey One of Luachair. My daughter has spoken much of you.'

'She ...'

'She lives.' Fíne Surehands' forehead creased momentarily. 'Although her head bears a painful reminder of the true brutality of this world in which we live.' She sniffed and regarded the Grey One with poorly concealed distaste. 'But this, of course, you would know.'

Liath Luachra said nothing but, unconsciously, her hand had reached out to the right of her bedding, the spot where she habitually placed *Gléas gan Ainm* when retiring at night. This time of course, there was no weapon for her fingertips to detect. The older woman spotted the movement and apparently recognised it for what it was for she gave a bitter smile.

'You seek your weapon?'

Liath Luachra paused. Sensing that it would be pointless to practice deceit with this woman, she answered truthfully. 'Yes.'

'You will not find it here.'

The Grey One frowned. Taking possession of another warrior's weapon was a breach of custom and the act could be construed as a direct insult. That had certainly been Conall Cacach's intent when he'd taken her weapons in the clearing by the river and at the beach.

'Your weapons are in a safe place,' the *Éblána* woman continued. 'But you are not known to me and therefore, not my friend. If you are not my friend, you are a potential enemy. If trust can be realised between us, then your weapons will be returned.' The expression on her face inspired no great confidence of such an event occurring.

Liath Luachra regarded the scar-faced woman with care, recognizing toughness and no-nonsense competence when she saw it. 'Muirenn told me you were a warrior.'

Fíne Surehands seemed to consider her response before she finally conceded a nod. 'My daughter has always been overgenerous with her trust and her words but, yes, I was a warrior. Now I am a mother and it is my children's safety that preoccupies me.' She leaned forward so abruptly that Liath Luachra had to fight the impulse to pull backwards. 'So tell me, Grey One. Are my children safe?'

Liath Luachra felt herself wither under that ferocious gaze. The throbbing headache suddenly returned and intensified, making it difficult to think.

'Why have you come to *Éblána* territories?' There was no let up from the *Éblána* woman's piercing stare. 'Were you with these men?'

The Grey One nodded.

'You are *díberg*.'

Liath Luachra's jaw clenched involuntarily at that. She was about to spit a heated denial but then stopped herself, belatedly realising that she too had already come to a similar conclusion. Her shoulders slumped and she let her eyes slide to the ground. 'No.'

'But it was your intention to raid Gort Na Meala.' The manner in which Fíne Surehands expressed it left little doubt in her mind that this was not a question so much as a request for confirmation. Liath Luachra felt her cheeks burn and kept her eyes to the floor of the hut. Neither woman spoke. Finally the *Éblána* woman clicked her tongue with impatience. 'Why did you turn on your comrades?'

The Grey One closed her eyes and raised her hands to her face. The question was one she couldn't even start to answer for it was one she hardly understood herself. Sensing the other woman's mounting impatience, she responded with a shrug.

Fíne Surehands' lips turned down but, holding her temper in check, she tried a different tack. 'Two of the dead men were not known to us. But one – the man with the black circle on his forehead – him I knew.' She waited, scrutinising the Grey One's features for any expression, any display of emotion. Finally, frustrated in her efforts, she continued. 'Flannán An Scian, they call him. Flannán The Knife.' She was unable to disguise the distaste in her voice.

'He is not your friend?' Liath Luachra's voice was hollow.

The *Éblána* woman lips gave a wry twist. 'He is not my friend. He's Rógallach Mór's cur, his strong right hand.' Fíne Surehands brought her own hands together, her fingers forming the tip of a triangle that she used to tap her lips in contemplation. 'The presence of Flannán An Scian suggests many things to me. It suggests that Rógallach Mór was not only aware of your presence in *Éblána* territory but complicit in bringing it about. You were here at his bidding.' With this, she settled back on her haunches, rested her hands in her lap and waited.

Unsure what to say, Liath Luachra remained silent.

'Are you bound to Rógallach Mór?'

The Grey One shook her head vehemently. Glancing up, she was relieved to see belief in the *Éblána* woman's eyes, her stance relaxing ever so slightly. 'Then why are you here?'

'I am bound to another. One that Rógallach Mór sought service of. I cannot tell you who it is.'

'Bressal Binnbhéalach.'

She sees right through me!

The Grey One crumbled, her initial shock transforming to anger as she saw the triumph of confirmation in the other woman's eyes. Fíne

169

Surehands seemed amused at having made a dent in her captive's impassive demeanour for she chuckled softly. 'Come now, Grey One. It was no great test. Rógallach Mór almost certainly sought such service from outside the tribe. A *díberg* or *fían,* with their men and women of violence, are the most natural places to seek that service. You say you are not *díberg* – which I sense is true – and *Na Cinéaltaí* is the only *fían* I have heard of that might offer such a service.'

Feeling outwitted at every turn, Liath Luachra scowled but this only provoked a fresh chuckle from the scar-faced woman. Fíne Surehands reached in under the folds of her cloak and pulled out a doubled, faded blue garment. 'Take this. My men retrieved your weapon but your clothing was taken with the tide. My daughter offers you this dress to wear in their stead.'

Liath Luachra accepted the clothing gingerly and bit her tongue, unsure what was going to happen next. The *Éblána* woman sucked on her lower lip before speaking again.

'So now that fresh facts are drawn from the shadows, let us examine them more closely. Rógallach Mór has obtained the service of foreign killers, dispatching them without remorse to lay waste to Gort Na Meala, a settlement of his own people.'

'Our service was to clear Gort Na Meala of *díberg* activity,' Liath Luachra interjected. 'We …I … had no knowing of Rógallach Mór's intent until I met Muirenn on …' She stopped then, realising that she'd inadvertently admitted more than she'd intended.

Fíne Surehands however did not look surprised. 'Rógallach Mór is not my friend, Grey One. And his intent is not unknown to me. I have known him as a threat for over three years.'

The Grey One looked at her blankly. 'What do you mean?'

'I am a mother. With a mother's instincts. Three years past, during the Imbolg celebrations, I saw Rógallach Mór's gaze fall on my oldest child.' The *Éblána* woman grew silent for a moment, as though reliving the incident once more. 'There was no disguising the cruel desire in that man's heart.'

Fíne Surehands cleared her throat as though to expunge the memory. When she looked at Liath Luachra again, that earlier intensity was back

170

in her eyes. 'Even then, I knew Rógallach Mór for a callous and merciless man. War leader and *tánaiste* to the previous *rí*, he was already a man of fearsome reputation and recognised ambition, poised to take succession of leadership. I knew it was but a matter of time before he sought Muirenn out. Just as I knew that any resistance on my part would be dealt to.'

She sighed.

'Some time after the festival, I started my preparations. At that time, our previous *rí* still held power so Rógallach Mór could not make his move. Even now, he is not so strong that he can do as he wishes with absolute impunity. My people may have been fooled by honeyed words or subdued by steel-tipped threats but they will not follow a man who murders or mistreats his own kin.

'Two years ago, I made a *margadh* – a deal – with Barra ua Éblána and during the autumn, I brought my family and retainers to Gort Na Meala for Muirenn to take Barra as her man.'

'He does not have her heart.' Liath Luachra blurted the words without reflection, not even knowing how she knew it was true.

Fíne Surehand's eyebrows raised perceptibly at the younger woman's outburst and, although she made no comment, she seemed to consider her more closely with those shrewd, measuring eyes.

'Such matters are of little consequence. It is a good match. Barra receives a wife as well as my sword and that of my two warriors. My daughter receives a man she likes well enough and who treats her with care and kindness. And Gort Na Meala offers the protection of distance from Rógallach Mór.' She looked at Liath Luachra with displeasure. 'Or so we had believed.'

Liath Luachra recalled the two warriors she'd seen from the outlook on the southern ridge what now seemed like a lifetime ago. She shivered involuntarily as the enormity of what had happened since then finally hit her. Her entire existence, the life she'd struggled to create with *Na Cinéaltaí* had fallen apart, crumbling away with all the consistency of mud in hard rain. Her time as *rígfénnid* had been a disaster. She'd failed her mission, her men were dead. She could not see Bressal forgiving such failure.

But Bressal lied to you!

Or had he? Overwhelmed by the breadth of possible machinations, she momentarily closed her eyes. When she opened them again Fíne Surehands was observing her with a bleak expression that did little to reassure her. 'What will you do with me?' she asked the *Éblána* woman.

'I have not yet decided.'

'I am not dead,' Liath Luachra pointed out.

This did not seem to be a subject of great satisfaction for Fíne Surehand's lips compressed. 'I have no love of raiders, Grey One. If Muirenn had not vouched for you and the tracks not confirmed your actions on the beach, you would lie on the sand beside your comrades instead of on this bed.'

Liath Luachra shivered.

'At present, your injuries mean you pose no meaningful threat but we will talk more on this matter. If your answers satisfy me then, you may live. If not …' A dagger suddenly appeared in Fíne Surehands right hand and shifting forward with shocking swiftness, she slid its sharp tip up under the Grey One's jaw. 'If not, that smooth throat offers tempting potential.'

Releasing the shaken warrior woman, Fíne Surehands pulled back and lowered the knife. Slipping it inside her sleeve, she rose smoothly to her feet. Moving towards the entranceway, she brushed the flap aside and made as though to leave but then paused to look back. 'You are young, Grey One,' she said. 'And you lack guile. Yours will be a short-known name should you choose to remain on the warrior path.'

With this she disappeared though the narrow entrance.

The leather flap slid back with decisive finality.

***

Hunger drove Liath Luachra from her bed later that afternoon. Hunger and a desperation to escape the encroaching walls that tightened further with every passing moment. Somehow, she managed to make it to her feet and even got as far as the entranceway before she collapsed onto the reed-strewn floor. She was still there when Muirenn entered and found her shivering, ashen-faced and close to fainting from the pain.

Gasping, she allowed the *Éblána* woman to help her back to the bedding. When she was horizontal once more and weighed down by heavy layers of furs, she squinted up to see Muirenn considering the folded blue dress with an odd look on her face. 'It is an old dress,' the fair-haired woman apologised. 'Old and shabby. But I had no other.'

Too spent to speak, the Grey One turned her head and let the fog of hunger and fatigue take her away.

***

The fair-haired woman was still there when Liath Luachra awoke again, sitting by the rekindled fire, a wooden bowl balanced precariously on one knee. The smell of the broth steaming over the curved lip of the container struck her a mouth-watering slap. She stared at it with silent, desperate eyes, her stomach gurgling in famished sympathy.

Muirenn made no comment as she passed the bowl over but watched in silence as the Grey One raised it to her lips with shaking hands, swallowing the contents in a single gulp. Dropping the empty bowl onto the ground, she belched and sighed dreamily for the broth had tasted even better than it smelled.

'More.'

Muirenn shook her head. Rising to her feet, she brushed snippets of reeds from the lower folds of her dress. 'You stomach will not bear the weight. It's been several days since solids passed your lips.'

Loath though she was to concede the point, Liath Luachra knew Muirenn had the right of it. 'I've lost blood,' she said anyway. 'Food will fill the empty space, make me whole.'

The *Éblána* woman was unmoved. 'Later.'

The woman warrior went quiet and an awkward silence settled in between them. 'You've met my mother?' the fair-haired woman asked at last.

'Of course. I am her prisoner.'

'You are *not* her prisoner. You are my friend.'

The emphatic nature of Muirenn's declaration made Liath Luachra consider her with mixed emotions. Although the fair-haired woman's association with her most recent misfortunes prompted feelings of bitterness, she found herself genuinely moved by the offer of

173

comradeship. She chewed carefully on her lower lip, loath to offer a response that could be construed one way or the other.

My friend.

No-one had ever been close enough to call her 'friend' before. She'd had her brothers, of course. And the *fénnid* from *Na Cinéaltaí* but never a friend in the manner in which others seemed to speak of it.

Except, perhaps, Sean Fergus.

She thought about that for a moment, ignoring the prickle of guilt that accompanied it. She hadn't spared a single thought for the old warrior since he'd passed to the Dark Lands.

Reluctant to deal with such uncomfortable considerations, she levered herself up off the bedding and onto her elbow, wincing at the bite of pain in her side.

'What are you doing?'

'I'm going outside. These walls … crowd me.'

'You cannot. Your stitches will …' The fair-haired woman's voice trailed off as she realised Liath Luachra was ignoring her. With a sigh of resignation, she offered her arm and the woman warrior accepted it gratefully, using the support to pull herself off the bedding.

When she was upright, Muirenn lifted the dress from the floor and helped her to pull it on. It sagged a little loose around the chest but otherwise it was a relatively good fit.

The *Éblána* woman regarded her critically. 'I will take it in at the bust,' she decided.

Liath Luachra didn't care. Shambling painfully towards the entrance, she brushed the flap aside and stood momentarily luxuriating in the touch of natural light and a fresh breeze across her face. Stepping outside the hut however, she paused to look around in bewilderment, taking in the view of the narrow lake, the hill, the swathes of yellow flowers and the nearby forest.

'This isn't Gort Na Meala!' She looked around again as though to ensure her eyes weren't deceiving her. 'This is the land beyond *Carraig An Fhírinne Buí*, the land past the wood of whispers.'

'You've been here before?' exclaimed Muirenn. 'How did you pass through the wood of whispers?'

'I was angry. I did not notice the voices at first.'

'You must have been very angry.' Muirenn frowned, an expression that did not look natural on her attractive face. 'Everyone avoids the wood of whispers. Even the wolves bypass this place. That is why my mother chose to set you here.'

'Set me here?'

Muirenn hesitated and looked uncomfortable, evidently struggling with a topic of some delicacy. 'Barra and my mother would not have you at Gort Na Meala. They do not trust you as I do.'

Liath Luachra was staring at her blankly when, suddenly, the *Éblána* woman lurched forward and wrapped her arms around her. Taken by surprise and still weak from her injuries, Liath Luachra was too slow to fend her off. Disconcerted, she started struggling to pull her arms free but found herself increasingly distracted by the other woman's physical proximity: the scent of freshly-washed skin flushing her nostrils, the softness of a cheek against her lips, the firm breasts pressed up against her own. Flustered, she turned her head away, looking towards the trees to avoid eye contact. It wasn't that the sensations were unpleasant, for they weren't. It was just that they were intimate – more intimate than she could cope with. For the first time she could remember, she felt herself blush.

'Thank you, thank you,' Muirenn was whispering in her ear, clearly torn with emotion. 'My family do not trust you but you saved my life. More than that, you saved me from whatever cruel fate Rógallach Mór had in mind for- '

She stopped then for the Grey One's body had stiffened. Pulling back in surprise, she stared at the woman warrior then turned her head to follow her gaze. Liath Luachra's eyes were locked on a dark figure watching them from the treeline shadow, less than ten paces from where they were standing. A tall man, their silent observer wore a brown cloak and held a long spear with a jagged metal point.

The man's head was large, with close-cropped, receding hair. A pockmarked face with thick lips and tattooed cheeks had a pair of dark, deeply inset eyes that regarded her with malice. Despite the evident animosity however, he made no threatening advance towards the women.

Muirenn grasped the woman warrior's waist, making her wince in pain. 'Hold, Liath Luachra. It is Cappa. One of my mother's fighting men.'

The Grey One's eyes never left the watching warrior but she relaxed slowly at the other woman's words.

Of course. Fíne Surehands would hardly risk her precious daughter without a competent guard.

Not, at least, in the company of a raider.

Albeit a raider whose injuries meant she posed no meaningful threat.

She bristled then and perceiving her anger, Muirenn continued to hold her, apparently imagining that she could pose a credible threat to the watching warrior. 'Liath Luachra, you must not blame my mother for having you watched. She does this out of concern for me.'

Observing no lessening of the vitriol in the woman warrior's eyes, she tried again. 'It was my mother who saved your life, Grey One. She fed you watered gruel and tended your injuries every day. She has the knowing of battle wounds and prevented the blood from poisoning.'

Liath Luachra stared, surprised and distressed by this fresh disclosure. Her vision momentarily blurred and she had to grasp the *Ébláná* woman to remain upright. She let Muirenn guide her to a nearby tree stump where she collapsed onto its solid support. Breathing deeply, she worked on loosening the shadows that clogged up the edges of her sight.

When her head finally cleared, she glanced over at the watching guard, aggrieved that he was able to perceive her at her weakest. 'Help me inside,' she instructed Muirenn. 'I need to rest.'

'Very well,' the fair-haired woman agreed. 'Take my hand and I'll help you return to the hut and I'll tend to your wounds while you sleep.'

Nodding sharply, the woman warrior took her hand and rose to her feet, trembling from the effort. 'And tomorrow,' continued Muirenn, 'once you have rested, you can meet Barra ua Ébláná.'

***

176

She was tired after another night of intense sleep, tired of being abed, tired of pain but, most of all, tired at the continuing constriction of the little hut.

Despite the hurt it cost her, the Grey One manoeuvred herself out from underneath the furs and managed to make it to the entranceway without stumbling. Outside, it was a drab morning, the hill and forest framed between the low-lying cloud and its mirrored reflection in the placid lake waters. Despite the absence of wind, there was a distinct chill to the air. Winter was upon them.

She turned her eyes up towards the sky.

A grey day.

Like her name. Like her mood.

Her lips cracked in a cynical grimace at the aptness of this as she recalled an old story from her childhood. According to her mother, the night was created by magic weavers who gathered up the colours of the world, stuffing them inside a great wicker basket until nothing was left but blackness. To create the morning, the colours were released again, their brightness and intensity dependent on the mood of the weavers. On grey days like this, her mother said, the weavers were sad and less generous with their magic hues.

She frowned at that. She'd never been entirely sure about a giant wicker basket that could fit all the colours of the world inside. As a child however, she'd always derived too much pleasure from the story to question its more fantastical elements.

Moving a few paces outside the hut, she found someone had built a small fire-pit, sheltered from the worst of the elements by a crude lean-to. It looked as though the fire had recently been fed, for it was crackling nicely and a partially-sealed metal pot sat in the ashes off to the side. The Grey One stared at it for a moment, sniffing the odour of freshly made porridge.

They are oddly thoughtful in their care of a prisoner.

Tottering slowly and excruciatingly stiffly towards the fire, she spotted the guard up at the treeline. It was a different man this time. Another bearded warrior in his forties, he had dark brown hair tied up in braids but his beard was a tangle of dense, grey bush. From the way

177

his hand was resting on the hilt of his sword she could tell he was a seasoned warrior. Injured though she was, Fíne Surehands was taking no chances.

For some reason that pleased her.

At the fire, she poured the steaming porridge into a wooden bowl and made a great show of rubbing her hands over the flames. 'Ho! Dark watcher,' she called mockingly up at the guard. 'Did you pass a cold night in the shadows?'

The warrior eyed her coldly but made no reply.

With a provocative smirk, she took the bowl and turned away to eat her porridge only to discover a second man standing off to the left of the hut. He'd been observing her in silence the whole time.

Tall and broad shouldered, this second individual had a handsome, intelligent face that was unfamiliar to her although the bright red cloak wrapped over his shoulders confirmed the identity of whom she was facing. She stared at Barra ua Éblána, surprised to find that he was older than she'd expected, with twenty-eight to thirty years on him at least. For some reason she'd always assumed Muirenn would be with a man her own age.

Despite his years, she had to admit that he was an attractive man with his strong jaw, fine chiselled features, short-cropped brown hair and broad moustache. The single noticeable imperfection – a small scar that bisected one of his heavy eyebrows – in an odd way served only to highlight the pleasantness of his other features.

'I see you,' said the *Éblána* man. He nodded in greeting and although his smile seemed relaxed, the stiffness in his stance told a different story.

'I see you,' she answered cautiously.

'I am Barra ua Éblána. The man Rólgallach Mór sent you to dispatch.' His lower jaw seemed to tense at that and when he spoke again his voice was harsher although markedly more forthright. 'I would have you put beneath the sod already had Muirenn not convinced me you'd protected her, turned on your own comrades to save her life.' He stopped and swallowed then as though trying to ingest something distinctly unpalatable. 'She says you have a good heart.'

He didn't sound convinced but because there was nothing to say, Liath Luachra said nothing. She stood looking at him, conscious of the porridge cooling in its bowl and wishing he would leave her in peace so that she could eat.

'Muirenn also says that you've been to Talamh An Fhírinne Buí.'

She cleared her throat nervously, unsure what he was referring to.

'Talamh An Fhírinne Buí,' he repeated, gesturing with his right hand to indicate the valley around them. Land of the Yellow Truth.

She nodded.

He harrumphed. 'That surprises me. Few people come this way for they fear to pass through the haunted woods. My father told me there'd been a massacre of innocents in those trees many years ago, long before his own grandfather's time. Once, during the Samhain festivities, he entered the woods to prove his courage and found rusted weapons and bones beneath the moss of the forest floor. He was also the one who passed me the secret of the hidden trail past *Carraig An Fhírinne Buí*, the path that bypasses the woods and allows us to travel here in safety.'

He stopped then and looked at her with unwavering intensity. 'These are my lands,' he said. 'They have been in my family for many generations and I will fight to keep them, to pass them down to my own children. Neither you nor Rólgallach Mór will ever take them from me.'

***

She remained beside the fire for the rest of the morning, adding more wood to keep the flames high for the air had an icy edge to it and she was reluctant to return inside. To her relief, the warrior watching her from the trees had disappeared, apparently fading back into the woods while she'd been talking with Barra. It felt good to be alone at last and she briefly revelled in the freedom from being monitored.

Her solitude was broken later that afternoon when a call sounded from the woods to the north-east. Raising her eyes, she spotted Muirenn at the edge of the trees, accompanied by the sour-faced Cappa. As the *Éblána* woman made her way towards the fire, the warrior lagged behind to offer some semblance of privacy. Liath Luachra noted that he kept his spear poised, ready to pin her on its jagged tip should she make any threatening gesture towards the fair-haired woman.

179

'Shall we walk?' the Grey One asked. Despite the pain, she was eager to test her mobility, to get a sense for how fast her wounds were healing. Initially, she'd been fearful of leaving the shelter but now, with someone to assist her should the need arise, she felt more confident.

Muirenn seemed surprised by the proposal but she nodded enthusiastically enough. 'We can go to Brú na Tanalachtaí'– the Bend of the Shallows – she suggested brightly, pointing south to a point where the long lake narrowed and curved off to the east. 'It's a short pacing. And there's a pleasant view from this side of the bank.'

They started walking slowly and although Liath Luachra moved with care, by the time they'd travelled little more than a hundred paces, her wound was aching again. She masked all sign of her discomfort however, determined to make the distant curve even if she was reduced to hobbling like a sickly cripple.

By the time they got to Brú na Tanalachtaí, she was sweating heavily and her wound was aggravated from the constant movement. Exhausted, the woman warrior sank onto a boulder beside a still pool. Her face was white and tight with pain as she awkwardly scooped up a handful of water to wash the sweat from her brow.

Taking a deep breath, she looked around and saw that the *Éblána* woman hadn't exaggerated. The spot where they'd stopped was quite beautiful, the lake narrowing to a river that veered due east, cut through a wide gap in the distant ridge and emptied straight into the sea. Liath Luachra stared. She'd known they were still somewhere near the coast but she hadn't realised they were so close. The great green bulk of the sea was clearly visible through the gap in the ridge and off the coast she could make out a dark lump that had a number of other, smaller, lumps gathered around its most southerly point.

While she rested, the Grey One watched Muirenn stroll along the bank of the lake, admiring her serene composure, the sheer svelte naturalness of the woman. Every now and again, she'd pause to crouch and pick up some odd-shaped stone or piece of wood that caught her fancy, secreting them in the small satchel that dangled from her shoulder. While she gathered her treasures, the *Éblána* woman sang softly to herself, a pleasant lilting melody that hung on the still air. Liath

Luachra listened with interest for although the tune was one she hadn't heard before, parts of it struck her as oddly familiar.

Sensing that she was being watched, Muirenn turned her head, pushed the long silver-blond hair back from her face and gave her a dazzling smile.

She is beautiful.

Struck and somewhat perturbed at having been caught staring, Liath Luachra felt her cheeks grow warm. She quickly turned away, redirecting her eyes back along the river to where her shadow – the warrior Cappa – stood watching. Her lips formed a thin line.

'*Féach ort,*' said Muirenn. Look.

Liath Luachra turned to find the *Éblána* woman had come closer and was pointing down at the still waters of the pool. 'See how your hair has lengthened in the short time you've been here. I told you it would soften your features. Now you can see for yourself.'

Curious, Liath Luachra bowed her head to examine the shimmering reflection. She stared, her breath catching for she hardly recognised the face staring back at her. The last time she'd seen her own image had been almost two years earlier, at a similar riverside pool shortly after joining *Na Cinéaltaí*. Back then she'd looked very different; her hair shorn close to the skull, crude streaks of war paint and blood splayed across her face, grey eyes flaring with hatred and madness.

In contrast, the young woman in the pool resembled a farmer's daughter: a little intense and ragged at the edges to be sure but relatively sane and human for all that.

This is the person I would have been!

'Even in that old dress,' laughed Muirenn, 'you are fair and comely. If you let them, men would form a line for you.'

And with that, the illusion fell away. The Grey One said nothing but felt a shudder of revulsion pass through her. As a slave for the *díberg*, men had formed a line for her on occasion. But not in the manner Muirenn had intended. Or probably even understood.

Feeling her mood darken, Liath Luachra looked away again, this time turning her gaze towards the sea. '*Cad iad sin?*' she asked, pointing towards the distant blue-grey lumps, eager to change the topic. What are they?

'*An Cearc 's a Sicíní*,' Muirenn answered. The Hen and its Chickens. 'They're Islands, closer than they appear in this light.' Her lips turned down and her face took on a serious air. 'The waters just beyond then are treacherous for that is where the currents meet.' She gestured towards the gap through which the river flowed. 'Strange things are found on the beach where the river empties into the sea. The storms throw up dead men or animals, boats with unusual shapes and, sometimes, odd containers with liquids or food spoiled by the sea-water.' She paused in quiet reflection. 'Once a box with a silver comb was washed onshore. My mother gave it as a gift to a person she greatly respected.'

Her eyes took on a faraway look as she continued to stare eastwards. 'Do you ever dream, Liath Luachra? Do you ever dream of exploring what lies across the waters, what's hidden over the next hill or obscured by the woods and forest?'

The woman warrior shook her head. 'This land can be bitter and dangerous. I want nothing more than a sheltered refuge, a secure place where I can hide and live in safety.'

'Gort Na Meala is safe. You could live here.'

Liath Luachra stared at her companion, unable to hide her incredulity at the extent of her naivety. Rólgallach Mór's desire for the fair-haired woman meant that Gort Na Meala's days were numbered. Of this, there was no doubt.

'I speak no lie,' responded Muirenn, misinterpreting the Grey One's reaction. 'Were you to swear allegiance to my mother, I'm sure she'd relent in her suspicions and grant you permission to remain. You would have your own section of land to settle and we … we could be friends.'

Liath Luachra got to her feet and considered Muirenn closely for she'd detected a slight tremor in her voice, an unsettling tinge of desperation or loneliness. The *Éblána* woman must be very lonely, she decided, if she found the companionship of someone with her limited social ability in any way appealing.

The two women stood close together in the gloom, considering one another in silence. Liath Luachra nervously clenched and unclenched her hands, unsure why she felt so tense. For her part, she sensed that Muirenn too, was experiencing similar discomfort given the stiff manner in which she held herself.

Although she did not turn, Liath Luachra could feel the eyes of the *Éblána* warrior drilling into her back. 'I'm tired,' she said. 'We should return now.'

***

The short walk to Brú na Tanalachtaí had taken its toll. When Liath Luachra returned to the warmth of the hut and collapsed on her bedding, she fell into a profound slumber that coalesced different elements of the day to produce a dream of disturbing character.

She found herself sitting by a fire-pit at the centre of a longhouse, an unfamiliar building but one she somehow knew to be part of the pair at Gort Na Meala. For some reason, she was holding a polished brass mirror in one hand. With the other, she was feeding the fire with long yellow sticks that burned instantaneously on touching the red-orange flames.

This is not real.

It felt strange to be in a dream where she was conscious it was a dream but even stranger was that when she looked into the mirror, she saw her old, shaven-headed, wild-eyed self staring back out at her. Even within the parameters of the dream, this scared her. Nervous, she plucked the hem of her blue dress – Muirenn's dress – and raised her hand to touch her short black hair as though to confirm it was still there.

In the shadows at the far end of the longhouse, her two brothers – her brothers from Luachair – were playing rough and tumble, laughing animatedly as they wrestled and mock-fought over possession of a wooden sword. Her jaw dropped in shock as she recognised them but then a loud laugh of delight escaped her. Excited, she was about to rise to her feet to join them when a figure stepped in from her left and sat down alongside her. The weight of a slender arm draped affectionately

183

around her shoulders and pulled her close. Turning her head, she stared at the exquisite features of the woman sitting beside her.

Muirenn!

She stiffened in surprise but then, slowly, felt her heart subside and soften for those beautiful blue eyes regarded her with great affection.

And need.

Heedless of the playing children, the *Éblána* woman reached one hand up to cup the Grey One's left breast and she felt her breath catch at the sudden swell of heat between her thighs. Keeping her eyes locked on hers, Muirenn lifted the hem of the dress she'd gifted her, took Liath Luachra's right hand in hers and placed it between the woman warrior's own legs, unlocking her middle and index fingers so that she could work them inside her. Liath Luachra felt her nipples harden as the *Éblána* woman smiled reassuringly, manipulating her hand, encouraging her to take the initiative and when she finally did, releasing her.

As she stroked the moistness inside her lips, Muirenn reached her hand around the back of her neck, drawing her forward to pepper her lips with hard, urgent kisses. Too aroused to speak, Liath Luachra turned her face away but the fair-haired woman followed greedily, running her tongue around and into her ear, down her collar bone then licking the warm skin of her neck.

Liath Luachra moaned softly as Muirenn slid down to her chest, undoing the fastenings of her dress to allow her breasts to drop free. She sucked on both nipples, stroking the inside of her thigh as the Grey One continued to massage her plump moistness. She felt the *Éblána* woman's tongue flick over her left breast, hitched a breath even as her fingers worked her right nipple.

Her own fingers were wet by then, saturated as the deep-rooted tingling intensified. Meanwhile, Muirenn had dropped lower again, trailing her tongue down the Grey One's belly, down beside her probing fingers. Liath Luachra felt the fair-haired woman slip her tongue inside her, explore her, and shuddered with the first wave of pleasure.

She awoke in the cold, dark hut on the crest of the orgasm, fingers pressing her clitoris, leg muscles rippling.

Afterwards, eyes half-open, she lay trembling, shocked and frightened by the sheer bliss her body had experienced, confused by her enjoyment of the fantasy.

Rolling onto her side, she wondered dozily what it would be like to live like the *Éblána* woman, to wear her clothing, grow her hair long, lie in the hollow of her bed beside some handsome warrior: serene, svelte, eternally composed.

Liath Luachra curled into a ball beneath the furs. The fantasy unwound within her as the world drained away, drip by drip, and there was nothing – nothing – left to think.

Chapter Nine

Fíne Surehands returned to Talamh An Fhírinne Buí ten days later, accompanied by a small contingent of followers from Gort Na Meala. Liath Luachra was alerted of their arrival by the sound of a child's laugh ringing through the dark trees. Raising her head, she watched them emerge from that section of the woods concealing the hidden path from *Carraig An Fhírinne Buí*, the same spot where Muirenn and Cappa had first appeared some days earlier.

Fíne Surehands was the first to step out of the trees, a small, woven wicker basket casually slung over one shoulder. She was followed almost immediately by her two warriors, a pair of slaves from Gort Na Meala and the little girl that Liath Luachra assumed was her younger daughter. She felt the pressure in her chest subside as they advanced towards the hut and breathed a sigh of relief. Muirenn was not with them.

Wrapped in the furs from her bedding, the Grey One was sitting in the shelter of the little lean-to, as close to the fire as she dared. It was bitterly cold. The summit of the ridge to the east was coated in snow and several white patches, ankle-deep, dotted the ground alongside the shallow, ice-frosted pools at the edge of the lake.

Although the air was calm that morning, a vicious storm had rolled in from the north-east the previous evening, lashing the land with a ferocious, hail-laced gale that had sent the temperature tumbling. In the shelter of the wicker refuge, Liath Luachra had passed a fearful night huddled over the feeble fire as the walls flexed violently with each pummelling gust. Now, weary from lack of sleep, she watched the little group circle the hut towards her with dull, unwelcoming eyes.

Fíne Surehands raised one hand in greeting. 'I see you, Grey One.'

Liath Luachra maintained a sullen silence. The previous days had been hard and not only because of the storm. Confined to the hut's immediate environs by her injuries and the deteriorating weather, there'd been little else for her to do to pass the time but dwell on old memories, reliving old failures, picking at them over and over, as a *gealtach* – a Stricken One – might pick at an unhealed scab. Since she'd

186

last seen the *Éblána* woman she'd come to loathe the little hut and the valley to which she'd been restricted, dreading the prospect of remaining there as much as her winter cave in Luachair.

Ignoring the Grey One's frosty response, Fíne Surehands came to a halt before the lean-to but as her companions clustered around her she threw her hands in the air. '*Imeacht libh! Ar aghaidh libh go dtí an Trá Mhór.*' Off with ye! Away to The Big Beach with you. 'The Grey One and I have matters to discuss.'

As the *Éblána* people dispersed, Fíne Surehands turned to Liath Luachra and gestured towards the hut. 'Let us talk inside, Grey One. I am no lively fawn and these bones have a fondness for the warmth.'

Liath Luachra silently stared at her departing companions, now following the lakeside path she'd previously walked with Muirenn.

'The storm came from the east,' the scar-faced woman told her.

Liath Luachra looked at her, cocked one puzzled eyebrow.

'When there's a storm from the east, we scour the beach for treasures tossed up from the sea.'

The Grey One's face remained guarded but she turned slowly and started for the hut. Pushing her way through the flap, she entered and eased herself cautiously onto the mat by the fire-pit. Her wounds were healing well but some physical movements still had the capacity to leave her gasping in pain.

Adjusting her position to reduce her discomfort, she watched as Fíne Surehands entered to join her. The *Éblána* woman paused by the fire to remove the flax basket from her shoulder then stooped and laid it gingerly on the beaten earth floor. Opening the woven cover of the basket, she dipped her hands inside and withdrew a small clay pot with a matching lid secured in place by flax fibre. Placing this on the ground alongside the basket, she flicked her wrist and a knife appeared in her hand. With a single nick of the blade, the fibre was parted.

Slipping the knife back up her sleeve, she lifted the pot and offered it to Liath Luachra. 'I bring you a gift,' she said.

Liath Luachra regarded the proffered pot, her eyes heavy with suspicion.

'Take it,' the other woman insisted. 'It's a harmless herbal drink but it eases the pain of lingering wounds. Barra's people make it from the petals of the yellow flowers that grow so profusely here. I'm sure you'll find it to your taste.'

With evident reluctance, the Grey One accepted the little container and held it against her chest. The heat of the contents had passed through the clay and it was still warm to the touch. Lifting the lid, she released a small cloud of steam. When the hot vapour had cleared, she looked inside at the yellow-tinted liquid it contained and swirled it about to cool.

Returning her gaze to Fíne Surehands, she found the *Éblána* woman's eyes fixed on her forehead, something that didn't particularly surprise her given the prominent gash and bruise it now sported. Three nights earlier, she'd had a particularly bad nightmare of her time as a slave with the *díberg*. For what seemed like an age, she'd relived that brutal period of beatings and abuse before waking in the darkness, bewildered, disorientated but driven by a primal urge to flee. Oblivious to her wounds, she'd lunged to her feet and smashed her head against the hut's central support pole.

Momentarily stunned by the force of the blow, she'd stumbled backwards, blood from the wound streaming down her forehead to the corner of her mouth. Surprisingly, despite the pain, the blow had helped to calm her, replacing the desperate panic with a numbness that allowed her to lie down and sleep again.

Liath Luachra let out a low, wavering breath, pushing the incident to the back of her mind as she sniffed at the remaining steam. It smelled a little odd but not repellent. Rather than delay the inevitable, she raised the container to her lips and took a deep gulp.

To her surprise, the liquid was surprisingly palatable, the flavour of the flower petals complimented by the sweetness of added honey. She glanced towards the *Éblána* woman and grudgingly nodded her head. 'Good.'

Fíne Surehands acknowledged the comment with a distracted wave of her hands before curtly coming to the point of her visit. 'You have asked my daughter not to come here.'

Liath Luachra's eye narrowed. She inhaled sharply through her nose then shrugged listlessly, a response that did not appear to satisfy the scar-faced woman. 'Why would you do that?' she persisted. 'Muirenn was wounded by your abrupt dismissal.'

The Grey One regarded her and although her face betrayed no emotion, her eyes remained cold and bitter. 'I would have thought my absence from your daughter's company was something to please you.'

'Oh, it does please me. But now your motive snags my curiosity as blackthorn snags a passing dress hem.' Here, she paused and considered the woman warrior with palpable scepticism. 'For reasons I do not understand, Muirenn considers you worthy of friendship. And yet, this is a proposal you appear to have rejected, despite turning against your own comrades to save her.'

Both women glared. Finally, realising that the *Éblána* woman wouldn't be satisfied until she had her answer, Liath Luachra sighed and dropped her eyes. 'I like Muirenn,' she said.

'And?' demanded Fíne Surehands as the silence stretched on.

'And she will die. It is not my wish to see that fate played out.'

The *Éblána* woman laughed out loud. 'Muirenn will not die. I will not let her die. Anyone who threatens her will find a bed on the forest floor, their life's blood pooling in a wet cushion about them.'

Liath Luachra tapped her knee in irritation, riled by the other woman's brusque interruption. 'Then why do you disregard the threat of Rólgallach Mór? The *rí* of the *Éblána* must be impatient to learn the fate of his man and his prize.'

The tissue of Fíne Surehands' scar seemed to stretch as her skin grew taut from a tensing jaw. 'That is true,' she conceded soberly. 'But he will not risk open conflict by sending warriors. Not until he knows with certainty how events have conspired.'

'He'll send scouts.'

'Even scouts cannot travel the southern path until spring. Winter snows have blocked the passes, the southern trail is reduced to mud and all sane men huddle close to the fire. I keep a watchful guard on the trail. For now, rest assured, Gort Na Meala has a reprieve to plan its response to Rólgallach Mór's aggression.'

Liath Luachra said nothing. Even pre-warned, she did not think much of their chances. The people of Gort Na Meala were facing a far superior enemy. Their valley, pleasant though it was, had too many routes of access, rendering it indefensible. The community there had insufficient fighting men to protect their territory and no allies. Despite Barra's defiant chest-thumping and Fíne Surehands apparent indifference, they would be fools if they hadn't already initiated preparations for flight come spring. Their single other option was to negotiate a surrender.

And hand Muirenn to Rólgallach Mór.

Fíne Surehands drew closer to the hut's small fire-pit. Even within the walls of the little shelter, it was perceptibly cold. 'Meanwhile, I have made my decision. You will winter at Gort Na Meala for you'll freeze to death should I leave you here. Gort Na Meala offers a warm hearth to pass the winter and respite enough to allow the healing of your wounds.'

And, more importantly, you can keep a watchful eye on me.

The Grey One sipped another mouthful from the pot, enjoying the sweet aftertaste on her tongue as she considered Fíne Surehands, an inspection that was duly returned with stony scrutiny. If she'd ever had doubts as to the *Éblána* woman's abilities as a warrior leader she did not have them now. The scar-faced woman had reverted to carrying a sword, wearing the weapon in a metal scabbard at her belt with an ease that spoke of great familiarity. Her natural authority had also become more pronounced since the last time Liath Luachra had seen her. A blooded warrior and *conradh* – champion – of the Gort Na Meala people, command was something that would have come naturally but now her eyes conveyed a far greater sense of purpose, an inevitable consequence from the prospect of war, she supposed.

For a moment the Grey One was tempted to say something, to deny her intent to hurt those at Gort Na Meala or return to Rólgallach Mór. In the end however, she kept her silence. Her words would make little difference. Fíne Surehands was unlikely to trust her under any circumstances.

'But no weapons,' the *Éblána* woman continued. 'Should those hands of yours clasp any pointed object larger than a pin, my men will strike you down.'

Resentment smouldered inside the Grey One like an ill-quenched fire but she swallowed her anger. Cappa or Darra – the warrior with the grey beard – had been her constant shadow any time she'd ventured from the hut. They'd remained discreetly within the trees but at no point did they ever let her move beyond the range of spear cast. For that reason alone she didn't doubt Fíne Surehands' threat would be carried through.

This abrupt recognition of her own vulnerability triggered an uncharacteristic fit of panic. Liath Luachra felt her face flush, her heart start to pound and, for a moment, her tongue seemed too large to fit inside her mouth. Determined not to display any weakness in front of the older woman, she disguised her anxiety by swallowing several mouthfuls of the beverage, gulping down the fear even as it seemed to grow inside her.

It struck her then how strange it was, how despite all the commotion and upheaval in her existence, so little had really changed. She was still under the leash, her existence defined and determined by others. Even now, after everything that had happened, she remained subject to the whims of Fíne Surehands just as she'd been subject to Bressal's and, before that, to those of the *díberg* leader who'd abducted her.

And before that again, to the frenzies of my father.

The realisation caused a sour bubble of fury to swell in her chest. Her world was spinning out of her control and she was powerless to prevent it. Assailed by a flurry of contradicting emotions, she instinctively grasped out for thoughts of comfort, for succour and once again, the first thing that came to mind was the soothing mental image of the *Éblána* land promised by Bressal and Rólgallach Mór. On this occasion however, even that tranquil vision failed her, the fleeting reminder of potential freedom so cruelly lost, serving only to make her angrier.

Conscious of the other woman's eyes on her, she stared at the fire and somehow pulled herself together.

'Come spring, I may yet decide to let you leave.'

Liath Luachra raised her eyes and regarded Fíne Surehands with fresh antipathy. Despite her chaotic emotions and her scepticism at the *Éblána* woman's words, she managed to keep her face blank. Gratitude for Muirenn's life or not, she could not envisage a blooded warrior like Fíne Surehands releasing her. The risk of her prisoner heading back to join her enemy's forces was simply too great.

No. Despite any feelings the scar-faced woman's daughter might have on the matter, Liath Luachra expected little more than one last quiet walk in the trees, a blade across the throat and a shallow grave in the deepest shadows of the forest.

'But first,' the other woman continued. 'I would require assurance of your friendly intentions towards Gort Na Meala. If you were released, for example, where would you go?'

Liath Luachra eyed her. Infuriated by days of confinement, she fought down the desire to throw herself at Fíne Surehands and batter her to a bloody pulp. That, she knew, would not end well for her. 'Far away.'

'Where?'

'I do not know,' she snarled. 'I have nowhere to go. *Na Cinéaltaí* will not take me back. Without the *fian* I have nothing, I am nothing.'

'You have no clan?'

The Grey One shook her head. '*Éclann*,' she said shortly.

Fíne Surehands' thoughtfully tapped her index finger against her lips. 'No clan, then. No clan, no possessions and without even a skill for trade.'

'I can kill.'

Fíne Surehands looked startled by the response but, surprisingly, her features softened and pursing her lips, she released a weary sigh. 'Yes,' she said. 'I read the battle-story of your combat on the tracks at the beach. To overcome and kill three warriors was no small feat. So, yes, you clearly are a killer.' That initial softness faded. 'But I have no need for a killer.'

'Given your current circumstance, it seems to me that is exactly what you need.'

Fíne Surehands' gaze did not waver. 'Then let me rearrange my words to avoid confusion. I have no use for a killer I cannot trust.'

Liath Luachra frowned. Barra had two warriors and had armed his two elderly slaves. With Fíne Surehands and her two warriors that made a total of six fighters and two sword fodder – not enough to provide credible opposition to the forces Rólgallach Mór would bring with him. An experienced warrior, Fíne Surehands must have considered this reality yet she appeared determined to ignore it.

'Will you negotiate a capitulation?'

'What do you think?'

'Flight then.'

Her silence confirmed Liath Luachra's suspicions.

'To fight is foolish. You cannot win.'

'And what would you have us do, oh Great Slayer?' There was no mistaking the acid in the *Éblána* woman's voice.

'Survive. Yield.'

Fíne Surehands laughed harshly at that. 'Yield Muirenn to Rólgallach Mór? I will not see my eldest child destroyed by that foul smear of shit.'

'If you fight, you will see all your children destroyed.'

'When you have a child of your own you can advise me on such matters.'

There was no clear response to that so Liath Luachra lapsed into her habitual silence. Folding back onto her haunches, she drew away from the fire but the *Éblána* woman's eyes continued to follow her. 'Tell me,' she asked suddenly. 'Do you enjoy the act of slaying?'

Liath Luachra eyed her cautiously for the question was an odd one although she could detect no obvious trap to it. She swallowed the last few drops from the pot and set the container on her lap. 'Sometimes,' she admitted. 'I am good at it.'

'And given this … skill at slaying, do you still judge yourself an upright person?'

Liath Luachra stared at her, confused. 'I don't understand. How can one make judgement on being an upright person or not?'

'I have heard the elders say that peaceful lives are the just rewards of an upright life.'

Liath Luachra's lips turned up with a cynicism that made her look many years older than she was. 'Well, then, I am hardly an upright person.' She paused, her fingers tightening on a rough wrinkle in the material of her dress. 'My mother was upright. My brothers at Luachair were upright, perhaps. They hurt no one and led peaceful lives. Until the flux and the *díberg* descended on them, at least.' With that, she raised her eyes and glared at Fíne Surehands as though expecting some argument from her. 'So, maybe they were not upright after all. For that was no just reward.'

She paused then, confused and angry at herself for allowing such personal revelations to slide so easily from her lips. Before she could reflect on the matter further, the older woman reached over and placed a callused palm against her cheek. Startled, Liath Luachra flinched and slapped the hand away.

If the *Éblána* woman was affronted by the reaction, she made no show of it. Instead she considered Liath Luachra with a sad expression and slowly shook her head. 'There is no lightness to you, Grey One. You are a storm tree, a scorched husk, a grey shadow of the person you might once have been.'

Liath Luachra stared, bewildered by this new direction the conversation had taken.

'You should not fret. *Na Cinéaltaí* will take you back. Men like Bressal Binnbhéalach l will always hold a place for one such as you for they like warriors that are broken. Broken warriors make good fighters but, more importantly, they're far easier to manipulate.'

Liath Luachra opened her mouth, feeling a sudden compulsion to refute what the *Éblána* woman was saying. She abruptly closed it again. She did not know what to say. 'I don't like you,' she growled at last.

'That is sad to hear,' said Fíne Surehands calmly, infuriatingly composed. 'I quite enjoy our talks.'

Liath Luachra stared at the old woman with mounting frustration, vexed at being so consistently outmanoeuvred. She looked down at the little clay pot in her hands, suddenly conscious of how tightly she was clenching it. In one foul flash of insight it all became clear.

'You have poisoned me!' She tossed the pot aside causing it hit the ground hard and smash into several pieces. The last of the yellow liquid seeped into the reeds that covered the floor.

The *Éblána* woman snorted. 'It's no poison. I've already told you it's a drink from the yellow flowers. Although …' She glanced sideways at the warrior woman. 'It is true Barra told me it has a tendency to loosen lips. Perhaps that is the origin of the name Talamh An Fhírinne Buí – Land of the Yellow Truth.'

The Grey One stared at her in horror.

'I bear no pride in such a ruse, Grey One. I am not one to twist complex words but neither are you one to share your thoughts and I did not have the luxury of drawing them from you softly.'

With that, Fíne Surehands got to her feet, the brusqueness of the movement signalling that, from her perspective at least, the conversation was at an end.

'Move yourself, Grey One. Injured or not, you return to Gort Na Meala with us.'

***

Despite her resentment at Fíne Surehands' deception, subsequent events forced Liath Luachra to reconsider her overall fortune. Within a day of her brusque eviction from Talamh An Fhírinne Buí, the winter weather revealed its true extremes. Snow dropped thick and heavy from leaden clouds, creating great swathes of white that smothered the ridges on either side of Gort Na Meala. For four days, gales smashed the land, funnelling blustery gusts though the valley and it grew so cold no-one ventured outside except for the most urgent of tasks: caring for the cattle or maintaining the supply of firewood. When the winds finally ceased and the woman warrior was able to step out into the watery winter sunlight, she regarded the height of the snowdrifts in sombre silence. She did not need to be told she would have perished had she remained at Talamh An Fhírinne Buí.

I owe Fíne Surehands my life a second time.

She cursed and spat on the ground before returning inside.

Such grudging acceptance did not otherwise improve her situation. For the most part, the people at Gort Na Meala treated her with courtesy but it was a courtesy tainted with frosty distrust. Liath Luachra could appreciate that. These people knew what she was, after all. They knew she'd been sent to kill them, to destroy their home. She could hardly have expected them to greet her with open arms.

There was one however, who did greet her with open arms: Muirenn. The fair-haired girl had embraced her joyously on her arrival, expressing no rancour for the distress she must have felt at the woman warrior's harsh rejection. In addition to the warmth of her welcome, she took it upon herself to shield Liath Luachra from the latent hostility of the community by acting as her constant companion. This was a gesture for which the Grey One was grateful but one that left her markedly uncomfortable.

Like most communities, the people of Gort Na Meala lived in close proximity. They slept as groups in the two longhouses, ate communally in the larger one, worked and spent all of their time together. Unaccustomed to the presence of others in such close and extended proximity, the constant pressure to interact was something the Grey One struggled with. It seemed ironic but here, hemmed in by the constant bustle and chatter, her sense of isolation was exacerbated in comparison to the solitude she'd endured back in Talamh An Fhírinne Buí. In that isolated valley, although it had been hard to be trapped with her thoughts, they had at least been *her* thoughts.

With no other alternative open to her, the Grey One stamped her frustration down deep, retreated to her habitual silence and stared longingly towards the dense forest to the west. She would have liked nothing more than to flee, to make a break for the dark shelter of the trees but her circumstances meant that any such attempt was unfeasible. She had no weapon. Her wounds were healing but not healing fast enough. She was slow, weak, unable to defend herself or hunt for food effectively. Now, in the growing heart of the winter, wolf howls echoed from the ridges at night, as the animals were drawn by the presence of cattle. Without shelter or refuge she knew that she'd most likely starve and freeze to death. Or be eaten. Possibly all three.

***

By her seventh day at Gort Na Meala, Liath Luachra had fallen into a gentle routine of domestic housework, helping out – where her wounds permitted – on the less physical but necessary tasks to be carried out at the holding. At first, this consisted of little more than maintaining the longhouse fires but by the ninth day she was also able to assist Muirenn and two slave women prepare the evening meals.

On the evening of the tenth day, she presented herself as usual at the larger longhouse where a sizeable stack of tubers sat waiting to be peeled and cut for the cauldron stew. Taking a seat on the mats where the women were gathered, Liath Luachra awaited her instructions, glancing up in surprise when Muirenn held a knife, handle first, towards her.

'We have a wrist's ache of peeling work this evening.'

Liath Luachra considered the knife briefly before turning her eyes to the longhouse entrance where Cappa stood watching, picking his teeth with a splinter of wood. The warrior looked relaxed but she could sense the tension beneath that calm demeanour, the muscles ready to uncoil if she reached out to touch the weapon.

'Gods, Cappa!' Muirenn declared loudly, deciphering the warrior's body language just as accurately as Liath Luachra. 'She cannot peel them with her teeth.'

Cappa glowered then turned a resentful eye to the warrior woman. Of Fíne Surehands' two warriors, he was the one who'd seemed to take a more personal dislike towards her. 'I'm watching you,' he said simply.

Muirenn turned back to face the woman warrior, screwing her face up in a comical mimicry of the grimacing warrior.

The Grey One wordlessly took the knife and started to peel.

They worked quietly for a time, peeling, carving, slicing and dicing the tubers until the pleasant hush was broken by the young *Éblána* woman. 'You never smile.'

Liath Luachra paused and although her posture didn't change, her eyes flickered up to where the fair-haired girl was watching her.

'No.'

'But why?'

The woman warrior frowned at the question, irked that Muirenn could be preoccupied with such inanities when the dark threat of Rólgallach Mór loomed above them all like an incoming storm.

'You fear Rólgallach Mór.'

Although thrown by this unexpected insightfulness, Liath Luachra maintained her neutral countenance.

'There's no need to be afraid. My mother promised that she and Barra would keep us safe. She has never lied to me.' Muirenn brushed an errant strand of silver-blond hair from her face. 'Besides, Rólgallach Mór might not even come to threaten us. He knows my mother's reputation as a fighter.'

Liath Luachra said nothing but felt a hollow crease inside her stomach. Having met the *rí* of the *Éblána*, she judged the man's return not so much a possibility as a certainty. Unlike her fair-haired companion, she'd also seen Fíne Surehands by the fire of the longhouse late at night when she thought everyone else asleep. Contrary to the bravado and confidence she displayed during the day, at such times the face staring in the flames bore a haunted expression.

'I don't want to talk.'

She shifted position, her face angled away from the other woman. Bending her head over the peeling board, she directed her full attention to the mechanical action of peel-slice-dice-drop. Sometime later, consumed in the mindless physical repetition, she was vaguely conscious of the longhouse door opening but it was a sudden squeal form Muirenn that roused her from her trance. Looking up, she saw Barra standing behind the *Éblána* woman, thick hairy arms encircling her waist. A hearty guffaw echoed Muirenn's squeal.

'What's this?' Barra released her and stood back as though to examine her more closely. 'The womenfolk sit in warm comfort by the fire?' He made an exaggerated expression of disgust as he brushed a dusting of snow from his shoulder onto the floor.

'While the menfolk work to feed and protect the herd, the womenfolk sit at their ease and grow fat.'

Muirenn slapped at him playfully but he quickly leaned back and out of reach.

'I will go,' the Grey One said, preparing to rise.

'Stay, Liath Luachra! There is no reason to leave. Let us all eat together tonight.' Muirenn beamed at her, oblivious to the expression on the face of the man just above her left shoulder.

She shook her head. 'I am tired. In pain. I should rest.'

Slowly, awkwardly, she got to her feet.

'Leave the knife,' suggested Barra, nodding his head to indicate her right hand.

The Grey One's expression was chilling. Stabbing the blade deep into one of the largest tubers she wordlessly turned and left the longhouse.

***

That night, curled close to the fire-pit of the smaller longhouse shared with Fíne Surehands, her warriors and the slaves, the incessant sense of isolation chaffed worse than usual. Unable to get the memory of Muirenn and Barra out of her head, she lay unconsciously grinding her teeth as she replayed the interaction in the larger longhouse in her head. An unfathomable fury towards the *Éblána* couple had flared inside her, although she knew they hadn't done anything to deserve it. In fact, Muirenn had done everything in her power to help her while Barra had acted no differently than she herself would have done under similar circumstances.

But they'd seemed happy, laughing and oblivious to anything but each other.

Why do you torment yourself? Both will be with the worms soon.

Such certainties of course, proved little comfort.

Fortunately, the longhouse was empty so there was no one present to witness her agitation. All the other occupants were gathered for the evening meal in the larger longhouse, even Darra who usually sat guarding her at night. Secure in the knowledge that there was nowhere for her to run, he was now most likely stuffing his gut with the others.

In some respects it was almost a relief to be distracted by the longhouse door scraping open. She listened carefully as someone entered and quickly closed it behind them against the cold night air. She recognised Fíne Surehands' footsteps immediately for they were quite distinctive, regular but light and surprisingly nimble. They drew to a halt directly behind her.

Turning away from the fire, the Grey One looked up at her in curiosity.

'Here.' The scar-faced woman held out a morsel of leathery looking material.

Beacáin scammalach!

Liath Luachra repressed the initial desire to reach up to grab it. Over the previous days, she'd thought her ache for cloud mushroom had dissipated but tonight, trapped with her own thoughts, she'd sensed it lingering on the fringe of her mind. Her eyes narrowed as she returned Fíne Surehands' gaze.

'This is no trick. I have seen your hands shake, the wildness in your eyes. I recognise the signs.'

The Grey One remained mute.

'Do you believe yourself the only person to use *beacáin scammalach* to stem fear and despair?'

When it became evident no reaction was forthcoming, Fíne Surehands shrugged and tossed the desiccated fungus onto the furs over the Grey One's stomach. 'Take it. Or not. It matters little to me.'

With this, she turned and walked away to her sleeping platform at the eastern wall, a distance of some seven or eight paces.

Without thinking, Liath Luachra grasped the sliver of desiccated mushroom, clamping it tight in her fist as she rolled back to the fire so that her back would screen anything she did from the other woman's sight. Even then, untrusting as ever, she held off swallowing it until the others had returned and everyone had retired to their bedding. When nothing but snores filled the silence of the longhouse, she slipped the sliver of mushroom into her mouth and longed for a dream that would take her very far away.

***

Slipping out of the longhouse, she crossed the clearing to enter the surrounding forest and started uphill towards that site on the southern ridge she'd originally used as a vantage point. Thick snow coated the tops of the trees and lay heavy on the ground between them. Despite

200

this, she felt no touch of cold against the soles of her feet, no sensation but a soft crunch when she stepped on those areas where the upper layer had frozen to a fine crust.

Fortunately the night sky was clear and the silver glow from a three-quarter moon leaked through the canopy to illuminate her path. Reaching the crest of the ridge, she quickly located the path along the northern edge, following it west until the little cluster of oak trees set back from the cliff came into view.

Suddenly something alerted her, some whispered ghost of instinct that told her she wasn't alone. Dropping to her belly, she crawled to the edge of the trees and peered through the foliage to where an indistinct figure was visible.

It was Sean Fergus, of course. Staring down at the rough, snow-covered mound where she'd laid him to rest. As she got to her feet and approached, he turned his head to give her a dispassionate glance before returning to brood over the grave.

'You're not here,' she told him as she drew up alongside. 'You rest lifeless beneath those stones.'

'Neither are you,' he countered sharply. 'You lie in drooling slumber beneath the furs by your fire.' Sean Fergus sniffed then ruefully considered the shadowed mound. 'You missed a bit.' He pointed towards the furthest end where the layer of stone did not lie as thickly as it did over the rest. 'There should be more stones to keep the wolves off.' He raised his right hand and wiped his nose. 'I don't want some gut-growling *mac tíre* gnawing on my bones.'

She gave him an irritated glare. 'It was no easy task. The ground was hard, the stones spread far. Other issues burdened my mind.'

'Even so. It is a poor thing to rush the burial of a friend.'

'So, you call me friend now?'

Sean Fergus frowned and considered that for a moment. 'Yes, he said at last. 'Although it is a sad day, Grey One, when your only friend is a dead one.'

'I have another friend.'

The old warrior's wrinkles creased up in a grim smile. 'Ah, yes. The fair-haired girl. The one you were told to rescue.'

201

'She needed no rescue.'

'Does that surprise you? You always suspected Rólgallach Mór's words were a wind of harsh breathing.' He looked down at his resting place once more and scraped his fingernails through his beard. Liath Luachra bit her lip.

'She is going to die.'

He grunted. 'Odd that. How all your friends die.'

She remained very still for a moment, stung by the warrior's comment. 'Rólgallach Mór will come at the spring thaw,' she said at last. 'The people of Gort Na Meala will resist or surrender but either way Muirenn will die. Killed in the fighting or beneath the thrusting weight of Rólgallach Mór's belly.'

The old warrior glanced sideways at her. 'I sense that this troubles you, Grey One. If you care for her then why don't you save her?'

'Because there is no saving her. Rólgallach Mór's forces are too strong. I could no more save her from her fate then I could halt the west wind.'

'Ah.' He gave a sympathetic shrug. 'What then of your own survival?'

'I don't know. Fíne Surehands may kill me for she grows ever desperate. Rólgallach Mór will certainly kill me should he learn of Flannán's death by my hand.' She paused. 'If I can keep my life until the thaw, I will try to escape and return to Bressal.' She glanced curiously at the old man as though waiting for him to protest or offer contrary advice. For once however, he remained steadfastly silent.

'I grow weary of being used,' she continued at last. 'A plaything for those who direct me as they will. Bressal will still have need of a *rígfénnid*. And he has promised me land. With that land I can be free.'

Sean Fergus snorted.

'Bressal promised! He gave me his word.'

Sean Fergus shook his head with a mocking grimace. 'Years ago,' he said. 'When I walked the centre lands, I found a man floating face down in the bog. He still had reeds in his hands, reeds from the side of the bog hole where he'd tried to pull himself out.' He held up his own fists in demonstration, clenching them tight in front of her. 'Like this. But the reeds had shallow roots. They came away in his hand.'

Liath Luachra regarded him in puzzlement. 'And?' she snapped.

'And … you grasp Bressal's promise in the same way. Despite knowing what you must offer him to recover his benevolence. Why else would the leader of the *fian* accept you back when you failed the task that he set you?'

The Grey One turned and stared at him directly, eyes dark and savage. 'Because I will fulfil the task.'

Sean Fergus' eyes widened. 'What?' he asked softly.

'I will fulfil the task. I will slay Barra. And his men. I will smooth Rólgallach Mór's entry to Gort Na Meala.' I am a killer after all. Killing is what I do.'

'And your blond-haired friend in all this?'

An unexpected tightness tingled her throat. 'If I could save her I would. But I cannot help her. She will die either way.'

Sean Fergus looked stunned. He continued to stare at her in disbelief.

'I am a single fighter,' she insisted. 'Hampered by wounds, without a weapon. I cannot save her. I can barely save myself.'

'We should discuss this matter further, come up with a plan before the dawn light rises '

'No.' She shook her head. There is no plan, no clever ruse or ploy to prevent this fate.'

'Then I was wrong about you, Grey One. For I expected better.' He exhaled heavily. 'Will you not stay to talk, at least until the sunrise?'

Liath Luachra could feel her jaw clench for she knew the ghost would try to dissuade her, just as she knew that he would fail. But she owed him enough to let him try. 'I liked you better,' she said, 'when there was silence between us.'

'Plenty of that now,' he replied.

Chapter Ten

Sixty days later.

By the time Liath Luachra reached the intersection with *Carraig An Fhírinne Buí*, a column of black smoke was visible above Gort Na Meala, bruising the sky with an oily smear. Even from that distance, it was obvious the smoke didn't originate from a campfire but from a conflagration, a blaze of destruction.

Instinctively, the Grey One sniffed at the air but the dark column was too far away, the wind shifting it even further to the north-west.

You know what it smells like.

With a cold heart, she continued to stare as she pulled the grey cloak tight around her shoulders one hand resting on the hilt of *Gléas Gan Ainm*. It calmed her to have the weapon's weight back against her hip. During her time at Gort Na Meala, its absence had been an almost physical loss, particularly at those moments when she'd felt most scared or vulnerable. Retrieved at last, its touch soothed her and offered reassuring assent for the task awaiting them both.

With one last glance towards the drifting smoke, she started south along the trail, pulling her hood down onto the small wicker basket strapped to her back. It was still bitingly cold but the tingle of her ear tips had faded and the hood muffled her hearing, something she couldn't afford on the perilous route towards the centre of *Éblána* territory.

Although winter's hard grip upon the land had been broken, evidence of its ongoing grasp remained. The forest on either side of the path was stark, devoid of any colour but washed-out browns and endless swathes of grey or mottled green. The trunks, dark brown or black in the winter shadow-light, looked hostile, the moss-coated branches eerily tortured.

The forest was also empty of sound apart from the drip of melting snow and ice from the higher branches or the occasional twitter of the *smólach ceoil* – the song thrush. The cold and the lack of undergrowth kept most of the smaller animals deep in their burrows and there was no sign of the larger ones.

Except the wolves, of course.

Always the wolves.

She'd seen the grey shapes slink between the shadows of the trees earlier that morning but since then, nothing. She suspected they'd faded back into the gloom, drawn by the blaze at Gort Na Meala. The animals had an excellent sense of smell and although generally repelled by fire, knew that where such a sizeable blaze existed, there was also likely to be bodies.

And they would eat well.

Liath Luachra travelled south at a slow trot, keeping to the trail for it was impractical to make rapid headway through the forest on either side. Feeling exposed on the open track, she took the precaution of stopping every twenty paces or so to cock her head, listen and scan the trail ahead. Where possible, she also kept to the more solid ground at the treeline to limit the tracks she left in passing.

Although her progress was much slower than she'd have liked, it couldn't be avoided. The spring thaw had started some days earlier and over the course of her journey it was inevitable she'd encounter scouts from Rógallach Mór coming the other way. To achieve the goal she'd set herself, it was important they didn't see her and, to avoid them, she was willing to compromise on speed.

It took her a while to get back into a rhythm and develop a comfortable breathing pattern. Her extended convalescence at Gort Na Meala and the lack of rigorous exercise meant her leg muscles had grown soft and the capacity of her lungs had contracted. In the past, she could have run comfortably for the better part of the day without stopping. Now she was obliged to stop regularly, as much to relieve the strain on her legs as to catch her breath.

Despite the regular pauses, by late morning she was struggling, falling back on anger and the desire for vengeance to keep herself moving. There, at least, she had a joint focus in Rólgallach Mór for thinking of the burly *Éblána* leader generated an intense rage that helped to propel her forwards. *Rí* of the *Éblána*, foul taint in the milk. Through his obsession with planting his *slat* in an unwilling woman, he'd extinguished the only chance of a life Liath Luachra ever had. Even worse, the stain of his actions had erased any hope for what might have been and now she had nothing but hatred and her sword and short-lived potential for both.

In the early afternoon her caution was finally rewarded when she heard the distant sound of running feet. Without thinking, she slid into the forest three trees deep and crouched low beside one of the moss-coated oaks. There, she pressed against the trunk, knowing that she'd be indistinguishable from the shadows provided she did not move.

The pounding of feet – a single runner – was almost on her by the time she'd taken her position and she just had time to catch sight of him racing north along the track, vapour from his mouth streaming in the frigid air behind him. A youth with no more than eighteen or nineteen years on him, as he flitted in and out of sight between the trees, she could make out his war paint, the axe grasped in his right hand and the quiver of javelins strapped to his back. Someone prepared for battle then.

The sound of the runner faded into the distance but Liath Luachra remained in hiding for she doubted any warrior would run so openly through enemy territory without support. Sure enough, within moments, the heavy tread of feet once again reached her ears. Pushing close to the tree, she watched as two more warriors raced by. One, about the same age as the first runner, was bare-chested despite the cold, his torso coated with a sheen of sweat. The other, an older warrior with a forked beard, wore a fur tunic but his shaven head too was wet and shiny from exertion.

Rógallach Mór demands urgent answers of his scouts.

The Grey One waited until she was absolutely certain the men were gone, before moving out of the trees and back onto the trail. She stared after them but there was no sign, no sound of the running warriors.

They move fast.

She found herself nodding in approval at their travelling technique. It wasn't a bad way to cover ground quickly in enemy territory. In fact, it was similar to one *Na Cinéaltaí* used on occasion. Send one man on ahead to draw out any potential ambush while supporting him from the rear with additional warriors, just far enough behind not to be seen. Of course it wasn't so good for the person out front acting as bait but, no doubt, like *Na Cinéaltaí,* these men took the role in turns to make the risk more tolerable.

Removing the basket, she stuffed her cloak inside, restrapped the wicker container to her back and set off again, this time at a brisk pace. With the scouts out of the way, the chances of another encounter in such poor weather were slim and it was essential she put some distance between herself and the *Éblána* men.

Despite her fatigue, she forced herself to continue for she had a great distance to cover and she wanted to reach the *Éblána* stronghold before the returning scouts. Having travelled most of the way north, they'd be weary by the time they reached Gort Na Meala and more than likely would pass the night in the forest before venturing into the valley. When they did enter Gort Na Meala, they'd take time to examine the remains of the settlement. In essence, that gave her more than a full day's start but, given her poor level of fitness, she'd need that lead to stay ahead of them.

Maintaining a steady stride, she continued south but by late afternoon her lungs were burning, her legs trembling. She stopped to camp earlier than she'd have liked but accepted that her body needed respite. She had to rest if she was to endure the physical effort of the next few days and be prepared for a final face-to-face with Rólgallach Mór.

There was also the issue of the dark clouds clumping up to the south-east. She could already smell rain on the air and knew a heavy downpour wasn't far off. Given the cold and the prospect of hail, she'd need shelter and a fire if she was to survive the night.

She settled on a rocky hillside just off the trail as it offered the best potential for shelter. Bordered by a stand of oak trees, the cliff face was shielded from the prevailing wind and peppered with clefts that offered refuge from the rain. Good fortune remained with her for she located a suitable shelter almost immediately. Little more than a crack in the grey steep face, it penetrated the rock in a ragged V-shape for a distance of six or seven paces before terminating abruptly at a space just wide enough for her to squeeze into.

Ignoring the ache in her legs, Liath Luachra collected dry deadwood, lit a fire using old leaves and twigs from the floor of the cleft and constructed a small spit to warm the cooked beef wrapped in leaves at the bottom of her basket. While the fire built up, she watched the storm clouds lurch in like a band of arrogant *óglaigh*, the darkness closing in around her like an undeclared threat.

When the meat was ready, she chewed it without appetite. Because of the distance she had to cover, there'd be no opportunity to hunt over the following days and this would be her last fresh meat for some time.

For ever, in fact.

She pushed that thought away for there was little benefit to dwelling on death. As someone overly familiar with some of the more violent routes to the Dark Lands, she was aware that solitary journey awaited everyone. The only aspect that could be influenced to any degree was its timing and, often enough, not even that.

When she'd finished eating, she shuffled into the rear of the cleft and sat wrapped in her cloak, enjoying the warmth of the fire reflected off the walls on either side. The hail started just as she was starting to drift off, the seething hiss of it against the canopy of the oak trees briefly startling her awake. Groggy, she stared out from her shelter but could see nothing in the darkness beyond the fire. When she finally worked out what had woken her, she grunted, satisfied in the knowledge that any tracks would now be completely washed away.

Reviving the fire, she pressed back against the rock but a creeping fear of the future kept sleep at bay. Once again, she did her best not to think, to distract herself by focussing on individual tongues of flame licking the edges of the woody. That attempt proved laughably ineffectual. Trying to disregard thoughts of her own inevitable journey to the Dark Lands was like a flying bird trying to ignore a relentless headwind.

The woman warrior sighed and, looking down at her trembling hands, felt a sudden longing for the oblivion of *beacáin scammalach*.

Until she remembered how much worse that substance could make it.

Over sixty days earlier, under the influence of cloud mushroom, she'd spoken in depth with the ghost of Sean Fergus, formulating plans to save the life of the fair-haired *Éblána* woman. At the time, the vagaries of dream logic had tricked her, seduced her into believing that some of the options he'd raised were actually feasible. The resulting sensation of accomplishment, of relief, had filled her with joy, a joy that faded abruptly when she awoke in the muted light of the longhouse. There, in the stark reality of day, she'd felt the soft edge of the dream slide away and her plans lay exposed for the fantasies they truly were. There were no feasible options. Muirenn, Fíne Surehands, Rólgallach Mór and even she herself, were aligned like pieces on a *fidchell* board. There were a limited number of restricted moves available and none of them offered any hope.

That erosion of hope, so close on the footsteps of joy, had broken her for a time, plunging her into a silent and impenetrable withdrawal. Someone had apparently informed Muirenn of her odd behaviour for the fair-haired woman had visited later that morning, attempting to cheer her up with the joyous news of her pregnancy.

Initially roused by the *Éblána* woman's presence, that announcement had sent the Grey One reeling even further into dark places, plunging her so deep that no-one could touch her.

And she finally understood what she had to do.

As she listened to the hail beyond the fire, the Grey One used her tongue to work a piece of gristle loose from between her molars. Spitting it out, she replaced it with a twig, chewing grimly as she recalled the dream talk with the old warrior.

What would Sean Fergus say now?

Nothing. For Sean Fergus was gone. Like Muirenn was gone.

The Grey One pulled her cloak tighter for a chill had pierced her to the bone. She hoped that, wherever he was, the old warrior might forgive her for what she'd done. For now she had nothing, nothing but a hole in her heart and a steely determination to keep her sword arm steady for one final, bloody purpose.

***

The next morning she awoke to mist floating through the dark cluster of oak trees, the moist air chill and slick against her face. Cold and stiff from her hard bed, she struggled to get upright, stamping her feet in their fur-lined boots to warm herself.

Eager to move on, she ate a few scraps of cold meat, removed all trace of her fire and paused only long enough to drink her fill from a pool of rainwater in the hollow of a nearby rock. Throwing one last glance at her little shelter, she headed down to the trail and started running south once more.

She settled into a rhythm slowly for her leg muscles still tingled from the strain of the previous day. As her body warmed up, the sensation faded and after that it was an easy enough to lose herself in the simple task of following the trail. Towards mid-day, fatigue forced her to slow her pace but she still felt strong and no longer feared being overtaken by the returning *Éblána* scouts. At some point on the way back to their master, they'd spot her tracks and work out she was headed in the same direction but because of the rain they wouldn't know where she'd joined the trail.

She ran, slowed to a walk, stopped every now and again to rest or to eat and then ran again, repeating the pattern until early evening. That night, she set camp on a clearing at the edge of a cliff overlooking verdant forest that spread south from its base. There was no trace of rain and the wind had all but disappeared so she was happy to sit watching the sun sink behind the western hills. Later, as she roasted tubers in the embers of the fire sat, she stared up at the heavens, a dark mantle sprinkled with flickering dust mites. As a rule, she'd always preferred not to set camp in open spaces with such an unrestricted view of the night sky. There was something about the vastness of that panorama overhead that terrified her, that had always made her feel small and very vulnerable.

That night however, knowing the inevitable touch of death was but an arm's reach away, the skies no longer held any fear for her. As she sat marvelling at the beauty of the glittering stars and the occasional spark that shot across the dark backdrop, she wondered why she'd never forced herself to look at it more keenly before.

Gnawing on the last of the roasted tubers, she pulled the folds of her cloak closer about her shoulders. Over the years, she'd heard various elders claim that the glistening lights were the souls of loved ones gone to the embrace of Great Father Sky. That night, she grasped the comfort of that belief knowing that she too would soon be up in that sparkling realm with her mother and brothers, happy and eternally silent.

***

By the fourth day, Liath Luachra knew she was nearing the centre of the *Éblána* territories for she'd come across the first signs of occupation; a single footprint, an ancient symbol carved into the trunk of an elm tree, a dry dog turd. Just after mid-morning, she saw smoke from a nearby habitation. Shortly afterwards, she discovered signs of recent forest clearances and tilled fields, empty now but clearly used for arable cultivation. A little after that again, she came across a section of the trail that had been heavily trampled by cattle.

Liath Luachra slowed to a halt, taking time to catch her breath while she examined the tracks. From the number of cowpats and the extensive pugging, the trail was used on a relatively frequent basis, suggesting a large farm was located somewhere in the environs. Crouching beside one of the circular cowpats, she poked its crusted skin with her finger. It was still firm and dry. There had been no rain for two days so the cattle had to have passed earlier than that.

Rising to her feet she brushed her fingers against her leggings and expanded her area of inspection. From the tracks, she estimated a herd of twenty to thirty cattle accompanied by two or three herders. She couldn't be sure but she imagined they'd been moving the cattle to better winter grazing. There wasn't any other reason she could think of as to why they'd be out in such chilling conditions. That conclusion reminded her briefly of Fíne Surehands' comment:

In such weather, all sane men huddle close to the fire.

Which, she supposed, said much about herself.

211

She caught her first glimpse of other humans early that afternoon; two shepherds tending their flock on a hill south-west of the trail. Although they were some distance off, their elevation and the absence of trees in that particular spot gave them a rare, unimpeded view of the trail and Liath Luachra noticed how they stopped to stare when they spotted her. Heavily wrapped in fur hats and cloaks, it wasn't possible to make out their gender or their age but she saw one of them raise a hand to wave. She also thought she heard someone call out but they were simply too far away to be certain. Making no effort to return the greeting, she put her head down and kept on running.

Once she was back in the forest and out of sight, Liath Luachra slowed her pace. She was drawing close to her goal and would have to proceed more cautiously to avoid further encounters. Despite the extensive size of the *Éblána* tribe, most of its members – in this area at least – would be familiar with each other by sight. Strangers were rare and any sightings would invariably lead to investigation. With luck, the shepherds wouldn't have caught a good enough glimpse to identify her out as an outsider or if they had, they'd hold off reporting it long enough for her to achieve her goal.

Moving off the trail, she headed deeper into the forest in a south-westerly direction, using snatches of sun through the canopy to guide her progress. After a time, she felt the gradient of the land increase perceptibly and a break in the trees confirmed that she was nearing the western hill range where she'd first entered *Éblána* territory. As she recalled the day she'd first crested those hills and looked out at the eastern sea, the memory felt oddly dislocated, as though it had all happened many, many years ago.

Hampered by the increasing steepness of the terrain and density of the trees, Liath Luachra was obliged to slow her pace further but now, no longer pressed to keep ahead of the *Éblána* scouts, this didn't bother her. She continued south-west with quiet determination, clambering up the arduous slopes, working a route through the trees, and emerging onto the bare crest of a hill overlooking a shallow valley. There, finally, at the far end of the valley, she spotted her destination. Dún Mór! *Caiseal* of the *Éblána.*

Although the stronghold was still some distance away, the Grey One instinctively dropped to her belly and stared in fascination. Even from that far viewpoint, Dún Mór was an intimidating edifice. From conversations at Gort Na Meala she'd understood it to be a formidable fortification but the scale of the structure had still managed to take her by surprise.

Situated on a low hill, the stronghold overlooked a number of hut clusters and cultivated fields that stretched down the length of the valley towards her. Its dominant feature, the enormous, circular drystone wall that encircled the summit, appeared to be accessible only through a rectangular entranceway on its eastern side.

The ascent from the foot of the hill was gradual but the path looked to have been overlaid with wide flagstones and bordered on each side with a row of standing stones. This impressive access route continued towards the top of the hill but ended abruptly about forty paces from the entranceway.

The Grey One ripped a piece of grass from the nearest tussock and chewed on it while she reflected. An age-old structure created by the Ancient Ones, Dún Mór had supposedly been standing there long before the *Éblána* had even taken possession of the land. Since then, the tribe had predominantly used it as a place for assembly, for celebrations and festivals or as a refuge in times of battle. According to Fíne Surehands, the tribe's dominance amongst its neighbours meant that the latter hadn't actually happened for at least two generations. Fíne Surehands had also told her the *caiseal* wasn't generally inhabited on a permanent basis, most *Éblána* members preferring to live on agricultural land where food could be grown, or cattle raised more effectively. In recent years however, Rógallach Mór and his immediate supporters had gone against tradition by taking it over for use as his personal seat of power.

Given the size of the fortress and the number of farms below it, the Grey One wasn't surprised to see so many people within the valley, at least thirty men, women and children working the fields or managing cattle. She also noted smoke from five separate fires, one of them situated up at the fortress.

The number of warriors however, was something of a concern. By the stronghold entrance, she counted at least five men armed with spears and a further two were situated at the point where the stone pillars and the path to the fortress terminated. Two or three more figures were visible on the ramparts of the stronghold itself.

Staring at the intimidating structure and the great array of warriors, Liath Luachra felt her determination waver. When she'd departed Gort Na Meala, her goal had been simple and sufficiently compelling to stay the course of her journey. Now, confronted by the true extent of the obstacles and forces before her, she felt that earlier sense of purpose eroded by fear and uncertainty.

You could just go. Walk away. Let these Éblána destroy themselves.

Theoretically, this was true but, in reality it was all too late for that. There was nowhere she could go now except Luachair. The only world she'd ever felt part of was dead and she had little else to look forward to but an existence of hardship, fear and loneliness until that too drew to its miserable conclusion. Such a future was not one worth living.

Exhaling deeply, she pulled back from the lip of the hill and got to her feet. There was work to be done.

For the remainder of the afternoon, the Grey One busied herself seeking a shelter. She had to remain in the forest undetected for one, possibly two, days, however long it took the *Éblána* scouts to return from Gort Na Meala. Because of her proximity to the *caiseal*, she couldn't risk a fire which meant any refuge would need to be sufficiently snug and sheltered for her to retain her body heat at night.

After a long period of searching, she found a potential site further west into the forest, a patch of exposed earth on the side of small mound where a recent storm had uprooted an ancient tree. A gigantic but long-withered oak, it had tumbled to the foot of the mound, wrenching out a substantial section of its root system in the process. A number of cavities remained among the remnants of those enormous roots, some of them almost big enough for her to crawl into.

After examining them closely, she selected one and, using her knife, expanded it further until she could comfortably fit inside. As twilight fell, she hurriedly gathered moss, leaves and red fern, tossing them into the hole to create a thick layer into which she could burrow during the night. Finally, as darkness fell, she cut some leafy branches from a nearby holly tree and, dragging it to the hole, backed inside and pulled it in behind to act as a rudimentary plug.

Burying deep into the nest she'd created, she lay still as the forest grew quiet, listening to the occasional scurry of small animals in the underbrush or the hoot of a passing owl. Within the burrow the smell of freshly dug earth was mitigated by the woody scent of dried leaves and crushed fern and – surprisingly – the scent of burning pine from some far distant fire briefly wafted in by the breeze.

Stay alive two more nights, she told herself. Two more nights and it won't matter anymore.

***

It was late morning on the second day that she saw the scouts return from Gort Na Meala. Lying on her belly at the vantage point overlooking the valley, she recognised them straight away; the two youthful warriors and the bald man with the forked beard. All three were walking, practically staggering with fatigue after so many days traversing the wilds at speed.

She pulled a knot of crinkled leaves from her hair as she watched them stumble up the trail from the north, headed straight up the valley towards the *caiseal*. To her surprise, instead of continuing along the trail, all three suddenly veered off the track and turned east instead, making for a cluster of stone-walled huts to the side of the valley.

Announcing their return to their families?

She watched the trio approach the huts, once again surprised when didn't split up to go their separate ways but entered through the door of the largest structure.

Intrigued, Liath Luachra frowned and irritably tapped the ground with the sharp twig she'd been using to clean her teeth. It annoyed her when she didn't understand people's intentions or behaviours but unable to work it out, she eventually let the niggling puzzle go and thought no more about it. The return of the scouts would hardly go unnoticed and it was only a matter of time before news of Gort Na Meala travelled up to the *caiseal* to reach Rólgallach Mór's ears.

She remained on the hill top for a time to see if the scouts would reappear, studying the people working in the fields and counting the fires while she was waiting. That morning, smoke from only four fires was visible although at one point a fifth sputtered briefly to life on the northern ridge of the valley. This didn't last long however and quickly died out again.

Shortly before noon, the scouts re-emerged from the stone hut. This time they did split up and part in different directions although none of the three headed up to the *caiseal*.

It's nearly time.

She started shivering then and even cried for a time before she managed to quell the fear and get to her feet. Moving down to the foot of the hill, she located the small spring that she'd discovered the previous day. There, she stripped and washed the dirt and leaves from her hair, the grime and sweat from her face and body. Her appearance was of little importance to her but for this final battle, the simple cleansing ritual helped her to calm herself and muster the strength she needed to continue.

She dressed before her body had fully dried and returned to the summit of the hill. Chewing on the last of the roasted tubers, she sat honing the blade of *Gléas Gan Ainm* with a whet stone one last time. Testing the finish with the edge of her finger, she laid the sword aside and pulled the short-bladed knife from its sheath, regarding it for a moment with silent fondness. The blade of the knife was short but extremely sharp, the pommel overlaid with strips of red leather stretched about the hilt, the guard engraved with a design composed of interlinking straight lines. This particular weapon she'd named *Bás gan Trua* – Death without Mercy – and it had been the sole object in her possession before joining *Na Cineáltaí*. She'd originally obtained the weapon from the son of the man who'd led the *díberg* attack at Luachair, grasping it when he'd carelessly laid it aside and then subsequently using it to slice his throat. Slipping the weapon back into its sheath, she patted it. Soon, if all went well, the blade would be put to equally good use.

***

216

The Dún Mór watchmen evidently had keen eyesight for by the time she'd entered the valley and followed the trail to the base of the hill, three of them had already descended and stood there awaiting her. Making her way towards them, she was struck by the unusual nonchalance of their stance, the relaxed manner in which they held their weapons, as though they'd been expecting her or didn't consider her a threat.

Two of the warriors – both young men– regarded her with open curiosity and a certain degree of sexual interest. She ignored them as she focussed her attention on the third man standing in front of them, clearly their superior. A balding, middle-aged individual, he had a patchy beard that exposed several sores along his chin and upper lip. Despite his untidy leather tunic and torn cloak, the sheathed sword and dagger at his belt showed evidence of scrupulous care.

As she drew to a halt before them, Liath Luachra felt the familiar pre-battle queasiness sour her stomach and struggled against her natural urge to attack. Unaware of this internal conflict, the bearded man looked her up and down in an almost surly manner. 'You're late!' he said.

Thrown by the curt and peculiar greeting, the woman warrior stiffened although her impassive features concealed her consternation. She regarded him coldly. 'I am named Liath Luachra. I come to sp-'

'I know who you are,' the bald warrior interrupted. His lip curled up and he pressed both hands against the pommel of his sword, leaning his weight against it and using the leverage to support himself. 'I've heard the song and, besides, I've seen you before.'

Song?

The woman warrior studied the wind-burned features with its blotchy beard more closely and realised he had seen her before. He was one of the men who'd accompanied Rógallach Mór during their initial encounter at *Cloch a' Bhod.*

'Come on,' the warrior snapped impatiently. 'The others are already here.'

The others?

217

Before she had a chance to ask what he meant, the warrior had spun on his heel and started up the path towards the stronghold. Concealing her confusion, Liath Luachra hurried after him, casting a quick glance at the two younger men as she walked by. Both regarded her but neither said, or did, anything to clarify the situation.

Although the gentle incline meant the walk up to the fortress was an undemanding one, the odd behaviour of the *Éblána* warriors troubled her. She'd intentionally timed her arrival to the return of the scouts from Gort Na Meala, counting on Rólgallach Mór's curiosity being sufficiently whetted by the reports of what they'd seen to allow her close enough to strike. By now, the *Éblána* warriors should have been hurrying her into their leader's presence but, instead, she'd been greeted with bizzare references to a song and the kind of welcome normally reserved for an unwelcome guest.

She was still pondering the situation as they approached the entrance to the *caiseal*, a rectangular passage with a pair of large wooden doors folded back flush against the inner walls. Any further view of the interior was hindered by the group of chatting warriors clustered in front of it.

Her reluctant escort drew to a halt and Liath Luachra stopped alongside him, something that bizarrely seemed to offend him even further. 'In there,' he scowled. 'I have better things to do.'

With this, he turned sharply and started back down the trail.

Liath Luachra stared after the departing figure with some disquiet then glanced nervously at the warriors barring the entrance, now lapsed into silence and staring directly at her. Wary but resolute, she pushed her way through the little group and entered the fortress.

Although the passage was only two paces in width, the thickness of the wall meant it took the Grey One eight full paces to reach the *lis*, the circular interior of the *caiseal*. Before stepping into the open courtyard, she paused in the shadow at the end of the passage, taking time to inspect it more closely. The *lis* was larger than she'd anticipated, dominated at its centre by an impressively wide, stone-walled building with a straw roof flanked by two wicker huts to either side. A fire blazed in a deep fire-pit several paces in front of the stone-walled building, equidistant to the two huts. A steaming metal cauldron hung above it, dangling from the trestle of a solid wooden frame by an iron chain.

The woman warrior regarded the stone-walled building with a certain measure of wariness, one hand anxiously fingering the pommel of *Gléas Gan Ainm*. Was Rógallach Mór in the larger building? If so, why were there no guards, no-one to escort her in?

Only one way you'll ever know.

Stepping forward, she started across the gravel-lined surface of the *lis,* her feet producing a soft crunch on the compressed pebbles. As she walked, her gaze turned up to the impressive inner walls where three sets of ramparts ascended above each other to create a series of levelled terraces. These were accessed by a flight of steps on either side of the passage and an intricate series of staggered, interconnecting stone stairways. On the upper rampart directly above the entrance to the *caiseal,* two warriors were chatting quietly beside a rack of javelins and spears.

Arriving at the narrow entrance to the building, she pushed the heavy fur flap aside and entered an unexpectedly-spacious and circular room. Despite the limited illumination from a number of tallow-oil lamps set into the walls, she was able to make out stools and benches arranged in a rough circle to align with the shape of the room. No-one else was present.

Surprised and unsettled in equal measure, she gnawed nervously at her lower lip before turning back to the entrance and easing the flap aside. The *lis* remained empty but she caught a snatch of conversation that seemed to originate from somewhere to the rear of the building.

She was still attempting to decide on her next course of action when a tall man in a hooded black cloak ambled around from the left. Blinkered by his hood, he didn't notice her through the crack in the flap but continued onwards to the fire pit where he paused to serve himself to a bowl of the cauldron's steaming contents. Liath Luachra studied him closely. The figure didn't have Rógallach Mór's distinctive height or build but there was something decidedly familiar about his bearing.

Determined to take matters in hand, she stepped through the opening and into the *lis.* Hearing the crunch of her feet on the gravelled

219

surface, the dark-cloaked figure glanced back over his shoulder and stiffened. The bowl fell from his hands, landing with a clatter on the stones.

'Grey One!'

Bressal!

Liath Luachra stared open-mouthed at the *Uí Loinge* man, her chest pounding painfully as though she'd received a blow to the heart. The expression of utter astonishment on Bressal's face would have been comical had it not so perfectly mirrored her own.

'What are you doing here? We'd thought you dead an-' Bressal stopped and his eyes moved up to stare at her forehead. 'You have hair.'

Confused, Liath Luachra reverted to her habitual silence, unconsciously raising a hand to run her fingers through the short, black locks. She stared back at the *Uí Loinge* man. It seemed an odd thing to say and she wasn't sure how to respond.

'You look … fair, Grey One.' His voice was soft. 'Very fair.'

This time, the woman warrior shuffled uneasily, awkwardly hitching her sword belt. Bressal held both hands wide, palms turned out. 'By the Great Father's balls, what are you doing here?' he exclaimed again.

Liath Luachra's stomach cramped with sudden nausea. She'd come to Dún Mór to die, to kill Rógallach Mór and as many of his men as she could slaughter before they finally cut her down. Now, with Bressal standing so devastatingly unexpected before her, on top of the odd behaviour of the *Éblána* warriors, she could feel her careful plans scatter like apple petals in a violent spring storm. 'I come to speak with Rógallach Mór,' she said at last, articulating each word carefully, painstakingly slowly, fearful that he'd notice the catch in her voice. 'On the task assigned us.'

The *Uí Loinge* man rubbed his forehead with his hands. Clearly he was still struggling from the shock of seeing her for otherwise he'd almost certainly have detected her clumsy attempt at artifice. 'You … You succeeded?'

'Yes. I carry his blood-flecked cloak in my pack.'

Her answer seemed to jolt Bressal from his stupefaction for the stunned glaze left his eyes and he startled her with a bark of laughter.

'You succeeded!' This time he laughed long and hard and the echo of his mirth rang off the face of the surrounding wall. Flustered, Liath Luachra took an involuntary step backwards and, glancing up at the ramparts, saw the guards staring down at them, drawn by the unexpected sound of merriment.

'You succeeded?' He laughed again, shook his head. 'The task I set you is truly complete?'

She nodded, eyes darting around the *lis*, wondering what she was missing.

'And the others?'

'No longer a concern for the *rí* of the *Éblána*.'

With that, the *Uí Loinge* man's animated air seemed to deflate and he nodded slowly in sober approval. 'Good. Good, Grey One. I should never have doubted your ability. But...' An odd look appeared in his eyes, a kind of feral wariness. 'All this time. Where have you been?'

The Grey One paused but then lifted her tunic to reveal the thick triangular scar on her left side. The healed wound was puffy and wormlike at the point of entry and an ugly furrow ran along the surface of the skin where the slash had followed through. Bressal sucked air in through his teeth. 'That looks a cruel wound.'

Liath Luachra had nothing to say to that but it hardly mattered for Bressal recovered his composure, reverting back to that expansive heartiness she knew so well. 'Come!' he said, grabbing her arm. 'The others should learn of your return.'

The warrior woman reluctantly allowed herself to be led around the stone-walled building to the far side of the *lis* where a company of men were sprawled in a small patch of winter sunshine, eating from bowls of stew, talking amongst themselves or sharpening the blades of their weapons. She stood before them, stiff and apprehensive. Bressal, it seemed, had come to Dún Mór with a *fian* of eight men.

Three of the *fénnid* she recognised instantly; her old comrades Senach, Biotóg and even Murchú who, apparently, had decided not to remain with his wife after all. Their reactions on seeing her almost perfectly epitomised their individual personalities: Senach stared at her blankly, struggling to recognise her with longer hair; Biotóg looked at her in his usual passionless, creepy manner. Murchú was the only one who seemed genuinely pleased at her reappearance. Rising from the flat stone where he'd been seated, he approached to slap her awkwardly on the shoulder. 'It's good to see you breathe the sweet air of life, Grey One,' he said simply.

The five other *fénnid*, she didn't know. Three of them were stragglybearded youths whose names she'd forgotten within moments of being introduced. The two older men however, she considered with greater attention. Both had at least thirty years on them and stood with that unmistakable air of competency she always associated with experienced fighters. One, a bearded man by the name of Giobog, had several battle scars that ran down once side of his face and cleaved white gaps through a thick, black beard.

As he faced his men, Bressal became caught up in the spirit of the moment and clapped an arm about the Grey One, something he'd never have dared in the past.

'Comrades!' he declared cheerfully. 'This is your *rígfénnid*, Liath Luachra, the fearsome woman warrior of Luachair! She's the warrior we had believed lost but who now returns from the dead, her task complete.'

He beamed. The *fian* members stared at her. Nobody seemed to know exactly how they were meant to react. Up on the terraces, the two guards continued to look down with interest.

'And she has forestalled our task.'

He caught the quizzical glance she cast him at that and guffawed, delighted to have caught her by surprise once more. 'Of course,' he continued, 'the Grey One doesn't know that yet! She's unaware of Rógallach Mór's call for our service, unaware of the task to revenge a *díberg* attack on a settlement of *Éblána* kin.'

He glanced up at the ramparts to check that the warriors were listening. 'But, now ...' His voice momentarily trailed off before booming back again at full volume. 'But, now it seems the Grey One has beaten us to the post for she's already dealt with the raiders of her own volition. Our victory has already been achieved!' He raised one hand in the air and bellowed. '*Na Cinéaltaí, abú!*'

222

'*Abú!*' the *fénnid* echoed, the ferocity and volume of their response taking the woman warrior by surprise. Clearly this rousing battle cry had been introduced since her departure.

As the roar faded, Bressal abruptly dismissed the men with a curt wave of his hand and drew closer to the woman warrior. 'Come,' he told her. 'Let us share words apart.'

Once again, Liath Luachra found herself trailing in the *Uí Loinge* man's wake, this time skirting the opposite side of the stone-walled building to the smaller wicker hut. Bressal proceeded inside and as Liath Luachra followed him, he took a seat on a stool beside the fire-pit and added firewood to the dwindling flames.

Wordlessly, the woman warrior eased herself onto some wicker mats directly across from him and mentally prepared herself for the conversation ahead. If he was true to form, Bressal would lead her a circuitous route of inquiry and she'd have to take care where she tread to avoid revealing the true reason for her presence at the fortress.

Sitting cross-legged, she looked up at the cocky *Uí Loinge* man, struck by the peculiarity of the situation. Despite the extraordinary events that had taken place since she'd last seen Bressal and the shock of finding him in the *Éblána* stronghold, in some respects it felt as though they'd never been separated. Here she was, once again, sitting at his feet, his compliant creature, and although that surprised and disturbed her, she was even more surprised by the comforting sense of familiarity, the misplaced wistfulness for happier times the situation inspired.

Oblivious to the woman warrior's reflections, Bressal grinned like a buck goat in a pen full of nannies. But then, he had every reason to. He'd achieved the success he desired in the *rí* of the *Éblána's* service, he had his *rígfénnid* back and his 'task' with the so called *díberg* had been resolved without need for further effort or outlay. With a broad smile, the *Uí Loinge* man gestured around the hut to the baskets of food and supplies, the two double sleeping platforms. 'Rógallach Mór has offered the comfort of his *conradh's* – his champion's – lodging for myself and any I choose to share with. It is a restful place to pass the night, is it not?'

His eyes lingered on the sleeping platform a little too long before returning to the Grey One. Liath Luachra said nothing but felt that earlier wistfulness wither away. Her eyes dropped as the muscles of her face rearranged themselves, her features taking on their usual passive expression. She retreated into subdued silence. She'd always found it best to restrict any conversation with Bressal to a minimum. Any engagement with her only ever seemed to encourage him further.

Fortunately, on this occasion, Bressal seemed preoccupied with more practical matters.

'Having you back at my side is a honeyed draught on a coarse throat, Grey One. More so with the news of your success.' He exhaled heavily and rubbed his palms together. 'In truth I'd received harsh words from Rógallach Mór at the absence of any account from you or the man he'd sent with you. The *rí* of the *Éblána* was unhappy for he feared treachery or failure and held me to account for both.' Bressal released an affected sigh and shook his head dolefully as though wounded by the accusation.

'To assuage his anger, I was obliged to raise a fresh *fian* and make my way here to resolve that 'failure' under the pretext of a service to deal with a fictitious *díberg*.'

'Where is Rógallach Mór now?' The Grey One asked the question hesitantly, unwilling to encourage him but she needed to know.

'He travels here from the south-west.'

'He is not here?'

This time Bressal did not miss it, the stifled exclamation on her breath. His left eyebrow curled up in curiosity even as the Grey One belatedly clamped down on her frustration. The *Éblána* leader's absence was a devastating setback, particularly as she knew she couldn't continue to maintain her deceit with someone of Bressal's perspicacity.

The *Uí Loinge* man continued to study her, biding his time to see what else she might inadvertently reveal but he continued the conversation as though he'd noticed nothing amiss. 'Yes. His man Fingin – that sharp-faced dog with the pox-ridden beard – tells me his leader has been quelling disquiet from a minor sub-tribe somewhere to the south. They anticipate his return on the morrow.' His eyes suddenly grew more serious. 'So tell me,' he said with deliberate emphasis. 'Tell me everything that happened.'

Liath Luachra obediently summarised the events following her separation from Bressal and the *fian* on the *Uí Bairrche - Uí Loinge* trade route, their adventures traversing the Great Wild and the subsequent meeting with Rógallach Mór. After that, she briefly described the journey north, the surveillance of Gort Na Meala and Sean Fergus' death on the ridge overlooking the valley.

The *Uí Loinge* man rubbed his chin at that. 'I knew he was dying,' he said simply. 'More's the pity for he was a useful fighter in his day. 'Did you bury him with his sword?'

'Yes.'

He nodded in approval. 'Good. But enough of Sean Fergus.' He dismissed all memory of his old comrade with a fatalistic shrug. 'What happened next?'

She hesitated briefly to gather her thoughts then continued the story of her encounter with Muirenn, the battle on the beach and her subsequent slaying of the *fénnid* and Flannán An Scian. The death of the two *fian* members didn't seem to overly upset the *Uí Loinge* man but he was clearly disturbed by the news of Flannán's death. 'Why?' he demanded, his voice stern. 'Why did you kill him?'

'His intent was treacherous. He had it in mind to kill me and make claim on Barra ua *Éblána* for himself. With the willing aid of Canann and Conall Cacach,' she added.

'But why?'

Liath Luachra shook her head helplessly, although from the expression in Bressal's eyes she knew he'd insist on an answer. 'I cannot say. Perhaps Rógallach Mór's dog was eager for a pat from his master. As for Canann and Conall Cacach …' She shook her head. 'Those two would have gone with the emptiest of promises.'

Bressal spat into the fire. 'I should have gutted those black pigs at the close of the last season.' He fumed silently for several moments then leaned forward to address the woman warrior in a voice that was menacingly soft. 'You will not speak of this. Ever. Do you understand? This wretched tale lies in a quiet grave between you and I. No-one else must know.' He waited for her to confirm with a sharp dip of her head before sitting up straight again. 'And Gort Na Meala?'

The Grey One paused. 'A smoking ruin.'

'You achieved this through your own endeavours?' Bressal looked unconvinced. 'How?'

The woman warrior shifted her weight uncomfortably. 'The Gort Na Meala people found me wounded. They made me their prisoner.' She cleared her throat, swallowing the lump of cold phlegm that had formed there. 'Fíne Surehands – the Gort Na Meala battle leader – sought information and deceived me to reveal some of what I knew. My injuries were such that I couldn't leave the settlement but I was permitted to help with the preparation of food. Several days ago there was …' Again, the woman warrior paused. 'There was a feast … to celebrate the impregnation of Fíne Surehands' daughter by Barra ua Éblána. While making the stew for the celebrations, I added *beacáin scammalach* … And …' Her voice caught and she struggled to speak.

His earlier suspicions allayed, Bressal misinterpreted her sudden disarray for fatigue. 'Hold,' he said, raising one hand. Rising from the stool, he moved to retrieve a pair of wicker baskets lying on the nearest sleeping platform and carried both back to the fire. Placing one on the floor, he reached into the other to withdraw a leather waterskin, pulled the stopper loose with his teeth and spat it towards the entrance. Taking a deep *sliog*, he grunted, coughed and passed it to her. 'I have allowed you no respite from the ordeal of your journey here, Grey One. Take this! *Uisce beatha* will smooth the lumps on your tongue.'

Liath Luachra raised the skin to her own lips, took a great swig and swallowed it in a single gulp. Bressal watched silently as she coughed and spluttered, finally able to breathe once more. 'Continue, now,' he said.

The woman warrior wiped tears from her eyes. 'The Gort Na Meala people ate well of the stew and it took effect soon after the feast. Some managed to retire to their beds but others lost all sense and fell to the ground in a stupor. I killed them while they lay defenceless. I killed them all.' Her voice was hollow, her eyes fixed firmly on the flames of the fire.

Bressal grunted. 'An endeavour well served. You fulfilled the task you were set.'

The Grey One took a fresh *sliog* of *uisce beatha*. Bressal's eyes meanwhile, had taken on a faraway look, a sure sign he was scheming again.

'Your efforts will not go unrewarded, Grey One. And you have earned your name as *rígfénnid*.'

'My name,' she echoed, her voice thick with bitterness.

Distracted by whatever scheme absorbed him, the *Uí Loinge* man missed that rare expression of regret. 'When you departed for *Éblána* lands,' he told her, 'I returned to Briga and set our bard to composing a song for the new *rígfénnid* of *Na Cinéaltaí*. It was a good song, a song of the fearsome and beautiful woman warrior, Liath Luachra. It was sung about campfires much farther afield than I'd ever expected but it brought new recruits and all are now familiar with your name.'

He stretched across to take the skin from her unresisting hand. Placing it on the ground alongside him, he reached into the second basket and withdrew a large bundle wrapped in rough canvas and tied up with flax fibre.

'And then there is this. A gift to celebrate your new title.'

Taken aback, she wordlessly accepted the bundle, considering it in surprise as she weighed it in her hands for it was unexpectedly heavy.

'Open it,' Bressal instructed.

Unknotting the fibre, she peeled the canvas wrapping back to reveal an item of clothing, some kind of harness fashioned from red leather. Taking it in her hands, she lifted it up to examine it more closely. Whatever its purpose, it was finely made, the leather of good quality and the stitching skilfully done. She looked dully at Bressal.

'It's a battle harness, Grey One. Created specifically for you. I had thought you dead, so brought it here in the hope of mollifying Rógallach Mór by offering it as a gift to his son' He paused. 'But now that you're safely returned ...' His eyes dropped to her waist. 'Had you been wearing it at Gort Na Meala that harness might have turned the blade, deflected the cut that pierced your side.'

Liath Luachra looked at it dubiously. The harness looked to expose more skin than it protected.

'Put it on, Grey One. This is your reward.'

'And the land?' she asked.

'The land?' He looked at her blankly.

'The *Éblána* land you promised.'

'Ah, that land. Yes, yes. We'll discuss that later. Just put on the harness.'

The Grey One regarded him, her eyes dark and completely unreadable.

'Now,' he pressed.

The woman warrior did not move. Loathe to pander to the *Uí Loinge* man's request, she also knew she couldn't afford to alienate him just yet. In an odd way, it seemed as though Bressal too had instinctively sensed this quandary.

'You return more ripened than when you left, Grey One.'

With great misgiving, Liath Luachra got to her feet. Undoing her sword belt, she let it drop to the floor and turning away, pulled her leather tunic off over her head. Stiff and inflexible, the harness was difficult to get into but she finally managed to fit it on.

Turning back to face Bressal, she found him standing upright, observing her with undisguised hunger. The sharpness of his gaze cut a trail along her stomach then up to her chest. He started forward, prompting her to take an involuntary step back but then her eyes darkened and her jaw set firm. As her hands clenched into fists, Bressal paused in mid-step, clearly mindful of the last time he'd attempted to push himself on her. They considered each other in silence for several heartbeats then the *Uí Loinge* man's features took on a sly expression. 'I know why they call you the Grey One,' he said.

Liath Luachra returned his gaze bluntly, exhibiting no reaction to his words.

'While you were away, a man came to Briga with the song of Liath Luachra on his lips. Curiosity brought him seeking the truth behind the words'. He chuckled softly. 'This man now leads a sub-tribe of the *Uí*

Cailbhe far to the south of Briga but some years before he was their leader, he led a *díberg*, a *díberg* that raided Luachair'.

Liath Luachra said nothing but continued to regard him, her eyes grey and cold, her face like stone.

'That *Uí Cailbhe* man told me of the raid, of your abduction and how you escaped more than three years ago by killing his son.' Bressal paused and tight smile stretched across his face. 'He also told me how his son considered you his favourite, how he kept you in a soft stone cave where the grey clay stained your skin.' He chuckled suddenly. 'It seems that whenever he wanted something to fuck, he'd call out, "Bring me the Grey One".'

Liath Luachra's face displayed all the passion of granite although her eyes bored into those of the *Uí Loinge* man. Unsettled by the coldness of that regard, Bressal took a tentative step forward. 'I tell you this,' he continued, 'for I want you to know, I am not like those men. I do not take that which is not freely given. If anything, the converse is true for there's much I have to offer.'

He took another careful step forward, as though testing to see how she'd respond. When she didn't react, he reached one hand out and placed it on her right shoulder, his fingers caressing the smooth skin stretched across the clavicle.

'You know there's much I admire in you, much I would like to reward should that admiration be returned. You bear the title of *rígfénnid* as a result of my favour but there could be more, so much more.'

He reached out his second hand, placed it on her left shoulder and stared intently into her eyes, oblivious to the rigidity of her frame. 'It is now time to make that decision, to ask yourself what you truly want of the future.'

As he spoke, the Grey One felt him apply pressure to her shoulders, gently pushing her down until her head was level with his groin. The *Uí Loinge* man's *slat* was straining against the material of his leggings like an oversized tent pole.

'Do you remain with the *fian* and accept my favour or do you go your own way. Just remember th- '

'Bressal!'

The muffled shout and the sudden thump against the wall of the hut took them both by surprise but Bressal, in particular, got such a shock, he jolted back in alarm. He glanced towards the entranceway, his face a mask of rage. Liath Luachra glanced down at her sword belt where her fingers were wrapped around the hilt of *Bás gan Trua*.

'Bressal! It's Rógallach Mór.' She recognised the voice now. It was Senach. 'He's back. The *rí* of the *Éblána* has returned.'

Bressal looked momentarily stunned by the announcement but he was already reaching for his black cloak. '*Ar aghaidh linn!*' He snapped at the woman warrior. Let's go! 'This is a discussion to be completed later'. He paused to hold her eyes. 'Grey One.'

Chapter Eleven

Senach was scratching his arse when they stepped outside, scraping his fingernails through filthy woollen leggings as he blinked up at liquid sunlight dripping over the lip of the northern rampart.

'Senach!' Bressal demanded. 'What *ráméis* – nonsense – are you spouting, *a bhreall*? Rólgallach Mór's not due until tomorrow.' Interrupted at a moment of some personal consequence, the *Uí Loinge* man was in no mood for absurdities.

Stung by the insult, the stocky warrior scrubbed his forehead with the knuckles of both hands. 'It's not my fault. All I know is what that bearded cock Fingin told me. He says the *rí* of the *Éblána*'s making his way here.'

The Grey One stood quietly to one side, completely ignored as the two men bickered over the garbled content of Fingin's message. This was good for, at that moment, reeling from the realisation of how close she'd come to stabbing Bressal, she was no more capable of holding a conversation than she was of climbing the walls of the *caiseal* and flying from its ramparts.

'Grey One. Grey One. Are you with us?'

Startled, she looked up to find Bressal regarding her, a smouldering anger in his eyes. To placate him, she unthinkingly gave a sharp nod of her head but the *Uí Loinge* leader continued to study her closely. 'You are changed, Grey One.' He scratched at a scab on the end of his chin, peeling the flaky skin off and tossing it aside. 'Somehow different. I cannot put a finger on it.'

'I have more hair,' she suggested with an affected lightness that took even her by surprise. 'More scars.'

That uncharacteristic frivolity seemed to trouble him even further for she caught a flash of disquiet in his eyes. 'Perhaps. But for now I need you at your clearest. I need you alert, yes?'

She nodded again, this time with increased emphasis.

Bressal gave her another apprehensive look but, pressed by matters of greater urgency, discarded his concerns as he turned back to Senach. 'So did this Fingin tell you what Rógallach Mór wished to discuss?'

The lean, dark-haired warrior shook his head. 'Only that he's aware of the Grey One's success and keen to trade words with you.'

Bressal looked puzzled. 'How does he know of the Grey One's success if he's been down south all this time?'

Because he hasn't been down south. He's been concealed here. And his scouts have returned to tell him what they saw.

Somehow, through some instinctive flash of insight, she knew she had the truth of it for within that context everything suddenly made greater sense; the strange timing of Rógallach Mór's return, the scouts peculiar detour to the stone huts on their return. From everything she now knew of the *Éblána rí*, she had no doubts as to his capacity to instigate such devious manipulations. It was, in fact, quite possible that she'd inadvertently stumbled into a plan to avenge himself on Bressal for the apparent lack of success at Gort Na Meala.

Despite her suspicions, Liath Luachra did not voice them for to do so had the potential of disrupting her own goal, recharged with fresh purpose now that the *Éblána* leader was back in the environs. Bressal however, had ample suspicions of his own for he turned to Liath Luachra with a wary look upon his face. 'Could it be, that Flannán An Scian's treachery was prompted by purposes of his own?' He stroked the stubble of his jaw in reflection. 'Or did he but follow the directive of his master? What are your thoughts on this matter, Grey One?'

'I don't know.'

'Then think it through, *mo láireog léith*! I did not ask if you knew. I asked what you thought.'

The warrior woman felt herself bristle at his use of the despised diminutive and was obliged to turn her eyes down to disguise her anger. 'I think Flannán was a loyal man,' she answered, keeping her voice low enough to stifle the anger it contained.

'So it's possible,' the *Uí Loinge* man mused aloud, 'that Rógallach Mór never intended to hold to his agreement, that he ...' He scowled then, struck by some contradicting line of reasoning. 'And yet, the *rí* of the

232

Éblána is a long-time ally of the *Uí Loinge*. And he's displayed great generosity, even offering us the comfort of his own residence.'

'It may not be generosity that had us placed here,' suggested Senach.

Bressal looked at the warrior in surprise. Counsel from Senach – not a man known for his depth of insight – was a rarity indeed. He cocked one curious eyebrow. 'What do you mean?'

Senach jerked his head to indicate the terraced wall. 'Walls can keep you in just as surely as they keep you out. Two guards on the ramparts, five at the gate. We've ventured outside in one or twos but never pressed the issue of departure as a larger body.'

The *Uí Loinge* man chewed on that indubitable morsel of fact. 'It's true,' he admitted. 'On our arrival, Fingin displayed great eagerness to keep us separate from his people. Mind you, at the time it struck me as a sensible request. And you can't deny we've been well serviced with food and *Éblána* women.'

Senach gave an ambivalent shrug while Bressal followed that particular train of thought a little further. 'No,' the *Uí Loinge* leader decided at last. 'I don't doubt Rógallach Mór was unhappy with *Na Cinéaltaí* – and myself in particular – for the extended silence from Gort Na Meala. It's also possible he ordered our isolation here in the *caiseal* but I don't believe it was for treacherous reasons. No tribal leader can risk stirring such currents of distrust amongst his allies. Rógallach Mór may have wished to deride me for our perceived failure but he's too smart to risk outright confrontation. Word of any retribution would eventually leak back to our territories and the *Uí Loinge* would not fail to seek vengeance.' He paused and his lips turned down in a thoughtful frown. 'Besides, he has everything he asked for. His cousin is dead, the land's free to usurp. What more could he want?'

Liath Luachra bit her lip and said nothing.

A great shout from the wall caused all three to glance up to the rampart. The two guards standing above the entranceway were facing outwards and waving spears in the air, presumably in response to someone of note making their way up to the *caiseal*.

'Well,' said Senach. 'Looks as though we'll find out soon enough either way. Our host arrives.'

Bressal's eyes flickered uneasily towards the *Éblána* warriors at the exterior of the entrance passage. 'Best take no chances. Senach, get back to the men and have them ready themselves' He reached out to place a cautionary hand on the warrior's forearm. 'But gentle now. Move with a smile on your lips. Give the guards no cause for alarm but make sure there's no sipping of *uisce beatha* and the *fénnid* have their weapons to hand. I'll signal if there's any trouble.'

Senach dipped his head a single time then turned and sauntered away, circling out of sight around the stone-walled building. Bressal turned to the woman warrior.

'As for you, Grey One ... I want you standing behind me. Stay to my right and say or do nothing unless I direct you to. I will lead this discussion. You do not speak. Understand?'

Seething with tension in anticipation of the impeding violence, the woman warrior's body was already strung out, her muscles taut and stretched, ready to snap into action at a moment's notice. Unable to speak, she simply nodded and loosened the sword in its sheath. Standing with Bressal before the fire pit, she had a direct view through the entranceway passage and could see the sudden flurry of activity as the *Éblána* party arrived.

Pouring into the entrance, a great body of men surged through the passageway and spilled out onto the sunlit *lis*. Rógallach Mór led the way, his distinctive bulk almost a full head higher than most of his companions. Stalking towards them with a scowl on his face, he thundered to a halt with the patch-bearded Fingin on one side and the bald, fork-bearded scout on the other. The remainder of the dourfaced warriors fanned out around them in a wide semi-circle.

A tremor of excitement ran through the warrior woman and she repeatedly shifted her weight from one foot to the other to relieve the stress building up inside her. The leader of the *Éblána* was escorted by more than twelve warriors, an impossible force to overcome.

It doesn't matter. Your blade has but a single focus and you knew you were never going to survive this encounter.

Rógallach Mór glowered at them, his lips curled down in an unpleasant grimace. Despite the reported success of her endeavours at

234

Gort Na Meala, he was visibly displeased. Of course, she was the only one who knew the true reason behind that displeasure. She eyed his thick neck, fondled the hilt of her sword.

Hold back! Not yet. He's too well protected.

At first, the big *Éblána* man's attention was focussed uniquely on Bressal and he shot her little more than a fleeting glance. Some irking echo from that initial glimpse seemed to trigger a vague recollection however, for he did a swift double take to examine her more closely. The Grey One felt the scrape of those cruel, heavy-lidded eyes against her skin. Because of the longer hair and the bright red battle harness it took him a moment to recognise her but he spent several heartbeats staring at her before returning his attention to Bressal.

The *Uí Loinge* man, meanwhile, had stepped forward and lowered himself down on one knee, his head bowed in a subservient gesture.

'Rógallach Mór, *rí* of the *Éblána*,

great boar of the eastern wilds.

With hooves sharp as swords

to tusks of white-silver.'

If Rógallach Mór was impressed by the flattery, he showed little sign of it. Following tradition, he endured the praise with visible impatience until Bressal had finished and got to his feet. He gave a somewhat listless wave of acknowledgement at the *Uí Loinge* man's words before making a brief attempt at fulfilling his responsibilities as host.

'Bressal Binnbhéalach. It is pleasing to receive you as our guest at Dún Mór. You've tasted the full bounty of *Éblána* hospitality?'

'Yes, great *rí*. The *Éblána* reputation for generosity remains without equal.'

Rógallach Mór accepted the tribute without false modesty. 'Good. Then let us retire to the comfort of the meeting house. There are urgent matters to discuss.'

Without waiting for a response, he stalked past them, skirting the fire and entering the stone-walled structure. The majority of the *Éblána* warriors remained where they were but he was followed almost immediately by Fingin and the older scout. In the absence of Flannán

An Scian, these two were clearly the *rí* of the *Éblána's* strongest warriors and bodyguards.

Bressal and the Grey One gave them a moment then followed dutifully, entering the hut to find the *Éblána rí* already seated on a single stool, his two bodyguards arranging themselves to either side, hands on their swords. Liath Luachra cursed silently for, once again, she knew she couldn't reach him without being intercepted.

The pair paused but Rógallach Mór beckoned them forward with a crooked finger. Just as he was about to speak however, the flap was brushed aside again and two women entered – an old crone and a pretty young woman of less than twenty years – both bearing wooden goblets of water scented with flower petals.

Once more, Rógallach Mór was obliged to sit patiently as the *Éblána* women handed out the traditional goblets of welcome. As she accepted her container, Liath Luachra couldn't help but notice the bruise on the right side of the younger woman's face and how both kept as far from the *rí* as possible while fulfilling their duties. When the younger one finally approached Rógallach Mór to hand him his goblet, he glowered at her, causing her to flinch involuntarily like a dog beaten too many times.

Task completed, the women hastily left the hut.

'There is talk,' the *rí* of the *Éblána* said as soon as the flap had fallen back into place, 'that your task has been accomplished before you depart to complete it.'

Bressal nodded, a knowing smile on his lips. 'It seems the Great Boar has inherited not only the great strength of his animal counterpart but its superior hearing as well. Yes, our task is done. My *rígfénnid* has returned to confirm that your troublesome cousin is dead, his settlement burned, his cattle scattered.'

Despite his guest's satisfied beam, Rógallach Mór greeted his news with no visible surprise. But then, as Liath Luachra knew only too well, he'd already received confirmation on this matter from his own sources.

'I require more of a guarantee on these matters than the word of your *rígfénnid* alone, Bressal Binnbhéalach.' He turned his eyes to Liath

Luachra, his face flushed. Sensing the big man's growing antagonism, Bressal stepped in with admirable swiftness.

'Fortunately, the Grey One has evidence to prove the truth of her assertion.' He turned to the woman warrior. 'Show him.'

Stepping forward, Liath Luachra unslung the wicker basket from her shoulder. Withdrawing a large red cloak, she cast the garment wordlessly onto the ground before the *Éblána* men. They stared at the rumpled material, their attention focussed on the dirt stains and bloody patches that blemished the cloth.

Rógallach Mór raised his eyes. 'You did not bring me his head.'

'You did not ask for his head,' Bressal answered smoothly. 'You asked for his death. And that was accomplished. You also asked that this task take place with the greatest discretion. Returning to Dún Mór with your nephew's head would have shown poor appreciation of your request.'

'This,' the *rí* of the *Éblána* pointed at the cloak. 'This tells me only that you obtained my cousin's clothing. It's still possible he survived the raid.'

'And stood idly by while his kin were killed, his settlement burned?' Bressal shook his head. 'Come, Rógallach Mór. That makes little sense. And besides ...' His eyes took on a teasing glint and he released a fluttering laugh. 'I cannot believe the Great Boar did not send eyes of his own to verify the Grey One's work. They must have told you what she accomplished. Can you truly believe any man would allow such destruction of his home were he still alive?'

Despite the tension now painfully wracking her body, Liath Luachra couldn't help but be impressed by the sharpness of the *Uí Loinge* man's acuity. Somehow, he'd anticipated the *rí* of the *Éblána's* reactions, reading the man's mind more accurately than tracks in the winter snow.

The three *Éblána* men, unfortunately, did not appear to share her admiration. Rógallach Mór held the *Uí Loinge* man's eyes without blinking as the silence extended between them. Finally, mercifully, the *Éblána* leader conceded defeat, disarming the mounting friction by nodding to acknowledge the truth of the *Uí Loinge* man's words. He turned to address the fork-bearded scout on his left. 'Ólan. Tell them what you told me.'

Thrown by his leader's unexpected request, the bald man cleared his throat and glanced nervously at the others before answering. 'Gort Na Meara was destroyed, the longhouses reduced to ashes. Several cattle lay dead in the pens. A number of bodies were strewn about the longhouse ruins, charred to the bone and gnawed at by wolves.' He paused. 'We could not make out their features but from the size of the bodies we judged that there were six men, two – perhaps three – women and at least one child.'

Rógallach Mór gestured at his scout as though to emphasise what he'd just related. 'So you see, Bressal Binnbhéalach. I do know Gort Na Meala is no more. And I know many people died there. What I do not know with complete certainty is whether one of those steaming corpses is Barra ua Éblána.'

'But the Grey One has herself confirmed tha- '

'That flat-chested bitch,' he snapped. 'She is your creature, Bressal. Do not deny it. I have no certainty and Flannán An Scian, the one man who could provide this, has not returned.' He manufactured a false smile; a nasty, yellow-toothed sneer that augured happiness for no-one.

From the corner of her eyes, Liath Luachra watched Bressal's face take on an expression of exaggerated melancholy. Familiar with the *Uí Loinge* man's non-verbal cues, she could tell that he was fuming, despite his calm demeanour. No hint of that anger was displayed as he spoke however.

'Sadly, great *rí*, your warrior was killed during the raid on the settlement. The Grey One has described to me how bravely he fought, killing his opponent with a great thrust of his knife even as he fell from his own wounds. It is out of respect for your man that she buried him in a safe place separate from the others. Such a courageous warrior should not have to endure the callous gnashing of predators.'

Once again, he beckoned to the woman warrior. Liath Luachra took a few steps forward before the bodyguards stepped in to block her. Bending down, she placed Flannán's knife gently on the ground before them.

238

'Your man Flannán was an impressive fighter, Great Boar, 'Bressal continued with his effortless patter. 'And we return his knife as a token of his bravery. I'm sure his feats will continue to inspire pride amongst his people.'

Liath Luachra kept her head down as she retreated to her original position, conscious of the weight of bodyguards' eyes upon her. The *rí* of the *Éblána* grunted, unable to find a chink in Bressal's summary.

'And Muirenn ua Éblána?'

'Who?' There was genuine curiosity in Bressal's voice and Liath Luachra realised that, in her summary of events to the *Uí Loinge* man, she'd never mentioned the girl by name.

He doesn't know!

Her initial shock at the revelation was followed by a tremor of remorse. Bressal, it seemed, had known nothing of Rógallach Mór's desires for Muirenn. Had she been aware of that prior to her departure from Gort Na Meala, she'd never have come to Dún Mór but continued, instead, to Briga. She closed her eyes, overwhelmed with regret for what could have been.

A chilling silence followed the *Uí Loinge* man's response. Liath Luachra risked a quick glance up to see Rógallach Mór glaring at him, his great frame quivering at the effort required to control his temper. 'A woman of our kin. I instructed your … bitch,' He cast a quick glance at Liath Luachra. 'To free her and return her here to safety.'

Confidence momentarily dented by a lack of context to this particular issue, Bressal shot the woman warrior a quick look of enquiry. In response, Liath Luachra gave a tight, barely perceptible shake of her head. The *Uí Loinge* man held her eyes for the briefest of moments but it was sufficient to transmit his intent. If they survived this interview, she was going to face serious consequences.

Composing himself, Bressal quickly gathered his thoughts and arranged his brightest smile. 'It appears that request was not realized. But, then, neither did it form part of the original agreement between us when we last met. Moreover, you know full well that any demands regarding my *fian* are mine alone to decide. My *rígfénnid* has … more practical matters to contend with.

239

Unaccustomed to having his demands denied, Rógallach Mór did not take the rebuttal well. Surging to his feet, he flipped the stool back onto its side with such force that it skidded along the floor. '*Liathadh ort*!' he roared. Bad cess to you!

There was an instant heightening of tension as backs stiffened, shoulders adopted a fighting stance, hands dropped low to weapon hilts.

'Great Boar,' pleaded Bressal, adopting his most reassuring, and placatory voice. 'Let us not lose ourselves to pointless anger. The task you set was accomplished. Your cousin is no more, Gort Na Meala is no more. Half of my *fian* has been lost achieving this deed. And what worth to you some loose piece of th-'

'If Muirenn ua Éblána has not been brought to me, our agreement no longer holds.'

'That makes no sense!' Bressal protested, but Rógallach Mór was past listening. Striding across the floor to where Liath Luachra was still crouched, the hulking *Éblána* man grabbed the shoulder straps of her harness and violently yanked her upright. 'Muirenn ua Éblána!' he snarled. 'Where is she?'

The Grey One's eyes grew chillingly cold and she felt a malicious smile spread like an obscenity across her face. 'She lies with Barra ua *Éblána,*' she whispered softly, so softly only he could hear her. 'Her belly swollen with his seed.'

Whatever response Rógallach Mór had been expecting, it clearly wasn't that. Stung by the Grey One's vicious disclosure, he abruptly released her, staggering backwards in shock. Just as abruptly, the disbelief in those cruel, pig eyes faded, supplanted by a flare of utter fury.

Before the Grey One could react, one great meaty palm smashed into the side of her face, tumbling her onto the hard-packed earthen floor. The thickset *rí* followed up with impressive swiftness for a man of his size, clutching a handful of her hair and wrenching her up off the ground. The blow had been a violent one. Loaded with every ounce of his protracted frustration Rógallach Mór hadn't held back and her head was spinning. She was vaguely aware of Bressal protesting. 'Great Boar! Be reasonable!'

The grip on her hair loosened momentarily but then transferred to her harness, hauling her up off the floor once more. Despite her height, she felt herself lifted off her feet, her face smeared with a lather of foamy spittle as Rógallach Mór screamed in her face.'

'Muirenn ua Éblána! Where is she?'

'I killed her! You cannot have her!'

This time she yelled it, so loud that everyone in the room heard her clearly. The dumbfounded *Éblána* men stared, struggling to absorb the enormity of this shocking revelation. Bressal however, faster to react, turned on her with a face distorted by rage. 'Not again! By the Gods! You insane, fucking sow!'

Rógallach Mór glanced sideways, distracted by the *Uí Loinge* man's despairing exclamation, his grip loosening just enough for the Grey One to wrench *Bas Gan Trua* from its scabbard. Before the *Éblána* leader could twist back to give fresh vent to his fury, she thrust the blade straight into his throat, just below the jaw.

The big man spluttered, coughed wetly and groaned, more out of shock then pain. Releasing her, he stumbled backwards, eyes wild with panic and despair as both hands grasped the hilt of the weapon lodged in his epiglottis. A high-pitched liquid whine emerged from his shattered throat as blood spewed between his fingers, several little sprays spreading scarlet life-fluid all over the room.

The *Éblána* men stared, frozen, as their leader stumbled backwards, tripping over the very stool he'd earlier kicked aside and hitting the ground with a heavy thump. One wretched, blood-soaked hand reached up in a pleading gesture but by then everyone knew there was no hope. The Great Boar's rule was done.

While the others struggled to break free of the shock that held them fast, Liath Luachra took the initiative. Charging Ólan, she shoulder-bashed him, bowling him backwards over one of the benches even as she wrenched *Gléas Gan Ainm* free of its scabbard.

'Murder!' roared Fingin, finally finding his voice. 'Treachery! *Éblána* to arms!'

Conscious that his cries would be heard throughout the *caiseal*, Liath Luachra rushed for the entranceway, barging through with such force

241

the flap was ripped free of its fixings. She staggered to a halt in the *lis*, discovering to her dismay that her route to the passage, the single egress from the *caiseal*, was impeded by the body of *Éblána* force. Ten warriors stared at her in surprise even as their hands reached for their weapons in response to Fingin's call.

'*Na Cinéaltaí*!' she screamed in desperation. '*Na Cinéaltaí, abú*!'

'*Abú*!' She heard the responding cry but had no time to appreciate it. Three of the warriors were already rushing her and cut-off on all sides by the spread of opponents, she was obliged to retreat, back into the stone-walled building. As she ducked inside, another *abú* sounded, taken up and repeated by a number of different voices.

Inside the murky structure, Bressal and the bearded warrior Fingin were thrashing about on the floor, walloping and pounding each other without mercy. The *Uí Loinge* man had apparently reacted with a lethal alacrity that exceeded that of his adversaries for Fingin's sword remained in its scabbard and Ólan was strewn on the ground beside Rógallach Mór's corpse. The bald *Éblána* scout was still breathing but he lay on one side, coughing up blood while an even greater quantity streamed from the wound where Flannán's knife protruded from his ribcage.

'Bressal, help me!'

The woman warrior had twisted back to hold the entrance, edging to the side to remain out of sight. Her three pursuers skidded to a halt before the narrow opening. Unable to see into the gloomy interior, two of them jabbed their swords through, probing, testing to draw her out in case she was awaiting them.

Which she was.

Liath Luachra slammed the lower edge of her own weapon against the tip of the nearest blade, producing a clash of metal that resounded through the hut and most likely numbed the hand of the person holding it. Both blades immediately whipped out of sight.

Behind her, she could hear the crash and grunts of the ongoing struggle between Bressal and the *Éblána* warrior but didn't dare take her eyes from the entrance to see what was happening. The entrance was tight, wide enough for a single person to fit through but impossible to rush and rendering anyone who tried, vulnerable to attack. She was confident she could hold the warriors off for a time but it wouldn't take them long to figure out that if they used spears, they'd have the reach on her. With that, they could drive her back far enough to enter without risk.

She hissed furiously over her shoulder. 'Despatch him, Bressal. Quickly!'

It was at that point that *Na Cinéaltaí* launched their attack, surging around the left side of the building, howling bloodthirsty ululation as they slammed into the assembled *Éblána* warriors.

'*Na Cinéaltaí, abú!*'

Following that initial crash of metal on metal and the screams of anger and pain, Liath Luachra risked a quick glance outside, relieved to see that her three assailants now had worries of their own. Fighting in close quarters with Senach and the big *fénnid* Giobog, they'd withdrawn from the entrance to the building, creating a clear route of escape.

Unlike the *fian*, which Senach had primed for combat, the *Éblána* force had been taken by surprise and struggled to establish a workable defence against the ferocious assault of the mercenaries. Unfortunately, what the *Éblána* lacked in experience and preparedness, they more than made up for in numbers and placement. Even as she watched the battle unfold, the woman warrior saw one of the new young *fénnid* slammed back off his feet by a javelin that took him full in the stomach. As he tumbled onto the ground, a second javelin smashed into the side of the wicker hut, just missing Biotóg, who'd crouched to pull his sword free from the guts of a fallen *Éblána* warrior.

The men on the ramparts.

They'd had javelins, she remembered. Several javelins and spears.

Her eyes narrowed as she glanced back over her shoulder to where Bressal was now straddling the bearded Fingin, hands wrapped tight about his neck, furiously throttling him. The *Éblána* man wasn't giving in without a fight however. Burdened though he was by the weight of the *Uí Loinge* man, his long arms still reached up to pummel Bressal viciously in the face.

Go! You owe him nothing.

She stepped closer to the entrance.

Go, now! Bressal has made the conditions of your service clear.

Another javelin slammed into the ground, this time only three paces from the hut entrance. In response, the woman warrior's eyes iced over and without thinking, she charged through the opening, slipping on a patch of blood at the exterior before deftly recovering her balance. Wrenching the javelin free with her right hand, she spun on her heel, automatically scanning the rampart to locate and target the warriors, then judging the trajectory and letting fly in one smooth movement.

Even as the missile left her hand, she knew her aim was true but remained long enough to see it strike one of the rampart guards in the left thigh. Walloped off balance, the *Éblána* warrior spun from the highest terrace, falling head over heels down the next two terraces and off the wall. Before he hit the ground the Grey One was already moving, rushing around the wicker hut on her right to evade the bloody fighting.

Hurtling around the curve of the structure, she crashed headlong into an *Éblána* warrior coming the other way, a sly man who'd had the brains to think of flanking the *fian* and taking them from behind. The impact as the two crashed into each other was enough to send both tumbling onto their arses. The warrior writhed desperately, struggling to get to his feet. Liath Luachra, knowing she wasn't going to beat him in time, twisted on the ground and thrust herself forward, skewering him in the lower leg with *Gléas Gan Ainm* just as he was almost upright. The *Éblána* warrior wailed and fell against the side of the hut, grasping its woody material with one hand to prevent himself from falling while shakily baring his sword with the other to fend off her next attack.

But there was no attack. Bounding to her feet, Liath Luachra simply skirted her opponent as she circled the hut. Cling though he might to the wall, he was unable to move and, therefore, out of the fight.

Around the curve of the hut and out of sight, Liath Luachra slewed to a halt for, almost directly ahead, a rough wooden ladder was lying against the southern section of the first stone terrace. Panting, the Grey One stared in disbelief. Here was her escape route. By climbing onto the terrace, she could make her way to the upper rampart and, from there, drop to the ground outside. It would be a great leap of course. At its lowest point the wall was at least twice the height of a normal man but she was confident she could make it and cut loose of the death-trap the *caiseal* had become.

Making a break for the ladder, she traversed the open section of *lis* at a run but seven paces from the wall, the crunch of gravel alerted her to the presence of pursuers in her wake. Cursing, the Grey One spun on her heel for her back was unprotected. She couldn't take the risk her pursuers were preparing to cast a javelin.

Her heart sank as she took in the two *Éblána* warriors rushing towards her, both armed with swords, not javelins, but close enough now that they could cut her down if she tried to turn and climb. Behind the two men, the entranceway to the *caiseal* was obscured by the central buildings but several bodies were visible between the structures, at least two of them recognisable as *Na Cinéaltaí* men. From the noise of battle, it sounded as though the *Éblána* forces had been pushed back to the passage but, given the inevitable reinforcements, it was only a matter of time before they counterattacked and the *fian* was overcome.

Despite the great wave of despair that threatened to engulf her, Liath Luachra released a peal of hysterical laughter, struck by the irony that now, having planned and prepared so carefully for death, she suddenly, desperately, wanted to live. In an odd way, that acknowledgement released something inside her and she felt an uncoiling of darkness as some kind of stifled tension slipped free of her body. Exhaling hard, she regarded the two warriors and smiled a happily, malevolent smile.

Unnerved by her laughter and the manic grin across her face, the *Éblána* men halted uncertainly. Liath Luachra, for her part, didn't hesitate and did the one thing they weren't expecting. She attacked.

Launching herself forward, she traversed the short distance between them like a blur, veering to the right at the last moment to slash her sword at her nearest opponent. She made no contact of course. Both warriors had the sense to draw back from her wild attack. Nevertheless, it gave her the opportunity to position herself so that one of them ended up blocking the other.

This was the technique to fighting two or more opponents she'd learned from the old warrior Bressal had employed to train her on joining *Na Cinéaltaí*. That wizened old fighter had stressed the need to constantly shift position, to move so that only one of your opponents could engage with you at any time. There were limitations, of course, limitations she'd learned to appreciate over the subsequent years. The technique required enough free space to be able to manoeuver for a protracted period and that wasn't always possible. The most serious limitation however was that in essence, the technique was little more than a holding pattern, a temporary measure to stay alive until you came up with some cunning means of escape or circumstances changed to equalise the opposition.

In this case, fortunately, it was the latter. She saw it immediately in the warriors' faces, sensed it in the sudden lessening of their attack. For just the briefest of moments, the eyes of her immediate opponent flickered over her shoulder and she took that moment to drive forward instead of retreating, her sword scraping along his as she blocked it high and slid underneath to head-butt him in the face.

As the warrior staggered back, his comrade treacherously deserted him, taking off at a run to scamper up the ladder. The Grey One didn't wait to see what he did next for a great surge of violence had overtaken her as she attacked the first warrior. Stunned by the blow to the head, his defence was clumsy, his laboured response to an obvious feint leaving him wide open on his left flank. Once again, Liath Luachra moved almost impossibly fast, her body responding to circumstances faster than her head could register them. She stabbed the warrior hard in the left side, felt the sword sink two finger lengths deep into his torso. He was screaming as she smashed him back off his feet and even the blow as he hit the ground didn't shut him up.

It was at that point that the battle frenzy overtook her and she was down, hacking and stabbing, barely able to see through the red mist in her eyes, sensing rather than seeing the spatter of blood and gobbets of flesh against her face and chest. It was several moments before the fit subsided and she found herself crouched, weak and breathless, beside the warrior's corpse, gasping for air as her vision finally started to clear.

'Grey One!'

Turning her head, she stared blearily through the bloody haze at the figure standing before her, the one who'd distracted her opponent. Whoever it was, he looked vaguely familiar but with her blurred eyesight, it was difficult to tell.

'Grey One,' the figure repeated. 'Victory! We have victory!'

It was Murchú, the *Uí Loinge* youth. Bressal's nephew. She recognised him now but numbed from battle frenzy, she stared at him, glassy-eyed. Murchú stood panting, almost as heavily as her, blood trailing down his sword arm. 'We have the *caiseal*, Grey One. The *Éblána* are defeated.'

She continued to stare blearily at him, barely able to hear what he was saying through the drone of the blood rush in her ears. What little she could hear seemed to make little sense.

Somehow, she managed to get to her feet and, chest heaving, looked down at the warrior she'd butchered. Even through the emotional detachment of the after-battle stupor, it was an unpleasant sight. The man's belly had been sliced open and entrails splayed the ground around him. In several place, white bone from his rib cage protruded up from the bloody mess. It looked as though he'd been savaged by a pack of wild animals yet, somehow, the body was still moving, caught in the final death spasms. She watched impassively as the legs twitched weakly, the stink of bile and voided bowels filling her nostrils.

She shook her head in an effort to clear it and drive the physical aftereffects of battle from her mind. Her lungs were heaving, her eyes watering. Her stomach was churning and she had a full bladder that she urgently needed to relieve.

But there was no time for that.

'We have the *caiseal*?' she repeated dumbly, unable to come up with any words of her own. Despite the dullness in her head, she was able to recognise the irony of using the word 'we'. Mere moments earlier, she'd been callously abandoning the *fian*, leaving them to their own bloody fate as she fled desperately to save herself. That realisation didn't provoke any subsequent sense of guilt however.

Absorbed in the elation of his own post-battle rapture, the youth seemed oblivious to her befuddled state for he was nodding excitedly, talking again. 'We drove them back, into the passage. They were about to rally when another force took them from the rear.'

That jolted her back to full alertness.

'Another force?'

'Yes!' he beamed, his eyes still alight, high on the excitement of victory.

'What other force?'

'I don't know. Whoever they are, they managed to convince the *Éblána* to yield. Their forces have withdrawn and we've barred the doors against them. They're calling out to speak with us but Bressal's unconscious and Senach sent me to find you.' He looked at her and, for a moment, the reality of their situation seemed to sink through the layer of euphoria. 'What should we do?'

It took her a moment to realise he was asking a direct question.

'Show me,' she said.

***

The *lis* was thick with the stink of blood, strewn with bodies and severed limbs. A few wispy tendrils of black smoke rose from the fire-pit, almost quenched now from the spilled contents of the fallen cauldron. The passage out of the *caiseal* was empty, the doors at the far end barred and fortified with spars, just as Murchú had reported.

Biotóg was sitting on the ground by the stone-walled building, grasping his chest in pain but she didn't spare him a second glance as she stared up at Senach on the highest rampart, crouched low behind the wall to avoid being observed from outside. The two surviving *fénnid* recruits were hunched, grim faced, beside him. All three held javelins in preparation for any attempt to retake the *caiseal*.

Spotting her, Senach waved her up to join him and, leaving Murchú to keep an eye on the passage, she mounted the steps at the side. The lean *Uí Loinge* warrior looked grim and sported bloody cuts to his forehead and left arm. He breathed a sigh of relief as she ducked in beside him, the other *fénnid* automatically pulling back to give her space.

248

'I'm glad you're here, Grey One.' He clucked his tongue nervously. 'They've been calling for someone to talk with them.'

'Who've been calling?'

He shrugged and gestured to a slit in the stone he'd been using to observe what was happening outside.

Drawing closer, the warrior woman peered through the little gap to see a large force gathered just beyond the *caiseal* entrance. Towards the rear, she saw two or three faces she recognised from the original group of warriors that accompanied Bressal but there were several others she hadn't seen before.

Adjusting her position, she turned her attention to the forefront of the assembled warriors and there, spotted a man and a woman that she recognised immediately. With a start, she pulled back from the slit.

'What?' asked Senach. 'What is it, Grey One?'

Ignoring him, she chewed thoughtfully on the inside of her cheek. Finally, to her comrade's horror, she got to her feet and stepped up onto the wall. In full view of those gathered outside, she stood with her hands on her hips and called down. 'Fíne Surehands. And Barra ua Éblána. What are you doing here?'

The *conradh* of Gort Na Meala Looked up in surprise and, catching sight of the woman warrior, a tight smile spread across her face. Dressed for battle, she was wearing a thick leather tunic with strips of metal stitched into the material and her hair was tied up in tight braids. 'You told us to expect some activity,' she called back. 'Some bustle should you succeed in killing Rógallach Mór. You mentioned nothing about a full-pitched battle. What did you expect us to do?'

Liath Luachra scowled then glanced at Barra who was standing beside his battle leader, a battle-axe gripped in both hands. 'There was not meant to be any "us". You were – ' She paused then for, in the midst of the warriors, she'd just spotted Cappa and Darra as well. 'You were supposed to come alone.'

She ground her teeth together, annoyed despite the conflicting sense of relief she felt. Fíne Surehands' presence outside the fortress with a band of warrior hadn't been part of the plan she'd proposed when she'd offered to kill the *rí* of the *Éblána*. The *conradh* of Gort Na Meala was supposed to have followed the scouts back to Dún Mór on her own, to remain hidden only long enough to confirm the successful assassination. That very morning, the Grey One had seen the pre-arranged signal confirming she was in place, the smokey fire on the northern ridge that had extinguished within moments of being started.

'You were supposed to come alone.'

'You did not fight Rógallach Mór's warriors on your own, Grey One. The survivors tell me there's a *fian* in there with you.'

'They were here when I arrived. I did not arrange for them to be present, just as I didn't arrange for a band of warriors to accompany me.'

Fíne Surehands shrugged the gibe aside with insoucicant ease. 'Such are the realities when holding the role of *conradh*, Grey One. You become accustomed to giving orders, not taking them. And you listen to your instincts. My instincts whispered that I should bring as many warriors as I could spare. I'm glad I did for without them we couldn't have intervened.'

'Some of those warriors served Rólgallach Mór,' Liath Luachra pointed out, indicating the men to the rear of her group.

'Some of them did,' Fíne Surehands admitted. 'But they are all *Éblána*. Most followed their *rí* with reluctance and misplaced loyalty. When they learned of his betrayal of his own people, they were happy to withdraw their support. They no longer pose a threat to you or your comrades.'

Liath Luachra chewed that over for a moment. She was still annoyed by the deviation from the scheme agreed to with the *conradh* but it made little sense to argue the point, particularly as that deviation had saved her life. She gave a brusque nod. 'Very well. I'll open the gates.'

Descending to the *lis*, she entered the passage with a nervous Murchú and, together, they worked the spar loose and dragged the heavy gates open. Fíne Surehands and Barra were waiting directly outside, looking both relieved and pleased with themselves.

'I see you, Fíne Surehands.'

'I see you Grey One,' the *conradh* answered, stepping into the shadow of the passage. 'And great is the pleasure it gives me.' She paused to consider the layers of blood and entrails that coated the Grey One's face and clothing. 'Although it seems you are once again in need of my healing skills.'

'Not my blood,' Liath Luachra answered bluntly.' But there are others here that would gladly use your people's help.'

'They will be treated as heroes.' This from Barra, who'd stepped forward, interpolating himself into the conversation. The handsome warrior was smiling broadly, greatly satisfied with how things had worked out. 'I must admit, Grey One, when you first approached with your proposal, I didn't truly believe you'd sacrifice yourself for us.'

Liath Luachra regarded him coldly. She hadn't approached Barra with the proposal but, instead, had spoken to Fíne Surehands. It'd taken twelve days, using the woman's love for her daughter, to convince her it was the only way to save Muirenn from the clutches of Rólgallach Mór. The Gort Na Meala *conradh* had immediately recognised the sincerity of the Grey One's offer. Barra would never have believed her. Not without his battle leader's intercession at least and, even then, he'd probably only truly believed it when he saw the proof of it with his own eyes.

'I speak of the *fian, Na Cinéaltaí*. Will they be treated with safety and the hospitality of *Éblána* guests?'

Barra's eyes took on a frosty glow at the mention of that name. 'Is this not the same *fian* who sent you to attack Gort Na Meala?'

'Yes,' she admitted.' But they too were deceived by Rógallach Mór's duplicity. They do not deserve to suffer your vengeance.'

Barra's earlier satisfaction seemed to waver but, on the wave of a great victory, he found it within himself to display benevolence. 'Very well, Grey One. We owe you that at least. *Na Cinéaltaí* will hold the status of honoured guests provided they offer no further threat.'

The warrior woman turned to Fíne Surehands to confirm the matter. 'You can guarantee this?' she asked.

'No, but Barra can. The tribe have now named him *rí* of the *Éblána*.'

The Gort Na Meala battle leader must have sensed the shock behind the Grey One's impassive expression or seen it in the glance she gave the *Éblána* man.

'This morning, Barra met secretly with elders from two of the larger *Éblána* sub-clans. It didn't take much to convince them of Rólgallach Mór's betrayal given the arduous yoke of his leadership. With an alternative leader to rally behind, they were quick to offer what warriors they had.'

Liath Luachra considered the warriors standing beyond the doors. 'This is how you obtained your force?'

The *conradh* nodded. 'Combined with those I'd brought from Gort Na Meala, we had less than fifteen fighters but we took the opportunity the battle at the stronghold presented. I led the charge and the Great Boar's warriors were trapped in the passage between your *fian* and our forces.' She shrugged. 'They were quick enough to yield when they saw they'd have to fight their cousins.'

The Grey One looked at her coldly. 'You told me nothing of this,' she said, her voice hard with accusation. 'Even knowing what I sacrificed, you told me nothing.'

Fíne Surehands sighed and she self-consciously brushed some grass from her battledress. 'I told you once that you lacked guile, Grey One. And that advice still holds true. It gave me no pleasure to conceal our plan from you but you were set on tackling Rólgallach Mór head on. I couldn't risk the possibility you might reveal the truth if you failed, if you were taken and tortured.'

'Enough!' Barra declared, his voice loud and ringing with false cheer in an attempt to overcome the tension now crackling in the air between the two women. 'This is a day for celebration. We've broken the chokehold of Rólgallach Mór's rule. Grey One, you and your comrades are welcome to *Éblána* hospitality, although you should remain within the *caiseal* until you leave. Many in our tribe have lost family and friends today and I cannot account for their behaviour beyond the wall.'

Appreciating the growing importance of this moment, he adjusted his stance to address the warriors as well as those inside the passage. 'Cousins! Today we care for our wounded and bury our dead but come two days hence, the skies will shake with the noise of our celebration. I promise you, the feasting and festivity to mark this event will be spoken of for generations by our people.'

The warriors cheered enthusiastically and slowly started to disperse but, looking at the two *Éblána,* Liath Luachra felt a gaping hollow grow inside her. She was exhausted and in pain but all of that now seemed trivial compared to the great emptiness that had blossomed in her chest. She'd decided to die but had not. She'd scarified herself for a cause where all was not as she'd originally believed. Deep down in her soul, her relief at escaping the call of the Dark Lands was genuine but any elation had been tarnished by Fíne Surehands' disclosure. Now, sick of bloodshed, sick of fighting, sick of these people and their lethal machinations, she wanted nothing more to do with them. Looking up towards the forest-coated ridges of the valley, she suddenly yearned for the isolation and the honest simplicity of the Great Wild.

Crouching down, she retrieved a loose cloak that had been discarded in the passage during the battle and then turned to address the *Uí Loinge* youth. 'Murchú, go to Senach and tell him what has been agreed. He can put any questions to Fíne Surehands. I will speak with him tomorrow.'

Murchú looked at her with a faceful of questions but she turned away before he could ask them and started through the doors of the stronghold. Ignoring the baleful glares of the remaining *Éblána* warriors, she made for the path leading down to the valley floor.

Grey One,' called Fíne Surehands, her voice high-pitched with incomprehension. 'What are you doing? Where are you going?'

Liath Luachra paused to look back, her eyes heavy with emotion. 'I go to the forest, great *conradh.* There at least, the trees don't lie.'

***

She spent that night in the forest, back at the burrow she'd created near the vantage point overlooking the shallow valley. Prior to entering the hidey-hole, she'd dropped to all fours and retched, spewing up everything she'd eaten that morning, expelling all remaining fear and battle violence in one noxious discharge of reeking bile.

Afterwards, wiping the vomit from her lips, she crawled into the little refuge, buried herself deep in the folds of the cloak and the scented nest of moss and leaves, trembling violently until exhaustion took her.

The following morning, she was awake before dawn but stayed huddled in her nest, brooding and nursing her face, now badly swollen from Rólgallach Mór's blow. When it was finally bright enough to see clearly, she left the burrow, retracing her steps out of the forest, down into the valley and following the trail back up to Dún Mór.

Two of the *fénnid* – Murchú and Giobog – were up when she entered the fortress, standing guard just inside the passage entrance with cloaks wrapped about them against the cold. They greeted her eagerly and although she answered with a mute dip of the chin she was pleased Senach hadn't taken any chances. When she went on to enter the *lis* however, she found two *Éblána* warriors guarding the entrance to the stone hut despite the *fían's* apparent control of *caiseal*. No-one, it seemed, was taking any chances.

Senach was sitting on a log beside the fire-pit, wolfing down a helping of porridge from the righted cauldron that someone had replaced over the fire. The dark-haired warrior looked haggard and deep furrows were etched across his forehead. He looked as though he hadn't slept all night and grunted when he saw her approach but seemed too weary or too hungry to pull his attention away from his meal.

They Grey One stood rubbing her palms together over the fire for a moment before helping herself to a wooden bowl and dolloping in a substantial serving of her own. Taking a seat by the chomping *Uí Loinge* man, both ate in silence while the other survivors of the *fían* slowly drifted back to join them.

By the time she'd eaten her fill and tossed the bowl aside, the remaining *fénnid* had gathered, the obvious exception being Bressal Binnbhéalach. 'He's in there,' Senach informed her, as though reading her thoughts. He gestured towards the stone building where the two guards were looking tersely back at them. 'He was cut bad, gushing blood all over the place. The *Éblána* healers took him in there with the others but we haven't been permitted to enter. We could have forced our way in, I suppose, but ...' He shrugged and let the sentence trail away, too weary to make the effort of completing his thought.

The Grey One looked around at the battered remnants of the *fían*. They all looked exhausted, deflated, at a loss to know what to do next. In an odd way it also seemed as though they were waiting for her to say something, suggest something. With a sigh, she leaned forward, closer to the fire as though to draw on its heat. 'Well,' she said and eyed each of them individually to ensure she had their attention. 'I suppose, there are things that we should discuss.'

***

Converted to a makeshift shelter for those too badly wounded to leave the *caiseal*, the stone-walled building no longer held benches but six beds of heather. Occupying one of those, directly opposite the entrance, was Bressal Binnbhéalach. Propped on some canvas bags that had been pushed against the wall, the *Uí Loinge* man was leaning up at angle that allowed him to look around the hut. Nervously twisting a sprig of heather between his fingers, he was eyeing the two women tending to the other injured men with distrust.

When she entered the hut, the Grey One was taken aback by how ragged he looked. His handsome features were marred from the fight, pale where it was free of the deep purple and black bruising. His eyes were puffed and black from Fingin's brutal pounding. A bloodstained woollen bandage was bound about his hip and groin. A second bandage was wrapped around his lower leg. From the tender manner in which he was holding himself, she could tell he was in great pain.

When he noticed her, he did his best to disguise that discomfort. 'Weeell,' he drawled, his voice heavy with false affability. 'Grey One. You live, then.'

'Yes.'

He grunted. 'As succinct as ever. Where and the others?'

'Camped at the far side of the *lis*. They have their weapons and freedom to come and go but they're not allowed to enter this hut.'

'And yet I see you have managed to do so.'

She ignored the scathing jab. 'Two of your new recruits – the younger ones – breathe no more. One of the older ones …' She pointed to another makeshift bed by the doorway where a man with a bloody bandage around his head, lay stretched out and unmoving. 'They say he will not last the night.'

Pulling up a stool, she eased herself onto it, putting her at a slightly higher level. It felt strange to sit above the *Uí Loinge* man for once, an odd circumstance that seemed to underline the reversal of fortunes since they'd last sat together. 'Biotóg has a shallow wound to the chest, the rest of us count new cuts and gashes but nothing serious. Of all *Na Cinéaltaí* injuries, yours seem by far the worst.'

'For which I have you to thank.'

The Grey One went quiet at that, nervously tapping the hut floor with her foot. 'I had no choice.'

Bressal tried to feign indifference with a casual shrug but winced at the stab of pain the movement produced. A bitter curse squeezed from between his lips. 'That poxy-bearded Fingin! I thought I had him but he carried a hidden weapon. Got the blade in twice before I squeezed the last breath from his shit-licking mouth.'

He grew quiet for a time and Liath Luachra could see that a sheen of sweat had broken out on his forehead from the simple effort of talking. 'You had the luck,' she said.

Bressal regarded her with indignation. 'The luck?' he snorted.

'The *Éblána* women are good healers. If you survive the fevers you'll walk again. But the wounds are deep. They'll take time to mend.'

'Pah!' he spat, glancing across the room at those tending the wounded. 'Those *Éblána* women can't be trusted. We killed enough of their husbands and sons for them to wish us a painful death.'

'Some,' she conceded. 'But many of Rógallach Mór's supporters were not so well liked.'

Bressal did not deign to respond to that. Instead, he sighed and lapsed into a protracted silence. Knowing the *Uí Loinge* man wouldn't be able to stay quiet for long, Liath Luachra held her own tongue and waited. Sure enough, a few moments later, he irritably tossed the sprig of heather aside. 'I saw Barra ua Éblána this morning. I must say, he looked remarkably hale for a dead man. He had the cheek to introduce himself when he came in looking for his cloak. It seems he's quite fond of it.' He scowled and regarded her with fresh resentment. 'Nothing you told me was true.'

'Most of it was true.'

'But Barra is still alive.'

'Yes.'

'And you never destroyed Gort Na Meala. That too was a lie, I suppose.' His lips compressed in a thin line and he scratched feverishly at his neck, although this seemed more out of need to do something than out of any genuine irritation on the skin. 'Although, by the Gods, I don't understand how you managed to fool Rógallach Mór's scouts.'

Liath Luachra shook her head. 'It was no lie. I destroyed the settlement but I had the help of its people to set fire to the thatch. It was a gruelling task, most particularly for Barra. He had to destroy the home his grandfather built, slaughter a portion of the herd his family raised over generations.'

She sat back on the stool, sniffed and wiped her nose with her sleeve. 'But it was the only way Rógallach Mór would be convinced to drop his guard, to let me come close. Although...' This time it was her turn to consider the *Uí Loinge* man with open censure. 'Your presence at Dún Mór came close to disrupting everything.'

Bressal disregarded the criticism. 'How did you do it? The scouts reported several bodies. Did Barra kill some of his own?'

Her lips twisted up in a cynical half-smile. 'It was a bitter winter. The frozen ground kept them well.'

Bressal looked at her blankly.

'The bodies the scouts saw were those of Flannán An Scian and the *fénnid*. So Conall Cacach finally proved himself useful.' She gave a mirthless chuckle that sounded like the rattle of stones. 'There were also four bodies from a wreck tossed up by the storms; another man, two women and a child. It wasn't my wish to treat them so but circumstances left us little choice. Even worse, because we lacked sufficient corpses, I had to dig up Sean Fergus as well.' She sank briefly into a silent reverie before looking up again. 'Wherever he rests now, I think ... I hope he'll understand.'

The *Uí Loinge* man nodded slowly, clearly impressed despite his obvious rancour. '*Ana ghlic,*' he said. Very sly. '*Ana ghlic, ar fad.*' Very sly altogether. He nodded again. 'It is a safe assumption then, that you didn't kill the *Éblána* woman.'

Liath Luachra shook her head provoking a fresh sigh from the perspiring *Uí Loinge* man. 'You know, Grey One, I've always recognised

257

the potential within you, always trusted your judgement when it comes to battle but ...' His eyes narrowed. 'Until now, I've never had reason to distrust you. Falsehoods are rare but unpleasant stones on the path of the true *gaiscíoch*.'

Liath Luachra regarded him wryly, unsure if he was mocking her or simply oblivious to the complete hypocrisy of his grievance. 'It's true,' she admitted. 'Untruths stick fast in my throat but most *gaiscíoch* do not sit in fear of their own comrades. I regret that you were here, Bressal. I regret that you were sucked into the undertow of my scheme and injured, but there was no other choice. For Muirenn ua Éblána to live, Rógallach Mór had to die.'

'Had *Na Cinéaltaí* not been present at *Dún Mór* you would now be dead.'

'Yes. But I'd prepared myself in that expectation.'

That took him by surprise. His eyes widened and he studied her face with care for a time. In the end, unable to read her he came straight out with the question that burdened the tip of his tongue. 'You were willing to die?' He paused. 'To save this *Éblána* woman from Rógallach Mór?'

Liath Luachra turned her face away, offering no answer but silence.

Bressal grunted in surprise. 'I see. Well ... Then I look forward to setting eyes on this particular creature. If Rógallach Mór's lust drove him to such extremes and a frigid assassin like you was willing to throw her life away then ...well, she must be very fair indeed.' He raised his hand and coughed with surprising delicacy. 'Nevertheless, there is the issue of a reckoning between you and I.'

'A reckoning?' The Grey One's head snapped back to glare at him.

'You betrayed me.'

The Grey One's stony expression concealed her thoughts on that particular matter.

'You swore fealty to me. I treated you with kindness. I named you *rígfénnid* of *Na Cinéaltaí*, created your name in song, gifted you a fine leather battle harness. I ...' His voice trailed off and he made a spinning gesture with his finger as though to indicate the list of kindnesses ran on an endless spool.

'Such offerings were for your benefit, not mine. I sought and asked for none of them. All I wanted was to be left alone.'

They both lapsed into angry silence but, as usual, Bressal could not contain himself for long. 'Almost half of my new *fénnid* have been lost as a result of your personal grudge with the Great Boar. To regain my good favour you'll remain in my service and do my bidding.'

'I will never slap buttock skin with you, Bressal.'

'And what will you do if you leave *Na Cineáltaí*? Do you truly believe your new *Éblána* friends will accept you? You're a fighter, a killer. Your very nature means you have nothing, are nothing without the *fían*. If you leave, you'll end your days taking a cold blade to your own throat.' He glared at her, daring her to deny it but she didn't give him that satisfaction.

'What you say is true. That's why I'm taking the *fían* with me.'

'What!' For the first time in all the years she'd known him, Bressal looked completely lost for words. 'What?' he spluttered hoarsely.

'The *fían* season recommences but your injuries mean you'll rest abed for the better part of it. The men hunger for battle and booty. They have asked me to lead them.'

'You?' roared Bressal. 'They wouldn't follow you.'

When she looked at him then there was a just a trace of righteousness – or possibly retribution – in her regard. 'You said it yourself. You created a name for me, a reputation. It's hardly my fault they now ask to follow? Even some of the *Éblána* warriors we fought now approach me.' Suddenly exhausted, the warrior woman seemed to sink back on her seat.

'Sean Fergus offered me advice at one time. *Cén maitheas uisce nuair atá uisce beatha le fáil?*' Why have the water when you can have the whiskey? 'It didn't really make sense at the time and it was only when speaking with the *fénnid* that I finally understood what he meant.'

Bressal's eyes boggled. His cheeks turned red beneath the bruises and he looked as though he was about to explode into convulsions of rage. 'It is my *fían*!'

She shook her head. 'No more.'

'You will receive no tasks, no call for services. I am the only one with connections to the other tribes, the only one with access to the ears of powerful men.'

'Hence my willingness for you to remain with us. If you're disposed, we can create that very *fian* you've always wanted. You could use your connections to the tribes to set us tasks, I would see those tasks accomplished. The single difference is that I'd make the final decision on the tasks that we accept. No more murder of innocents for the likes of Rógallach Mór.'

'I spit on you, Grey One. I spit on your breath that stinks of shit!'

Liath Luachra shrugged. 'The choice is yours. You can lose all you had and end up the laughing stock whose *fian* deserted him or you can help to benefit us both. Either way, I leave with the men at first light tomorrow.'

As she got to her feet, the *Uí Loinge* man followed through on his threat and spat but it was a feeble effort and she brushed the spittle carelessly from her leg.

She left him then without speaking again, emerging outside onto the *lis* where the sun had broken through the morning cloud. Standing alone, she sighed and closed her eyes, enjoying the play of sunlight against her face. She felt tired. The conversation had been one of the longest and most intense she'd ever had with Bressal and it had left her feeling sad and empty yet, in a strange way, hopeful.

Making her way back to the fire, she found the *fénnid* awaiting her and sat down to join them. Five faces looked at her, waiting on her words. Before she spoke, she paused to look up at the sky where the clouds had cleared, a flock of geese were on the wing and the promise of spring was beckoning.

Epilogue

Fíne Surehands was waiting outside the *caiseal* when Liath Luachra and her *fian* emerged, a short time after dawn. It was a good day for partings, dreary and grey, the valley smothered with low-lying cloud, a light drizzle eating up the distance.

Off to the left of the entranceway, a group of ten *Éblána* warriors were also waiting, watching warily as the surviving members of *Na Cinéaltaí* gathered outside their stronghold. Liath Luachra scrutinised their faces with interest. A certain softness to their features suggested some residue of gratitude for the toppling of Rógallach Mór but any goodwill had been tempered by the bloodshed and the death of extended family. Either way, they'd be well pleased to see the back of their 'guests'.

Fíne Surehands displayed no such concerns. Standing alone at the south-west section of the wall, she beckoned the warrior woman over. Leaving her men, the Grey One trotted lithely across the short grass of the summit to join her.

The Gort Na Meala *conradh* looked well. She'd swapped her battlesdress for a soft green dress and an oiled wool cloak. Her dark hair had been freed from its braids and hung loose, restricted only by a bronze headband. The result rendered her less ... hawkish, almost regal in an odd way. Despite the drizzle, she had her hood down and her hair was patterned with a delicate web of fine, silver drops.

'Did you truly think to slip away without farewell, Grey One?'

Unable to deny the obvious, Liath Luachra picked self-consciously at a loose thread on her tunic, the battle harness now safely stored away in her travel pack. 'I did not know what to say. I did not know what you would say.'

'I would say thank you. I would offer you the immeasurable appreciation of Barra and the *Éblána*, I would offer you the appreciation of all those at Gort Na Meala. Most of all however, I would offer you the gratitude of my own heart and my sorrow for deceiving you. Your actions saved my children and for that alone I'll always hold you close to my thoughts.' She paused for a moment as though to allow the Grey One an opportunity to speak. When she didn't, the *Éblána* woman filled that unspoken space for her. 'And Muirenn, of course. Muirenn will never forget you. Trust me when I tell you she knows how much you've done, how much you've sacrificed for her.'

An uncomfortable silence followed the older woman's words. Liath Luachra turned her eyes away, looked down the valley to avoid her gaze. She sniffed in the cold morning air. 'Barra didn't join you, then?'

'He is *rí* of the *Éblána* now. He has to keep his distance, not be seen to support the spilling of *Éblána* blood. Besides,' she added wryly. 'There are the festivities to be prepared.'

Liath Luachra snorted.

Fíne Surehands accepted the scorn with grace. 'You do not have to leave, you know. The *Éblána* may not want you here but there is always a place for you at Gort Na Meala. There's much to rebuild. You could build with us, create a new life of your own.'

Liath Luachra gave her a furtive, sideways glance but made no response.

Fíne Surehands gave a heavy sigh. 'Do you have a boon at least? Something you would like to ask of me before you leave?'

The Grey One thought about that for a moment. 'Don't kill Bressal. Heal him well. As you healed me.'

The older woman pursed her lips, unconvinced at the wisdom of the warrior woman's request. 'You should kill that one. No man suffers humiliation or the supplanting of authority easily. You took his *fian*. He'll never forgive you for that.'

'I know Bressal. He'll come around once he's had the time to think it through and sees the benefits of what I offer. He may be a schemer but he's nothing if not pragmatic and I can handle him… now.'

She lapsed into silence for what seemed like a very long time.

'Besides,' she added, at last. 'He did save my life once.'

Fíne Surehands nodded, acceding to the request. 'Very well. But what of you now, Grey One?' What route will take you from Dún Mór?'

'I take the *fian* to Malla. Senach tells me that Bressal promised a service there before coming to Dún Mór. After that, we travel to Dún

Baoiscne seeking service with *Clann Baoiscne*.' She hesitated. 'But first we travel south of Briga. There's a man of the *Uí Cailbhe* at that place I'd have words with.'

If the *Éblána* woman noticed the sudden coldness in her voice she made no mention of it. 'And so the legend of *Na Cinéaltaí* will spread. Like the song of Liath Luachra.'

Liath Luachra shrugged. The subject was not one that held any interest for her.

'I have one further request of you,' Fíne Surehands continued. 'My daughter asked that I seek your true name, the name you had before you took the mantle of the Grey One.'

Liath Luachra cocked one eyebrow in curiosity.

'Her child,' Fíne Surehands explained. 'If the child is a girl she would like to name her in your honour.'

At this, the Grey One' eyes gave the briefest of twitches. She coughed and awkwardly shifted her weight from one leg to the other. 'Grey One is my true name. The person who was before is dead. Long dead.'

'Then my heart weeps for you.'

The woman warrior looked at her in surprise.

'All parents see the potential of their own children, Grey One. And through that, they learn the potential of all children.' She lifted her hands in a gesture of helplessness. 'You are younger than my own daughter and I grieve for the person who is gone. I console myself with the knowledge that you are a person of standing and with that, no matter how bleak, there is always hope.' She paused and regarded the Grey One with unexpected softness. 'Can I embrace you before you go?'

Without waiting, she raised her hands to step forward but Liath Luachra had unthinkingly backed away, hands up, palms held out before her like a shield. Somewhat embarrassed by the excessive reaction, she gave an apologetic shake of her head.

The two women stood looking at one another. A bleak smile formed on Fíne Surehands lips and she shook her head sadly. 'Then there's no more to be said. Go safe, Grey One.' She turned and started walking towards the trail of standing stones that led down to the bottom of the hill.

Liath Luachra watched her go, an unfathomable, indecipherable sense of loss bubbling in her chest. 'Fíne Surehands!'

The *Éblána* woman stopped and turned to look back over her shoulder.

'Tell Muirenn … 'She paused. 'Tell Muirenn I liked her. Tell her I'm glad she was my friend.'

Fíne Surehands looked at her wordlessly for a moment then her lips curled into an odd half-smile. With a nod, she turned and continued on her way.

The Grey One watched her for a time before returning to the *caiseal* entrance where the *fénnid* were awaiting. Picking up her wicker basket, she looked to the west and felt a kind of tired ache drawing her in that direction, pulling her towards something she couldn't completely understand.

'*Ar aghaidh linn*,' she said at last. Let's go.

The little group set off at a trot, circling the stronghold, descending to the floor of the valley and continuing west towards the misted ridge. Within a few moments the haze began to soak them up, the distant figures fading further and further until they had completely disappeared. And there was no sound but the desolate keen of a circling falcon.

The character Liath Luachra also appears in the Fionn mac Cumhaill series which commences with **Fionn: Defence of Ráth Bládhma**.
I produce a number of other works (all related to Irish history, mythology and folklore) through Irish Imbas Books so please feel free to contact me there with any suggestions or comments

Glossary

Some of the Irish terms/concepts used in this novel:

Abú! – A victory cry (Connelly, abú! = Connelly forever!/ Up with Connelly!)

Bás gan Trua – Death without Mercy

Beacáin scammalach – Literally, 'cloudy mushroom'. A fungus with hallucinogenic properties.

Bod – A penis

Conradh – A champion/ battel leader

Cabóg – A clumsy, awkward person

Caiseal – A circular defensive fort, usually made out of stone

Díberg – A band of warriors, usually a raiding party or reavers

Draoi – A druid

Éblána – A clan/tribe

Éclann – Clanless/tribeless state. A person not affiliated to any particular clan

Fian – A band of warriors or war party

Fidchell – an ancient board game used in Ireland believed to be similar to chess

Fénnid – a member of a fian. The noun can be plural or singular)

Gaiscíoch – a hero warrior, a fighter of great prowess

Gléas Gan Ainm – Literally 'Tool Without a Name'

Lis – Circular courtyard of a *caiseal* or *ráth*

Mo láireog léith – My Grey Mare

Na Cinéaltaí – The Friendly Ones

Óglach – A young, unblooded warrior (plural: Óglaigh)

Ráméis – Nonsense talk

Rí – Literally 'king' but generally a tribal leader

Rígfénnid – Leader of a fian

Seanstrompa – Derogatory term for an old person (Old Fart)

Slat – Slang word for penis (cock/ dick)

Sliog – A slug (a great swallow) of a drink

Tánaiste – Deputy or successor to the *rí*

Tuirse croí – literally, 'tiring of the heart' –a wearing down of the spirit or the soul.

Uí Loinge – A clan/tribe

Uí Bairrche – A clan/tribe

Historical And Creative Notes:

This book came about predominantly as a result of queries from several people on one of the characters from the Fionn mac Cumhaill series. Most, in particular, wanted to know whether Liath Luachra was based on a real person or not.

The truth, unfortunately, is that very little information on the character has survived to say for sure. Most of the stories in which Liath Luachra played a part (and she was only ever a subsidiary character) were transmitted orally over hundreds (and possibly over a thousand) years before being collated in written form in texts such as the twelfth century *Macgnímartha Finn* (the Boyhood Deeds of Fionn). The fact that the Fenian Cycle tales still retain such a consistent kernel of narrative is actually a minor miracle in itself.

The relevant section of the *Macgnímartha Finn* text reads as follows:

> *Cumall left his wife Muirne pregnant. And she brought forth a son, to whom the name of Demne was given. Fiacal mac Conchinn, and Bodball the druidess, and the Gray One of Luachar came to Muirne, and carried away the boy, for his mother durst not let him be with her. Muirne afterwards slept with Gleor Red-hand, king of the Lamraige, whence the saying, "Finn, son of Gleor." Bodball, however, and the Gray One, and the boy with them, went into the forest of Sliab Bladma. There the boy was secretly reared.*

That's pretty much it.

The name 'Liath Luachra', literally, means the 'Grey One of Luachair'. Why the character was known as 'The Grey One' – is impossible to say after all this time. Generally speaking, names at that period had a direct reference to a person's heritage, occupation, physical or mental attributes and so on. For this reason, it's possible the character was meant to be an old woman (i.e. grey-haired) or the name was a moniker associated with a particular kind of grey clothing or other possession.

267

Another possibility was that she had a 'grey' personality and of course there's a different reason again suggested in this particular story.

'Luachair', meanwhile, is an Irish word that means 'rushes' (as in, reed plants) but could also be taken to mean 'a place of rushes'. There was a Luachair in West Kerry mentioned in many of the early texts (Luachair Deaghaidh – Sliabh Luachra) but, of course, it's impossible to tell if that was the area the author of *Macgnímartha Finn* was referring to in relation to Liath Luachra.

One of the additional frustrations with the Fenian Cycle tales is that sometimes, because of the 'Chinese Whisper' effects on a story over such an extended period of time, you can end up with a confused narrative where one character reappears later as a completely different character (but with the same name). This is why, in the ongoing story of Fionn mac Cumhaill, a second Liath Luachra turns up (this time a fearsome male warrior). Part of the reason I was keen to write this novel was to prepare the groundwork for a credible solution to deal with that narrative confusion (which will probably take place in Book 4 or 5 of the series).

Throughout this book I've used what historical information is available to recreate the world in which Liath Luachra and her contemporaries lived. In some cases however, for creative purposes, I've added elements that are clearly fictitious. It's unlikely, for example, that the skills required to make *uisce beatha* (whiskey) came to Ireland prior to the mid-Medieval period. Similarly, there's no reference to *beacáin scammalach* anywhere in the source historical documents, although given what we know of equivalent contemporary cultures, it's very likely our ancestors had some similar narcotic. Unlike contemporary society, this substance would probably have been used for ritualistic practices as opposed to intentional self-intoxication.

Some people have expressed surprise at the young age of the lead character in this story but, again, the context of the period has to be taken into account. During the Iron Age, people died much younger than they do nowadays and it was important for the survival of the tribe that it continually replenished its numbers. This was particularly important where a large proportion of a tribe's fighting force was killed off in inter-tribal warfare. As a result, warriors were blooded from a very early age.

Where to next?

'Liath Luachra – The Grey One' was originally written as a stand-alone novel but because of the scope of the story I wanted to tell, space was intentionally left for a second volume that covers the events prior to the events in *Fionn:Defence at Ráth Bládhma*. Given the large volume of writing projects I have to juggle however, I've made a call to wait to see if there's demand for a second Liath Luachra novel before committing to it (over my other work). If a sequel is something you'd like to see, please feel free to send a flare up either through your book review comments or by sending me a comment through the Irish Imbas Books website.

At the website (irishimbasbooks.com) you can also sign up for our newsletter on future works (books and audio not available elsewhere), elements of Irish folklore, culture and the creative process we use.

Brian O'Sullivan: December 2015

Other Books by Brian O'Sullivan

See Brian's blog and website at _irishimbasbooks.com_ for contact details and updates on new and upcoming titles.

Fionn: Defence of Ráth Bládhma:

[The Fionn mac Cumhaill Series: Book 1]

Ireland: 192 A.D. A time of strife and treachery. Political ambition and inter-tribal conflict has set the country on edge, testing the strength of long-established alliances. Following their victory at the battle of Cnucha, Clann Morna are hungry for power. Meanwhile, a mysterious war party roams the 'Great Wild' and a ruthless magician is intent on murder.

In the secluded valley of Glenn Ceoch, disgraced female druid Bodhmhall and her lover Liath Luachra have successfully avoided the bloodshed for many years. Now, the arrival of a pregnant refugee threatens the peace they have created together. The odds are overwhelming and death stalks on every side.

Based on the ancient Irish Fenian Cycle texts, the Fionn mac Cumhaill Series recounts the fascinating and pulse-pounding tale of the birth and adventures of Ireland's greatest hero, Fionn mac Cumhaill.

A sample of what the reviewers say:

"An Ireland of centuries ago, threaded through with myth and magic, but very 'real' for all that. Dark and at times very violent, it is balanced by affirming friendships and relationships, and a very strong female cast."

270

"*The violence and brutality of ancient Ireland presented on a very human scale, with real characters of depth and substance.*"

"*If you're sick of elves, chivalrous knights and arcane quests like me, this is probably the most exciting and refreshing book you'll read in a long time!*"

"*Powerful female characters are all too rare in literature. The druidess Bodhmhall, and her lover the warrior Liath Luachra will inspire current and future generations of women. O'Sullivan keeps a cracking pace in this, the first of his Fionn mac Cumhaill series.*'

"*The characters are richly drawn and there is plenty of change and tension in the relationship dynamics to suggest that it's a character piece. However, it's the plot that makes this book impossible to put down as you rush towards the end.*"

Fionn: Traitor of Dún Baoiscne:

[The Fionn mac Cumhaill Series – Book 2]

Ireland: 198 A.D. Six years have passed since the brutal attack on the community of Ráth Bládhma. The isolated valley of Glenn Ceoch is at peace once more but those who survived still bear the scars of that struggle. Now, new dangers threaten the settlement.

Troubling signs of strangers have been discovered in the surrounding wilderness. Disgraced druid Bodhmhall fears a fresh attempt to abduct her talented nephew. A summons from the fortress of Dún Baoiscne sets them on a perilous traverse of the Great Wild where enemies, old and new, await them.

And Muirne has returned to reclaim her son.

Come what may, there will be blood.

Based on the ancient Fenian Cycle texts, the Fionn mac Cumhaill Series recounts the fascinating and pulse-pounding tale of the birth and adventures of Ireland's greatest hero, Fionn mac Cumhaill.

A sample of what the reviewers say:

"An impressive follow on from the first of the series. Once again I love the descriptive scenery, you walk but mostly run with the characters through the Great Wild."

"I slipped back into the story of Fionn mac Cumhaill as though I had never been away. Again such a strong sense of place, culture, and magic, woven together with wonderful characters, both good and evil, and an un-put-downable plot. I can't think of anything else I've read that so successfully makes the fantastic so believable."

"Like the first volume, this book delivers edge-of-your-seat thrills and is written in a welcoming style meant to draw you in from the first page. O'Sullivan transports us back to the misty beginnings of Ireland, a land of forest and bog and sea, of druids and superstition, supernatural happenings and warring tribes sequestered in hill forts."

"The yin and yang relationship between the two female protagonists in these books is particularly captivating. Liath Luachra, the warrior woman, plays foil to Bodhmhall, the wise and considered leader, as they face violent and uncertain times."

The Irish Muse and Other Stories

This intriguing collection of stories puts an original twist on foreign and familiar territory. Merging the passion and wit of Irish storytelling with the down-to-earth flavour of other international locations around the world, these stories include:

- a ringmaster's daughter who is too implausible to be true — despite all the evidence to the contrary

- an ageing nightclub gigolo in one last desperate bid to best a younger rival

- an Irish consultant whose uncomplicated affair with a public service colleague proves anything but

- an Irish career woman in London stalked by a mysterious figure from her past

- a sleep-deprived translator struggling to make sense of bizarre events in a French city